W9-AYK-908

A prolific author of more than one hundred books, **Diana Palmer** got her start as a newspaper reporter. A *New York Times* bestselling author and voted one of the top ten romance writers in America, she has a gift for telling the most sensual tales with charm and humor. Diana lives with her family in Cornelia, Georgia. Visit her website at dianapalmer.com.

B.J. Daniels is a *New York Times* and *USA TODAY* bestselling author. She wrote her first book after a career as an award-winning newspaper journalist and author of thirty-seven published short stories. She lives in Montana with her husband, Parker, and three springer spaniels. When not writing, she quilts, boats and plays tennis. Contact her at bjdaniels.com, on Facebook or on Twitter, @bjdanielsauthor.

New York Times Bestselling Author

DIANA PALMER

TEXAS BORN

**HARLEQUIN
BESTSELLING
AUTHOR
COLLECTION**

**HARLEQUIN®
BESTSELLING
AUTHOR
COLLECTION**

Recycling programs
for this product may
not exist in your area.

ISBN-13: 978-1-335-99641-1

Texas Born
First published in 2014. This edition published in 2021.
Copyright © 2014 by Diana Palmer

Smokin' Six-Shooter
First published in 2009. This edition published in 2021.
Copyright © 2009 by Barbara Heinlein

This edition published by arrangement with Harlequin Books S.A.

For questions and comments about the quality of this book, please contact us at CustomerService@Harlequin.com.

Harlequin Enterprises ULC
22 Adelaide St. West, 40th Floor
Toronto, Ontario M5H 4E3, Canada
www.Harlequin.com

Printed in U.S.A.

CONTENTS

Visit her Author Profile page on Harlequin.com,
or dianapalmer.com, for more titles!

TEXAS BORN

Diana Palmer

For our friends Cynthia Burton and Terry Sosebee

Chapter 1

Michelle Godfrey felt the dust of the unpaved road all over her jeans. She couldn't really see her pants. Her eyes were full of hot tears. It was just one more argument, one more heartache.

Her stepmother, Roberta, was determined to sell off everything her father had owned. He'd only been dead for three weeks. Roberta had wanted to bury him in a plain pine box with no flowers, not even a church service. Michelle had dared her stepmother's hot temper and appealed to the funeral director.

The kindly man, a friend of her father's, had pointed out to Roberta that Comanche Wells, Texas, was a very small community. It would not sit well with the locals if Roberta, whom most considered an outsider, was disrespectful of the late Alan Godfrey's wishes that he be buried in the Methodist church cemetery beside his first wife. The funeral director was soft-spoken but eloquent. He also pointed out that the money Roberta would save with her so-called economy plans, would be a very small amount compared to the outrage she would provoke. If she planned to continue living in Jacobs County, many doors would close to her.

Roberta was irritated at the comment, but she had a shrewd mind. It wouldn't do to make people mad when she had many things to dispose of on the local market, including some cattle that had belonged to her late husband.

She gave in, with ill grace, and left the arrangements to Michelle. But she got even. After the funeral, she gathered up Alan's personal items while Michelle was at school and sent them all to the landfill, including his clothes and any jewelry that wasn't marketable.

Michelle had collapsed in tears. That is, until she saw her stepmother's wicked smile. At that point, she dried her eyes. It was too late to do anything. But one day, she promised herself, when she was grown and no longer under the woman's guardianship, there would be a reckoning.

Two weeks after the funeral, Roberta came under fire from Michelle's soft-spoken minister. He drove up in front of the house in a flashy red older convertible, an odd choice of car for a man of the cloth, Michelle thought. But then, Reverend Blair was a different sort of preacher.

She'd let him in, offered him coffee, which he refused politely. Roberta, curious because they never had visitors, came out of her room and stopped short when she saw Jake Blair.

He greeted her. He even smiled. They'd missed Michelle at services for the past two weeks. He just wanted to make sure everything was all right. Michelle didn't reply. Roberta looked guilty. There was this strange rumor he'd heard, he continued, that Roberta was preventing her stepdaughter from attending church services. He smiled when he said it, but there was something about him that was strangely chilling for a religious man. His eyes, ice-blue, had a look that Roberta recognized from her own youth, spent following her father around the casinos in Las Vegas, where he made his living. Some of the patrons had that same penetrating gaze. It was dangerous.

"But of course, we didn't think the rumor was true," Jake Blair continued with that smile that accompanied the unblinking blue stare. "It isn't, is it?"

Roberta forced a smile. "Um, of course not." She faltered, with a nervous little laugh. "She can go whenever she likes."

"You might consider coming with her," Jake commented. "We welcome new members in our congregation."

"Me, in a church?" She burst out laughing, until she saw the two bland faces watching her. She sounded defensive when she added, "I don't go to church. I don't believe in all that stuff."

Jake raised an eyebrow. He smiled to himself, as if at some private joke. "At some point in your life, I assure you, your beliefs may change."

"Unlikely," she said stiffly.

He sighed. "As you wish. Then you won't mind if

my daughter, Carlie, comes by to pick Michelle up for services on Sunday, I take it?"

Roberta ground her teeth together. Obviously the minister knew that since Michelle couldn't drive, Roberta had been refusing to get up and drive her to church. She almost refused. Then she realized that it would mean she could have Bert over without having to watch for her stepdaughter every second. She pursed her lips. "Of course not," she assured him. "I don't mind at all."

"Wonderful. I'll have Carlie fetch you in time for Sunday school each week and bring you home after church, Michelle. Will that work for you?"

Michelle's sad face lit up. Her gray eyes were large and beautiful. She had pale blond hair and a flawless, lovely complexion. She was as fair as Roberta was dark. Jake got to his feet. He smiled down at Michelle.

"Thanks, Reverend Blair," she said in her soft, husky voice, and smiled at him with genuine affection.

"You're quite welcome."

She walked him out. Roberta didn't offer.

He turned at the steps and lowered his voice. "If you ever need help, you know where we are," he said, and he wasn't smiling.

She sighed. "It's just until graduation. Only a few more months," she said quietly. "I'll work hard to get a scholarship so I can go to college. I have one picked out in San Antonio."

He cocked his head. "What do you want to do?"

Her face brightened. "I want to write. I want to be a reporter."

He laughed. "Not much money in that, you know.

Of course, you could go and talk to Minette Carson. She runs the local newspaper."

She flushed. "Yes, sir," she said politely, "I already did. She was the one who recommended that I go to college and major in journalism. She said working for a magazine, even a digital one, was the way to go. She's very kind."

"She is. And so is her husband," he added, referring to Jacobs County sheriff Hayes Carson.

"I don't really know him. Except he brought his iguana to school a few years ago. That was really fascinating." She laughed.

Jake just nodded. "Well, I'll get back. Let me know if you need anything."

"I will. Thank you."

"Your father was a good man," he added. "It hurt all of us to lose him. He was one of the best emergency-room doctors we ever had in Jacobs County, even though he was only able to work for a few months before his illness forced him to quit."

She smiled sadly. "It was a hard way to go, for a doctor," she replied. "He knew all about his prognosis and he explained to me how things would be. He said if he hadn't been so stubborn, if he'd had the tests sooner, they might have caught the cancer in time."

"Young lady," Jake said softly, "things happen the way they're meant to. There's a plan to everything that happens in life, even if we don't see it."

"That's what I think, too. Thank you for talking to her," she added hesitantly. "She wouldn't let me learn how to drive, and Dad was too sick to teach me. I don't really think she'd let me borrow the car, even if I could drive. She wouldn't get up early for anything, especially on a Sunday. So I had no way to get to church. I've missed it."

"I wish you'd talked to me sooner," he said, and smiled. "Never mind. Things happen in their own time."

She looked up into his blue eyes. "Does it…get better? Life, I mean?" she asked with the misery of someone who'd landed in a hard place and saw no way out.

He drew in a long breath. "You'll soon have more control over the things that happen to you," he replied. "Life is a test, Michelle. We walk through fire. But there are rewards. Every pain brings a pleasure."

"Thanks."

He chuckled. "Don't let her get you down."

"I'm trying."

"And if you need help, don't hold back." His eyes narrowed and there was something a little chilling in them. "I have yet to meet a person who frightens me."

She burst out laughing. "I noticed. She's a horror, but she was really nice to you!"

"Sensible people are." He smiled like an angel. "See you."

He went down the steps two at a time. He was a tall man, very fit, and he walked with a very odd gait, light and almost soundless, as he went to his car. The vehicle wasn't new, but it had some kind of big engine in it. He started it and wheeled out into the road with a skill and smoothness that she envied. She wondered if she'd ever learn to drive.

She went back into the house, resigned to several minutes of absolute misery.

"You set that man on me!" Roberta raged. "You went over my head when I told you I didn't want you to bother with that stupid church stuff!"

"I like going to church. Why should you mind? It isn't hurting you…"

"Dinner was always late when you went, when your father was alive," the brunette said angrily. "I had to take care of him. So messy." She made a face. In fact, Roberta had never done a thing for her husband. She left it all to Michelle. "And I had to try to cook. I hate cooking. I'm not doing it. That's your job. So you'll make dinner before you go to church and you can eat when you get home, but I'm not waiting an extra hour to sit down to a meal!"

"I'll do it," Michelle said, averting her eyes.

"See that you do! And the house had better be spotless, or I won't let you go!"

She was bluffing. Michelle knew it. She was unsettled by the Reverend Blair. That amused Michelle, but she didn't dare let it show.

"Can I go to my room now?" she asked quietly.

Roberta made a face. "Do what you please." She primped at the hall mirror. "I'm going out. Bert's taking me to dinner up in San Antonio. I'll be very late," she added. She gave Michelle a worldly, patronizing laugh. "You wouldn't know what to do with a man, you little prude."

Michelle stiffened. It was the same old song and dance. Roberta thought Michelle was backward and stupid.

"Oh, go on to your room," she muttered. That wide-eyed, resigned look was irritating.

Michelle went without another word.

She sat up late, studying. She had to make the best grades she could, so that she could get a scholarship. Her father had left her a little money, but her step-mother had control of it until she was of legal age. Probably by then there wouldn't be a penny left.

Her father hadn't been lucid at the end because of the massive doses of painkillers he had to take for his condition. Roberta had influenced the way he set up his will, and it had been her own personal attorney who'd drawn it up for her father's signature. Michelle was certain that he hadn't meant to leave her so little. But she couldn't contest it. She wasn't even out of high school.

It was hard, she thought, to be under someone's thumb and unable to do anything you wanted to do. Roberta was always after her about something. She made fun of her, ridiculed her conservative clothes, made her life a daily misery. But the reverend was right. One day, she'd be out of this. She'd have her own place, and she wouldn't have to ask Roberta even for lunch money, which was demeaning enough.

She heard a truck go along the road, and glanced out to see a big black pickup truck pass by. So he was back. Their closest neighbor was Gabriel Brandon. Michelle knew who he was.

She'd seen him for the first time two years ago, the last summer she'd spent with her grandfather and grandmother before their deaths. They'd lived in this very house, the one her father had inherited. She'd gone to town with her grandfather to get medicine for a sick calf. The owner of the store had been talking to a man, a very handsome man who'd just moved down the road from them.

He was very tall, muscular, without it being obvious, and he had the most beautiful liquid black eyes she'd ever seen. He was built like a rodeo cowboy. He had thick, jet-black hair and a face off of a movie poster. He was the most gorgeous man she'd ever seen in her life.

He'd caught her staring at him and he'd laughed. She'd never forgotten how that transformed his hard face. It had melted her. She'd flushed and averted her eyes and almost run out of the store afterward. She'd embarrassed herself by staring. But he was very good-looking, after all—he must be used to women staring at him.

She'd asked her grandfather about him. He hadn't said much, only that the man was working for Eb Scott, who owned a ranch near Jacobsville. Brandon was rather mysterious, too, her grandfather had mused, and people were curious about him. He wasn't married. He had a sister who visited him from time to time.

Michelle's grandfather had chided her for her interest. At fifteen, he'd reminded her, she was much too young to be interested in men. She'd agreed out loud. But privately she thought that Mr. Brandon was absolutely gorgeous, and most girls would have stared at him.

By comparison, Roberta's friend, Bert, always looked greasy, as if he never washed his hair. Michelle couldn't stand him. He looked at her in a way that made her skin crawl and he was always trying to touch her. She'd jerked away from him once, when he'd tried to ruffle her hair, and he made a big joke of it. But his eyes weren't laughing.

He made her uncomfortable, and she tried to stay out of his way. It would have been all right if he and Roberta didn't flaunt their affair. Michelle came home from school one Monday to find them on the sofa together, half-dressed and sweaty. Roberta had almost doubled up with laughter at the look she got from her stepdaughter as she lay half across Bert, wearing nothing but a lacy black slip.

"And what are you staring at, you little prude?" Roberta had demanded. "Did you think I'd put on black clothes and abandon men for life because your father died?"

"He's only been dead two weeks," Michelle had pointed out with choking pride.

"So what? He wasn't even that good in bed before he got sick," she scoffed. "We lived in San Antonio and he had a wonderful practice, he was making loads of money as a cardiologist. Then he gets diagnosed with terminal cancer and decides overnight to pull up stakes and move to this flea-bitten wreck of a town where he sets up a free clinic on weekends and lives on his pension and his investments! Which evaporated in less than a year, thanks to his medical bills," she added haughtily. "I thought he was rich…!"

"Yes, that's why you married him," Michelle said under her breath.

"That's the only reason I did marry him," she muttered, sitting up to light a cigarette and blow smoke in Michelle's direction.

She coughed. "Daddy wouldn't let you smoke in the house," she said accusingly.

"Well, Daddy's dead, isn't he?" Roberta said pointedly, and she smiled.

"We could make it a threesome, if you like," Bert offered, sitting up with his shirt half-off.

Michelle's expression was eloquent. "If I speak to my minister…"

"Shut up, Bert!" Roberta said shortly, and her eyes dared him to say another word. She looked back at Michelle with cold eyes and got to her feet. "Come on, Bert, let's go to your place." She grabbed him by the hand and led him to the bedroom. Apparently their clothes were in there.

Disgusted beyond measure, Michelle went into her room and locked the door.

She could hear them arguing. A few minutes later they came back out.

"I won't be here for dinner," Roberta said.

Michelle didn't reply.

"Little torment," Roberta grumbled. "She's always watching, always so pure and unblemished," she added harshly.

"I could take care of that," Bert said.

"Shut up!" Roberta said again. "Come on, Bert!"

Michelle could feel herself flushing with anger as she heard them go out the door. Roberta slammed it behind her.

Michelle had peeked out the curtains and watched them climb into Bert's low-slung car. He pulled out into the road.

She closed the curtains with a sigh of pure relief.

Nobody knew what a hell those two made of her life. She had no peace. Apparently Roberta had been seeing Bert for some time, because they were obviously obsessed with each other. But it had come as a shock to walk in the door and find them kissing the day after Michelle's father was buried, to say nothing of what she'd just seen.

The days since then had been tense and uncomfortable. The two of them made fun of Michelle, ridiculed the way she dressed, the way she thought. And Roberta was full of petty comments about Michelle's father and the illness that had killed him. Roberta had never even gone to the hospital. It had been Michelle who'd sat with him until he slipped away, peacefully, in his sleep.

She lay on her back and looked at the ceiling. It was only a few months until graduation. She made very good grades. She hoped Marist College in San Antonio would take her. She'd already applied. She was sweating out the admissions, because she'd have to have a scholarship or she couldn't afford to go. Not only that, she'd have to have a job.

She'd worked part-time at a mechanic's shop while her father was alive. He'd drop her off after school and pick her up when she finished work. But his illness had come on quickly and she'd lost the job. Roberta wasn't about to provide transportation.

She rolled over restlessly. Maybe there would be something she could get in San Antonio, perhaps in a convenience store if all else failed. She didn't mind hard work. She was used to it. Since her father had

married Roberta, Michelle had done all the cooking
and cleaning and laundry. She even mowed the lawn.

Her father had seemed to realize his mistake toward
the end. He'd apologized for bringing Roberta into their
lives. He'd been lonely since her mother died, and Roberta had flattered him and made him feel good. She'd
been fun to be around during the courtship—even Michelle had thought so. Roberta went shopping with the
girl, praised her cooking, acted like a really nice person. It wasn't until after the wedding that she'd shown
her true colors.

Michelle had always thought it was the alcohol that
had made her change so suddenly for the worse. It
wasn't discussed in front of her, but Michelle knew that
Roberta had been missing for a few weeks, just before
her father was diagnosed with cancer. And there was
gossip that the doctor had sent his young wife off to
a rehabilitation center because of a drinking problem.
Afterward, Roberta hadn't been quite so hard to live
with. Until they'd moved to Comanche Wells, at least.

Dr. Godfrey had patted Michelle on the shoulder
only days before the cancer had taken a sudden turn for
the worse and he was bedridden. He'd smiled ruefully

"I'm very sorry, sweetheart," he'd told her. "If I
could go back and change things…"

"I know, Daddy. It's all right."

He'd pulled her close and kissed her forehead.
"You're like your mother. She took things to heart,
too. You have to learn how to deal with unpleasant people. You have to learn not to take life so seriously…"

"Alan, are you ever coming inside?" Roberta had
interrupted petulantly. She hated seeing her husband

and her stepdaughter together. She made every effort to keep them apart. "What are you doing, anyway, looking at those stupid smelly cattle?"

"I'll be there in a moment, Roberta," he called back.

"The dishes haven't been washed," she told Michelle with a cold smile. "Your job, not mine."

She'd gone back inside and slammed the screen.

Michelle winced.

So did her father. He drew in a deep breath. "Well, we'll get through this," he said absently. He'd winced again, holding his stomach.

"You should see Dr. Coltrain," she remarked. Dr. Copper Coltrain was one of their local physicians. "You keep putting it off. It's worse, isn't it?"

He sighed. "I guess it is. Okay. I'll see him tomorrow, worrywart."

She grinned. "Okay."

Tomorrow had ended with a battery of tests and a sad prognosis. They'd sent him back home with more medicine and no hope. He'd lasted a few weeks past the diagnosis.

Michelle's eyes filled with tears. The loss was still new, raw. She missed her father. She hated being at the mercy of her stepmother, who wanted nothing more than to sell the house and land right out from under Michelle. In fact, she'd already said that as soon as the will went through probate, she was going to do exactly that.

Michelle had protested. She had several months of school to go. Where would she live?

That, Roberta had said icily, was no concern of hers. She didn't care what happened to her stepdaughter.

Roberta was young and had a life of her own, and she wasn't going to spend it smelling cattle and manure. She was going to move in with Bert. He was in be-tween jobs, but the sale of the house and land would keep them for a while. Then they'd go to Las Vegas where she knew people and could make their fortune in the casino.

Michelle had cocked her head and just stared at her stepmother with a patronizing smile. "Nobody beats the house in Las Vegas," she said in a soft voice.

"I'll beat it," Roberta snapped. "You don't know anything about gambling."

"I know that sane people avoid it," she returned.

Roberta shrugged.

There was only one real-estate agent in Coman-che Wells. Michelle called her, nervous and obviously upset.

"Roberta says she's selling the house," she began.

"Relax." Betty Mathers laughed. "She has to get the will through probate, and then she has to list the prop-erty. The housing market is in the basement right now, sweetie. She'd have to give it away to sell it."

"Thanks," Michelle said huskily. "You don't know how worried I was…" Her voice broke, and she stopped.

"There's no reason to worry," Betty assured her. "Even if she does leave, you have friends here. Some-body will take the property and make sure you have a place to stay. I'll do it myself if I have to."

Michelle was really crying now. "That's so kind…!"

"Michelle, you've been a fixture around Jacobs County since you were old enough to walk. You spent summers with your grandparents here and you were always doing things to help them, and other people. You spent the night in the hospital with the Harrises' little boy when he had to have that emergency appendectomy and wouldn't let them give you a dime. You baked cakes for the sale that helped Rob Meiner when his house burned. You're always doing for other people. Don't think it doesn't get noticed." Her voice hardened. "And don't think we aren't aware of what your stepmother is up to. She has no friends here, I promise you."

Michelle drew in a breath and wiped her eyes. "She thought Daddy was rich."

"I see," came the reply.

"She hated moving down here. I was never so happy," she added. "I love Comanche Wells."

Betty laughed. "So do I. I moved here from New York City. I like hearing crickets instead of sirens at night."

"Me, too."

"You stop worrying, okay?" she added. "Everything's going to be all right."

"I will. And thanks."

"No thanks necessary."

Michelle was to remember that conversation the very next day. She got home from school that afternoon and her father's prized stamp collection was sitting on the coffee table. A tall, distinguished man was handing Roberta a check.

"It's a marvelous collection," the man said.

"What are you doing?" Michelle exclaimed, dropping her books onto the sofa, as she stared at the man with horror. "You can't sell Daddy's stamps! You can't! It's the only thing of his I have left that we both shared! I helped him put in those stamps, from the time I was in grammar school!"

Roberta looked embarrassed. "Now, Michelle, we've already discussed this…"

"We haven't discussed anything!" she raged, red-faced and weeping. "My father has only been dead three weeks and you've already thrown away every single thing he had, even his clothes! You've talked about selling the house… I'm still in school—I won't even have a place to live. And now this! You…you… mercenary gold digger!"

Roberta tried to smile at the shocked man. "I do apologize for my daughter…"

"I'm not her daughter! She married my father two years ago. She's got a boyfriend. She was with him while my father was dying in the hospital!"

The man stared at Michelle for a long moment, turned to Roberta, snapped the check out of her hands and tore it into shreds.

"But…we had a deal," Roberta stammered.

The man gave her a look that made her move back a step. "Madam, if you were kin to me, I would disown you," he said harshly. "I have no wish to purchase a collection stolen from a child."

"I'll sue you!" Roberta raged.

"By all means. Attempt it."

He turned to Michelle. "I am very sorry," he said gently. "For your loss and for the situation in which you find yourself." He turned to Roberta. "Good day."

He walked out.

Roberta gave him just enough time to get to his car. Then she turned to Michelle and slapped her so hard that her teeth felt as if they'd come loose on that side of her face.

"You little brat!" she yelled. "He was going to give me five thousand dollars for that stamp collection! It took me weeks to find a buyer!"

Michelle just stared at her, cold pride crackling around her. She lifted her chin. "Go ahead. Hit me again. And see what happens."

Roberta drew back her hand. She meant to do it. The child was a horror. She hated her! But she kept remembering the look that minister had given her. She put her hand down and grabbed her purse.

"I'm going to see Bert," she said icily. "And you'll get no lunch money from me from now on. You can mop floors for your food, for all I care!"

She stormed out the door, got into her car and roared away.

Michelle picked up the precious stamp collection and took it into her room. She had a hiding place that, hopefully, Roberta wouldn't be able to find. There was a loose baseboard in her closet. She pulled it out, slid the stamp book inside and pushed it back into the wall.

She went to the mirror. Her face looked almost blistered where Roberta had hit her. She didn't care. She had the stamp collection. It was a memento of happy times when she'd sat on her father's lap and carefully tucked stamps into place while he taught her about them. If Roberta killed her, she wasn't giving the stamps up.

But she was in a hard place, with no real way out. The months until graduation seemed like years. Roberta would make her life a living hell from now on because she'd opposed her. She was so tired of it. Tired of Roberta. Tired of Bert and his innuendoes. Tired of having to be a slave to her stepmother. It seemed so hopeless.

She thought of her father and started bawling. He was gone. He'd never come back. Roberta would torment her to death. There was nothing left.

She walked out the front door like a sleepwalker, out to the dirt road that led past the house. And she sat down in the middle of it—heartbroken and dusty with tears running down her cheeks.

Chapter 2

Michelle felt the vibration of the vehicle before she smelled the dust that came up around it. Her back was to the direction it was coming from. Desperation had blinded her to the hope of better days. She was sick of life. Sick of everything.

She put her hands on her knees, brought her elbows in, closed her eyes, and waited for the collision. It would probably hurt. Hopefully, it would be quick...

There was a squealing of tires and a metallic jerk. She didn't feel the impact. Was she dead?

Long, muscular legs in faded blue denim came into view above big black hand-tooled leather boots.

"Would you care to explain what the hell you're doing sitting in the middle of a road?" a deep, angry voice demanded.

She looked up into chilling liquid black eyes and grimaced. "Trying to get hit by a car?"

"I drive a truck," he pointed out.

"Trying to get hit by a truck," she amended in a matter-of-fact tone.

"Care to elaborate?"

She shrugged. "My stepmother will probably beat me when she gets back home because I ruined her sale."

He frowned. "What sale?"

"My father died three weeks ago," she said heavily. She figured he didn't know, because she hadn't seen any signs of life at the house down the road until she'd watched his truck go by just recently. "She had all his things taken to the landfill because I insisted on a real funeral, not a cremation, and now she's trying to sell his stamp collection. It's all I have left of him. I ruined the sale. The man left. She hit me…"

He turned his head. It was the first time he'd noticed the side of her face that looked almost blistered. His eyes narrowed. "Get in the truck."

She stared at him. "I'm all dusty."

"It's a dusty truck. It won't matter."

She got to her feet. "Are you abducting me?"

"Yes."

She sighed. "Okay." She glanced at him ruefully. "If you don't mind, I'd really like to go to Mars. Since I'm being abducted, I mean."

He managed a rough laugh.

She went around to the passenger side. He opened the door for her.

"You're Mr. Brandon," she said when he climbed into the driver's seat and slammed the door.

"Yes."

She drew in a breath. "I'm Michelle."

"Michelle." He chuckled. "There was a song with that name. My father loved it. One of the lines was 'Michelle, *ma belle*.'" He glanced at her. "Do you speak French?"

"A little," she said. "I have it second period. It means something like 'my beauty.'" She laughed. "And that has nothing to do with me, I'm afraid. I'm just plain."

He glanced at her with raised eyebrows. Was she serious? She was gorgeous. Young, and untried, but her creamy complexion was without a blemish. She was nicely shaped and her hair was a pale blond. Those soft gray eyes reminded him of a fog in August...

He directed his eyes to the road. She was just a child, what was he thinking? "Beauty, as they say, is in the eye of the beholder."

"Do you speak French?" she asked, curious.

He nodded. "French, Spanish, Portuguese, Afrikaans, Norwegian, Russian, German and a handful of Middle Eastern dialects."

"Really?" She was fascinated. "Did you work as a translator or something?"

He pursed his lips. "From time to time," he said, and then laughed to himself.

"Cool."

He started the truck and drove down the road to the house he owned. It wasn't far, just about a half mile. It was a ranch house, set back off the road. There were oceans of flowers blooming around it in the summer, planted by the previous owner, Mrs. Eller, who had died. Of course, it was still just February, and very cold. There were no flowers here now.

"Mrs. Eller loved flowers."

"Excuse me?"

"She lived here all her life," she told him, smiling as they drove up to the front porch. "Her husband worked as a deputy sheriff. They had a son in the military, but he was killed overseas. Her husband died soon afterward. She planted so many flowers that you could never even see the house. I used to come over and visit her when I was little, with my grandfather."

"Your people are from here?"

"Oh, yes. For three generations. Daddy went to medical school in Georgia and then he set up a practice in cardiology in San Antonio. We lived there. But I spent every summer here with my grandparents while they were alive. Daddy kept the place up, after, and it was like a vacation home while Mama was alive." She swallowed. That loss had been harsh. "We still had everything, even the furniture, when Daddy decided to move us down here and take early retirement. She hated it from the first time she saw it." Her face hardened. "She's selling it. My stepmother, I mean. She's already talked about it."

He drew in a breath. He knew he was going to regret this. He got out, opened the passenger door and waited for her to get out. He led the way into the house, seated her in the kitchen and pulled out a pitcher of iced tea. When he had it in glasses, he sat down at the table with her.

"Go ahead," he invited. "Get it off your chest."

"It's not your problem…"

"You involved me in an attempted suicide," he said with a droll look. "That makes it my problem."

She grimaced. "I'm really sorry, Mr. Brandon…"

"Gabriel."

She hesitated.

He raised an eyebrow. "I'm not that old," he pointed out.

She managed a shy smile. "Okay."

He cocked his head. "Say it," he said, and his liquid black eyes stared unblinking into hers.

She felt her heart drop into her shoes. She swallowed down a hot wave of delight and hoped it didn't show. "Ga… Gabriel," she obliged.

His face seemed to soften. Just a little. He smiled, showing beautiful white teeth. "That's better."

She flushed. "I'm not…comfortable with men," she blurted out.

His eyes narrowed on her face, her averted eyes. "Does your stepmother have a boyfriend?"

She swallowed, hard. The glass in her hand trembled.

He took the glass from her and put it on the table. "Tell me."

It all poured out. Finding Roberta in Bert's arms just after the funeral, finding them on the couch together that day, the way Bert looked and her and tried to touch her, the visit from her minister…

"And I thought my life was complicated," he said heavily. He shook his head. "I'd forgotten what it was like to be young and at the mercy of older people."

She studied him quietly. The expression on his face was…odd.

"You know," she said softly. "You understand."

"I had a stepfather," he said through his teeth. "He was always after my sister. She was very pretty, almost fourteen. I was a few years older, and I was bigger than he was. Our mother loved him, God knew why. We'd moved back to Texas because the international company he worked for promoted him and he had to go to Dallas for the job. One day I heard my sister scream. I went into her room, and there he was. He'd tried to…" He stopped. His face was like stone. "My mother had to get a neighbor to pull me off him. After that, after she knew what had been going on, she still defended him. I was arrested, but the public defender got an earful. He spoke to my sister. My stepfather was arrested, charged, tried. My mother stood by him, the whole time. My sister was victimized by the defense attorney, after what she'd already suffered at our stepfather's hands. She was so traumatized by the experience that she doesn't even date."

She winced. One small hand went shyly to cover his clenched fist on the table. "I'm so sorry."

He seemed to mentally shake himself, as if he'd been locked into the past. He met her soft, concerned gaze. His big hand turned, curled around hers. "I've never spoken of it, until now."

"Maybe sometimes it's good to share problems. Dark memories aren't so bad when you force them into the light."

"Seventeen going on thirty?" he mused, smiling at her. It didn't occur to her to wonder how he knew her age.

She smiled. "There are always people who are in worse shape than you are. My friend Billy has an alcoholic father who beats him and his mother. The police are over there all the time, but his mother will never press charges. Sheriff Carson says the next time, he's going to jail, even if he has to press charges himself."

"Good for the sheriff."

"What happened, after the trial?" she prodded gently.

He curled his fingers around Michelle's, as if he enjoyed their soft comfort. She might have been fascinated to know that he'd never shared these memories with any other woman, and that, as a rule, he hated having people touch him.

"He went to jail for child abuse," he said. "My mother was there every visiting day."

"No, what happened to you and your sister?"

"My mother refused to have us in the house with her. We were going to be placed in foster homes. The public defender had a maiden aunt, childless, who was suicidal. Her problems weren't so terrible, but she tended to depression and she let them take her almost over the edge. So he thought we might be able to help each other. We went to live with Aunt Maude." He chuckled. "She was not what you think of as anybody's maiden aunt. She drove a Jaguar, smoked like a furnace, could drink any grown man under the table, loved bingo parties and cooked like a gourmet. Oh, and she spoke about twenty languages. In her youth, she was in the army and mustered out as a sergeant."

"Wow," she exclaimed. "She must have been fascinating to live with."

"She was. And she was rich. She spoiled us rotten. She got my sister into therapy, for a while at least, and me into the army right after I graduated." He smiled. "She was nuts about Christmas. We had trees that bent at the ceiling, and the limbs groaned under all the decorations. She'd go out and invite every street person she could find over to eat with us." His face sobered. "She said she'd seen foreign countries where the poor were treated better than they were here. Ironically, it was one of the same people she invited to Christmas dinner who stabbed her to death."

She winced. "I'm so sorry!"

"Me, too. By that time, though, Sara and I were grown. I was in the…military," he said, hoping she didn't notice the involuntary pause, "and Sara had her own apartment. Maude left everything she had to the two of us and her nephew. We tried to give our share back to him, as her only blood heir, but he just laughed and said he got to keep his aunt for years longer because of us. He went into private practice and made a fortune defending drug lords, so he didn't really need it, he told us."

"Defending drug lords." She shook her head.

"We all do what we do," he pointed out. "Besides, I've known at least one so-called drug lord who was better than some upright people."

She just laughed.

He studied her small hand. "If things get too rough for you over there, let me know. I'll manage something."

"It's only until graduation this spring," she pointed out.

"In some situations, a few months can be a lifetime," he said quietly.

She nodded.

"Friends help each other."

She studied his face. "Are we? Friends, I mean?"

"We must be. I haven't told anyone else about my stepfather."

"You didn't tell me the rest of it."

His eyes went back to her hand resting in his. "He got out on good behavior six months after his conviction and decided to make my sister pay for testifying against him. She called 911. The police shot him."

"Oh, my gosh."

"My mother blamed both of us for it. She moved back to Canada, to Alberta, where we grew up."

"Are you Canadian?" she asked curiously.

He smiled. "I'm actually Texas born. We moved to Canada to stay with my mother's people when my father was in the military and stationed overseas. Sara was born in Calgary. We lived there until just after my mother married my stepfather."

"Did you see your mother again, after that?" she asked gently.

He shook his head. "Our mother never spoke to us again. She died a few years back. Her attorney tracked me down and said she left her estate, what there was of it, to the cousins in Alberta."

"I'm so sorry."

"Life is what it is. I had hoped she might one day realize what she'd done to my sister. She never did."

"We can't help who we love, or what it does to mess us up."

He frowned. "You really are seventeen going on thirty."

She laughed softly. "Maybe I'm an old soul."

"Ah. Been reading philosophy, have we?"

"Yes." She paused. "You haven't mentioned your father."

He smiled sadly. "He was in a paramilitary group overseas. He stepped on an antipersonnel mine."

She didn't know what a paramilitary group was, so she just nodded.

"He was from Dallas," he continued. "He had a small ranch in Texas that he inherited from his grandfather. He and my mother met at the Calgary Stampede. He trained horses and he'd sold several to be used at the stampede. She had an uncle who owned a ranch in Alberta and also supplied livestock to the stampede." He stared at her small hand in his. "Her people were French-Canadian. One of my grandmothers was a member of the Blackfoot Nation."

"Wow!"

He smiled.

"Then, you're an American citizen," she said.

"Our parents did the whole citizenship process. In short, I now have both Canadian and American citizenship."

"My dad loved this Canadian television show, *Due South.* He had the whole DVD collection. I liked the Mountie's dog. He was a wolf."

He laughed. "I've got the DVDs, too. I loved the show. It was hilarious."

She glanced at the clock on the wall. "I have to go. If you aren't going to run over me, I'll have to fix supper in case she comes home to eat. It's going to be gruesome. She'll still be furious about the stamp collection." Her face grew hard. "She won't find it. I've got a hiding place she doesn't know about."

He smiled. "Devious."

"Not normally. But she's not selling Daddy's stamps."

He let go of her hand and got up from his chair. "If she hits you again, call 911."

"She'd kill me for that."

"Not likely."

She sighed. "I guess I could, if I had to."

"You mentioned your minister. Who is he?"

"Jake Blair. Why?"

His expression was deliberately blank.

"Do you know him? He's a wonderful minister. Odd thing, my stepmother was intimidated by him."

He hesitated, and seemed to be trying not to laugh. "Yes. I've heard of him."

"He told her that his daughter was going to pick me up and bring me home from church every week. His daughter works for the Jacobsville police chief."

"Cash Grier."

She nodded. "He's very nice."

"Cash Grier?" he exclaimed. "Nice?"

"Oh, I know people talk about him, but he came to speak to my civics class once. He's intelligent."

"Very."

He helped her back into the truck and drove her to her front door.

She hesitated before she got out, turning to him. "Thank you. I don't think I've ever been so depressed. I've never actually tried to kill myself before."

His liquid black eyes searched hers. "We all have days when we're ridden by the 'black dog.'"

She blinked. "Excuse me?"

He chuckled. "Winston Churchill had periods of severe depression. He called it that."

She frowned. "Winston Churchill…"

"There was this really big world war," he said facetiously, with over-the-top enthusiasm, "and this country called England, and it had a leader during—"

"Oh, give me a break!" She burst out laughing.

He grinned at her. "Just checking."

She shook her head. "I know who he was. I just had to put it into context is all. Thanks again."

"Anytime."

She got out and closed the door, noting with relief that Roberta hadn't come home yet. She smiled and waved. He waved back. When he drove off, she noticed that he didn't look back. Not at all.

She had supper ready when Roberta walked in the door. Her stepmother was still fuming.

"I'm not eating beef," she said haughtily. "You know I hate it. And are those mashed potatoes? I'll bet you crammed them with butter!"

"Yes, I did," Michelle replied quietly, "because you always said you liked them that way."

Roberta's cheeks flushed. She shifted, as if the words, in that quiet voice, made her feel guilty.

In fact, they did. She was remembering her behavior with something close to shame. Her husband had only been dead three weeks. She'd tossed his belongings, refused to go to the funeral, made fun of her stepdaughter at every turn, even slapped her for messing up the sale of stamps which Alan had left to Michelle. And after all that, the child made her favorite food.

Her behavior should be raising red flags, but her step-daughter was, thankfully, too naive to notice it. Bert's doing, she thought bitterly. All his fault.

"You don't have to eat it," Michelle said, turning away.

Roberta made a rough sound in her throat. "It's all right," she managed tautly. She sat down at the table. She glanced at Michelle, who was dipping a tea bag in a cup of steaming water. "Aren't you eating?"

"I had soup."

Roberta made inroads into the meat loaf and mashed potatoes. The girl had even made creamed peas, her favorite.

She started to put her fork down and noticed her hand trembling. She jerked it down onto the wood and pulled her hand back.

It was getting worse. She needed more and more. Bert was complaining about the expense. They'd had a fight. She'd gone storming up to his apartment in San Antonio to cry on his shoulder about her idiot step-daughter and he'd started complaining when she dipped into his stash. But after all, he was the one who'd gotten her hooked in the first place.

It had taken more money than she'd realized to keep up, and Alan had finally figured out what she was doing. They'd argued. He'd asked her for a divorce, but she'd pleaded with him. She had no place to go. She knew Bert wouldn't hear of her moving in with him. Her whole family was dead.

Alan had agreed, but the price of his agreement was that she had to move down to his hometown with him after he sold his very lucrative practice in San Antonio.

She'd thought he meant the move to be a temporary one. He was tired of the rat race. He wanted something quieter. But they'd only been in his old family homestead for a few days when he confessed that he'd been diagnosed with an inoperable cancer. He wanted to spend some time with his daughter before the end. He wanted to run a free clinic, to help people who had no money for doctors. He wanted his life to end on a positive note, in the place where he was born.

So here was Roberta, stuck after his death with a habit she could no longer afford and no way to break it. Stuck with Cinderella here, who knew about as much about life as she knew about men.

She glared at the girl. She'd really needed the money from those stamps. There was nothing left that she could liquidate for cash. She hadn't taken all of Alan's things to the landfill. She'd told Michelle that so she wouldn't look for them. She'd gone to a consignment shop in San Antonio and sold the works, even his watch. It brought in a few hundred dollars. But she was going through money like water.

"What did you do with the stamps?" Roberta asked suddenly.

Michelle schooled her features to give away nothing, and she turned. "I hitched a ride into town and asked Cash Grier to keep them for me."

Roberta sucked in her breath. Fear radiated from her. "Cash Grier?"

Michelle nodded. "I figured it was the safest place. I told him I was worried about someone stealing them while I was at school."

Which meant she hadn't told the man that Roberta

had slapped her. Thank God. All she needed now was an assault charge. She had to be more careful. The girl was too stupid to recognize her symptoms. The police chief wouldn't be. She didn't want anyone from law enforcement on the place. But she didn't even have the grace to blush when Michelle made the comment about someone possibly "stealing" her stamp collection.

She got up from the table. She was thirsty, but she knew it would be disastrous to pick up her cup of coffee. Not until she'd taken what she needed to steady her hands.

She paused on her way to the bathroom, with her back to Michelle. "I'm… I shouldn't have slapped you," she bit off.

She didn't wait for a reply. She was furious with herself for that apology. Why should the kid's feelings matter to her, anyway? She pushed away memories of how welcoming Michelle had been when she first started dating Alan. Michelle had wanted to impress her father's new friend.

Well, that was ancient history now. She was broke and Alan had died, leaving her next to nothing. She picked up her purse from the side table and went into the bathroom with it.

Michelle cleaned off the table and put the dishes into the dishwasher. Roberta hadn't come out of the bathroom even after she'd done all that, so she went to her room.

Michelle had been surprised by the almost-apology. But once she thought about it, she realized that Roberta might think she was going to press charges. She was afraid of her stepmother. She had violent mood swings and she'd threatened to hit Michelle several times.

It was odd, because when she'd first married Dr. Alan Godfrey, Michelle had liked her. She'd been fun to be around. But she had a roving eye. She liked men. If they went to a restaurant, someone always struck up a conversation with Roberta, who was exquisitely groomed and dressed and had excellent manners. Roberta enjoyed masculine attention, without being either coarse or forward.

Then, several months ago, everything had changed. Roberta had started going out at night alone. She told her husband that she'd joined an exercise club at a friend's house, a private one. They did aerobics and Pilates and things like that. Just women.

But soon afterward, Roberta became more careless about her appearance. Her manners slipped, badly. She complained about everything. Alan wasn't giving her enough spending money. The house needed cleaning, why wasn't Michelle doing more when she wasn't in school? She wasn't doing any more cooking, she didn't like it, Michelle would have to take over for her. And on it went. Alan had been devastated by the change. So had Michelle, who had to bear the brunt of most of Roberta's fury.

"Some women have mood swings as they get older," Alan had confided to his daughter, but there was something odd in his tone of voice. "But you mustn't say anything about it to her. She doesn't like thinking she's getting on in years. All right?"

"All right, Daddy," she'd agreed, with a big smile. He'd hugged her close. "That's my girl."

* * *

Roberta had gone away for a few weeks after that. Then, not too long after her return, they'd moved to Comanche Wells, into the house where Michelle had spent so many happy weeks with her grandparents every summer.

The elderly couple had died in a wreck only a few years after Michelle's mother had died of a stroke. It had been a blow. Her father had gone through terrible grief. But then, so had Michelle.

Despite the double tragedy, Comanche Wells and this house seemed far more like home than San Antonio ever had, because it was so small that Michelle knew almost every family who lived in it. She knew people in Jacobsville, too, of course, but it was much larger. Comanche Wells was tiny by comparison.

Michelle loved the farm animals that her grandparents had kept. They always had dogs and cats and chickens for her to play with. But by the time Alan moved his family down here, there was only the small herd of beef cattle. Now the herd had been sold and was going to a local rancher who was going to truck the steers over to his own ranch.

Her door opened suddenly. Roberta looked wild-eyed. "I'm going back up to San Antonio for the night. I have to see Bert."

"All…" She had started to say "all right," but the door slammed. Roberta went straight out to her car, revved it up and scattered gravel on the way to the road.

It was odd behavior, even for her.

Michelle felt a little better than she had. At least

she and Roberta might be able to manage each other's company until May, when graduation rolled around.

But Gabriel had helped her cope with what she thought was unbearable. She smiled, remembering his kindness, remembering the strong, warm clasp of his fingers. Her heart sailed at the memory. She'd almost never held hands with a boy. Once, when she was twelve, at a school dance. But the boy had moved away, and she was far too shy and old-fashioned to appeal to most of the boys in her high school classes. There had been another boy, at high school, but that date had ended in near disaster.

Gabriel was no boy. He had to be at least in his mid-twenties. He would think of her as a child. She grimaced. Well, she was growing up. One day...who knew what might happen?

She opened her English textbook and got busy with her homework. Then she remembered with a start what she'd told Roberta, that lie about having Cash Grier keep the stamp book. What if Roberta asked him?

Her face flamed. It would be a disaster. She'd lied, and Roberta would know it. She'd tear the house apart looking for that collection...

Then Michelle calmed down. Roberta seemed afraid of Cash Grier. Most people were. She doubted very seriously that her stepmother would approach him. But just to cover her bases, she was going to stop by his office after school. She could do it by pretending to ask Carlie what time she would pick her up for church services. Then maybe she could work up the nerve to tell him what she'd done. She would go without lunch. That would give her just enough money to pay for a cab home from Jacobsville, which was only a few miles away. Good thing she already had her lunch money for the week, because Roberta had told her there wouldn't be any more. She was going to have to do without lunch from now on, apparently. Or get a job. And good luck to that, without a car or a driver's license.

She sighed. Her life was more complicated than it had ever been. But things might get better. Someday.

Chapter 3

Michelle got off the school bus in downtown Jacobsville on Friday afternoon. She had to stop by the newspaper office to ask Minette Carson if she'd give her a reference for the scholarship she was applying for. The office was very close to police chief Grier's office, whom she also needed to see. And she had just enough money to get the local cab company to take her home.

Minette was sitting out front at her desk when Michelle walked in. She grinned and got up to greet her.

"How's school?" she asked.

"Going very well," Michelle said. "I wanted to ask if I could put you down as a reference. I'm applying for that journalism scholarship we spoke about last month, at Marist College in San Antonio."

"Of course you can."

"Thanks. I'm hoping I can keep my grades up so I'll have a shot at it."

"You'll do fine, Michelle. You have a way with words." She held up a hand when Michelle looked as if she might protest. "I never lie about writing. I'm brutally honest. If I thought you didn't have the skill, I'd keep my mouth shut."

Michelle laughed. "Okay. Thanks, then."

Minette perched on the edge of her desk. "I was wondering if you might like to work part-time for me. After school and Saturday morning."

Michelle's jaw dropped. "You mean, work here?" she exclaimed. "Oh, my gosh, I'd love to!" Then the joy drained out of her face. "I can't," she groaned. "I don't drive, and I don't have cab fare home. I mean, I do today, but I went without lunch…" Her face flamed.

"Carlie lives just past you," she said gently. "She works until five. So do we. I know she'd let you ride with her. She works Saturday mornings, too."

The joy came back into her features. "I'll ask her!"

Minette chuckled. "Do that. And let me know."

"I will, I promise."

"You can start Monday, if you like. Do you have a cell phone?" Minette asked.

Michelle hesitated and shook her head with lowered eyes.

"Don't worry about it. We'll get you one."

"Oh, but…"

"I'll have you phoning around town for news. Junior reporter stuff," she added with a grin. "A cell's an absolute necessity."

"In that case, okay, but I'll pay you back."

"That's a deal."

"I'll go over and talk to Carlie."

"Stop back by and let me know, okay?"

"Okay!"

She didn't normally rush, but she was so excited that her feet carried her across the street like wings.

She walked into the police station. Cash Grier was perched on Carlie's desk, dictating from a paper he held in his hand. He stopped when he saw Michelle.

"Sorry," Michelle said, coloring. She clutched her textbooks to her chest almost as a shield. "I just needed to ask Carlie something. I can come back later..."

"Nonsense," Cash said, and grinned.

She managed a shy smile. "Thanks." She hesitated. "I told a lie to my stepmother," she blurted out. "I think you should know, because it involved you."

His dark eyebrows arched. "Really? Did you volunteer me for the lead in a motion picture or something? Because I have to tell you, my asking price is extremely high..."

She laughed with pure delight. "No. I told her I gave you my father's stamp collection for safekeeping." She flushed again. "She was going to sell it. She'd already thrown away all his stuff. He and I worked on the stamp collection together as long as I can remember. It's all I have left of him." She swallowed. Hard.

Cash got up. He towered over her. He wasn't laughing. "You bring it in here and I'll put it in the safe," he said gently. "Nobody will touch it."

"Thanks." She was trying not to cry. "That's so kind..."

"Now, don't cry or you'll have me in tears. What

would people think? I mean, I'm a big, tough cop. I can't be seen standing around sobbing all over the place. Crime would flourish!"

That amused her. She stopped biting her lip and actually grinned.

"That's better." His black eyes narrowed quizzically. "Your stepmother seems to have some issues. I got an earful from your minister this morning."

She nodded sadly. "She was so different when we lived in San Antonio. I mean, we went shopping together, we took turns cooking. Then we moved down here and she got mixed up with that Bert person." She shivered. "He gives me cold chills, but she's crazy about him."

"Bert Sims?" Cash asked in a deceptively soft tone.

"That's him."

Cash didn't say anything else. "If things get rough over there, call me, will you? I know you're outside the city limits, but I can get to Hayes Carson pretty quick if I have to, and he has jurisdiction."

"Oh, it's nothing like that…"

"Isn't it?" Cash asked.

She felt chilled. It was as if he was able to see Roberta through her eyes, and he saw everything.

"She did apologize. Sort of. For hitting me, I mean."

"Hitting you?" Cash stood straighter. "When?"

"I messed up the sale of Daddy's stamps. She was wild-eyed and screaming. She just slapped me, is all. She's been excitable since before Daddy died, but now she's just…just…nuts. She talks about money all the time, like she's dying to get her hands on some. But she doesn't buy clothes or cosmetics, she doesn't even dress well anymore."

"Do you know why?"

She shook her head. She drew in a breath. "She doesn't drink," she said. "I know that's what you're thinking. She and Daddy used to have drinks every night, and she had a problem for a little while, but she got over it."

Cash just nodded. "You let me know if things get worse. Okay?"

"Okay, Chief. Thanks," she added.

The phone rang. Carlie answered it. "It's your wife," she said with a big grin.

Cash's face lit up. "Really? Wow. A big-time movie star calling me up on the phone. I'm just awed, I am." He grinned. Everybody knew his wife, Tippy, had been known as the Georgia Firefly when she'd been a super-model and, later, an actress. "I'll take it in my office. With the door closed." He made a mock scowl. "And no eavesdropping."

Carlie put her hand over her heart. "I swear."

"Not in my office, you don't," he informed her. "Swearing is a misdemeanor."

She stuck out her tongue at his departing back.

"I saw that," he said without looking behind him. He went into his office and closed the door on two giggling women.

"He's a trip to work for," Carlie enthused, her green eyes sparkling in a face framed by short, dark, wavy hair. "I was scared to death of him when I interviewed for the job. At least, until he accused me of hiding his bullets and telling his men that he read fashion magazines in the bathroom."

Michelle laughed.

"He's really funny. He says he keeps files on aliens in the filing cabinet and locks it so I won't peek." The smile moderated. "But if there's an emergency, he's the toughest guy I've ever known. I would never cross him, if I was a criminal."

"They say he chased a speeder all the way to San Antonio once."

She laughed. "That wasn't the chief. That was Kilraven, who worked here undercover." She leaned forward. "He really belongs to a federal agency. We're not supposed to mention it."

"I won't tell," Michelle promised.

"However, the chief—" she nodded toward his closed door "—got on a plane to an unnamed foreign country, tossed a runaway criminal into a bag and boated him to Miami. The criminal was part of a drug cartel. He killed a small-town deputy because he thought the man was a spy. He wasn't, but he was just as dead. Then the feds got involved and the little weasel escaped into a country that didn't have an extradition treaty with us. However, once he was on American soil, he was immediately arrested by Dade County deputies." She grinned. "The chief denied ever having seen the man, and nobody could prove that it was him on the beach. And," she added darkly, "you never heard that from me. Right?"

"Right!"

Carlie laughed. "So what can I do for you?"

"I need a ride home from work."

"I've got another hour to go, but…"

"Not today," Michelle said. "Starting Monday. Minette Carson just offered me a part-time job, but I don't have a way to get home. And she said I could work part-time Saturday, but I can't drive and I don't have a car."

"You can ride with me, and I'd welcome the company," Carlie said easily.

"I'll chip in for the gas."

"That would really help! Have you seen what I drive?" She groaned. "My dad has this thing about cars. He thinks you need an old truck to keep you from speeding, so he bought me a twelve-year-old tank. At least, it looks like a tank." She frowned. "Maybe it was a tank and he had it remodeled. Anyway, it barely gets twelve miles to a gallon and it won't go over fifty." She shook her head. "He drives a vintage Ford Cobra," she added with a scowl. "One of the neatest rides on the planet and I'm not allowed to touch it, can you believe that?"

Michelle just grinned. She didn't know anything about cars. She did recall the way the minister had peeled out of the driveway, scattering gravel. That car he drove had one big engine.

"Your dad scared my stepmother." Michelle laughed. "She wasn't letting me go to church. Your dad said I could ride with you." She stopped and flushed. "I really feel like I'm imposing. I wish I could drive. I wish I had a car…"

"It's really not imposing," Carlie said softly, smiling. "As I said, I'd like the company. I go down lots of back roads getting here from Comanche Wells. I'm not spooky or anything, but this guy did try to kill my Dad with a knife." She lowered her eyes. "I got in the way."

Michelle felt guilty that she hadn't remembered. "I'll learn karate," she promised. "We can go to a class together or something, and if anybody attacks us we can fight back!"

"Bad idea," Cash said, rejoining them. "A few weeks of martial arts won't make you an expert. Even an expert," he added solemnly, "knows better than to fight if he can get away from an armed man."

"That isn't what the ads say," Carlie mused, grinning.

"Yes, I know," Cash replied. "Take it from me, disarming someone with a gun is difficult even for a black belt." He leaned forward. "Which I am."

Carlie stood up, bowed deeply from the waist, and said, "Sensei!" Cash lost it. He roared with laughter.

"You could teach us," Michelle suggested. "Couldn't you?"

Cash just smiled. "I suppose it wouldn't hurt. Just a few basics for an emergency. But if you have an armed opponent, you run," he said firmly. "Or if you're cornered, scream, make a fuss. Never," he emphasized, "get into a car with anyone who threatens to kill you if you don't. Once he's got you in a car, away from help, you're dead, anyway."

Michelle felt chills run down her spine. "Okay."

Carlie looked uncomfortable. She knew firsthand about an armed attacker. Unconsciously, she rubbed the shoulder where the knife had gone in. She'd tried to protect her father. Her assailant had been arrested, but had died soon afterward. She never knew why her father had been the target of an attack by a madman.

"Deep thoughts?" Michelle asked her.

She snapped back. "Sorry. I was remembering the guy who attacked my father." She frowned. "What sort of person attacks a minister, for goodness' sake!"

"Come on down to federal lockup with me, and I'll show you a baker's dozen who have," Cash told her. "Religious arguments quite often lead to murder, even in families. That's why," he added, "we don't discuss politics or religion in the office." He frowned. "Well, if someone died in here, we'd probably say a prayer. And if the president came to see me, and why wouldn't he, we'd probably discuss his foreign policy."

"Why would the president come to see you?" Michelle asked innocently.

Cash pursed his lips. "For advice, of course. I have some great ideas about foreign policy."

"For instance?" Carlie mused.

"I think we should declare war on Tahiti."

They both stared at him.

"Well, if we do, we can send troops, right?" he continued. "And what soldier in his right mind wouldn't want to go and fight in Tahiti? Lush tropical flowers, fire-dancing, beautiful women, the ocean…"

"Tahiti doesn't have a standing army, I don't think," Michelle ventured.

"All the better. We can just occupy it for like three weeks, let them surrender, and then give them foreign aid." He glowered. "Now you've done it. You'll repeat that everywhere and the president will hear about it and he'll never have to come and hear me explain it.

You've blown my chances for an invitation to the White House," he groaned. "And I did so want to spend a night in the Lincoln bedroom!"

"Listen, break out those files on aliens that you keep in your filing cabinet and tell the president you've got them!" Carlie suggested, while Michelle giggled. "He'll come right down here to have a look at them!"

"They won't let him," Cash sighed. "His security clearance isn't high enough."

"What?" Carlie exclaimed.

"Well, he's only in the office for four years, eight tops. So the guys in charge of the letter agencies—the really secretive ones—allegedly keep some secrets to themselves. Particularly those dealing with aliens." He chuckled.

The girls, who didn't know whether to believe him or not, just laughed along with him.

Michelle stopped back by Minette's office to tell her the good news, and to thank her again for the job.

"You know," she said, "Chief Grier is really nice."

"Nice when he likes you," Minette said drily. "There are a few criminals in maximum-security prisons who might disagree."

"No doubt there."

"So, will Monday suit you, to start to work?" Minette asked.

"I'd really love to start yesterday." Michelle laughed. "I'm so excited!"

Minette grinned. "Monday will come soon enough. We'll see you then."

"Can you write me a note? Just in case I need one?"

She was thinking of how to break it to Roberta. That was going to be tricky.

"No problem." Minette went to her desk, typed out an explanation of Michelle's new position, and signed it. She handed it to the younger woman. "There you go."

"Dress code?" Michelle asked, glancing around the big open room where several people were sitting at desks, to a glass-walled room beyond in which big sheets of paper rested on a long section like a chalkboard.

"Just be neat," Minette said easily. "I mostly kick around in jeans and T-shirts, although I dress up when I go to political meetings or to interviews with state or federal politicians. You'll need to learn how to use a camera, as well. We have digital ones. They're very user-friendly."

"This is very exciting," Michelle said, her gray eyes glimmering with delight.

Minette laughed. "It is to me, too, and I've done this since I was younger than you are. I grew up running around this office." She looked around with pure love in her eyes. "It's home."

"I'm really looking forward to it. Will I just be reporting news?"

"No. Well, not immediately, at least. You'll learn every aspect of the business, from selling ads to typing copy to composition. Even subscriptions." She leaned forward. "You'll learn that some subscribers probably used to be doctors, because the handwriting looks more like Sanskrit than English."

Michelle chuckled. "I'll cope. My dad had the worst handwriting in the world."

"And he was a doctor," Minette agreed, smiling.

The smile faded. "He was a very good doctor," she said, trying not to choke up. "Sorry," she said, wiping away a tear. "It's still hard."

"It takes time," Minette said with genuine sympathy. "I lost my mother, my stepfather, my stepmother—I loved them all. You'll adjust, but you have to get through the grief process first. Tears are healing."

"Thanks."

"If you need to talk, I'm here. Anytime. Night or day."

Michelle wiped away more tears. "That's really nice of you."

"I know how it feels."

The phone rang and one of the employees called out. "For you, boss. The mayor returning your call."

Minette grimaced. "I have to take it. I'm working on a story about the new water system. It's going to be super."

"I'll see you after school Monday, then. And thanks again."

"My pleasure."

Michelle went home with dreams of journalism dancing in her head. She'd never been so happy. Things were really looking up.

She noted that Roberta's car was in the driveway and she mentally braced herself for a fight. It was suppertime and she hadn't been there to cook. She was going to be in big trouble.

Sure enough, the minute she walked in the door, Roberta threw her hands up and glared at her. "I'm not cooking," she said furiously. "That's your job. Where the hell have you been?"

Michelle swallowed. "I was in...in town."

"Doing what?" came the tart query.

She shifted. "Getting a job."

"A job?" She frowned, and her eyes didn't seem to quite focus. "Well, I'm not driving you to work, even if somebody was crazy enough to hire you!"

"I have a ride," she replied.

"A job," she scoffed. "As if you're ever around to do chores as it is. You're going to get a job? Who's going to do the laundry and the housecleaning and the cooking?"

Michelle bit her tongue, trying not to say what she was thinking. "I have to have money for lunch," she said, thinking fast.

Roberta blinked, then she remembered that she'd said Michelle wasn't getting any more lunch money. She averted her eyes.

"Besides, I have to save for college. I'll start in the fall semester."

"Jobs. College." Roberta looked absolutely furious. "And you think I'm going to stay down here in this hick town while you sashay off to college in some big city, do you?"

"I graduate in just over three months..."

"I'm putting the house on the market," Roberta shot back. She held up a hand. "Don't even bother arguing. I'm listing the house with a San Antonio broker, not one from here." She gave Michelle a dirty look.

"They're all on your side, trying to keep the property off the market. It won't work. I need money!"

For just one instant, Michelle thought about letting her have the stamps. Then she decided it was useless to do that. Roberta would spend the money and still try to sell the house. She comforted herself with what the local Realtor had told her—that it would take time for the will to get through probate. If there was a guardian angel, perhaps hers would drag out the time required for all that. And even then, there was a chance the house wouldn't sell.

"I don't imagine a lot of people want to move to a town this small," Michelle said out loud.

"Somebody local might buy it. One of those ranchers." She made it sound like a dirty word.

That made Michelle feel better. If someone from here bought the house, they might consider renting it to her. Since she had a job, thanks to Minette, she could probably afford reasonable rent.

Roberta wiped her face. She was sweating.

Michelle frowned. "Are you all right?"

"Of course I'm all right, I'm just hungry!"

"I'll make supper." She went to her room to put her books away and stopped short. The place was in shambles. Drawers had been emptied, the clothes from the shelves in the closet were tossed haphazardly all over the floor. Michelle's heart jumped, but she noticed without looking too hard that the baseboards in the closet were still where they should be. She looked around but not too closely. After all, she'd told Roberta that Chief Grier had her father's stamp collection. It hadn't stopped Roberta from searching the room. But it was obvious that she hadn't found anything.

She went back out into the hall, where her stepmother was standing with folded arms, a disappointed look on her face. She'd expected that the girl would go immediately to where she'd hidden the stamps. The fact that she didn't even search meant they weren't here. Damn the luck, she really had taken them to the police chief. And even Roberta wasn't brash enough to walk up to Cash Grier and demand the stamp collection back, although she was probably within her legal rights to do so.

"Don't tell me," Michelle said, staring at her. "Squirrels?"

Roberta was disconcerted. Without meaning to, she burst out laughing at the girl's audacity. She turned away, shaking her head. "All right, I just wanted to make sure the stamp collection wasn't still here. I guess you were telling the truth all along."

"Roberta, if you need money so much, why don't you get a job?"

"I had a job, if you recall," she replied. "I worked in retail."

That was true. Roberta had worked at the cosmetics counter in one of San Antonio's most prestigious department stores.

"But I'm not going back to that," Roberta scoffed. "Once I sell this dump of a house, I'll be able to go to New York or Los Angeles and find a man who really is rich, instead of one who's just pretending to be," she added sarcastically.

"Gosh. Poor Bert," Michelle said. "Does he know?"

Roberta's eyes flashed angrily. "If you say a word to him…!"

Michelle held up both hands. "Not my business."

"Exactly!" Roberta snapped. "Now, how about fixing supper?"

"Sure," Michelle agreed. "As soon as I clean up my room," she added in a bland tone.

Her stepmother actually flushed. She took a quick breath. She was shivering. "I need…more…" she mumbled to herself. She went back into her own room and slammed the door.

They ate together, but Michelle didn't taste much of her supper. Roberta read a fashion magazine while she spooned food into her mouth.

"Where are you getting a job? Who's going to even hire a kid like you?" she asked suddenly.

"Minette Carson."

The magazine stilled in her hands. "You're going to work for a newspaper?"

"Of course. I want to study journalism in college."

Roberta looked threatened. "Well, I don't want you working for newspapers. Find something else."

"I won't," Michelle said firmly. "This is what I want to do for a living. I have to start somewhere. And I have to save for college. Unless you'd like to volunteer to pay my tuition…"

"Ha! Fat chance!" Roberta scoffed.

"That's what I thought. I'm going to a public college, but I still have to pay for books and tuition."

"Newspapers. Filthy rags." Her voice sounded slurred.

She was picking at her food. Her fork was moving in slow motion. And she was still sweating.

"They do a great deal of good," Michelle argued. "They're the eyes and ears of the public."

"Nosy people sticking their heads into things that don't concern them!"

Michelle looked down at her plate. She didn't mention that people without things to hide shouldn't have a problem with that.

Roberta took her paper towel and mopped her sweaty face. She seemed disoriented and she was flushed, as well.

"You should see a doctor," Michelle said quietly. "There's that flu still going around."

"I'm not sick," the older woman said sharply. "And my health is none of your business!"

Michelle grimaced. She sipped milk instead of answering.

"It's too hot in here. You don't have to keep the thermostat so high!"

"It's seventy degrees," Michelle said, surprised. "I can't keep it higher or we couldn't afford the gas bill." She paid the bills with money that was grudgingly supplied by Roberta from the joint bank account she'd had with Michelle's father. Roberta hadn't lifted a finger to pay a bill since Alan had died.

"Well, it's still hot!" came the agitated reply. She got up from the table. "I'm going outside. I can't breathe in here."

Michelle watched her go with open curiosity. Odd. Roberta seemed out of breath and flushed more and more lately. She had episodes of shaking that seemed very unusual. She acted drunk sometimes, but Michelle knew she wasn't drinking. There was no liquor in the house. It probably was the flu. She couldn't understand why a person who was obviously sick wouldn't just go to the doctor in the first—

There was a loud thud from the general direction of the front porch.

Chapter 4

Michelle got up from her chair and went out onto the porch. It sounded as if Roberta had flung a chair against the wall, maybe in another outburst of temper.

She opened the door and stopped. Roberta was lying there, on her back on the porch, gasping for breath, her eyes wide, her face horrified.

"It's all right, I'll call 911!" She ran for the phone and took it outside with her while she pushed in the emergency services number.

Roberta was grimacing. "The pain!" she groaned. "Hurts…so…bad! Michelle…!"

Roberta held out her hand. Michelle took it, held it, squeezed it comfortingly.

"Jacobs County 911 Center," came a gentle voice on the line. "Is this an emergency?"

"Yes. This is Michelle Godfrey. My stepmother is

complaining of chest pain. She's short of breath and barely conscious."

"We'll get someone right out there. Stay on the line."

"Yes, of course."

"Help me," Roberta sobbed.

Michelle's hand closed tighter around her stepmother's. "The EMTs are on the way," she said gently. "It will be all right."

"Bert," Roberta choked. "Damn Bert! It's…his… fault!"

"Please don't try to get up," Michelle said, holding the older woman down. "Lie still."

"I'll…kill him," Roberta choked. "I'll kill him…!"

"Roberta, lie still," Michelle said firmly.

"Oh, God, it hurts!" Roberta sobbed. "My chest… my chest…!"

Sirens were becoming noticeable in the distance.

"They're almost there, dear," the operator said gently. "Just a few more minutes."

"Yes, I hear them," Michelle said. "She says her chest hurts."

There was muffled conversation in the background, on the phone.

Around the curve, the ambulance shot toward her leaving a wash of dust behind it. Roberta's grip on Michelle's hand was painful.

The older woman was white as a sheet. The hand Michelle was holding was cold and clammy. "I'm… sorry," Roberta bit off. Tears welled in her eyes. "He said it wasn't…pure! He swore…! It was too…much…" She gasped for breath. "Don't let Bert…get away…with it…" Her eyes closed. She shivered. The hand holding Michelle's went slack.

The ambulance was in the driveway now, and a man and a woman jumped out of it and ran toward the porch.

"She said her chest hurt." Michelle faltered as she got out of the way. "And she couldn't breathe." Tears were salty in her eyes.

Roberta had never been really kind to her, except at the beginning of her relationship with Michelle's father. But the woman was in such pain. It hurt her to see anyone like that, even a mean person.

"Is she going to be all right?" Michelle asked.

They ignored her. They were doing CPR. She recognized it, because one of the Red Cross people had come to her school and demonstrated it. In between compressions one EMT ran to the truck and came back with paddles. They set the machine up and tried to restart Roberta's heart. Once. Twice. Three times. In between there were compressions of the chest and hurried communications between the EMTs and a doctor at the hospital.

After a few minutes, one EMT looked at the other and shook his head. They stood up. The man turned to Michelle. "I'm very sorry."

"Sorry. Sorry?" She looked down at the pale, motionless woman on the dusty front porch with a blank expression. "You mean, she's…?"

They nodded. "We'll call the coroner and have him come out, and we'll notify the sheriff's department, since you're outside the city limits. We can't move her until he's finished. Do you want to call the funeral home and make arrangements?"

"Yes, uh, yes." She pushed her hair back. She couldn't believe this. Roberta was dead? How could she be dead? She just stood there, numb, while the EMTs loaded up their equipment and went back out to the truck.

"Is there someone who can stay with you until the coroner gets here?" the female EMT asked softly, staring worriedly at Michelle.

She stared back at the woman, devoid of thought. Roberta was dead. She'd watched her die. She was in shock.

Just as the reality of the situation really started to hit her, a pickup truck pulled up into the driveway, past the EMT vehicle, and stopped. A tall, good-looking man got out of it, paused to speak to the male EMT and then came right up to the porch.

Without a word, he pulled Michelle into his arms and held her, rocked her. She burst into tears.

"I'll take care of her," he told the female EMT with a smile.

"Thanks," she said. "She'll need to make arrangements…"

"I'll handle it."

"We've notified the authorities," the EMT added. "The sheriff's department and the coroner should arrive shortly." The EMTs left, the ambulance silent and grim now, instead of alive with light and sound, as when it had arrived.

Michelle drank in the scent that clung to Gabriel, the smells of soap and spicy cologne, the leather smell of his jacket. Beneath that, the masculine odor of his skin. She pressed close into his arms and let the tears fall.

* * *

Zack Tallman arrived just behind the coroner. Michelle noted the activity on the front porch, but she didn't want to see Roberta's body again. She didn't go outside.

She heard Gabriel and the lawman and the coroner discussing things, and there was the whirring sound a camera made. She imagined that they were photographing Roberta. She shivered. It was so sudden. They'd just had supper and Roberta went outside because she was hot. And then Roberta was dead. It didn't seem real, somehow.

A few minutes later, she heard the coroner's van drive away. Gabriel and Zack Tallman came in together. Zack was handsome, tall, lean and good-looking. His eyes were almost as dark as Gabriel's, but he looked older than Gabriel did.

"The coroner thinks it was a heart attack," Zack was saying. "They'll have to do an autopsy, however. It's required in cases of sudden death."

"Hayes told me that Yancy Dean went back to Florida," Gabriel said. "He was the only investigator you had, wasn't he?"

"He was," Zack said, "so when he resigned, I begged Hayes on my knees for the investigator's position. It's a peach of a job."

"Pays about the same as a senior deputy," Gabriel mused, tongue in cheek.

"Yes, but I get to go to seminars and talk to forensic anthropologists and entomologists and do hard-core investigative work," he added. He chuckled. "I've been after Yancy's job forever. Not that he was bad at it—he was great. But his parents needed him in Florida and he was offered his old job back with Dade County SO," he added, referring to the sheriff's office.

"Well, it worked out for both of you, then," Gabriel said.

"Yes." He sobered as Michelle came into the living room from the kitchen. "Michelle, I'm sorry about your stepmother. I know it must be hard, coming so close on the heels of your father passing."

"Thanks, Mr. Tallman," she replied gently. "Yes, it is." She shook her head. "I still have to talk to the funeral director."

"I'll take care of that for you," Gabriel told her.

"Thanks," she added.

"Michelle, can you tell me how it happened?" Zack asked her.

"Of course." She went through the afternoon, ending with Roberta feeling too hot and going out on the porch to cool off.

He stopped her when she mentioned what Roberta had said about Bert and had her repeat Roberta's last words. He frowned. "I'd like to see her room."

Michelle led the way. The room was a mess. Roberta never picked anything up, and Michelle hadn't had time to do any cleaning. She was embarrassed at the way it looked. But Zack wasn't interested in the clutter. He started going through drawers until he opened the one in the bedside table.

He pulled out his digital camera and shot several photos of the drawer and its contents before he put on a pair of gloves, reached into it and pulled out an oblong case. He dusted the case for fingerprints before he opened it on the table and photographed that, too, along with a small vial of white powder. He turned to Gabriel who exchanged a long look with him.

"That explains a lot," Zack said. "I'll take this up to the crime lab in San Antonio and have them run it for us, but I'm pretty sure what it is and where she got it."

"What is it?" Michelle asked, curious.

"Something evil," Zack said.

Michelle wasn't dense. "Drugs," she said icily. "It's drugs, isn't it?"

"Hard narcotics," Zack agreed.

"That's why she was so crazy all the time," Michelle said heavily. "She drank to excess when we lived in San Antonio. Dad got her into treatment and made her quit. I was sure she was okay, because we didn't have any liquor here. But she had these awful mood swings, and sometimes she hit me..." She bit her lip.

"Well, people under the influence aren't easy to live with," Zack replied heavily. "Not at all."

Zack sat down with Michelle and Gabriel at the kitchen table and questioned Michelle further about Roberta's recent routine, including trips to see Bert Sims in San Antonio. Roberta's last words were telling. He wrote it all down and gave Michelle a form to fill out with all the pertinent information about the past few hours. When she finished, he took it with him.

There was no real crime scene, since Roberta died of what was basically a heart attack brought on by a drug overdose. The coroner's assistant took photos on the front porch, adding to Zack's, so there was a record of where Roberta died. But the house wasn't searched, beyond Zack's thorough documentation of Roberta's room.

"Bert Sims may try to come around to see if Roberta had anything left, to remove evidence," Zack said solemnly to Michelle. "It isn't safe for you to be here alone."

"I've got that covered," Gabriel said with a smile. "Nobody's going to touch her."

Zack smiled. "I already had that figured out," he mused, and Gabriel cleared his throat.

"I have a chaperone in mind," Gabriel replied. "Just so you know."

Zack patted him on the back. "I figured that out already, too." He nodded toward Michelle. "Sorry again."

"Me, too," Michelle said sadly.

Michelle made coffee while Gabriel spoke to his sister, Sara, on the phone. She couldn't understand what he was saying. He was speaking French. She recognized it, but it was a lot more complicated than, "My brother has a brown suit," which was about her level of skill in the language.

His voice was low, and urgent. He spoke again, listened, and then spoke once more. *"C'est bien,"* he concluded, and hung up.

"That was French," Michelle said.

"Yes." He sat down at the table and toyed with the thick white mug she'd put in front of him. There was good china, too—Roberta had insisted on it when she and Alan first married. But the mug seemed much more Gabriel's style than fancy china. She'd put a mug at her place, as well. She had to have coffee in the morning or she couldn't even get to school.

"This morning everything seemed much less complicated," she said after she'd poured coffee. He refused cream and sugar, and she smiled. She didn't take them, either.

"You think you're going in a straight line, and life puts a curve in the way," he agreed with a faint smile. "I know you didn't get along with her. But she was part of your family. It must sting a bit."

"It does," she agreed, surprised at his perception. "She was nice to me when she and Daddy were dating," she added. "Taught me how to cook new things, went shopping with me, taught me about makeup and stuff." She grimaced. "Not that I ever wear it. I hate the way powder feels on my face, and I don't like gunking up my eyes and mouth with pasty cosmetics." She looked at him and saw an odd expression on his face. "That must sound strange…"

He laughed and sipped coffee before he spoke. "Actually, I was thinking how sane it sounded." He quietly studied her for a couple of moments. "You don't need makeup. You're quite pretty enough without it."

She gaped at him.

"Michelle, *ma belle*," he said in an odd, soft, deep tone, and he smiled.

She went scarlet. She knew her heart was shaking her to death, that he could see it, and she didn't care. He was simply the most gorgeous man she'd ever seen, and he thought she was pretty. A stupid smile turned her lips up, elongating the perfect bow shape they made.

"Sorry," he said gently. "I was thinking out loud, not hitting on you. This is hardly the time."

"Would you like to schedule a time?" she asked with wide, curious eyes. "Because my education in that department is really sad. This one boy tried to kiss me and missed and almost broke my nose. After that, I didn't get another date until the junior prom." She leaned forward. "He was gay and so sweet and shy about it...well, he asked me and told me the reason very honestly. And I said I'd go with him to the prom because of the way my other date had ended. I mean, he wasn't likely to try to kiss me and break my nose and all... Why are you laughing?"

"Marshmallow," he accused, and his smile was full of affectionate amusement.

"Well, yes, I guess I am. But he's such a nice boy. Several of us know about him, but there are these two guys on the football squad that he's afraid of. They're always making nasty remarks to him. He thought if he went with a girl to a dance, they might back off."

"Did they?" he asked, curious.

"Yes, but not because he went with me," she said. She glowered at the memory. "One of them made a nasty remark to him when we were dancing, next to the refreshment table, and I filled a big glass with punch and threw it in his face." She grinned. "I got in big trouble until the gym coach was told why I did it. His brother's gay." The grin got bigger. "He said next time I should use the whole pitcher."

He burst out laughing. "Well, your attitude toward modern issues is...unique. This is a very small town," he explained when her eyebrows went up.

"Oh, I see. You think we treat anybody different like a fungus." She nodded.

"Not exactly. But we hear things about small towns," he began.

"No bigots here. Well, except for Chief Grier."

He blinked. "Your police chief is a bigot?"

She nodded. "He is severely prejudiced against people from other planets. You should just hear him talk about how aliens are going to invade us one day to get their hands on our cows. He thinks they have a milk addiction, and that's why you hear about cattle mutilations... You're laughing again."

He wiped his eyes. She couldn't know that he rarely laughed. His life had been a series of tragedies. Humor had never been part of it. She made him feel light inside, almost happy.

"I can see the chief's point," he managed.

"Cow bigot," she accused, and he almost fell on the floor.

She wrapped her cold hands around her mug. "I guess I shouldn't be cracking jokes, with Roberta dead..." Her eyes burned with tears. "I still can't believe it. Roberta's gone. She's gone." She drew in a breath and sipped coffee. "We've done nothing but argue since Daddy died. But she wanted me to hold her hand and she was scared. She said she was sorry." She looked at him. "She said it was Bert's fault. Do you think she was delirious?"

"Not really," he replied quietly.

"Why?"

"That can wait a bit." He grew somber. "You don't have any other family?"

She shook her head. She looked around. "But surely I can stay here by myself? I mean, I'm eighteen now…"

He frowned. "I thought you were seventeen."

She hesitated. Her eyes went to the calendar and she grimaced. "I just turned eighteen. Today is my birthday," she said. She hadn't even realized it, she'd been so busy. Tears ran down her cheeks. "What an awful one this is."

He caught her hand in his and held it tight. "No cousins?"

She shook her head. "I have nobody."

"Not quite true. You have me," he said firmly. "And Sara's on her way down here."

"Sara. Your sister?"

He nodded.

"She'll stay with me?" she asked.

He smiled. "Not exactly. You'll stay with us, in my house. I won't risk your reputation by having you move in with just me."

"But…we're strangers," she pointed out.

"No, we're not," he said, and he smiled. "I told you about my stepfather. That's a memory I've never shared with anyone. And you won't mention it to Sara, right?"

"Of course not." She searched his black eyes. "Why would you do this for me?"

"Who else is there?" he asked.

She searched her mind for a logical answer and couldn't find one. She had nobody. Her best friend, Amy, had moved to New York City with her parents during the summer. They corresponded, and they were still friends, but Michelle didn't want to live in New

York, even if Amy's parents, with their five children, were to offer her a home.

"If you're thinking of the local orphanage," he said, tongue in cheek, "they draw the line at cow partisans."

She managed a laugh. "Oh. Okay."

"You can stay with us until you graduate and start college."

"I can't get in until fall semester, even if they accept me," she began.

"Where do you want to go?"

"Marist College in San Antonio. There's an excellent journalism program."

He pulled out his cell phone, punched a few buttons and made a phone call. Michelle listened with stark shock. He was nodding, laughing, talking. Then he thanked the man and hung up.

"You called the governor," she said, dumbfounded.

"Yes. We were in the same fraternity in college. He's on the board of trustees at Marist. You're officially accepted. They'll send a letter soon."

"But they don't have my grades...!"

"They will have, by the time you go. What's on the agenda for summer?" he continued.

"I... Well, I have a job. Minette Carson hired me for the rest of the school year, after school and on Saturdays. And I'm sure she'll let me work this summer, so I can save for college."

"You won't need to do that."

"What?"

He shrugged. "I drive a truck here because it helps me fit in. But I have an apartment in San Antonio with a garage. In the garage, there's a brand-new Jaguar

XKE." He raised an eyebrow. "Does that give you a hint about my finances?"

She had no idea what an XKE was, but she knew what a Jaguar was. She'd priced them once, just for fun. If it was new...gosh, people could buy houses around here for less, she thought, but she didn't say it.

"But, I'm a stranger," she persisted.

"Not for long. I'm going to petition the court to become your temporary legal guardian. Sara will go with us to court. You can wear a dress and look helpless and tragic and in desperate need of assistance." He pursed his lips. "I know, it will be a stretch, but you can manage it."

She laughed helplessly.

"Then we'll get you through school."

"I'll find a way to pay you back," she promised.

He smiled. "No need for that. Just don't ever write about me," he added. It sounded facetious, but he didn't smile when he said it.

"I'd have to make up something in order to do that." She laughed.

She didn't know, and he didn't tell her, that there was more to his life than she'd seen, or would ever see. Sara knew, but he kept his private life exactly that—private.

Just for an instant, he worried about putting her in the line of fire. He had enemies. Dangerous enemies, who wouldn't hesitate to threaten anyone close to him. Of course, there was Sara, but she'd lived in Wyoming for the past few years, away from him, on a ranch they co-owned. Now he was putting her in jeopardy along with Michelle.

But what could he do? The child had nobody. Now

that her idiot stepmother was dead, she was truly on her own. It was dangerous for a young woman to live alone, even in a small community. And there was Roberta's boyfriend, Bert.

Gabriel knew things about the man that he wasn't eager to share with Michelle. The man was part of a criminal organization, and he knew Michelle's habits. He also had a yen for her, if what Michelle had blurted out to him once was true—and he had no indication that she would lie about it. He might decide to come and try his luck with her now that her stepmother was out of the picture. That couldn't be allowed.

He was surprised by his own affection for Michelle. It wasn't paternal. She was, of course, far too young for anything heavy, being eighteen to his twenty-four. She was a beauty, kind and generous and sweet. She was the sort of woman he usually ran from. No, strike that, she was no woman. She was still unfledged, a dove without flight feathers. He had to keep his interest hidden. At least, until she was grown up enough that it wouldn't hurt his conscience to pursue her. Afterward…well, who knew the future?

At the moment, however, his primary concern was to make sure she had whatever she needed to get through high school and, then, through college. Whatever it took.

Sara called him back. She wouldn't be able to get a flight to Texas for two days, which meant that Michelle would be on her own at night. Gabriel wasn't about to leave her, not with Bert Sims still out there.

But he couldn't risk her reputation by having her stay alone with him.

"You don't want to be alone with me," Michelle guessed when he mentioned Sara's dilemma and frowned.

"It wouldn't look right," he said. "You have a spotless reputation here. I'm not going to be the first to put a blemish on it."

She smiled gently. "You're a very nice man."

He shrugged. "Character is important, regardless of the mess some people make of theirs in public and brag about it."

"My dad used to say that civilization rested on the bedrock of morality, and that when morality went, destruction followed," she recalled.

"A student of history," he said approvingly.

"Yes. He told me that first go the arts, then goes religion, then goes morality. After that, you count down the days until the society fails. Ancient Egypt. Rome. A hundred other governments, some more recently than others," she said.

"Who's right? I don't know. I like the middle of the road, myself. We should live the way that suits us and leave others to do the same."

She grinned. "I knew I liked you."

He chuckled. He finished his coffee. "We should stop discussing history and decide what to do with you tonight."

She stared at her own cooling coffee in the thick mug. "I could stay here by myself."

"Never," he said shortly. "Bert Sims might show up, looking for Roberta's leftovers, like Zack said."

She managed a smile. "Thanks. You could sleep in Roberta's room," she offered.

"Only if there's someone else in the house, too." He pursed his lips. "I have an idea." He pulled out his cell phone.

Carlie Blair walked in the door with her overnight bag and hugged Michelle close. "I'm so sorry," she said. "I know you and your stepmother didn't get along, but it's got to be a shock, to have it happen like that."

"It was." Michelle dashed away tears. "She apologized when she was dying. She said one other thing," she added, frowning, as she turned to Gabriel. "She said don't let Bert get away with it. You never told me what you thought that meant."

Gabriel's liquid black eyes narrowed. "Did she say anything else?"

She nodded slowly, recalling the odd statement. "She said he told her it wasn't pure and he lied. What in the world did that mean?"

Gabriel was solemn. "That white powder in the vial was cocaine," he explained. "Dealers usually cut it with something else, dilute it. But if it's pure and a user doesn't know, it can be lethal if they don't adjust the dose." He searched Michelle's eyes. "I'm betting that Bert gave her pure cocaine and she didn't know."

Carlie was surprised. "Your stepmother was using drugs?" she asked her friend.

"That's what they think," Michelle replied. She turned back to Gabriel. "Did he know it was pure? Was he trying to kill her?"

"That's something Zack will have to find out."

"I thought he cared about her. In his way," she faltered.

"He might have, even if it was only because she was a customer."

Michelle bit her lower lip. "That would explain why she was so desperate for money. I did wonder, you know, because she didn't buy new clothes or expensive cosmetics or things like she used to when Daddy was alive." She frowned. "She never bought anything, but she never had any money and she was always desperate for more. Like when she tried to sell my father's stamp collection."

"It's a very expensive habit," Gabriel said quietly.

"But… Bert might have meant to kill her…?"

"It's possible. Maybe she made threats, maybe she tried to quit or argued over the price. But, whether he meant to kill her or not, he's going to find himself in a lot of hot water pretty soon."

"Why?" Michelle asked curiously.

He grimaced. "I'm sorry. That's all I can say. This is more complicated than it seems."

She sighed. "Okay. I won't pry. Keep your secrets." She managed a smile. "But don't you forget that I'm a reporter in training," she added. "One day, I'll have learned how to find out anything I want to know." She grinned.

"Now you're scaring me," he teased.

"Good."

He just shook his head. "I have to go back to my place and get a razor. I'll be right back. Lock the door," he told Michelle, "and don't open it for anybody. If Bert Sims shows up, you call me at once. Got that?"

"Got it," she said.

"Okay."

He left. Carlie got up from the sofa, where she'd been perched on the arm, and hugged Michelle. "I know this is hard for you. I'm so sorry."

"Me, too." Michelle gave way to tears. "Thanks for coming over. I hope I'm not putting you in any danger."

"Not me," Carlie said. "And neither of us is going to be in danger with that tall, dark, handsome man around. He is so good-looking, isn't he?" she added with a theatrical sigh.

Michelle dried her tears. "He really is. My guardian angel."

"Some angel."

She tried to think of something that might restore a little normalcy into her routine. Roberta was lying heavily on her mind. "I have to do dishes. Want to dry?"

"You bet!"

Chapter 5

Carlie and Michelle shared the double bed in Michelle's room, while Gabriel slept in Roberta's room. Michelle had insisted on changing the bed linen first. She put Roberta's clothes in the washing machine, the ones that had been scattered all over the room. When she'd washed them, she planned to donate them to charity. Michelle couldn't have worn them even if she'd liked Roberta's flamboyant style, which she didn't.

The next morning, Gabriel went to the local funeral home and made the arrangements for Roberta. She had an older sister in Virginia. The funeral home contacted her, but the woman wanted nothing to do with any arrangements. She and Roberta had never gotten along, and she couldn't care less, she said, whether they cremated her or buried her or what. Gabriel arranged for her to be cremated, and Reverend Blair offered a plot in the cemetery of his church for her to be interred. There would be no funeral service, just a graveside one. Michelle thought they owed her that much, at least.

Reverend Blair had invited Michelle to come and stay at his house with Carlie, but Michelle wanted familiar things around her. She also wanted Gabriel, on whom she had come to rely heavily. But she couldn't stay with Gabriel alone. It would not look right in the tiny community of Comanche Wells, where time hadn't moved into the twenty-first century yet.

"Sara will be here tomorrow," Gabriel told the girls as they sat down to supper, which Michelle and Carlie had prepared together. He smiled as he savored hash browns with onions, perfectly cooked, alongside a tender cut of beef and a salad. "You two can cook," he said with admiration. "Hash browns are hard to cook properly. These are wonderful."

"Thanks," they said in unison, and laughed.

"She did the hash browns," Carlie remarked, grinning at Michelle. "I never could get the hang of them. Mine just fall apart and get soggy."

"My mother used to make them," Michelle said with a sad smile. "She was a wonderful cook. I do my best, but I'm not in her league."

"Where do your parents live, Gabriel?" Carlie asked innocently.

Gabriel's expression went hard.

"I made a cherry pie for dessert," Michelle said, quickly and neatly deflecting Carlie's question. "And we have vanilla ice cream to go on it."

Carlie flushed, realizing belatedly that she'd made

a slight faux pas with her query. "Michelle makes the best cherry pie around," she said with enthusiasm.

Gabriel took a breath. "Don't look so guilty," he told Carlie, and smiled at her. "I'm touchy about my past, that's all. It was a perfectly normal question."

"I'm sorry, just the same," Carlie told him. "I get nervous around people and I babble." She flushed again. "I don't...mix well."

Gabriel laughed softly. "Neither do I," he confessed.

Michelle raised her hand. "That makes three of us," she remarked.

"I feel better," Carlie said. "Thanks," she added, intent on her food. "I have a knack for putting my foot into my mouth."

"Who doesn't?" Gabriel mused.

"I myself never put my foot into my mouth," Michelle said, affecting a haughty air. "I have never made a single statement that offended, irritated, shocked or bothered a single person."

The other two occupants of the table looked at her with pursed lips.

"Being perfect," she added with a twinkle in her eyes, "I am unable to understand how anyone could make such a mistake."

Carlie picked up her glass of milk. "One more word..." she threatened.

Michelle grinned at her. "Okay. Just so you remember that I don't make mistakes."

Carlie rolled her eyes.

It was chilly outside. Michelle sat on the porch steps, looking up at the stars. They were so bright, so perfectly clear in cold weather. She knew it had something to do with the atmosphere, but it was rather magical. There was a dim comet barely visible in the sky. Michelle had looked at it through a pair of binoculars her father had given her. It had been winter, and most hadn't been visible to the naked eye.

The door opened and closed behind her. "School is going to be difficult on Monday," she said. "I dread it. Everyone will know…you sure you don't mind giving me rides home after work?" she added.

"That depends on where you want to go," came a deep, amused masculine voice from behind her.

She turned quickly, shocked. "Sorry," she stammered. "I thought you were Carlie."

"She found a game show she can't live without. She's sorry." He chuckled.

"Do you like game shows?" she wondered.

He shrugged. He came and sat down beside her on the step. He was wearing a thick black leather jacket with exquisite beadwork. She'd been fascinated with it when he retrieved it from his truck earlier.

"That's so beautiful," she remarked, lightly touching the colorful trim above the long fringes with her fingertips. "I've never seen anything like it."

"Souvenir from Canada," he said. "I've had it for a long time."

"The beadwork is gorgeous."

"A Blackfoot woman made it for me," he said.

"Oh." She didn't want to pursue that. The woman he mentioned might have been a lover. She didn't want to think of Gabriel with a woman. It was intensely disturbing.

"My cousin," he said, without looking down at her. "She's sixty."

"Oh." She sounded embarrassed now.

He glanced at her with hidden amusement. She was so young. He could almost see the thoughts in her mind. "You need somebody young to cut your teeth on, kid. They'd break on my thick hide."

She flushed and started to jump up, but he caught her hand in his big, warm one, and pulled her gently back down.

"Don't run," he said softly. "No problem was ever solved by retreat. I'm just telling you how it is. I'm not involved with anyone. I haven't been for years. You're a bud, just opening on a rosebush, testing the air and the sunlight. I like my roses in full bloom."

"Oh."

He sighed. His fingers locked into hers. "These one syllable answers are disturbing," he mused.

She swallowed. The touch of his big, warm hand was causing some odd sensations in her young body. "I see."

"Two syllables. Better." He drew in a long breath. "Until you graduate, we're going to be living in close proximity, even with Sara in the house. I'll be away some of the time. My job takes me all over the world. But there are going to have to be some strict ground rules when I'm home."

"Okay," she faltered. "What?"

"No pajamas or nightgowns when you walk around the house. You put them on when you go to bed, in your room. No staying up late alone. Stuff like that."

She blinked. "I feel like Mata Hari."

"You feel like a spy? An old one, at that." He chuckled.

"A femme fatale, then," she amended. "Gosh, I don't even own pajamas or a gown..."

"You don't wear clothes in bed?" He sounded shocked.

"Oh, get real," she muttered, glad he couldn't see her face. "I wear sweats."

"To bed?" he exclaimed.

"They're comfortable," she said. "Nobody who wanted a good night's sleep ever wore a long gown, they just twist you up and constrict you. And pajamas usually have lace or thick embroidery. It's irritating to my skin."

"Sweats." Of all the things he'd pictured his young companion in at night, that was the last thing.

She looked down at his big hand in the light from the living room. It burned out onto the porch like yellow sun in the darkness, making shadows of the chairs behind them on the dusty boards of the porch. He had good hands, big and strong-looking, with square nails that were immaculate. "I guess the women you know like frilly stuff."

They did, but he wasn't walking into that land mine. He turned her hand in his. "Do you date?"

Her heart jumped. "Not since the almost-broken-nose thing."

He laughed softly. "Sorry. I forgot about that."

"There aren't a lot of eligible boys in my school who live in the dark ages like I do," she explained. "At least two of the ones who go to my church are wild as bucks and go to strip parties with drugs." She grimaced. "I don't fit in. Anywhere. My parents raised me with certain expectations of what life was all about." She turned to look at him. "Is it wrong, to have a belief system? Is it wrong to think morality is worth something?"

"Those are questions you should be asking Carlie's dad," he pointed out.

"Do you believe in…in a higher power?"

His fingers contracted around hers. "I used to."

"But not anymore?"

His drawn breath was audible. "I don't know what I believe anymore, *ma belle*," he said softly. "I live in a world you wouldn't understand, I go to places where you couldn't survive."

"What kind of work do you do?" she asked.

He laughed without humor. "That's a discussion we may have in a few years."

"Oh, I see." She nodded. "You're a cannibal."

He stilled. "I'm…a what?"

"Your work embarrasses you," she continued, unabashed, "which means you don't work in a bank or drive trucks. If I had a job that embarrassed me, it would be involved with cannibalism."

He burst out laughing. "Pest," he muttered.

She grinned.

His big thumb rubbed her soft fingers. "I haven't laughed so much in years, as I do with you."

She chuckled. "I might go on the stage. If I can make a hardcase like you laugh, I should be able to do it for a living."

"And here I thought you wanted to be a reporter."

"I do," she said. She smiled. "More than anything. I can't believe I'm actually going to work for a newspaper starting Monday," she said. "Minette is getting me my own cell phone and she's going to teach me to use a camera…it's like a dream come true. I only asked her for a reference for college. And she offered me a job." She shook her head. "It's like a dream."

"I gather you'll be riding with Carlie."

"Yes. I'm going to help with gas."

He was silent for a minute. "You keep your eyes open on the road, when you're coming home from work."

"I always do. But why?"

"I don't trust Roberta's boyfriend. He's dangerous. Even Carlie is in jeopardy because of what happened to her father, so you both have to be careful."

"I don't understand why someone would want to harm a minister," she said, shaking her head. "It makes no sense."

He turned his head toward her. "Michelle, most ministers started out as something else."

"Something else?"

"Yes. In other words, Reverend Blair wasn't always a reverend."

She hesitated, listening to make sure Carlie wasn't at the door. "What did he do before?" she asked.

"Sorry. That's a confidence. I never share them."

She curled her hand around his. "That's reassuring. If I ever tell you something dreadful in secret, you won't go blabbing it to everyone you know."

He laughed. "That's a given." His hand contracted. "The reverse is also applicable," he added quietly. "If you overhear anything while you're under my roof, it's privileged information. Not that you'll hear much that you can understand."

"You mean, like when you were talking to Sara in French," she began.

"Something like that." His eyes narrowed. "Did you understand what I said?"

"I can say, where's the library and my brother has a brown suit," she mused. "Actually, I don't have a brother, but that was in the first-year French book. And it's about the scope of my understanding. I love languages, but I have to study very hard to learn anything."

He relaxed a little. He'd said some things about Michelle's recent problems to Sara that he didn't want her to know. Not yet, anyway. It would sound as if he were gossiping about her to his sister.

"The graveside service is tomorrow," she said. "Will Sara be here in time, do you think?"

"She might. I'm having a car pick her up at the airport and drive her down here."

"A car?"

"A limo."

Her lips parted. "A limousine? Like those long, black cars you see politicians riding around in on television? I've only seen one maybe once or twice, on the highway when I was on the bus!"

He laughed softly at her excitement. "They also have sedans that you can hire to transport people," he told her. "I use them a lot when I travel."

He was talking about another world. In Michelle's world, most cars were old and had plenty of mechanical problems. She'd never even looked inside a limousine. She'd seen them on the highway in San Antonio. Her father told her that important businessmen and politicians and rich people and movie stars rode around in them. Not ordinary people. Of course, Gabriel wasn't ordinary. He'd said he owned a new Jaguar. Certainly he could afford to ride in a limousine.

"Do you think they'd let me look inside, when it brings her here?" she asked.

Gabriel was amused at her innocence. She knew nothing of the world at large. He couldn't remember being that young, or that naive about life. He hoped she wouldn't grow up too quickly. She made him feel more masculine, more capable, more intriguing than he really was. He liked her influence. She made him laugh. She made him want to be all the things she thought he was.

"Yes," he said after a minute. "Certainly you can look inside."

"Something to put in my diary," she mused.

"You keep a diary?" he asked, with some amusement.

"Oh, yes," she said. "I note all the cows I've seen abducted, and the strange little men who come out of the pasture at night..."

"Oh, cool it." He chuckled.

"Actually, it's things like how I did on tests, and memories I have of my father and mother," she confessed. "And how I feel about things. There's a lot about Roberta and Bert in there, and how disgusting I thought they were," she added.

"Well, Roberta's where she can't hurt you. And Bert is probably trying to find a way out of the country, if he's smart."

"What do you mean?" she asked.

He stood up and pulled her up beside him. "That's a conversation for another time. Let's go see if Carlie's game show is off."

"Don't you like game shows?" she wondered aloud.

"I like the History Channel, the Nature Channel, the Military Channel, and the Science Channel."

"No TV shows?"

"They're not TV shows. They're experiments in how to create attention deficit disorders in the entire population with endless commercials and ads that pop up right in the middle of programs. I only watch motion pictures or DVDs, unless I find something interesting enough to suffer through. I like programs on World War II history and science."

She pondered that. "I guess there's five minutes of program to fifteen minutes of commercials," she agreed.

"As long as people put up with it, that will continue, too." He chuckled. "I refuse to be part of the process."

"I like history, too," she began.

"There was this big war…" he began with an exaggerated expression.

She punched his arm affectionately. "No cherry pie and ice cream for you."

"I take it back."

She grinned up at him. "Okay. You can have pie and ice cream."

He smiled and opened the door for her.

She hesitated in the opening, just staring up at him, drinking in a face that was as handsome as any movie star's, at the physique that could have graced an athlete.

"Stop ogling me, if you please," he said with exaggerated patience. "You have to transfer that interest to someone less broken."

She made a face at him. "You're not broken," she

pointed out. "Besides, there's nobody anywhere who could compare with you." She flushed at her own boldness. "Anyway, you're safe to cut my teeth on, and you know it." She grinned. "I'm off-limits, I am."

He laughed. "Off-limits, indeed, and don't you forget it."

"Spoilsport."

She went inside ahead of him. He felt as if he could fly. Dangerous, that. More dangerous, his reaction to her. She was years too young for anything more than banter. But, he reminded himself, the years would pass. If he lived long enough, after she graduated from college, who knew what might happen?

There was a grim memorial service at the Comanche Wells Cemetery. It was part of the land owned by the Methodist church where Reverend Blair was the minister. He stood over the small open grave, with an open Bible in his hands, reading the service for the dead. The urn containing Roberta's ashes was in the open grave, waiting for the funeral home's maintenance man, standing nearby, to close after the ceremony.

Gabriel stood beside Michelle, close, but not touching. He was wearing a suit, some expensive thing that fit him with delicious perfection. The navy darkness of the suit against the spotless white shirt and blue patterned tie only emphasized his good looks. His wavy black hair was unruly in the stiff breeze. Michelle's own hair was tormented into a bun because of the wind. But it blew tendrils down into her eyes and mouth while she tried to listen to the service, while she tried even harder to feel something for the late Roberta.

It was sad that the woman's own sister didn't care enough to even send a flower. Total strangers from Jacobs County had sent sprays and wreathes and potted plants to the funeral home that had arranged for the cremation. The flowers were spread all around the grave. Some of them would go to the local hospital and nursing home in Jacobsville, others for the evening church service here. A few of the potted plants would go home with Michelle.

She remembered her father, and how much he'd been in love with Roberta at first. She remembered Roberta in the days before Bert. More recently, she remembered horrible arguments and being slapped and having Roberta try to sell the very house under her feet. There had been more bad times than good.

But now that part of her life was over. She had a future that contained Gabriel, and the beginning of a career as a journalist. It was something to look forward to, something to balance her life against the recent death of her father and Roberta's unexpected passing.

Sara's plane had been held up due to an electrical fault. She'd phoned Gabriel just before he and Michelle went to the funeral with Carlie, to apologize and give an updated arrival time. Michelle looked forward to meeting her. From what Gabriel had said about his sister, she sounded like a very sweet and comfortable person.

Reverend Blair read the final verses, closed the Bible, bowed his head for prayer. A few minutes later, he paused to speak to Michelle, where she stood with Gabriel and Carlie, thanking the few local citizens who'd taken time to attend. There hadn't been time for the newspaper to print the obituary, so services had been announced on the local radio station. Everybody listened to it, for the obituaries and the country-western music. They also listened for the school closings when snow came. That didn't happen often, but Michelle loved the rare times when it did.

"I'm sorry for your loss," Reverend Blair said, holding Michelle's hand and smiling gently. "No matter how contrary some people are, we get used to having them in our lives."

"That's true," Michelle said gently. "And my father loved her," she added. "For a time, she made him happy." She grimaced. "I just don't understand how she changed so much, so quickly. Even when she drank too much—" she hesitated, looking around to make sure she wasn't overheard before she continued "—she was never really mean."

Gabriel and the minister exchanged enigmatic glances.

Michelle didn't notice. Her eyes were on the grave. "And she said not to let Bert get away with it," she added slowly.

"There are some things going on that you're better off not knowing about," Reverend Blair said softly. "You can safely assume that Bert will pay a price for what he did. If not in this life, then in the next."

"But what did he do?" Michelle persisted.

"Bad things." Reverend Blair smiled.

"My sister will be here in an hour," Gabriel said, reading the screen of his cell phone, with some difficulty because of the sun's glare. He grinned at the reverend. "You can have your daughter back tonight."

Reverend Blair grinned. "I must say, I miss the little touches. Like clean dishes and laundry getting done." He made a face. "She's made me lazy." He smiled with pure affection at his daughter, who grinned.

"I'll make you fresh rolls for supper," Carlie promised him.

"Oh, my, and I didn't get you anything," he quipped.

She hugged him. "You're just the best dad in the whole world."

"Pumpkin, I'm glad you think so." He let her go. "If you need anything, you let us know, all right?" he asked Michelle. "But you're in good hands." He smiled at Gabriel.

"She'll be safe, at least." Gabriel gave Reverend Blair a complicated look. "Make sure about those new locks, will you? I've gotten used to having you around."

The other man made a face. "Locks and bolts won't keep out the determined," he reminded him. "I put my trust in a higher power."

"So do I," Gabriel replied. "But I keep a Glock by the bed."

"Trust in Allah, but tie up your camel."

Everybody looked at Michelle, who blushed.

"Sorry," she said. "I was remembering something I read in a nonfiction book about the Middle East. It was written by a former member of the French Foreign Legion."

Now the stares were more complicated, from the two males at least.

"Well, they fascinate me," she confessed, flushing a little. "I read true crime books and biographies of military men and anything I can find about the Special Air Services of Great Britain and the French Foreign Legion."

"My, my," Gabriel said. He chuckled with pure glee, a reaction that was lost on Michelle.

"I lead a sheltered life." Michelle glanced at the grave. The maintenance man, a little impatient, had started to fill the grave. "We should go."

"Yes, we should." Reverend Blair smiled. "Take care."

"Thanks. The service was very nice," Michelle said.

"I'm glad you thought so."

Gabriel took her arm and led her back to the car. He drove her home first, so that she could change back into more casual clothes and get her overnight bag. Then he drove her to his own house, where Sara was due to arrive any minute.

Michelle had this picture of Sara. That she'd be dark-haired and dark-eyed, with a big smile and a very tender nature. Remembering what Gabriel had told her in confidence, about the perils Sara had survived when they were in school, she imagined the other woman would be a little shy and withdrawn.

So it came as something of a shock when a tall, beautiful woman with long black hair and flashing black eyes stepped out of the back of the limousine and told the driver where he could go and how fast.

Chapter 6

"I am very sorry, lady," the driver, a tall lanky man, apologized. "I truly didn't see the truck coming…"

"You didn't look!" she flashed at him in a terse but sultry tone. "How dare you text on your cell phone while driving a customer!"

He was very flushed by now. "I won't do it again, I swear."

"You won't do it with me in the car, and I am reporting you to the company you work for," she concluded.

Gabriel stepped forward as the driver opened the trunk. He picked up the single suitcase that Sara had brought with her. Something in the way Gabriel looked at the man had him backing away.

"Very sorry, again," he said, flustered. "If you'd just sign the ticket, ma'am…"

He fetched a clipboard and handed it to her, eyeing

Gabriel as if he expected him to leap on him any second. Sara signed it. The man obviously knew better than to look for a tip. He nodded, turned, jumped into the car and left a trail of dust as he sped away.

"That could have gone better," Sara said with a grim smile. She hugged Gabriel. "So good to see you again."

"You, too," he replied. His face changed as he looked at the younger woman. He touched her hair. "You only grow more beautiful with age."

"You only think so because you're my brother." She laughed musically. She looked past him at Michelle, who stood silent and wary.

"And you must be Michelle." Sara went to her, smiled and hugged her warmly. "I have a nasty temper. The silly man almost killed us both, texting some woman."

"I'm so glad he didn't," Michelle said, hugging her back. "It's very kind of both of you to do this for me," she added. "I...really don't have anyplace to go. I mean, the Reverend Blair said I could stay with him and Carlie, but..."

"You certainly do have someplace to go," Gabriel said with a grin. "Sara needed the change of scenery. She was vegetating up in Wyoming."

Sara sighed. "In a sense, I suppose so, although I like it better there than in British Columbia. I left our foreman in charge at the ranch in Catelow. That's in Wyoming," Sara told Michelle with a smile. "Anything that needs doing for the sale, I can do online." Her black eyes, so like Gabriel's, had a sad cast. "The change of scenery will do me good. I love to ride. Do you?" she asked the younger woman.

"I haven't been on a horse in years," Michelle confessed. "Mostly, horses try to scrape me off or dislodge me. I'm sort of afraid of them."

"My horses are very tame," Gabriel told her. "They'll love you."

"I hope you have coffee made," Sara sighed as they made their way into the sprawling house. "I'm so tired! Flying is not my favorite mode of travel."

"I've never even been on a plane," Michelle confessed.

Sara stopped and stared at her. "Never?"

"Never."

"She wanted to look inside the limo." Gabriel chuckled. "She's never seen one of those, either."

"I'm so sorry!" Sara exclaimed. "I made a fuss…"

"You should have made a fuss," Michelle replied. "There will be other times."

"I'll make sure of that." Sara smiled, and it was like the sun coming out.

School had been rough in the days after Roberta's death. People were kind, but there were so many questions about how she died. Gossip ran rampant. One of the girls she sat near in history class told her that Roberta's boyfriend was a notorious drug dealer. At least two boys in their school got their fixes from him.

Now the things Roberta had said started to make sense. And Michelle was learning even more about the networks and how they operated from Minette since she'd started working for the Jacobsville newspaper.

"It's a vile thing, drug dealing," Minette said harshly. "Kids overdose and die. The men supplying the drugs don't even care. They only care about the profit." She hesitated. "Well, maybe some of them have good intentions…"

"A drug dealer with good intentions?" Michelle laughed. "You have got to be kidding."

"Actually, I'm not. You've heard of the man they call El Jefe?"

"Who hasn't?" Michelle replied. "We heard that he helped save you and Sheriff Carson," she added.

"He's my father."

Michelle gaped at her. "He's…?"

"My father," Minette repeated. "I didn't know who my real father was until very recently. My life was in danger, even more than Hayes's was when he was shot, because my father was in a turf war with a rival who was the most evil man I ever knew."

"Your life is like a soap opera," Michelle ventured.

Minette laughed. "Well, yes, it is."

"I wish mine was more exciting. In a good way," she clarified. She drew in a long breath. "Okay, what about this camera?" she asked. It had more dials and settings than a spaceship.

"I know, it's a little intimidating. Let me show you how it works."

She did. It took a little time, and when they finished, a phone call was waiting for Minette. She motioned to Michelle. "I have a new reporter. I'm going to let her take this down, if you don't mind. Her name is Michelle… That's right. It's a deal. Thanks!" She put her hand over the receiver so that the caller wouldn't hear. "This is Ben Simpson. He's our Jacobs County representative in District 3 for the Texas Soil and Water

Conservation Board. He wants us to do a story on a local rancher who won Rancher of the Year for the Jacobs County Soil and Water Conservation District for his implementation of natural grasses and ponds. The award was made just before Christmas, but the rancher has been out of the country until now. I'm going to let you take down the details, and then I'll send you out to his ranch to take a photo of him with the natural grasses in the background. Are you up to it?" she teased.

Michelle was almost shaking, but she bit her lip and nodded. "Yes, ma'am," she said.

Minette grinned. "Go for it!"

Michelle was used to taking copious notes in school. She did well in her schoolwork because she was thorough. She took down the story, pausing to clarify the spelling of names, and when she was through she had two sheets of notes and she'd arranged a day and time to go out to photograph the rancher.

She hung up. Minette was still in the doorway. "Did I do that okay?" she asked worriedly.

"You did fine. I was listening on the other phone. I took notes, too, just in case. You write the story and we'll compare your notes to mine."

"Thanks!" Michelle said fervently. "I was nervous."

"No need to be. You'll do fine." She indicated the computer at the desk. "Get busy." She smiled. "I like the way you are with people, even on the phone. You have an engaging voice. It will serve you well in this business."

"That's nice of you to say," Michelle said.

"Write the story. Remember, short, concise sentences,

nothing flowery or overblown. I'll be out front if you need me."

She started to thank Minette again, but it was going to get tedious if she kept it up, so she just nodded and smiled.

When she turned in the story, she stood gritting her teeth while Minette read it and compared it with her own notes.

"You really are a natural," she told the younger woman. "I couldn't have done better myself. Nice work."

"Thank you!"

"Now go home," she said. "It's five, and Carlie will be peeling rubber any minute to get home."

Michelle laughed. "I think she may. I'll see you tomorrow, then. Do I go out to photograph the man tomorrow, too?"

"Yes."

Michelle bit her lip. "But I don't have a license or own a car…there's only Roberta's and she didn't leave it to me. I don't think she even had a will…and I can't ask Carlie to take off from work…" The protests came in small bursts.

"I'll drive you out there," Minette said softly. "We might drop by some of the state and federal offices and I'll introduce you to my sources."

"That sounds very exciting! Thanks!" She sounded relieved, and she was.

"One more thing," Minette said.

"Yes?"

"I'm printing the conservation story under your own byline."

Michelle caught her breath. "My first one. That's so kind of you."

"You'll have others. This is just the first." She grinned. "Have a good night."

"I will. Sara's making homemade lasagna. It's my favorite."

"Sara?"

"Gabriel's sister. She's so beautiful." Michelle shook her head. "The two of them have been lifesavers for me. I didn't want to have to pick up and move somewhere else. I couldn't have stayed here to finish school without them."

"Not quite true," Minette replied. "You could have come to us. Even Cash Grier mentioned that they could make room for you, if you needed a place to stay."

"So many," Michelle said, shaking her head. "They hardly know me."

"They know you better than you think," was the reply. "In small communities like ours, there are no secrets. Your good deeds are noted by many."

"I guess I lived in the city for too long. Daddy had patients but no real friends, especially after Roberta came into our lives. It was just the three of us." She smiled. "I love living here."

"So do I, and I've been here all my life." She cocked her head. "Gabriel seems an odd choice to be your guardian. He isn't what you think of as a family man."

"He's not what he seems," Michelle replied. "He was kind to me when I needed it most." She made a face. "I was sitting in the middle of the road hoping to get hit by a car. It was the worst day of my life. He took me home with him and talked to me. He made everything better. When Roberta…died…he was there to comfort me. I owe him a lot. He even got Sara down here to live with him so that he could be my legal guardian with no raised eyebrows around us."

Minette simply said, "I see." What she did see, she wasn't going to share. Apparently Gabriel had a little more than normal interest in this young woman, but he wasn't going to risk her reputation. It was going to be all by the book. Minette wondered what he had in mind for Michelle when she was a few years older. And she also wondered if Michelle had any idea who Gabriel really was, and how he earned his living. That was a secret she wasn't going to share, either. Not now.

"Well, I'll see you tomorrow, then," Michelle added.

"Tomorrow."

Carlie was waiting for her at the front door the next morning, which was Friday. She looked out of breath.

"Is something wrong?" Michelle asked.

"No. Of course not. Let's go."

Carlie checked all around the truck and even looked under it before she got behind the wheel and started it.

"Okay, now, what's going on?" Michelle asked.

"Daddy got a phone call earlier," Carlie said, looking both ways before she pulled carefully out of the driveway.

"What sort of call?"

"From some man who said Daddy might think he was out of the woods, but somebody else was coming to pay him a visit, and he'll never see it coming." She swallowed. "Daddy told me to check my truck out before I drove it. I forgot, so I looked underneath just in case." She shook her head. "It's like a nightmare," she groaned. "I have no idea in this world why anyone would want to harm a minister."

"It's like our police chief said," Michelle replied quietly. "There are madmen in the world. I guess you can't ever understand what motivates them to do the things they do."

"I wish things were normal again," Carlie said in a sad tone. "I hate having to look over my shoulder when I drive and look for bombs under my car." She glanced at Michelle. "I swear, I feel like I'm living in a combat zone."

"I know the feeling, although I've never been in any real danger. Not like you." She smiled. "Don't you worry. I'll help you keep a lookout."

"Thanks." She smiled. "It's nice, having someone to ride with me. These back roads get very lonely."

"They do, indeed." Michelle sighed as she looked out over the barren flat landscape toward the horizon as the car sped along. "I just wrote my first story for the newspaper," she said with a smile. "And Minette is taking me out to introduce me to people who work for the state and federal government. It's the most exciting thing that's ever happened to me," she added, her eyes starry with pleasure. "I get my own byline." She shook her head. "It really is true…"

"What's true?" Carlie asked.

"My dad said that after every bad experience, something wonderful happens to you. It's like you pay a price for great happiness."

"I see what you mean." She paused. "I really do."

* * *

Minette drove Michelle out to the Patterson ranch, to take photographs for her story and to see the rancher's award for conservation management. She also wanted a look at his prize Santa Gertrudis bull. The bull had been featured in a cattle magazine because he was considered one of the finest of his breed, a stud bull whose origins, like all Santa Gertrudis, was the famous King Ranch in Texas. It was a breed native to Texas that had resulted from breeding Shorthorn and Hereford cattle with Brahman cattle. The resulting breed was named for the Spanish land grant where Richard King founded the cattle empire in the nineteenth century: Santa Gertrudis.

Wofford Patterson was tall, intimidating. He had jet-black hair, thick and straight, and an olive complexion. His eyes, surprisingly, were such a pale blue that they seemed to glitter like Arctic ice. He had big hands and big feet and his face looked as if it had been carved from solid stone. It was angular. Handsome, in its way, but not conventionally handsome.

There were scars on his hands. Michelle stared at them as she shook his hand, and flushed when she saw his keen, intelligent eyes noting the scrutiny.

"Sorry," she said, although she hadn't voiced her curiosity.

"I did a stint with the FBI's Hostage Rescue Team," he explained, showing her the palms of both big hands. "Souvenirs from many rappels down a long rope from a hovering chopper," he added with a faint smile. "Even gloves don't always work."

Her lips fell open. This was not what she'd expected when Minette said they'd take pictures of a rancher. This man wasn't what he appeared to be.

"No need to look threatened," he told her, and his pale eyes twinkled as he shoved his hands into the pockets of his jeans. "I don't have arrest powers anymore." He scowled. "Have you done something illegal? Is that why you look intimidated?"

"Oh, no, sir," she said quickly. "It's just that I was listening for the sound of helicopters." She smiled vacantly.

He burst out laughing. He glanced at Minette. "I believe you said she was a junior reporter? You didn't mention that she was nuts, did you?"

"I am not nuts, I have read of people who witnessed actual alien abductions of innocent cows," she told him solemnly. But her eyes were twinkling, like his.

"I haven't witnessed any," he replied, "but if I ever do, I'll phone you to come out and take pictures."

"Would you? How kind!" She glanced at Minette, who was grinning from ear to ear. "Now about that conservation award, Mr. Patterson…"

"Mr. Patterson was my father," he corrected. "And he was Mister Patterson, with a capital letter. He's gone now, God rest his soul. He was the only person alive I was really afraid of." He chuckled. "You can call me Wolf."

"Wolf?"

"Wofford… Wolf," he said. "They hung that nickname on me while I worked for the Bureau. I have something of a reputation for tracking."

"And a bit more," Minette interrupted, tongue in cheek.

"Yes, well, but we mustn't put her off, right?" he asked in return, and he grinned.

"Right."

"Come on and I'll show you Patterson's Lone Pine Red Diamond. He won a 'bull of the year' award for conformation, and I'm rolling in the green from stud fees. He has nicely marbled fat and large—" he cleared his throat "—assets."

Minette glanced at Michelle and shook her head when Wolf wasn't looking. Michelle interpreted that as an "I'll tell you later" look.

The bull had his own stall in the nicest barn Michelle had ever seen. "Wow," she commented as they walked down the bricked walkway between the neat wooden stalls. There was plenty of ventilation, but it was comfortably warm in here. A tack room in back provided any equipment or medicines that might be needed by the visiting veterinarian for the livestock in the barn.

There were two cows, hugely pregnant, in two of the stalls and a big rottweiler, black as coal, lying just in front of the tack room door. The animal raised his head at their approach.

"Down, Hellscream," he instructed. The dog lay back down, wagging its tail.

"Hellscream?" Michelle asked.

He grinned. "I don't have a social life. Too busy with the bloodstock here. So in my spare time, I play World of Warcraft. The leader of the Horde—the faction that fights the Alliance—is Garrosh Hellscream.

I really don't like him much, so my character joined the rebellion to throw him out. Nevertheless, he is a fierce fighter. So is my girl, there," he indicated the rottweiler. "Hence, the name."

"Winnie Kilraven's husband is a gaming fanatic," Minette mused.

"Kilraven plays Alliance," Wolf said in a contemptuous tone. "A Paladin, no less." He pursed his lips. "I killed him in a battleground, doing player versus player. It was very satisfying." He grinned.

"I'd love to play, but my husband is addicted to the Western Channel on TV when he's not in his office being the sheriff," Minette sighed. "He and the kids watch cartoon movies together, too. I don't really mind. But gaming sounds like a lot of fun."

"Trust me, it is." Wolf stopped in front of a huge, sleek red-coated bull. "Isn't he a beaut?" he asked the women, and actually sighed. "I'd let him live in the house, but I fear the carpets would never recover."

The women looked at each other. Then he laughed at their expressions, and they relaxed.

"I read about a woman who kept a chicken inside once," Michelle said with a bland expression. "I think they had to replace all the carpets, even though she had a chicken diaper."

"I'd like to see a cow diaper that worked." Wolf chuckled.

"That's a product nobody is likely to make," Michelle said.

"Can we photograph you with the bull?" Michelle asked.

"Why not?"

He went into the stall with the bull and laid his long arm around his neck. "Smile, Red, you're going to be even more famous," he told the big animal, and smoothed his fur.

He and the bull turned toward the camera. Michelle took several shots, showing them to Minette as they went along.

"Nice," Minette said. She took the digital camera, pulled up the shots, and showed them to Wolf.

"They'll do fine," Wolf replied. "You might want to mention that the barn is as secure as the White House, and anyone who comes here with evil intent will end up in the backseat of a patrol car, handcuffed." He pursed his lips. "I still have my handcuffs, just in case."

"We'll mention that security is tight." Minette laughed.

"He really is a neat bull," Michelle added. "Thanks for letting us come out and letting us take pictures."

He shrugged broad shoulders. "No problem. I'm pretty much available until next week."

"What happens next week?" Michelle asked.

"A World Event on World of Warcraft," he mused. "The 'Love Is in the Air' celebration. It's a hoot."

"A world event?" Michelle asked, curious.

"We have them for every holiday. It's a chance for people to observe them in-game. This is the equivalent of Valentine's Day." He laughed. "There's this other player I pal around with. I'm pretty sure she's a girl. We do battlegrounds together. She gets hung on trees, gets lost, gets killed a lot. I enjoy playing with her."

"Why did you say that you think she's a girl?" Michelle asked.

"People aren't what they seem in video games," he replied. "A lot of the women are actually men. They think of it as playing with a doll, dressing her up and stuff."

"What about women, do they play men?" she persisted.

He laughed. "Probably. I've come across a few whose manners were a dead giveaway. Women are mostly nicer than some of the guys."

"What class is your Horde character?" Minette broke in.

"Oh, you know about classes, huh?"

"Just what I overheard when Kilraven was raving about them to my husband," she replied, chuckling.

"I play a Blood Elf death knight," he said. "Two-handed sword, bad attitude, practically invincible."

"What does the woman play?" Michelle asked, curious.

"A Blood Elf warlock. Warlocks cast spells. Deadliest class there is, besides mages," he replied. "She's really good. I've often wondered where she lives. Somewhere in Europe, I think, because she's on late at night, when most people in the States are asleep."

"Why are you on so late yourself?" Michelle asked.

He shrugged. "I have sleep issues." And for an instant, something in his expression made her think of wounded things looking for shelter. He searched her eyes. "You're staying with the Brandons, aren't you?"

"Well, yes," she said hesitantly.

He nodded. "Gabriel's a good fellow." His face tautened. "His sister, however, could drop houses on people."

She stared at him. "Excuse me?"

"I was backing out of a parking space at the county courthouse and she came flying around the corner and hit the back end of my truck." He was almost snarling. "Then she gets out, cussing a blue streak, and says it's my fault! She was the one speeding!"

Michelle almost bit her tongue off trying not to say what she was thinking.

"So your husband—" he nodded to Minette "—comes down the courthouse steps and she's just charming to him, almost in tears over her poor car, that I hit!" He made a face. "I get hit with a citation for some gold-arned thing, and my insurance company has to fix her car and my rates go up."

"Was that before or after you called her a broom-riding witch and indicated that she didn't come from Wyoming at all, but by way of Kansas...?"

"Sure, her and the flying monkeys," he muttered.

Michelle couldn't keep from laughing. "I'm sorry," she defended herself. "It was the flying monkey bit..." She burst out laughing again.

"Anyway, I politely asked her which way she was going and if she was coming back to town, so I could park my truck somewhere while she was on the road. Set her off again. Then she started cussing me in French. I guess she thought some dumb country hick like me wouldn't understand her."

"What did you do?" Michelle asked.

He shrugged. "Gave it back to her in fluent and formal French. That made her madder, so she switched to Farsi." He grinned. "I'm also fluent in that, and I know the slang. She called on the sheriff to arrest me for obscenity, but he said he didn't speak whatever language we were using so he couldn't arrest me." He smiled blithely. "I like your husband," he told Minette. "He was nice about it, but he sent her on her way. Her parting shot, also in Farsi, was that no woman in North America would be stupid enough to marry a man like me. She said she'd rather remain single forever than to even consider dating someone like me."

"What did you say to her then?" Michelle wanted to know.

"Oh, I thanked her."

"What?" Minette burst out.

He shrugged. "I said that burly masculine women didn't appeal to me whatsoever, and that I'd like a nice wife who could cook and have babies."

"And?" Minette persisted.

"And she said I wanted a malleable female I could chain to the bed." He shook his head.

"What did you say about that?"

"I said it would be too much trouble to get the stove in there."

Michelle almost doubled up laughing. She could picture Sara trying to tie this man up in knots and failing miserably. She wondered if she dared repeat the conversation when she got home.

Wolf anticipated her. He shook his finger at her. "No carrying tales, either," he instructed. "You don't arm the enemy."

"But she's nice," she protested.

"Nice. Sure she is. Does she keep her pointed hat in the closet or does she wear it around the house?" he asked pleasantly.

"She doesn't own a single one, honest."

"Make her mad," he invited. "Then stand back and watch the broom and the pointy hat suddenly appear."

"You'd like her if you got to know her," Michelle replied.

"No, thank you. No room in my life for a woman who shares her barn with flying monkeys."

Michelle and Minette laughed all the way back to the office.

"Oh, what Sara's missing," Minette said, wiping tears of mirth from her eyes. "He's one of a kind."

"He really is."

"I wish I could tell her what he said. I wouldn't dare. She's already scored a limousine driver. I expect she could strip the skin off Wofford Patterson at ten paces."

"A limousine?"

Michelle nodded. "The driver was texting someone at the wheel and almost wrecked the car. She reported him to the agency that sent him."

"Good for her," Minette said grimly. "There was a wreck a few months ago. A girl was texting a girlfriend and lost control of the car she was driving. She killed a ten-year-old boy and his grandmother who were walking on the side of the road."

"I remember that," Michelle said. "It was so tragic."

"It's still tragic. The girl is in jail, pending trial. It's going to be very hard on her parents, as well as those of the little boy."

"You have sympathy for the girl's parents?" Michelle ventured.

"When you work in this business for a while, you'll

learn that there really are two sides to every story. Normal people can do something impulsive and wrong and end up serving a life term. Many people in jail are just like you and me," she continued. "Except they have less control of themselves. One story I covered, a young man had an argument with his friend while he was skinning a deer they'd just killed in the woods. Impulsively, he stabbed his friend with the knife. He cried at his trial. He didn't mean to do it. He had one second of insanity and it destroyed his life. But he was a good boy. Never hurt an animal, never skipped school, never did anything bad in his life. Then he killed his best friend on an impulse that he regretted immediately."

"I never thought of it like that," Michelle said, dazed.

"Convicted felons have families," she pointed out. "Most of them are as normal as people can be. They go to church, give to charity, help their neighbors, raise good children. They have a child do something stupid and land in jail. They're not monsters. Although I must confess I've seen a few parents who should be sitting in jail." She shook her head. "People are fascinating to me, after all these years." She smiled. "You'll find that's true for you, as well."

Michelle leaned back. "Well, I've learned something. I've always been afraid of people in jail, especially when they work on the roadways picking up trash."

"They're just scared kids, mostly," Minette replied. "There are some bad ones. But you won't see them out on the highways. Only the trusted ones get to do that sort of work."

"The world is a strange place."

"It's stranger than you know." Minette chuckled. She pulled up in front of the newspaper office. "Now, let's get those photos uploaded and cropped and into the galleys."

"You bet, boss," Michelle said with a grin. "Thanks for the ride, too."

"You need to learn to drive," Minette said.

"For that, you need a car."

"Roberta had one, I'll talk to Blake Kemp. He's our district attorney, but he's also a practicing attorney. We'll get him going on probate for you."

"Thanks."

"Meanwhile, ask Gabriel about teaching you. He's very experienced with cars."

"Okay," she replied. "I'll ask him." It didn't occur to her to wonder how Minette knew he was experienced with cars.

Chapter 7

"No, no, no!" Gabriel said through gritted teeth. "Michelle, if you want to look at the landscape, for God's sake, stop and get out of the car first!"

She bit her lower lip. "Sorry. I wasn't paying attention."

The truck, his truck, was an inch away from going into a deep ditch.

"Put it in Reverse, and back up slowly," he instructed, forcing his voice to seem calm.

"Okay." She did as instructed, then put it in gear, and went forward very slowly. "How's this?"

"Better," he said. He drew in a breath. "I don't understand why your father never taught you."

Mention of her father made her sad. "He was too busy at first and then too sick," she said, her voice strained. "I wanted to learn, but I didn't pester him."

"I'm sorry," he said deeply. "I brought back sad memories for you."

She managed a faint smile. "It's still not that long since he, well, since he was gone," she replied. She couldn't bring herself to say "died." It was too harsh a word. She concentrated on the road. "This is a lot harder than it looks," she said. She glanced up in the rearview mirror. "Oh, darn."

He glanced behind them. A car was speeding toward them, coming up fast. The road was straight and clear, however. "Just drive," he told her. "He's got plenty of room to pass if he wants to."

"Okay."

The driver slowed down suddenly, pulled around them and gave her a sign that made her flush.

"And that was damned well uncalled for," Gabriel said shortly. He pulled out his cell phone, called the state highway police, gave them the license plate number and offered to press charges if they caught the man. "She's barely eighteen and trying to learn to drive," he told the officer he was speaking to. "The road was clear, he had room to pass. He was just being a jerk because she was female."

He listened, then chuckled. "I totally agree. Thanks."

He closed the cell phone. "They're going to look for him."

"I hope they explain manners to him. So many people seem to grow up without any these days," she sighed. She glanced at her companion. It had made him really angry, that other man's rudeness.

He caught her staring. "Watch the road."

"Sorry."

"What's wrong?"

"Nothing. I was just…well, it was nice of you, to care that someone insulted me."

"Nobody's picking on you while I'm around," he said with feeling.

She barely turned her head and met his searching black eyes. Her heart went wild. Her hands felt like ice on the wheel. She could barely get her breath.

"Stop that," he muttered, turning his head away. "You'll kill us both."

She cleared her throat. "Okay."

He drew in a breath. "You may be the death of me, anyway," he mused, giving her a covert glance. She was very pretty, with her blond hair long, around her shoulders, with that creamy complexion and those soft gray eyes. He didn't dare pay too much attention. But when she was fully grown, she was going to break hearts. His jaw tautened. He didn't like to think about that, for some reason.

"Now make a left turn onto the next road. Give the signal," he directed. "That's right. Look both ways. Good. Very good."

She grinned. "This is fun."

"No, fun is when you streak down the interstate at a hundred and twenty and nobody sees you. That's fun."

"You didn't!" she gasped.

He shrugged. "Jags like to run. They purr when you pile on the gas."

"They do not."

"You'll see." He smiled to himself. He already had plans for her graduation day. He and Sara had planned it very well. It was only a couple of months away. He glanced at his companion. She was going to be absolutely stunned when she knew what they had in mind.

The piece on Wofford Patterson ran with Michelle's byline, along with photos of his native grasses, his water conservation project and his huge bull. People she didn't even know at school stopped her in the hall to talk to her. And not only other students. Teachers paid her more attention, as well. She felt like a minor celebrity.

"I actually had someone to sit with at lunch," she told Sara, all enthusiasm, when she got home from school that day. "Mostly I'm always by myself. But one little article in the paper with my name and just look!"

Sara managed a smile. "It was well written. You did a good job. Considering the material you had to work with," she added with smoldering black eyes.

Then Michelle remembered. Wofford Patterson. Mortal enemy. Sara's nemesis.

"Sorry," she said, flushing.

"The man is a total lunatic," Sara muttered, slamming pans around as she looked for something to boil pasta in. Her beautiful complexion was flushed. "He backed into me and tried to blame me for it! Then he said I rode a broom and kept flying monkeys in the barn!"

Michelle almost bit through her lower lip. She couldn't laugh. She couldn't laugh...

Sara glanced at her, rolled her eyes, and dragged out a big pot. "You like him, I gather?"

"Well, he didn't accuse me of keeping flying monkeys," Michelle said reasonably. "He's very handsome, in a rough-cut sort of way, and he loves animals."

"Probably because he is one," Sara said under her breath.

"He has this huge rottweiler. You wouldn't believe what he calls her!"

"Have you seen my hammer?" Gabriel interrupted suddenly.

Both women turned.

"Don't you keep it in the toolbox?" Michelle asked.

"Yes. Where's my toolbox?" he amended.

The two women looked at each other blankly. Then Sara flushed.

"I, uh, had to find a pair of pliers to turn the water spigot on outside. Not my fault," she added. "You have big hands and when you turn the water off, I can't turn it back on. I took the whole toolbox with me so I'd have access to whatever I needed."

"No problem. But where is it?" Gabriel added.

"Um," Sara frowned. "I think I remember…just a sec." She headed out the back door.

"Don't, for God's sake, tell her the name of Patterson's dog!" Gabriel said in a rough whisper.

She stared at him. "Why?"

He gave her a speaking look. "Who do you think Patterson's unknown buddy in World of Warcraft is?" he asked patiently.

Her eyes widened with glee. "You mean, they're buddies online and they don't know it?"

"In a nutshell." He grinned. "Two lonely people who can't stand each other in person, and they're soul mates online. Let them keep their illusions, for the time being."

"Of course." She shook her head. "She'd like him if she got to know him."

"I know. But first impressions die hard."

Sara was back, carrying a beat-up brown toolbox. "Here." She set it down on the table. "Sorry," she added sheepishly.

"I don't mind if you borrow stuff. Just put it back, please." He chuckled.

She shrugged. "Sometimes I do. I'm just scatter-brained."

"Listen," he said, kissing the top of her head, "nobody who speaks six languages fluently could even remotely be called scatterbrained. You just have a lot on your mind all the time."

"What a nice way to put it. No wonder you're my favorite brother!"

He gave Michelle a droll look.

"Well, if I had other brothers, you'd still be my favorite," Sara amended.

"Are we going to drive some more today?" Michelle asked him hopefully.

"Maybe tomorrow," he said after a minute. He forced a smile. He left, quickly.

Michelle sighed. "I can't follow orders," she explained while Sara put water on to boil and got out spaghetti.

"He's just impatient," Sara replied. "He always was, even when we were kids." She shook her head. "Some habits you never grow out of."

Michelle knew a lot about Sara, and her childhood.

But she was too kindhearted to mention any of what Gabriel had told her. She just smiled and asked what she could do to help.

Graduation was only days away. So much had happened to Michelle that she could hardly believe how quickly the time had gone by. Marist College had accepted her, just as Gabriel had told her. She was scheduled for orientation in August, and she'd already had a conversation online with her faculty advisor.

"I'm so excited," she told Gabriel. They were sitting on the front porch, watching a meteor shower. There were a couple of fireballs, colorful and rare. "I'll be in college. I can't believe it."

He smiled. "You'll grow. College changes people. You see the world in a different way when you've studied courses like Western Civilization and math."

"I'm not looking forward to the math," she sighed. "People say college trig is a nightmare."

"Only if you don't have a tutor."

"But I don't…"

He glanced down at her. "I made straight A's."

"Oh." She grinned. "Okay. Thanks in advance."

He stretched. "No problem. Maybe you'll do better at math than you do at driving."

She thumped his arm. "Stop that. I can drive."

"Sort of."

"It takes practice," she reminded him. "How can I practice if you're always too busy to ride in the truck with me?"

"You could ask Sara," he pointed out.

She glowered at him. "I did."

"And?"

"She's always got something ready to cook." She pursed her lips. "In fact, she has pots and pans lined up, ready, in case I look like I'm even planning to ask her to ride with me." Her eyes narrowed suspiciously. "I have reason to believe you've been filling her head with irrelevant facts about how many times I've run into ditches."

"Lies."

"It was only one ditch," she pointed out.

"That reminds me." He pulled out his cell phone and checked a text message. He nodded. "I have a professional driving instructor coming out to work with you, starting Saturday afternoon."

"Coward," she accused.

He grinned. "I don't teach."

"I thought you were doing very well, except for the nonstop cursing."

"I thought you were doing well, except for the nonstop near accidents."

She threw up her hands and sighed. "Okay. Just push me off onto some total stranger who'll have a heart attack if I miss a turn. His family will sue us and we'll end up walking everywhere…"

He held up a hand. "I won't change my mind. I can't teach you how to drive with any efficiency. These people have been doing it for a long time."

She gave in. "Okay. I'll give it a shot." She looked up at him. "You and Sara are coming to graduation, aren't you?"

He smiled down at her. "I wouldn't miss it for the whole world, *ma belle*."

Her heart jumped up into her throat. She could walk

on air, because Gabriel teased her in that deep, soft tone that he used only with her.

He touched her long hair gently. "You're almost grown. Just a few more years."

"I'm eighteen."

He let go of her hair. "I know." He turned away. She was eighteen years old. Years too young for what he was thinking of. He had to let her go, let her grow, let her mature. He couldn't hold her back out of selfishness. In a few years, when she was through college, when she had a good job, when she could stand alone—then, yes, perhaps. Perhaps.

"You're very introspective tonight," she remarked.

"Am I?" He chuckled. "I was thinking about cows."

"Cows?"

"It's a clear night. If a UFO were to abduct a cow, we would probably see it."

"How exciting! Let's go looking for them. I'll drive!"

"Not on your life, and don't you have homework? Finals are coming up, I believe?"

She made a face. "Yes, they are, and I can't afford to make a bad grade." She glanced at him. "Spoilsport."

He shrugged. "I want you to graduate."

She folded her hands on her jeans-clad thighs. "I've never told you how much I appreciate all you and Sara have done for me," she said quietly. "I owe you so much…"

"Stop that. We were happy to help."

It had just occurred to her that she was going away, very soon, to college. She was going to live in the dormitory there. She wouldn't live with Sara and Gabriel again. Her holidays would be spent with fellow students, if anyone even stayed on campus—didn't the campus close for holidays?

"I can see the wheels turning," he mused, glancing down at her. "You'll come to us for holidays and vacations," he said. "Sara and I will be here. At least until you're through college. Okay?"

"But Sara has a place in Wyoming—" she began.

"We have a place in Wyoming, and we have a competent manager in charge of it," he interrupted. "Besides, she likes it here in Texas."

"I did notice she was up very late last night on the computer," she said under her breath.

"New expansion on her game," he whispered. "She and her unknown pal are running battlegrounds together. She's very excited."

Michelle laughed softly. "We should probably tell her."

"No way. It's the first time I've seen her happy, really happy, in many years," he said wistfully. "Dreams are precious. Let her keep them."

"I suppose it won't hurt," she replied. "But she's not getting a lot of sleep."

"She hasn't slept well in a long time, despite therapy and prescriptions. This gaming might actually solve a few problems for her."

"You think?"

"We can wait and see, at least." He glanced at his watch, the numbers glowing in the darkness. "I have some paperwork to get through. You coming in?"

"In just a minute. I do love meteor showers."

"So do I. If you like astronomy, we'll have to buy a telescope."

"Could we?" she asked enthusiastically.

"Of course. I'll see about it."

"I would love to look at Mars!"

"So would I."

"I would love to go there," she ventured.

He shrugged. "Not going to happen."

"It was worth a try."

He chuckled, ruffled her hair and went back inside.

Graduation day was going to be long and exciting. Michelle had gone to the rehearsal, which had to be held inside because it was pouring rain that day. She had hoped it wouldn't rain on graduation day.

Her gown and cap fit perfectly. She wasn't going to graduate with honors, but she was at least in the top 10 percent of her class. Her grades had earned her a small scholarship, which would pay for textbooks. She didn't want Gabriel and Sara to be out of pocket on her account, regardless of their financial worth.

Her gown was white. It made her look almost angelic, with her long blond hair down to her waist, her peaches-and-cream complexion delicately colored, her gray eyes glittering with excitement.

She didn't see Gabriel and Sara in the audience, but that wasn't surprising. There was a huge crowd. They were able to graduate outside because the skies cleared up. They held the graduation ceremonies on the football field, with faculty and students and families gathered for the occasion.

Michelle accepted her diploma from the principal, grinned at some of her fellow students and walked off the platform. On the way down, she remembered what a terrifying future she was stepping into. For twelve years, she'd gone to school every day—well, thirteen years if you counted kindergarten. Now, she was free. But with freedom came responsibility. She had to support herself. She had to manage an apartment. She had to pay bills...

Maybe not the bills part, totally. She would have to force Gabriel and Sara to let her pay rent. That would help her pride. She'd go off to college, to strangers, to a dormitory that might actually be unisex. That was a scary thought.

She ran to Gabriel and Sara, to be hugged and congratulated.

"You are now a free woman." Sara chuckled. "Well, mostly. Except for your job, and college upcoming."

"If it's going to be a unisex dorm," Michelle began worriedly.

"It's not," Gabriel assured her. "Didn't you notice? It's a Protestant college. They even have a chaplain."

"Oh. Oh!" She burst out laughing, and flushed. "No, I didn't really notice, until I thought about having to share my floor with men who are total strangers."

"No way would that happen," Gabriel said solemnly, and his dark eyes flashed. "I'd have you driven back and forth first."

"So would I," Sara agreed. "Or I'd move up to San Antonio, get an apartment and you could room with me."

Tears stung Michelle's cheeks. She was remembering how proud her father had been of her grades and her ambitions, how he'd looked forward to seeing her graduate. He should have been here.

"Now, now," Gabriel said gently, as if he could see the thoughts in her mind. He brushed the tears away and kissed her eyelids closed. "It's a happy occasion," he whispered.

She was tingling all over from the unexpectedly intimate contact. Her heart went wild. When he drew back, everything she felt and thought was right there, in her eyes. His own narrowed, and his tall, muscular body tensed.

Sara coughed. She coughed again, to make sure they heard her.

"Lunch," Gabriel said at once, snapping out of it. "We have reservations."

"At one of the finest restaurants in the country, and we still have to get to the airport."

"Restaurant? Airport?" Michelle was all at sea.

Gabriel grinned. "It's a surprise. Someone's motioning to you." He indicated a female student who was waving like crazy.

"It's Yvonne," Michelle told them. "I promised to have my picture taken with her and Gerrie. They were in my geography class. Be right back!"

They watched her go, her face alive with pleasure.

"Close call, masked man," Sara said under her breath.

He stuffed his hands into his slacks and his expression hardened.

"You have to be patient," Sara added gently, and touched his chest with a small hand. "Just for a little while."

"Just for years," he said curtly. "While she meets men and falls in love…"

"Fat chance."

He turned and looked down at her, his face guarded but full of hope.

"You know how she feels," Sara said softly. "That isn't going to change. But she has to have time to grow up, to see something of the world. The time will pass."

He grimaced and then drew in a breath. "Yes. I suppose so." He laughed hollowly. "Maybe in the meantime, I can work up to how I'm going to explain my line of work to her. Another hurdle."

"By that time, she'll be more likely to understand."

He nodded. "Yes."

She hugged him impulsively. "You're a great guy. She already knows it."

He hugged her back. "I'll be her best friend."

"You already are." She drew back, smiling. The smile faded and her eyes sparked with temper as she looked past him.

"My, my, did you lose your broom?" came a deep, drawling voice from behind Gabriel.

"The flying monkeys are using it right now," Sara snarled at the tall man. "Are you just graduating from high school, too?" she added. "And I didn't get you a present."

He shrugged. "My foreman's daughter graduated. I'm her godfather."

"So many responses come to mind. But choosing just one." She pondered for a minute. She pursed her full lips. "Do you employ a full-time hit man, or do you have to manage with pickups?"

He raised his thick eyebrows. "Oh, full-time, definitely," he said easily, hands deep in his jean pockets. He cocked his head. "But he doesn't do women. Pity."

Sara was searching for a comeback when Michelle came running back.

"Oh, hi, Mr. Patterson!" she said with a grin. "How's that bull doing?"

"Eating all he can get and looking better by the day, Miss Godfrey," he replied, smiling. "That was a good piece you wrote on the ranch."

"Thanks. I had good material to work with."

Sara made a sound deep in her throat.

"What was that? Calling the flying monkeys in some strange guttural language?" Wolf asked Sara with wide, innocent eyes.

She burst out in Farsi, things that would have made Michelle blush if she understood them.

"Oh, my, what a thing to say to someone!" Wolf said with mock surprise. He looked around. "Where's a police officer when you need one?"

"By all means, find one who speaks Farsi," Sara said with a sarcastic smile.

"Farsi?" Jacobsville police chief Cash Grier strolled up with his wife, Tippy. "I speak Farsi."

"Great. Arrest her," Wolf said, pointing at Sara. "She just said terrible things about my mother. Not to mention several of my ancestors."

Cash glanced at Sara, who was glowering at Wolf, and totally unrepentant.

"He started it," Sara said angrily. "I do not ride a broom, and I have never seen a flying monkey!"

"I did, once," Cash said, nodding. "Of course, a man threw it at me…"

"Are you going to arrest her?" Wolf interrupted.

"You'd have to prove that she said it," Cash began.

"Gabriel heard her say it," Wolf persisted.

Cash looked at Gabriel. So did Sara and Michelle and Tippy.

"I'll burn the pasta for a week," Sara said under her breath.

Gabriel cleared his throat. "Gosh, I'm sorry," he said. "I wasn't paying attention. Would you like to say it again, and this time I'll listen?" he asked his sister.

"Collusion," Wolf muttered. He glowered at Sara. "I still have my handcuffs from my FBI days..."

"How very kinky," Sara said haughtily.

Cash turned away quickly. His shoulders were shaking. Tippy hit him.

He composed himself and turned back. "I'm sorry, but I really can't be of any assistance in this particular matter. Congratulations, Michelle," he added.

"Thanks, Chief Grier," she replied.

"Why are you here?" Wolf asked the chief.

"One of my young brother-in-law's older gaming friends is graduating," he replied with a smile. "We came to watch him graduate." He shook his head. "He's awesome at the Halo series on Xbox 360."

"So am I," Wolf said with a grin. He glanced at Gabriel. "Do you play?"

Gabriel shook his head. "I don't really have time."

"It's fun. I like console games. But I also like..." Wolf began.

"The reservations!" Gabriel interrupted, checking his watch. "Sorry, but we've got a flight to catch. Graduation present," he added with a grin and a glance at Michelle. "See you all later."

"Sure," Wolf replied. He glanced at Sara and his

eyes twinkled. "An airplane, huh? Having mechanical problems with the broom…?"

"We have to go, right now," Gabriel said, catching Sara before she could move toward Wolf.

He half dragged her away, to the amusement of the others.

"You should have let me hit him," Sara fumed as they sat comfortably in the business-class section of an aircraft bound for New Orleans. "Just one little slap…"

"In front of the police chief, who would have been obliged to arrest you," Gabriel pointed out. "Not a good thing on Michelle's graduation day."

"No." She smiled at Michelle, who looked as amused as Gabriel did. "Sorry. That man just rubs me the wrong way."

"It's okay," Michelle said. "I can't believe we're flying to New Orleans for lunch." She laughed, shaking her head. "I've never been on a plane before in my life. The takeoff was so cool!" she recalled, remembering the burst of speed, the clouds coming closer, the land falling away under the plane as she looked out the window. They'd given her the window seat, so that she had a better view.

"It was fun, seeing it through your eyes," Sara replied, smiling. "I tend to take it for granted. So does he." She indicated Gabriel, who laughed.

"I spend most of my life on airplanes, of one type or another," Gabriel confessed. "I must admit, my flights aren't usually this relaxed."

"You never did tell me what you do," Michelle said.

"I'm sort of a government contractor," he said easily. "An advisor. I go lots of places in that capacity. I deal with foreign governments." He made it sound conventional. It really wasn't.

"Oh. Like businessmen do."

"Something like that," he lied. He smiled. "You have your first driving lesson tomorrow," he reminded her.

"Sure you wouldn't like to do it instead?" she asked. "I could try really hard to avoid ditches."

He shook his head. "You need somebody better qualified than I am."

"I hope he's got a good heart."

"I'm sure he'll be personable…"

"I hope he's in very good health," she amended.

Gabriel just chuckled.

They ate at a five-star restaurant downtown. The food was the most exquisite Michelle had ever tasted, with a Cajun spiced fare that teased the tongue, and desserts that almost made her cry they were so delicious.

"This is one of the best restaurants I've ever frequented," Gabriel said as they finished second cups of coffee. "I always stop by when I'm in the area." He looked around at the elegant decor. "They had some problems during Hurricane Katrina, but they've remodeled and regrouped. It's better than ever."

"It was delicious," Michelle said, smiling. "You guys are spoiling me rotten."

"We're enjoying it," Sara replied. "And there's an even bigger surprise waiting when we get home," she added.

"Another one? But this was the best present I've ever had! You didn't need to…"

"Oh, but we did," Gabriel replied. He leaned back in his chair, elegant in a navy blue jacket with a black turtleneck and dark slacks. Sara was wearing a simple black dress with pearls that made her look both expensive and beautiful. Michelle, in contrast, was wearing the only good dress she had, a simple sheath of off-white, with her mother's pearls. She felt dowdy compared to her companions, but they didn't even seem to notice that the dress was old. They made her feel beautiful.

"What is it?" Michelle asked suddenly.

She was met with bland smiles.

"Wait and see," Gabriel said with twinkling black eyes.

Chapter 8

It was very late when they got back to the ranch. There, sitting in the driveway, was a beautiful little white car with a big red ribbon tied around it.

Michelle gaped at it. Her companions urged her closer.

She touched the trunk, where a sleek silver Jaguar emblem sat above the keyhole.

"It's a Jag," she stammered.

"It's not the most expensive one," Sara said quickly when Michelle gave them accusing glances. "In fact, it's a midrange automobile. But it's one of the safest cars on the road. Which is why we got it for you. Happy Graduation!"

She hugged Michelle.

"It's too much," Michelle stammered, touching the body with awe. She fought tears. "I never dreamed… Oh, it's so…beautiful!" She turned and threw herself into Sara's arms, hugging her close. "I'll take such good care of it! I'll polish it by the inch, with my own hands…!"

"Don't I get a hug, too? It was my idea," Gabriel said.

She laughed, turned and hugged him close. "Of course you do. Thank you! Gosh, I never dreamed you'd get me a car as a present!"

"You needed one," Gabriel said at the top of her head. "You have to be able to drive to work for Minette in the summer. And you'll need one to commute from college to home on weekends. If you want to come home that often," he added.

"Why would I want to stay in the city when I can come down here and ride horses?" she asked, smiling up at him. He was such a dish, she thought dreamily.

Gabriel looked back at her with dark, intent eyes. She was beautiful. Men would want her. Other men.

"Well, try it out," Sara said, interrupting tactfully. "I'll help you untie the ribbon."

"I'm never throwing the ribbon away!" Michelle laughed. "Oh. Wait!" She pulled out her cell phone and took a picture of the car in its bow.

"Stand beside it. We'll get one of you, too," Gabriel said, pulling out his own cell phone. He took several shots, smiling all the time. "Okay. Now get inside and try it out."

"Who's riding shotgun?" Michelle asked.

They looked worriedly at each other.

"It's too late to take it out of the driveway," Gabriel said finally. "Just start it up."

Michelle stood at the door. It wouldn't open.

"The key," Sara prompted Gabriel.

"The key. Duh." He chuckled. He dug it out of his pants pocket and handed it to Michelle. It was still warm from his body.

She looked at the fob in the light from the porch. "There's no key."

"You don't need one."

She unlocked the car and got inside. "There's no gearshift!"

"See the start button?" Gabriel prompted. "Press it."

She did. Nothing happened.

"Hold down the brake with your foot and then press it," he added.

She did. The car roared to life. She caught her breath as the vents opened and the gearshift rose up out of the console. "Oh!" she exclaimed. She looked at the controls, at the instrument panel, at the leather seats. "Oh!" she said again.

Gabriel squatted by the door, on the driveway. "Its creator said something like, 'We will never come closer to building something that is alive.' Each Jaguar is unique. Each has its own little idiosyncrasies. I've been driving them for years, and I still learn new things about them. They purr when they're happy, they growl when they want the open road." He laughed self-consciously. "Well, you'll see."

She leaned over and brushed her soft mouth against his cheek, very shyly. "Thanks."

He chuckled and got to his feet. "You're welcome."

"Thanks, Sara," she called to the other woman.

"It was truly our pleasure." Sara yawned. "And now we really should get to bed, don't you think? Michelle has an early morning, and I'm quite tired." She hesitated. "Perhaps we should check to make sure the flying monkeys are locked up securely...?"

They both laughed.

The driving instructor's name was Mr. Moore. He had a small white round patch of hair at the base of his skull. Michelle wondered if his hair loss was from close calls by students.

He was very patient. She had a couple of near-misses, but was able to correct in time and avoid an accident. He told her that it was something that much practice would fix. She only needed to drive, and remember her lessons.

So she drove. But it was Sara, not Gabriel, who rode with her that summer. Gabriel had packed a bag, told the women goodbye, and rushed out without another word.

"Where is he going?" Michelle had asked Sara.

The other woman smiled gently. "We're not allowed to know. Some of what he does is classified. And you must never mention it to anyone. Okay?"

"Of course not," Michelle replied. She bit her lip. "What he does—it's just office stuff, right? I mean he advises. That's talking to people, instructing, right?"

Sara hesitated only a beat before she replied, "Of course."

Michelle put it out of her mind. Gabriel didn't phone home. He'd been gone several weeks. During that time, Michelle began to perfect her driving skills, with Sara's help. She got her driver's license, passing the test easily, and now she drove alternately to work with Carlie.

"This is just so great," Carlie enthused on the way

to work. "They bought you a Jaguar! I can't believe it!" She sighed, smoothing her hand over the soft leather seat. "I wish somebody would buy me a Jaguar."

Michelle chuckled. "It was a shock to me, too, let me tell you. I tried to give it back, but they wouldn't hear of it. They said I needed something safe. Like a big Ford truck wouldn't be safe?" she mused.

"I'd love a big brand-new Ford truck," Carlie sighed. "One of those F-Series ones. Or a Dodge Ram. Or a Chevy Silverado. I've never met a truck I didn't love."

"I like cars better," Michelle said. "Just a personal preference." She glanced at her friend. "I'm going to miss riding with you when I go to college."

"I'll miss you, too." Carlie glanced out the window. "Just having company keeps me from brooding."

"Carson is still giving you fits, I gather?" Michelle asked gently.

Carlie looked down at her hands. "I don't understand why he hates me so much," she said. "I haven't done anything to him Well, except make a few sarcastic comments, but he starts it," she added with a scowl.

"Maybe he likes you," Michelle ventured. "And he doesn't want to."

"Oh, sure, that's the reason." She shook her head. "No. That isn't it. He'd throw me to the wolves without a second thought."

"He spends a lot of time in Cash Grier's office."

"They're working on something. I'm not allowed to know what, and the chief makes sure I can't overhear him when he talks on the phone." She frowned. "My father's in there a lot, too. I can't imagine why. Carson isn't the praying sort," she added coldly, alluding to her father's profession. He was, after all, a minister.

"I wouldn't think the chief is the praying sort, either," Michelle replied. "Maybe it's something to do about that man who attacked your father."

"I've wondered about that," her companion replied. "Dad won't tell me anything. He just clams up if I mention it."

"You could ask the chief."

Carlie burst out laughing. "You try it," she replied with a grin. "He changes the subject, picks up the phone, drags someone passing by into the office to chat—he's a master at evasion."

"You might try asking Carson," she added.

The smile faded. "Carson would walk all over me."

"You never know."

"I know, all right." Carlie flushed a little, and stared out the window again.

"Sorry," Michelle said gently. "You don't want to talk about him. I understand."

"It's okay." She turned her head. "Is Gabriel coming back soon?"

"We don't know. We don't even know where he is," Michelle said sadly. "Some foreign country, I gather, but he didn't say." She shook her head. "He's so mysterious."

"Most men are." Carlie laughed.

"At least what he does is just business stuff," came the reply. "So we don't have to worry about him so much."

"A blessing," Carlie agreed.

Michelle did a story about the local fire department and its new fire engine. She learned a lot from the fire chief about how fires were started and how they were fought. She put it all into a nice article, with photos of the firemen. Minette ran it on the front page.

"Favoritism," Cash Grier muttered when she stopped by to get Carlie for the drive home that Friday afternoon.

"Excuse me?" Michelle asked him.

"A story about the fire department, on the front page," he muttered. He glared at her. "You haven't even done one about us, and we just solved a major crime!"

"A major crime." Michelle hadn't heard of it.

"Yes. Someone captured old man Jones's chicken, put it in a doll dress, and tied it to his front porch." He grinned. "We captured the perp."

"And?" Michelle prompted. Carlie was listening, too.

"It was Ben Harris's granddaughter." He chuckled. "Her grandmother punished her for overfilling the bathtub by taking away her favorite dolly. So there was this nice red hen right next door. She took the chicken inside, dressed it up, and had fun playing with it while her grandparents were at the store. Then she realized how much more trouble she was going to be in when they noticed what the chicken did, since it wasn't wearing a diaper."

Both women were laughing.

"So she took the chicken back to Jones's house, but she was afraid it might run off, so she tied it to the porch rail." He shook his head. "The doll's clothes were a dead giveaway. She's just not cut out for a life of crime."

"What did Mr. Jones do?" Michelle asked.

"Oh, he took pictures," he replied. "Want one? They're pretty cool. I'm thinking of having one blown up for my office. To put on my solved-crime wall." He grinned.

They were laughing so hard, tears were rolling down their cheeks.

"And the little girl?" Michelle persisted.

"She's assigned to menial chores for the next few days. At least, until all the chicken poop has been cleaned off the floors and furniture. They did give her back the doll, however," he added, tongue in cheek. "To prevent any future lapses. Sad thing, though."

"What is?"

"The doll is naked. If she brings it out of the house, as much as I hate it, I'll have to cite it for indecent exposure..."

The laughter could be heard outside the door now. The tall man with jet-black hair hanging down to his waist wasn't laughing.

He stopped, staring at the chief and his audience.

"Something?" Cash asked, suddenly all business.

"Something." Carson's black eyes slid to Carlie's face and narrowed coldly. "If you can spare the time."

"Sure. Come on in."

"If you don't need me, I'll go home," Carlie said at once, flushed, as she avoided Carson's gaze.

"I don't need you." Carson said it with pure venom.

She lifted her chin pugnaciously. "Thank God," she said through her teeth.

He opened his mouth, but Cash intervened. "Go on home, Carlie," he said, as he grabbed Carson by the arm and steered him into the office.

* * *

"So that's Carson," Michelle said as she drove toward Carlie's house.

"That's Carson."

Michelle drew in a breath. "A thoroughly unpleasant person."

"You don't know the half of it."

"He really has it in for you."

Carlie nodded. "Told you so."

There really didn't seem to be anything else to say. Michelle gave her a sympathetic smile and kept her silence until they pulled up in front of the Victorian house she shared with her father.

"Thanks for the ride," Carlie said. "My turn to drive tomorrow."

"And my turn to buy gas." She chuckled.

"You don't hear me arguing, do you?" Carlie sighed, smiling. "Gas is outrageously high."

"So is most everything else. Have a good night. I'll see you tomorrow."

"Sure. Thanks again."

Michelle parked her car in front of the house, noted that she really needed to take it through the car wash, and started toward the front door. Sara's car was missing. She hadn't mentioned being away. Not a problem, however, since Michelle had a key.

She started to put it into the lock, just as it opened on its own. And there was Gabriel, tanned and handsome and smiling.

"Gabriel!" She threw herself into his arms, to be lifted, and hugged, and swung around once, twice, three times, in an embrace so hungry that she never wanted to be free again.

"When did you get home?" she asked at his ear.

"About ten minutes ago," he murmured into her neck. "You smell of roses."

"New perfume. Sara bought it for me." She drew back just enough to see his face, her arms still around his neck, his arms still holding her close. She searched his eyes at point-blank range and felt her heart go into overdrive. She could barely breathe. He felt like heaven in her arms. She looked at his mouth, chiseled, perfect, and wondered, wondered so hard, how it would feel if she moved just a little, if she touched her lips to it…

His hand caught in her long hair and pulled. "No," he said through his teeth.

She met his eyes. She saw there, or thought she saw, the same burning hunger that was beginning to tauten her young body, to kindle needs she'd never known she had.

Her lips parted on a shaky breath. She stared at him. He stared back. There seemed to be no sound in the world, nothing except the soft rasp of her breathing and the increasing heaviness of his own. Against her flattened breasts, she could feel the warm hardness of his chest, the thunder of his heartbeat.

One of his hands slid up and down her spine. His black eyes dropped to her mouth and lingered there until she almost felt the imprint of them, like a hard, rough kiss. Her nails bit into him where her hands clung.

She wanted him. He could feel it. She wanted his mouth, his hands, his body. Her breath was coming in tiny gasps. He could feel her heartbeat behind the soft, warm little breasts pressed so hard to his chest. Her mouth was parted, moist, inviting. He could grind his own down into it and make her moan, make her want him, make her open her arms to him on the long, soft sofa that was only a few steps away…

She was eighteen. She'd never lived. There hadn't been a serious romance in her young life. He could rob her of her innocence, make her a toy, leave her broken and hurting and old.

"No," he whispered. He forced himself to put her down. He held her arms, tightly, until he could force himself to let go and step back.

She was shaky. She felt his hunger. He wasn't impervious to her. But he was cautious. He didn't want to start anything. He was thinking about her age. She knew it.

"I won't…always be eighteen," she managed.

He nodded, very slowly. "One day," he promised. "Perhaps."

She brightened. It was like the sun coming out. "I'll read lots of books."

His eyebrows arched.

"You know. On how to do…stuff. And I'll buy a hope chest and fill it up with frothy little black things."

The eyebrows arched even more.

"Well, it's a hope chest. As in, I hope I'll need it one day when you think I'm old enough." She pursed her lips and her gray eyes twinkled. "I could fake my ID…"

"Give it up." He chuckled.

She shrugged. "I'll grow up as fast as I can," she promised. She glowered at him. "I won't like it if I hear about you having orgies with strange women."

"Most women are strange," he pointed out.

She hit his chest. "Not nice."

"How's the driving?" he asked, changing the subject.

"I haven't hit a tree, run off the road or approached a ditch since you left," she said smugly. "I haven't even dinged the paint."

"Good girl," he said, chuckling. "I'm proud of you. How's the job coming along?"

"It's great! I'm working on this huge story! It may have international implications!"

Odd, how worried he looked for a few seconds. "What story?"

"It involves a kidnapping," she continued.

He frowned.

"A chicken was involved," she added, and watched his face clear and become amused. "A little girl whose doll was taken away for punishment stole a chicken and dressed it in doll's clothes. I understand she'll be cleaning the house for days to come."

He laughed heartily. "The joys of small-town reporting," he mused.

"They never end. How was your trip?"

"Long," he said. "And I'm starving."

"Sara made a lovely casserole. I'll heat you up some."

He sat down at the kitchen table and watched her work. She made coffee and put a mug of it, black, at his place while she dealt with reheating the chicken casserole.

She warmed up a piece of French bread with butter to go with it. Then she sat down and watched him eat while she sipped her own coffee.

"It sure beats fried snake," he murmured.

She blinked. "What?"

"Well, we eat what we can find. Usually, it's a snake. Sometimes, if we're lucky, a big bird or some fish."

"In an office building?" she exclaimed.

He glanced at her with amusement. "It's not always in an office building. Sometimes we have to go out and look at…projects, wherever they might be. This time, it was in a jungle."

"Wow." She was worried now. "Poisonous snakes?"

"Mostly. It doesn't really affect the taste," he added.

"You could get bitten," she persisted.

"I've been bitten, half a dozen times," he replied easily. "We always carry antivenin with us."

"I thought you were someplace safe."

He studied her worried face and felt a twinge of guilt. "It was just this once," he lied, and he smiled. "What I do is rarely dangerous." Another lie. A bigger one. "Nothing to concern you. Honest."

She propped her face in her hands, her elbows on the table, and watched him finish his meal and his coffee.

"Stop that," he teased. "I can take care of myself. I've been doing it for twenty-odd years."

She grimaced. "Okay. Just checking."

"I promise not to get killed."

"If you do, I'm coming after you. Boy, will you be sorry, too."

He laughed. "I hear you."

"Want dessert? We have a cherry pie."

He shook his head. "Maybe later. Where's Sara?"

"I have no idea. She didn't even leave a note."

He pulled out his cell phone and pressed the speed dial. He got up and poured more coffee into his cup while he waited.

"Where are you?" he asked after a minute.

There was a reply. He glanced at Michelle, his lips pursed, his eyes twinkling. "Yes, she's right here."

Another silence. He sat back down. He was nodding.

"No, I think it's a very good idea. But you might have asked for my input first… No, I agree, you have exquisite taste… Yes, that's true, returns are possible. I won't tell her. How long?… Okay. See you then." He smiled. "Me, too. Thanks."

He hung up.

"Where is she?" she asked.

"On her way home. With a little surprise."

"Something for me?" she asked, and her face brightened.

"I'd say so."

"But you guys have already given me so much," she began, protesting.

"You can take that up with my sister," he pointed out. "Not that it will do you much good. She's very stubborn."

She laughed. "I noticed." She paused. "What is it?"

"You'll have to wait and see."

Sara pulled up into the driveway and got out of her car. She popped the truck and dragged out several big shopping bags. She handed some to Gabriel and one to Michelle. She was grinning from ear to ear.

"What in the world…?" Michelle exclaimed.

"Just a few little odds and ends that you're going to need to start college. Come on inside and I'll show you. Gabriel, get your nose out of that bag, it's private!"

He laughed and led the way into the house.

* * *

Michelle was speechless. Sara had exquisite taste in clothing, and it showed in the items she'd purchased for their houseguest. There was everything from jeans and sweats to dresses and handbags and underwear, gossamer gowns and an evening gown that brought tears to Michelle's eyes because it was the loveliest thing she'd ever seen.

"You like them?" Sara asked, a little worried.

"I've never had things like this," she stammered. "Daddy was so sick that he never thought of shopping with me. And when Roberta took me, it was just for bras and panties, never for nice clothes." She hugged Sara impulsively. "Thank you. Thank you so much!"

"You might try on that gown. I wasn't sure about the size, but we can exchange it if it doesn't fit. I'll go have coffee with Gabriel while you check the fit." She smiled, and left Michelle with the bags.

They were sipping coffee in the kitchen when Michelle came nervously to the doorway. She'd fixed her hair, put on shoes and she was wearing the long, creamy evening gown with its tight fit and cap sleeves, revealing soft cleavage. There was faint embroidery on the bodice and around the hem. The off-white brought out the highlights in Michelle's long, pale blond hair, and accentuated her peaches-and-cream complexion. In her softly powdered face, her gray eyes were exquisite.

Gabriel turned his head when he caught movement in his peripheral vision. He sat like a stone statue, just staring. Sara followed his gaze, and her face brightened.

"It's perfect!" she exclaimed, rising. "Michelle, it's

absolutely perfect! Now you have something to wear to a really formal occasion."

"Thanks," she replied. "It's the most beautiful thing I've ever owned." She glanced at Gabriel, who hadn't spoken. His coffee cup was suspended in his hand in midair, as if he'd forgotten it. "Does it...look okay?" she asked him, wanting reassurance.

He forced his eyes away. "It looks fine." He put the mug down and got to his feet. "I need to check the livestock." He went out the back door without a glance behind him.

Michelle felt wobbly. She bit her lower lip. "He didn't like it," she said miserably.

Sara touched her cheek gently. "Men are strange. They react in odd ways. I'm sure he liked it, but he's not demonstrative." She smiled. "Okay?"

Michelle relaxed. "Okay."

Out in the barn, Gabriel was struggling to regain his composure. He'd never seen anything in his life more beautiful than Michelle in that dress. He'd had to force himself out the door before he reacted in a totally inappropriate way. He wanted to sweep her up in his arms and kiss her until her mouth went numb. Not a great idea.

He stood beside one of his horses, stroking its muzzle gently, while he came to grips with his hunger. It was years too soon. He would have to manage the long wait. Meanwhile, he worried about the other men, young men, who would see Michelle in that gown and want her, as he wanted her. But they would be her age, young and untried, without his jaded past. They would be like her, full of passion for life.

It wasn't fair of him to try to keep her. He must distance himself from her, give her the chance to grow away from him, to find someone more suitable. It was going to be hard, but he must manage it. She deserved the chance.

The next morning, he was gone when Michelle went into the kitchen to help Sara fix breakfast.

"His truck's gone," Michelle said, her spirits dropping hard.

"Yes. I spoke to him late last night," Sara replied, not looking at her. "He has a new job. He said he might be away for a few weeks." She glanced at the younger woman and managed a smile. "Don't worry about him. He can take care of himself."

"I'm sure he can. It's just…" She rested her hand on the counter. "I miss him, when he's away."

"I'm sure you do." She hesitated. "Michelle, you haven't started to live yet. There's a whole world out there that you haven't even seen."

Michelle turned, her eyes old and wise. "And you think I'll find some young man who'll sweep me off my feet and carry me off to a castle." She smiled. "There's only one man I'll ever want to do that, you know."

Sara grimaced. "There are so many things you don't know."

"They won't matter," Michelle replied very quietly. She searched Sara's eyes. "None of it will matter."

Sara couldn't think of the right words. So she just hugged Michelle instead.

Chapter 9

Michelle was very nervous. It was the first day of the semester on campus, and even with a map, it was hard to find all her classes. Orientation had given the freshmen an overview of where everything was off the quad, but it was so confusing.

"Is Western Civilization in Sims Hall or Waverly Hall?" she muttered to herself, peering at the map.

"Waverly," came a pleasant male voice from just behind her. "Come on, I'll walk you over. I'm Randy. Randy Miles."

"Michelle Godfrey," she said, shaking his hand and smiling. "Thanks. Are you in my class?"

He shook his head. "I'm a junior."

"Should you be talking to me?" she teased. "After all, I'm pond scum."

He stopped and smiled. He had dark hair and pale

eyes. He was a little pudgy, but nice. "No. You're not pond scum. Trust me."

"Thanks."

"My pleasure. Are you from San Antonio?"

"My family is from Jacobsville, but I lived here with my parents while they were alive."

"Sorry."

"They were wonderful people. The memories get easier with time." She glanced around. "This is a huge campus."

"They keep adding to it," he said. "Sims Hall is brand-new. Waverly is old. My father had history with old Professor Barlane."

"Really?"

He nodded. "Just a word of warning, never be late for his class. You don't want to know why."

She grinned. "I'll remember."

On the way to Waverly Hall, Randy introduced Michelle to two of his friends, Alan Drew and Marjory Wills. Alan was distantly pleasant. Marjory was much more interested in talking to Randy than being introduced to this new student.

"You're going to be late for class, aren't you?" Alan asked Michelle, checking his watch. "I'll walk you the rest of the way."

"Nice to have met you," Randy said pleasantly. Marjory just nodded.

Michelle smiled and followed Alan to the towering building where her class was located.

"Thanks," she said.

He shrugged and smiled. "Those two." He rolled his eyes. "They're crazy about each other, but neither one will admit it. Don't let them intimidate you, especially Marjory. She has…issues."

"No problem. I guess I'll see you around."

"You will." He leaned forward, grinning. "I'm in the class you're going to right now. And we'd better hurry!"

They barely made it before the bell. The professor, Dr. Barlane, was old and cranky. He gave the class a dismissive look and began to lecture. Michelle was grateful that she'd learned how to take notes, because she had a feeling that this class was going to be one of the more demanding ones.

Beside her, Alan was scribbling on scraps of paper instead of a notebook, like Michelle. He wasn't bad-looking. He had dark hair and eyes and a nice smile, but in her heart, there was only Gabriel. She might like other men as friends, but there was never going to be one to compare with Gabriel.

After class, Alan left her with a smile and whistled as he continued on to his next class. Michelle looked at her schedule, puzzled out the direction to go and went along the walkway to the next building.

"Well, how was it?" Sara asked that night on the phone.

"Very nice," she replied. "I made a couple of friends."

"Male ones?" Sara teased.

"What was that?" Gabriel spoke up in the background.

"She made friends," Sara called to him. "Don't have a cow."

He made a sarcastic sound and was quiet.

"How do you like your roommate?" Sara continued.

Michelle glanced into the next room, where Darla was searching frantically for a blouse she'd unpacked and couldn't find, muttering and ruffling her red hair.

"She's just like me. Disorganized and flighty," Michelle said, a little loudly.

"I heard that!" Darla said over her shoulder.

"I know!" Michelle laughed. Darla shook her head, laughing, too.

"We're going to get along just fine," Michelle told Sara. "Neither of us has half a mind, and we're so disorganized that we're likely to be thrown out for creating a public eyesore."

"Not likely," Sara replied. "Well, I'm glad things are going well. If you need us, you know where we are, sweetie."

"I do. Thanks. Thanks for everything."

"Keep in touch. Good night."

"Good night."

"Your family?" Darla asked, poking her head into the room.

Michelle hesitated, but only for a second. She smiled. "Yes. My family."

Michelle adjusted to college quite easily. She made some friends, mostly distant ones, and one good one—her roommate, Darla. She and Darla were both religious, so they didn't go to boozy parties or date promiscuous boys. That meant they spent a lot of time watching rented movies and eating popcorn in their own dorm room.

One thing Sara had said was absolutely true; college changed her. She learned things that questioned her own view of the world and things about other cultures. She saw the rise and fall of civilizations, the difference in religions, the rise of science, the fascination of history. She continued her study of French—mainly because she wanted to know what Sara and Gabriel spoke about that they didn't want her to hear—and she sweated first-year biology. But by and large, she did well in her classes.

All too soon, final exams arrived. She sat in the library with other students, she and Darla trying to absorb what they needed to know to pass their courses. She'd already lived in the biology lab for several days after school with a study group, going over material that was certainly going to come up when they were tested.

"I'm going to fail," she moaned softly to Darla. "I'll go home in disgrace. I'll have to hide my head in a paper sack…"

"Shut up," Darla muttered. "You're going to pass! So am I. Be quiet and study, girl!"

Michelle sighed. "Thanks. I needed that."

"I'm going to fail," one of the boys nearby moaned to Darla. "I'll go home in disgrace…"

She punched him.

"Thanks." He chuckled, and went back to his books.

Michelle did pass, with flying colors, but she didn't know it when she went back to Comanche Wells for the holidays.

"I'll have to sweat it out until my grades come through," she said to Sara, hugging her warmly. "But I think I did okay." She looked past Sara and then at her, curious.

"He's out of the country," Sara said gently. "He was

really sorry, he wanted to be home for the holidays. But it wasn't possible. This was a rush thing."

Michelle's heart fell. "I guess he has to work."

"Yes, he does. But he got your presents, and mine, and wrapped them before he left." Her dark eyes twinkled. "He promised that we'd love the gifts."

"I'd love a rock, if he picked it out for me," Michelle sighed. "Can we go shopping? Minette said I could work for her over the holidays while I'm home, so I'll have a little money of my own."

"Whenever you like, dear," Sara promised.

"Thanks!"

"Now come and have hot chocolate. I want to hear all about college!"

Minette had some interesting assignments for Michelle. One was to interview one of Jacobsville's senior citizens about Christmas celebrations in the mid-twentieth century, before the internet or space travel. It had sounded rather boring, honestly. But when she spoke to Adelaide Duncan, the old woman made the past come alive in her soft, mellow tones.

"We didn't have fancy decorations for the Christmas tree," Mrs. Duncan recalled, her pale blue eyes dancing with delightful memories. "We made them from construction paper. We made garlands of cranberries. We used candles set on the branches to light the tree, and we used soap powder mixed with a little water for snow. Presents were practical things, mostly fruit or nuts or handcrafted garments. One year I got oranges and a knit cap. Another, I got a dress my mother had made me in a beautiful lemon color. My husband kissed me under the mistletoe when we were still in school together, long before we married." Her face was wistful. "He was seventeen and I was fifteen. We danced to music that our parents and relatives made with fiddles and guitars. I wore the lemon-yellow dress, ruffled and laced, and I felt like I had possession of the whole world's treasures." She sighed. "We were married for fifty-five years," she added wistfully. "And one day, not too long away now, I'll see him again. And we'll dance together..."

Michelle had to fight tears. "Fifty-five years," she repeated, and couldn't imagine two people staying together for so long.

"Oh, yes. In my day, people got married and then had children." She shook her head. "The world has changed, my dear. Marriage doesn't seem to mean the same as it used to. History tends to repeat itself, and I fear when the stability of a civilization is lost, society crumbles. You'll study the results in your history classes in college," she added, nodding. "Do you have Dr. Barlane for history by any chance?"

"Yes," Michelle said, stunned.

The old woman laughed. "He and I graduated together from Marist College, both with degrees in history. But he went on to higher education and I got married and had a family. By and large, I think my life was happier than his. He never married."

"Do your children live here?" she asked.

"Oh, no, they're scattered around the world." She laughed. "I visit with them on Skype and we text back and forth every day, though. Modern technology." She shook her head. "It really is a blessing, in this day and time."

Michelle was surprised. "You text?" she asked.

"My dear," the old lady mused, laughing, "I not only text, I tweet and surf, and I am hell on wheels with a two-handed sword in World of Warcraft. I own a guild."

The younger woman's idea of elderly people had gone up in a blaze of disbelief. "You…play video games?"

"I eat them up." She shrugged. "I can't run and jump and play in real life, but I can do it online." She grinned from ear to ear. "Don't you dare tell Wofford Patterson, but I creamed one of his Horde toons last night on a battleground."

Michelle almost fell over laughing.

"And you thought you were going to interview some dried up old hulk who sat in a rocking chair and knitted, I bet," the woman mused with twinkling eyes.

"Yes, I did," Michelle confessed, "and I am most heartily sorry!"

"That's all right, dear," Mrs. Duncan said, patting her hand. "We all have misconceptions about each other."

"Mine were totally wrong."

"How nice of you to say so!"

Michelle changed gears and went back to the interview. But what she learned about elderly people that day colored her view of them forever.

"She plays video games," Michelle enthused to Minette, back at the office. She'd written her story and turned it in, along with her photos, while Minette was out of the office. Now she was elaborating on the story, fascinated with what she'd learned.

"Yes, there have been a lot of changes in the way

we perceive the elderly," Minette agreed. "I live with my great-aunt. She doesn't play video games, but I did catch her doing Tai Chi along with an instructor on public television. And she can text, too."

"My grandparents sat and rocked on the porch after supper," Michelle recalled. "He smoked a pipe and she sewed quilt tops and they talked." She shook her head. "It's a different world."

"It is." She hesitated. "Has Gabriel come home?"

Michelle shook her head. "It's almost Christmas, too. We don't know where he is, or what he's doing."

Minette, who did, carefully concealed her knowledge. "Well, he might surprise you and show up on Christmas day. Who knows?"

Michelle forced a smile. "Yes."

She and Sara decorated the tree. Two of the men who worked for Gabriel part-time, taking care of the horses and the ranch, had come in earlier with a big bucket, holding a tree with the root ball still attached.

"I can't bear to kill a tree," Sara confided as the men struggled to put it in place in the living room. "Sorry, guys," she added.

"Oh, Miss Sara, it's no trouble at all," the taller of the two cowboys said at once, holding his hat to his heart. He grinned. "It was our pleasure."

"Absolutely," the shorter one agreed.

They stood smiling at Sara until one thumped the other and reminded him that they had chores to do. They excused themselves, still smiling.

"You just tie them up in knots." Michelle laughed, when they were out of the room. "You're so pretty."

Sara made a face. "Nonsense."

"Hide your head in the sand, then. What are we going to decorate it with?" she added.

"Come with me."

Sara pulled down the ladder and the two women climbed carefully up into the attic.

Michelle caught her breath when she saw the heart of pine rafters. "My goodness, it's almost a religious experience to just look at them!" she exclaimed. "Those rafters must be a hundred years old!"

Sara glanced at her with amusement. "I believe they are. Imagine you, enthralled by rafters!"

"Heart of pine rafters," she replied. "My grandfather built houses when he was younger. He took me with him a time or two when he had to patch a roof or fix a leak. He was passionate about rafters." She laughed. "And especially those made of heart of pine. They're rare, these days, when people mostly build with green lumber that hasn't been properly seasoned."

"This house has a history," Sara said. "You probably already know it, since your people came from Jacobs County."

Michelle nodded, watching Sara pick up two boxes of ornaments and stack them together. "It belonged to a Texas Ranger."

"Yes. He was killed in a shoot-out in San Antonio. He left behind two sons, a daughter and a wife. There's a plaque in city hall in Jacobsville that tells all about him."

"I'll have to go look," Michelle said. "I haven't done any stories that took me there, yet."

"I'm sure you will. Minette says you're turning into a very good reporter."

"She does?" Michelle was all eyes. "Really?"

Sara looked at her and smiled. "You must have more confidence in yourself," she said gently. "You must believe in your own abilities."

"That's hard."

"It comes with age. You'll get the hang of it." She handed Michelle a box of ornaments. "Be careful going down the steps."

"Okay."

They spent the afternoon decorating the tree. When they finally plugged in the beautiful, colored fairy lights, Michelle caught her breath.

"It's the most breathtaking tree I've ever seen," she enthused.

"It is lovely, isn't it?" Sara asked. She fingered a branch. "We must keep it watered, so that it doesn't die. When Christmas is over, I'll have the men plant it near the front steps. I do so love white pines!"

"Do you ever miss Wyoming?" Michelle asked, a little worried because she knew Sara was only here so that Michelle could come home, so that she wouldn't be alone with Gabriel.

Sara turned to her. "A little. I lived there because Gabriel bought the ranch and one of us needed to run it. But I had no real friends. I'm happier here." Her dark eyes were soft. She smoothed over an ornament. "This belonged to my grandmother," she said softly. It was a little house, made of logs, hanging from a red silk ribbon. "My grandfather whittled it for her, when they were dating." She laughed. "Wherever I am, it always makes me feel at home when the holidays come."

"Your mother's parents?"

Sara's face went hard. "No. My father's."

"I'm sorry."

Sara turned back to her. In her lovely face, her dark eyes were sad. "I don't speak of my mother, or her people. I'm sorry. It's a sore spot with me."

"I'll remember," Michelle said quietly. "It's like my stepmother."

"Exactly."

Michelle didn't betray her secret knowledge of Sara's early life, of the tragedy she and Gabriel had lived through because of their mother's passion for their stepfather. She changed the subject and asked about the other ornaments that Sara had placed on the tree.

But Sara wasn't fooled. She was very quiet. Later, when they were sipping hot chocolate in the kitchen, her dark eyes pinned Michelle.

"How much did he tell you?" she asked suddenly.

In her hands, the mug jumped, almost enough to spill the hot liquid on her fingers.

"Careful, it's hot," Sara said. "Come on, Michelle. How much did Gabriel tell you?"

Michelle grimaced.

Sara took in a long breath. "I see." She sipped the liquid gingerly. "He never speaks of it at all. Yet he told you." Her soft eyes lifted to Michelle's worried gray ones. "I'm not angry. I'm surprised."

"That he told me?"

"Yes." She smiled sadly. "He doesn't warm to people. In fact, he's cold and withdrawn with almost everyone. You can't imagine how shocked I was when he phoned me and asked me to come down here because of a young girl he was going to get custody of." She laughed, shaking her head. "I thought he was joking."

"But he's not. Cold and withdrawn, I mean." Michelle faltered.

"Not with you." She stared into Michelle's eyes earnestly. "I haven't heard Gabriel laugh in years," she added softly. "But he does it all the time with you. I don't understand it. But you give him peace, Michelle."

"That would be nice, if it were true. I don't know if it is," Michelle replied.

"It's fairly obvious what you feel for him."

She flushed. She couldn't lift her eyes.

"He won't take advantage of it, don't worry," Sara added gently. "That's why I'm here." She laughed. "He's taking no chances."

"He doesn't want to get involved with a child," Michelle said heavily.

"You won't be a child for much longer," the other woman pointed out.

"I'm sure he meets beautiful women all the time," Michelle said.

"I'm sure it doesn't matter what they look like," Sara replied. She smiled. "You'll see."

Michelle didn't reply to that. She just sipped her hot chocolate and felt warm inside.

It was the week before Christmas, a Friday about lunchtime, when the women heard a truck pull up in the driveway.

Michelle, who was petting one of the horses in the corral, saw the truck and gasped and ran as fast as she could to the man getting out of it.

"Gabriel!" she cried.

He turned. His face lit up like floodlights. He held out his arms and waited until she ran into them to pick her up and whirl her around, holding her so close that she felt they were going to be joined together forever.

"Oh, I've missed you," she choked.

"I've missed you." His voice was deep at her ear. He lifted his head and set her on her feet. His black eyes were narrow, intent on her face. He touched her mouth with just the tip of his forefinger, teasing it apart. His eyes fell to it and lingered there while her heart threatened to jump right out of her throat.

"*Ma belle,*" he whispered roughly.

He framed her oval face in his big hands and searched her eyes. "*Ma belle,*" he repeated. His eyes fell to her mouth. "It's like falling into fire…"

As he spoke, his head started to bend. Michelle's heart ran away. She could hear her own breathing, feel his breath going into her mouth, taste the coffee and the faint odor of tobacco that came from him, mingled with some masculine cologne that teased her senses.

"Gabriel," she whispered, hanging at his mouth, aching to feel it come crashing down on her lips, crushing them, devouring him, easing the ache, the hunger that pulsed through her young, untried body…

"Gabriel!"

Sara's joyful cry broke them apart just in the nick of time. Gabriel cleared his throat, turned to his sister and hugged her.

"It's good to have you home," Sara said against his chest.

"It's good to be home." He was struggling to sound normal. His mind was still on Michelle's soft mouth and his hunger to break it open under his lips, back her into a wall and devour her.

"Have you eaten? I just made soup," Sara added.

"No. I'm starved." He made an attempt not to look at Michelle when he said that. He even smiled.

"I could eat, too," Michelle said, trying to break the tension.

"Let's go in." Sara took his arm. "Where did you come from?"

"Dallas, this time," he said. "I've been in the States for a couple of days, but I had business there before I could get home." He hesitated. "I got tickets to the ballet in San Antonio when I came through there this morning." He glanced at Michelle. "Want to go see *The Nutcracker* with me?" he added with a grin.

"Oh, I'd love to," she said fervently. "What do we wear?"

"A very dressy evening outfit," Sara said. "I bought you one once, and you never even wore it."

Michelle grinned. "Well, I haven't been anywhere I'd need to wear it," she replied, not guessing what it told Gabriel, whose eyes twinkled brightly.

Michelle flushed and then grinned at him. "No, I'm not dating anybody at college," she said. She shrugged. "I'm too busy studying."

"Is that so?" Gabriel laughed, and was relieved.

"When are you leaving?" Sara asked.

"At six, and you'd better start dressing as well, because we're all three going," Gabriel added, and he exchanged a speaking look with Sara.

"All of us? Oh. Oh! That's nice!" Michelle worked at sounding enthusiastic.

Sara just winked at her. "I'd better go through my closet."

Gabriel looked down at Michelle with the Christmas tree bright and beautiful behind her. "I wouldn't dare take you out alone, *ma belle*," he said under his breath. "You know it. And you know why."

Her eyes searched his hungrily. She knew. She'd felt it, when he held her beside the truck. She knew that he wanted her.

She'd had no idea what wanting really was, until Gabriel had come into her life. Now she was aware of a hunger that came around when he was close, that grew and surged in her when he looked at her, when he spoke to her, when he touched her...

"Yes, you know, don't you?" he breathed, standing a little too close. He rubbed his thumb against her lips, hard enough to make her gasp and shiver with delight. His black eyes narrowed. "It's too soon. You know that, too."

She ground her teeth together as she looked at him. He was the most perfect thing in her life. He was preaching caution when all she wanted to do was push him down on the floor and spread her body over him and...

She didn't know what would come next. She'd read books, but they were horribly lacking in preliminaries.

"What are you thinking about so hard?" he asked.

"About pushing you down on the floor," she blurted

out, and flushed. "But I don't know what comes next, exactly..."

He burst out laughing.

"You stop that," she muttered. "I'll bet you weren't born knowing what to do, either."

"I wasn't," he confessed. He touched her nose with the tip of his finger. "It's just as well that you don't know. Yet. And we aren't going to be alone. Yet."

She drew in a long sigh and smiled. "Okay."

He chuckled.

"I've never been to the ballet," she confessed.

"High time you went," he replied, and he laughed. "Go on."

Sara had laid out the most beautiful black velvet dress Michelle had ever seen. It had a discreet rounded neckline and long sleeves, and it fell to the ankles, with only a slight tuck where the waistline was.

"It's gorgeous!" Michelle enthused.

"And you'll look gorgeous in it," Sara replied. She hugged Michelle. "It's yours. I have shoes and a purse to match it."

"But, I have a dress," Michelle began.

"A summer dress," Sara said patiently, and smiled. "This one is more suitable for winter. I have one similar to it that I'm wearing. We'll look like twins." She grinned.

"Okay, then. And thank you!" Michelle said heartily.

"You're very welcome."

Chapter 10

Gabriel wore a dress jacket with dark slacks and a black turtleneck sweater. He looked classy and elegant. Sara wore a simple sheath of navy blue velvet with an expensive gold necklace and earrings and looked exquisite, with her silky black hair loose almost to her waist and her big, dark eyes soft in her beautiful face.

Michelle in her black velvet dress felt like royalty. The trio drew eyes as they filed into the auditorium where the ballet was being performed.

Up front, in the orchestra pit, the musicians were tuning up their instruments. Gabriel found their seats and let the women go in first before he took his place on the aisle.

"There's quite a crowd," Michelle remarked as more people filed in.

"Oh, dear." Sara's voice was full of consternation.

Before Michelle could ask what was wrong, she saw it for herself. Wofford Patterson, in a dinner jacket with a white tie and black slacks was escorting a beautiful blonde, in an elegant green velvet gown, down the aisle—directly to the seats beside Sara.

"Mr. Brandon," Wolf said, nodding. "This is Elise Jorgansen. Elise, Gabriel Brandon. That's his sister, Sara. And that's his ward, Michelle."

"Nice to meet you," Elise said, and smiled at them all with genuine warmth.

"I believe our seats are right there," Wolf told the pretty woman. He escorted her past Gabriel and the women with apologies, because it was a tight squeeze. He sat next to Sara, with Elise on his other side.

Sara tensed and glared straight ahead. Wolf grinned.

"I didn't know that you liked the ballet, Miss Brandon," Wolf said politely.

"I like this one. It's *The Nutcracker*," she added with a venomous look at the man beside her.

He pursed his lips. "Left the flying monkeys at home, did we?"

"I'd love to drop a house on you, dear man," she said under her breath.

"Now, now, it's the ballet," he pointed out. "We must behave like civilized people."

"You'd need so much instruction for that, Mr. Patterson," Sara said, her voice dripping honey.

"Isn't the music lovely?" Michelle broke in.

The music was the instruments being tuned, but it shattered the tension and everyone laughed.

"Behave," Gabriel whispered to his sister.

She gave him an irritated look, but she kept her

hands in her lap and sat quietly as the ballerinas came onstage one by one and the performance began, to Michelle's utter fascination and delight. She'd never seen a live performance of the ballet, which was her favorite.

At intermission, Sara excused herself and left the row.

"I'm not getting up," Wolf said. "I'd never get back in here."

"Neither am I," Gabriel mused. "It's quite a crowd."

"You seem to be enjoying the music, Miss Godfrey," Wolf said politely.

"I've never been to a ballet before," she replied, laughing. "It's so beautiful!"

"You should see it in New York City, at the American Ballet Company," Gabriel said gently.

"They do an excellent performance," Wolf agreed. "Have you seen it at the Bolshoi?" he added.

"Yes," Gabriel agreed. "Theirs is unbelievably beautiful."

"That's in Russia, isn't it?" Michelle asked, wide-eyed.

"Yes," Gabriel said. He smiled down at her. "One day, Sara and I will have to take you traveling."

"You should see the world," Elise agreed, from beside Wolf. "Or at least, some of it. Travel broadens your world."

"I can't think of anything I'd love more," Michelle replied, smiling back at the woman.

"Elise studied ballet when she was still in school," Wolf said. "She was in line to be a prima ballerina with the company she played with in New York."

"Don't," Elise said gently.

"Sorry," Wolf said, patting her hand. "Bad memories. I won't mention it again."

"That life is long over," she replied. "But I still love going to see the ballet and the theater and opera. We have such a rich cultural heritage here in San Antonio."

"We do, indeed," Gabriel agreed.

The musicians began tuning their instruments again, just as Sara came back down the aisle, so graceful and poised that she drew male eyes all the way.

"Your sister has an elegance of carriage that is quite rare," Elise said to Gabriel as she approached.

"She also studied ballet," Gabriel replied quietly. "But the stress of dancing and trying to get through college became too much. She gave up ballet and got her degree in languages." He laughed. "She still dances, though," he added. "She just doesn't put on a tutu first."

"It wouldn't go with the broom," Sara said to Wolf, and smiled coldly as she sat down.

"Broom?" Elise asked, curious.

"Never mind. I'll explain it to you later," Wolf replied.

Sara gave him a look that might have curdled milk and turned her attention to the stage as the curtain began to rise.

"Well, it was a wonderful evening," Michelle said dreamily as she followed them out to the car. "Thank you so much for taking us," she added to Gabriel.

He studied her in the lovely dress, smiling. "It was my pleasure. We'll have to do this more often."

"Expose you to culture, he means," Sara said in a stage whisper. "It's good for you."

"I really had a good time."

"I would have, except for the company," Sara muttered. She flushed. "Not you two," she said hastily when they gaped at her. "That...man! And his date."

"I thought Elise was very nice," Michelle ventured.

Sara clammed up.

Gabriel just chuckled.

Christmas Eve was magical. They sat around the Christmas tree, watching a program of Christmas music on television, sipping hot chocolate and making s'mores in the fireplace, where a sleepy fire flamed every now and then.

In all her life, Michelle couldn't remember being so happy. Her eyes kept darting to Gabriel, when she thought he wasn't looking. Even in jeans and a flannel shirt, he was the stuff of dreams. It was so hard not to appear starstruck.

They opened presents that night instead of the next morning, because Sara announced that she wasn't getting up at dawn to see what Santa had left.

She gave Michelle a beautiful scarf of many colors, a designer one. Michelle draped it around her neck and raved over it. Then she opened Gabriel's gift. It was pearls, a soft off-white set in a red leather box. They were Japanese. He'd brought them home from his last trip and hidden them to give at Christmas. The necklace was accompanied by matching drop earrings.

"I was right," he mused as Michelle tried them on enthusiastically. "They're just the right shade."

"They are, indeed. And thank you for mine, also, my sweet." Sara kissed his tan cheek, holding a strand of white ones in her hand. They suited her delicate coloring just as the off-white ones suited Michelle's.

"I like mine, too." He held up a collection of DVDs of shows he particularly liked from Michelle and a black designer turtleneck from Sara.

Sara loved her handmade scarf from Michelle. It was crocheted and had taken an age to finish. It was the softest white knit, with tassels. "I'll wear it all winter," she promised Michelle, and kissed her, too.

Michelle had hung mistletoe in strategic places, but she hadn't counted on Gabriel's determined reticence. He kissed her on the cheek, smiled and wished her the happiest of Christmases and New Years. She pretended that it didn't matter that he didn't drag her into an empty room and kiss her half to death. He was determined not to treat her as an adult. It was painful. But in some sense, she did understand.

So three years went by, more quickly than Michelle had dreamed they would. She got a job part-time with a daily newspaper in San Antonio and did political pieces for it while she got through her core courses and into serious journalism in college.

She went to class during summer to speed up her degree program, although she came home for the holidays. Gabriel was almost always away now. Sara was there, although she spent most of her time in Wyoming at the ranch she and Gabriel owned. Michelle had gone up there with her one summer for a couple of weeks during her vacation. It was a beautiful place.

Sara was different somehow. Something had happened between her and Wofford Patterson. She wouldn't talk about it, but she knew that it had changed Sara. Gabriel had mentioned something about Sara going back into therapy and there had been an argument in French that Michelle couldn't follow.

Wofford Patterson had also moved up to Catelow, Wyoming. He bought a huge ranch there near Sara's. He kept his place in Comanche Wells, but he put in a foreman to manage it for him. He had business interests in Wyoming that took up much of his time, he said, and it was hard to commute. Sara didn't admit that she was glad to have him as a neighbor. But Michelle suspected that she did.

Sara was still playing her online game with her friend, and they fought battles together late into the night. She still didn't know who he really was, either. Gabriel had made sure of it.

"He's such a gentleman," Sara mused over coffee one morning, her face bright with pleasure. "He wants to meet me in person." She hesitated. "I'm not sure about that."

"Why not, if you like him?" Michelle asked innocently, although she didn't dare let on that she knew exactly who Sara's friend was, and she knew that Sara would have a stroke if she saw him in person. It would be the end of a lovely online relationship.

"People aren't what they seem," Sara replied, and pain was in her eyes. "If it seems too good to be true, it usually is."

"He might be a knight in shining armor," Michelle teased. "You should find out."

"He might be an ogre who lives in a cave with bats, too." Sara chuckled. "No. I like things the way they are. I really don't want to try to have a relationship with a man in real life." Her face tensed. "I never wanted to."

Michelle grimaced. "Sara, you're so beautiful…"

"Beautiful!" She laughed coldly. "I wish I'd been born ugly. It would have made my life so much easier. You don't know…" She drew in a harsh breath. "Well, actually, you do know." She managed a soft smile. "We're all prisoners of our childhoods, Michelle. Mine was particularly horrible. It warped me."

"You should have been in therapy," Michelle said gently.

"I tried therapy. It only made things worse. I can't talk to total strangers."

"Maybe you just talked to the wrong person."

Sara's eyes were suddenly soft and dreamy and she flushed. "I think I did. So much has changed," she added softly.

Michelle, who had a good idea what was going on up in Wyoming, just grinned.

Sara's eyes took on an odd, shimmering softness. "Life is so much sweeter than I dreamed it could be." She smiled to herself and looked at her watch. "I have some phone calls to make. I love having you around." She added, "Thanks."

"For what?"

"For caring," Sara said simply.

Michelle was looking forward to her last Christmas in college. She got talked into a blind date with Darla's boyfriend's friend. He turned out to be a slightly haughty man who worked as a stockbroker and never stopped talking on his cell phone for five seconds. He was at it all through dinner. Bob, Darla's boyfriend, looked very uncomfortable and apologetic.

"Bob feels awful," Darla whispered to Michelle in the restroom after they'd finished eating. "Larry seemed to be a normal guy."

"He just lives and breathes his job. Besides," she added, "you know there's only one man who interests me at all. And it's never going to be someone like Larry."

"Having seen your Mr. Brandon, I totally understand." Darla giggled. She shook her head. "He is a dreamboat."

"I think so."

"Well, we'll stop by the bar for a nightcap and go home. Maybe we can pry Larry away from his phone long enough to say good-night."

"I wish I was riding with you and Bob," Michelle sighed. "At least he stops talking while he's driving."

"Curious, that he didn't want to ride with Bob," Darla said. "Well, that's just men, I guess."

But Larry had an agenda that the girls weren't aware of. He knew that Bob and Darla were going dancing and wouldn't be home soon. So when he walked Michelle to the door of the apartment she and Darla shared, he pushed his way in and took off his jacket.

"Finally, alone together," he enthused, and reached for her. "Now, sweetie, let's have a little payback for the meal and the drinks..."

"Are you out of your mind?" she gasped, avoiding his grasping arms.

"I paid for the food," he said, almost snarling. "You owe me!"

"I owe you? Like hell I owe you!" She got to the door and opened it. "I'll send you a check for my part of the meal! Get out!"

"I'm not leaving. You just want to play hard to get." He started to push the door closed. And connected with a steely big hand that caught him by the arm, turned him around and booted him out into the night.

"Gabriel!" Michelle gasped.

"You can't do that to me…!" Larry said angrily, getting to his feet.

Gabriel fell into a fighting stance. "Come on," he said softly. "I could use the exercise."

Larry came to his senses. He glanced at Michelle. She went back inside, got his jacket, and threw it at him.

"Dinner doesn't come with bed," she told him icily.

Larry started to make a reply, but Gabriel's expression was a little too unsettling. He muttered something under his breath, turned, slammed into his car and roared away.

Gabriel went inside with Michelle, who was tearing up now that the drama had played itself out.

"Ah, no, *ma belle*," he whispered. "There's no need for tears." He pulled her into his arms, bent his head, and kissed her so hungrily that she forgot to breathe.

He lifted his head. His black eyes were smoldering, so full of desire that they mesmerized Michelle. She tasted him on her mouth, felt the heavy throb of his heart under her hands.

"Finally," he breathed, pulling her close. He brushed his lips over her soft mouth. "Finally!"

She opened her mouth to ask what he meant, and the kiss knocked her so off balance that she couldn't manage a single word in reply. She held on with all her might, clung to him, pushed her body into his so that she could feel every movement of his powerful body against her. He was aroused, very quickly, and even that didn't intimidate her. She moaned. Which only made matters worse.

He picked her up, still kissing her, and laid her out on the couch, easing his body down over hers in a silence that throbbed with frustrated desire.

"Soft," he whispered. "Soft and sweet. All mine."

She would have said something, but he was kissing her again, and she couldn't think at all. She felt his big, rough hands go under her dress, up and up, touching and exploring, testing softness, finding her breasts under the lacy little bra.

"You feel like silk all over," he murmured. He found the zipper and eased her out of the dress and the half slip under it, then out of the bra, so that all she had left on were her briefs. He kissed his way down her body, lingering on her pert breasts with their tight little crowns, savoring her soft, helpless cries of pleasure.

It excited him to know that she'd never done this. He ate her up like candy, tasting her hungrily. He nuzzled her breasts, kissing their soft contours with a practiced touch that made her rise up in an aching arch to his lips.

Somehow, his jacket and shirt ended up on the floor.

She felt the rough, curling hair on his chest against her bare breasts as his body covered hers. His powerful legs eased between her own, so that she could feel with him an intimacy she'd never shared with anyone.

She cried out as he moved against her. Sensations were piling on each other, dragging her under, drowning her in pleasure. She clung to him, pleading for more, not even knowing exactly what she wanted, but so drawn with tension that she was dying for it to ease.

She felt hot tears run down her cheeks as his mouth moved back onto hers. He touched her as he never had before. She shivered. The touch came again. She sobbed, and opened her mouth under his. She felt his tongue go into her mouth, as his hands moved on her more intimately.

Suddenly, like a fall of fire, a flash of agonized pleasure convulsed the soft body under his. He groaned and had to fight the instinctive urge to finish what he started, to go right into her, push inside her, take what was his, what had always been his.

But she was a virgin. His exploration had already told him that. He'd known already, by her reactions. She was very much a virgin. He didn't want to do this. Not yet. She was his. It must be done properly, in order, in a way that wouldn't shame her to remember somewhere down the line.

So he forced his shivering body to bear the pain. He held her very close while she recovered from her first ecstasy. He wrapped her up tight, and held her while he endured what he must to spare her innocence.

She wept. He kissed away the tears, so tenderly

that they fell even harder, hot and wet on her flushed cheeks.

She was embarrassed and trying not to let him see.

He knew. He smiled and kissed her eyes shut. "It had to be with me," he whispered. "Only with me. I would rather die than know you had such an experience with any other man."

She opened her eyes and looked up into his. "Really?"

"Really." He looked down at her nudity, his eyes hungry again at the sight of her pink-and-peach skin, silky and soft and fragrant. He touched her breasts tenderly. "You are the most beautiful woman I will ever see."

Her lips parted on a shaky breath.

He bent and kissed her breasts. "And now we have to get up."

She stared at him.

"Or not get up," he murmured with a laugh. "Because I can't continue this much longer."

"It would be…all right," she whispered. "If you wanted to," she added.

"I want to," he said huskily. "But you won't be happy afterward. And you know it. Not like this, *ma belle*. Not our first time together. It has to be done properly."

"Properly?"

"You graduate from college, get a job, go to work. I come to see you bringing flowers and chocolates," he mused, tracing her mouth. "And then, eventually, a ring."

"A ring."

He nodded.

"An…engagement…ring?"

He smiled.

"People do it all the time, even before they get engaged," she said.

He got to his feet. "They do. But we won't."

"Oh."

He dressed her, enjoying the act of putting back onto her lovely body the things he'd taken off it. He laughed at her rapt expression. "You have a belief system that isn't going to allow a more modern approach to sex," he said blandly. "So we do it your way."

"I could adjust," she began, still hungry.

"Your happiness means a lot to me," he said simply. "I'm not going to spoil something beautiful with a tarnished memory. Not after I've waited so long."

She stared up into his black eyes. "I've waited for you, too," she whispered.

"I know." He smoothed back her hair just as they heard a car door slam and footsteps approaching.

Michelle looked horrified, thinking what could have happened, what condition they could have been in as Darla put her key into the lock.

Gabriel burst out laughing at her expression. "Now was I right?" he asked.

The door opened. Darla stopped with Bob in tow and just stared at Gabriel. Then she grinned. "Wow," she said. "Look what Larry changed into!"

And they all burst out laughing.

Michelle graduated with honors. Gabriel and Sara were both there for the ceremony, applauding when she walked down the aisle to accept her diploma. They went out to eat afterward, but once they were home, Gabriel couldn't stay. He was preoccupied, and very worried, from the look of things.

"Can you tell me what's wrong?" Michelle asked.

He shook his head. He bent to kiss her, very gently. "I'm going to have to be out of the country for two or three months."

"No!" she exclaimed.

"Only that. Then I have a job waiting, one that won't require so much travel," he promised. "Bear with me. I'm sorry. I have to do this."

She drew in a long breath. "Okay. If you have to go."

"You've got a job waiting in San Antonio, anyway," he reminded her with a smile. "On a daily newspaper. It has a solid reputation for reporting excellence. Make a name for yourself. But don't get too comfortable there," he added enigmatically. "Because when I get back, we need to talk."

"Talk." She smiled.

"And other things."

"Oh, yes, especially, other things," she whispered, dragging his mouth down to hers. She kissed him hungrily. He returned the kiss, but drew back discreetly when Sara came into the room. He hugged her, too.

He paused in the doorway and looked back at them, smiling. "Take care of each other." He grinned at his sister. "Happy?" he asked, referring to the changes in her life.

Sara laughed, tossing her long hair. "I could die of it," she sighed.

"I'll be back before you miss me," he told Michelle, who was looking sad. He wanted to kiss her, right there in front of the world. But it wasn't the time. And he wasn't sure he could stop.

"Impossible," Michelle said softly. "I miss you already."

He winked and closed the door.

Michelle liked the job. She had a desk and three years of solid education behind her to handle the assignments she was given.

A big story broke the second month she'd been with the newspaper. There was a massacre of women and children in a small Middle Eastern nation, perpetrated, it was said, by a group of mercenaries led by a Canadian national named Angel Le Veut. He had ties to an anti-terrorism school run by a man named Eb Scott in, of all places, Jacobsville, Texas.

Michelle went on the offensive at once, digging up everything she could find about the men in the group who had killed the women and children in the small Muslim community that was at odds with a multinational occupation force.

The name of the man accused of leading the assault was ironic. One of the languages she'd studied was French. And if loosely translated, the man's name came out as "Angel wants it." It was an odd play on words that was used most notably in the sixteenth century by authorities when certain cases were tried and a guilty verdict was desired. The phrase *"Le Roi le Veut"* meant that the king wanted the accused found guilty—whether or not he really was, apparently. The mysterious Angel was obviously an educated man with a knowledge of

European history. Michelle was puzzled over why such a man would choose a lifestyle that involved violence.

Her first stop was Jacobsville, Texas, where she arranged an interview with Eb Scott, the counterterrorism expert, whose men had been involved in the massacre. Michelle knew him, from a distance.

Her father had gone to school with him and they were acquaintances. Her father had said there wasn't a finer man anywhere, that Eb was notorious for backing lost causes and fighting for the underdog. That didn't sound like a man who would order the murder of helpless women and children.

Eb shook her hand and invited her into his house. His wife and children were gone for the day, shopping in San Antonio for summer clothing. It was late spring already.

"Thank you for seeing me," Michelle said when they were seated. "Especially under the circumstances."

"Hiding from the press is never a good idea, but at times, in matters like this, it's necessary, until the truth can be ferreted out," Eb said solemnly. His green eyes searched hers. "You're Alan Godfrey's daughter."

"Yes," she said, smiling.

"You used to spend summers in Comanche Wells with your grandparents." He smiled back. "Minette Carson speaks well of you. She did an interview with me yesterday. Hopefully, some of the truth will trickle down to the mass news media before they crucify my squad leader."

"Yes. This man, Angel," she began, looking over her notes while Eb Scott grimaced and tried not to reveal what he really knew about the man, "his name is quite odd."

"Le Veut?" He smiled again. "He gets his way. He's something of an authority on sixteenth-century European history. He and Kilraven, one of the feds who's married to a local girl, go toe-to-toe over whether or not Mary Queen of Scots really helped Lord Bothwell murder her husband."

"Has this man worked for you, with you, for a long time?" she asked.

He nodded. "Many years. He's risked his life time and time again to save innocents. I can promise you that when the truth comes out, and it will, he'll be exonerated."

She was typing on her small notebook computer as he spoke. "He's a Canadian national?"

"He has dual citizenship, here and in Canada," he corrected. "But he's lived in the States most of his life."

"Does he live in Jacobsville?"

Eb hesitated.

She lifted her hands from the keyboard. "You wouldn't want to say, would you?" she asked perceptibly. "If he has family, it could hurt them, as well. There wouldn't be a place they could go where the media wouldn't find them."

"The media can be like a dog after a juicy bone," Eb said with some irritation. "They'll get fed one way or the other, with truth or, if time doesn't permit, with lies. I've seen lives ruined by eager reporters out to make a name for themselves." He paused. "Present company excepted," he added gently. "I know all about you from Minette."

She smiled gently. "Thanks. I always try to be fair and present both sides of the story without editorializing. I don't like a lot of what I see on television, presented as fair coverage. Most of the commentators seem quite biased to me. They convict people and act as judge, jury and executioner." She shook her head. "I like the paper I work for. Our editor, even our publisher, are fanatics for accurate and fair coverage. They fired a reporter last month whose story implicated an innocent man. He swore he had eyewitnesses to back up the facts, and that he could prove them. Later, when the editor sent other reporters out to recheck—after the innocent man's attorneys filed a lawsuit—they found that the reporter had ignored people who could verify the man's whereabouts at the time of the crime. The reporter didn't even question them."

Eb sighed, leaning back in his recliner. "That happens all too often. Even on major newspapers," he added, alluding to a reporter for one of the very large East Coast dailies who'd recently been let go for fabricating stories.

"We try," Michelle said quietly. "We really try. Most reporters only want to help people, to point out problems, to help better the world around us."

"I know that. It's the one bad apple in the barrel that pollutes the others," he said.

"This man, Angel, is there any way I could interview him?"

He almost bit through his lip. He couldn't tell her that. "No," he said finally. "We've hidden him in a luxury hotel in a foreign country. The news media will have a hell of a time trying to ferret him out. We have armed guards in native dress everywhere. Meanwhile, I've hired an investigative firm out of Houston—Dane Lassiter's—to dig out the truth. Believe me, there's no one in the world better at it. He's a former Houston policeman."

"I know of him," she replied. "His son was involved in a turf war between drug lords in the area, wasn't he?"

"Yes, he was. That was a while back."

"Well, tell me what you can," she said. "I'll do my best not to convict the man in print. The mercenaries who were with Angel," she added, "are they back in the States?"

"That's another thing I can't tell you right now," he replied. "I'm not trying to be evasive. I'm protecting my men from trial by media. We have attorneys for all of them, and our investigator hopes to have something concrete for us, and the press, very soon."

"That's fair enough."

"Here's what we know right now," Eb said. "My squad leader was given an assignment by a State Department official to interview a local tribesman in a village in Anasrah. The man had information about a group of terrorists who were hiding in the village— protected by a high-ranking government official, we were told. My squad leader, in disguise, took a small team in to interview him, but when he and his men arrived, the tribesman and his entire family were dead. One of the terrorists pointed the finger at Angel and accused his team of the atrocity. I'm certain the terrorist was paid handsomely to do it."

Michelle frowned. "You believe that?"

Eb stared her down with glittering green eyes. "Miss Godfrey, if you knew Angel, you wouldn't have to ask me that question."

"Sorry," she said. "It's my job, Mr. Scott."

He let out a breath. "You can't imagine how painful this is for me," he said. "Men I trained, men I've worked with, accused of something so inhuman." His face hardened. "Follow the money. It's all about the money, I assure you," he added curtly. "Someone stands to lose a lot of it if the truth comes out."

"I can only imagine how bad it must be," she said, and not without sympathy.

She asked questions, he answered them. She was impressed by him. He wasn't at all the sort of person that she'd pictured when she heard people speak of mercenaries. Even the word meant a soldier for hire, a man who sold his talents to the highest bidder. But Eb Scott's organization trained men in counterterrorism. He had an enormous operation in Jacobsville, and men and women came from around the world to learn from his experts. There were rumors that a few government agents had also availed themselves of his expertise.

The camp was state-of-the-art, with every electronic gadget known to modern science—and a few things that were largely experimental. They taught everything from evasive driving techniques to disarming bombs, improvised weapons, stealth, martial arts, the works. Michelle was allowed to photograph only a small section of the entire operation, and she wasn't allowed to photograph any of his instructors or the students. But even with the reservations on what she was shown, what she learned fascinated her.

"Well, I'll never think of mercenaries the same way again, Mr. Scott," she said when she was ready to leave. "This operation is very impressive."

"I'm glad you think so."

She paused at the door and turned. "You know, the electronic media have resources that those of us in print journalism don't. I mean, we have a digital version of our paper online, like most everyone does. But the big networks employ dozens of experts who can find out anything. If they want to find your man, they will. And his family."

"Miss Godfrey, for the sake of a lot of innocent people, I hope you're wrong."

The way he said it stayed on her mind for hours after she left.

Chapter 11

Michelle wrote the story, and she did try to be fair. But when she saw the photographs of the massacre, the bodies of small children with women and men weeping over them, her heart hardened. If the man was guilty, he should be hanged for this.

She didn't slant the story. She presented the facts from multiple points of view. She interviewed a man in Saudi Arabia who had a friend in Anasrah with whom he'd recently spoken. She interviewed a representative of the State Department, who said that one of their staff had been led into the village by a minor government official just after the attack and was adamant that the mercenaries had been responsible for the slaughter. She also interviewed an elder in the village, through an interpreter, who said that an American had led the attack.

There was another man, also local, who denied that a foreigner was responsible. He was shouted down by the others, but Michelle managed to get their representative in Saudi Arabia to go to Anasrah, a neighboring country, and interview the man in the village. His story contradicted the others. He said that it was a man well-known in terrorist circles who had come into the village and accused the tribesmen of betraying their own people by working with the government and foreigners. He said that if it continued, an example, a horrible example, would be made, he would see to it personally.

The local man said that he could prove that the terrorists themselves had perpetrated the attack, if he had time.

Michelle made the first big mistake of her career in journalism by discounting the still, small voice in the wilderness. The man's story didn't ring true. She took notes, and filed them on her computer. But when she wrote the story, she left out what sounded like a made-up tale.

The story broke with the force of bombs. All of a sudden, it was all anyone heard on the media. The massacre in Anasrah, the children murdered by foreigners, the mercenaries who had cut them down with automatic weapons while their parents pleaded for mercy. On television, the weeping relatives were interviewed. Their stories brought even hardened commentators to tears on-screen.

Michelle's story, with its unique point of view and Eb Scott's interview—which none of the national media had been able to get, because he refused to talk to them—put her in the limelight for the first time. Her story was reprinted partially in many national papers, and she was interviewed by the major news networks, as well. She respected Eb Scott, she added, and she thought he was sincere, but she wept for the dead children and she thought the mercenary responsible should be tried in the world court and imprisoned for the rest of his life.

Her impulsive comment was broadcast over and over. And just after that came the news that the mercenary had a sister, living in Wyoming. They had her name, as well. Sara.

It could have been a coincidence. Except that suddenly she remembered that the man, Angel, had both American and Canadian citizenship. Now she learned that he had a sister named Sara. Gabriel was gone for long periods of time overseas on jobs. Michelle still tried to persuade herself that it wasn't, couldn't, be Gabriel.

Until Sara called her on the phone.

"I couldn't believe it when they said you broke the story," she said in a cold tone. "How could you do this to us?"

"Sara, it wasn't about anyone you know," she said quickly. "It was about a mercenary who gunned down little children in a Middle Eastern village…!"

"He did nothing of the sort," Sara said, her voice dripping ice. "It was the tribesman's brother-in-law, one of the terrorists, who killed the man and his family and then blamed it on Angel and his men."

"Do you know this man Angel?" Michelle asked, a sick feeling in her stomach because Sara sounded so harsh.

"Know him." Her laugh was as cold as death. "We both know him, Michelle. He uses Angel as an alias when he goes on missions for Eb Scott's clients. But his name is Gabriel."

Michelle felt her blood run cold. Images flashed through her mind. Dead children. The one dissenting voice, insisting that it was the terrorists not the Americans who perpetrated the horror. Her refusal to listen, to print the other side of the story. Gabriel's side. She'd convinced herself that it couldn't be Gabriel. Now she had to face facts.

"I didn't know," she said, her voice breaking. "Sara, believe me, I didn't know!"

"Eb told you it wasn't him," Sara said furiously. "But you wouldn't listen. I had a contact in the State Department send a man to tell your newspaper's agent about the dead man's brother-in-law. And you decided not to print it. Didn't you? God forbid you should run against the voice of the world press and risk your own glowing reputation as a crusader for justice by dissenting!"

"I didn't know," Michelle repeated through tears.

"You didn't know! If Gabriel ends up headfirst in a ditch somewhere, it will be all right, because you didn't know! Would you like to see the road in front of our ranch here in Wyoming, Michelle?" she added. "It looks like a tent city, surrounded by satellite trucks. They're certain they'll wear me down and I'll come out and accuse my brother for them!"

"I'm so sorry." Michelle didn't have to be told that Gabriel was innocent. She knew he was. But she'd helped convict him.

"You're sorry. I'll be certain to tell him when, and if, I see him again." There was a harshly indrawn breath. "He phoned me two days ago," she said in a haunted voice. "They're hunting him like an animal, thanks to you. When I told him who sold him out, he wouldn't believe me. It wasn't until I sent him a link to your story that he saw for himself."

Michelle felt every drop of blood draining out of her face. "What…did he say?"

"He said," Sara replied, enunciating every word, "that he'd never been so wrong about anyone in his life. He thought that you, of all people, would defend him even against the whole world. He said," she added coldly, "that he never wanted to see you or hear from you again as long as he lived."

The words were like bullets. She could actually feel their impact.

"I loved you like my own sister," Sara said, her voice breaking. "And I will never, never forgive you!" She slammed down the phone.

Michelle realized after a minute that she hadn't broken the connection. She hung up her own telephone. She sat down heavily and heard the recriminations break over her head again and again.

She remembered Eb Scott's certainty that his man would never do such a thing. Sara's fierce anger. It had been easy to discount them while Angel was a shadowy figure without substance. But Michelle knew Gabriel. And she was certain, absolutely certain, that the man who'd saved her from suicide would never put another human being in harm's way.

It took two days for the effects of Sara's phone call to wear off enough that she could stop crying and blaming herself. The news media was having a field day with the story, running updates about it all day, every day, either in newscasts or in banners under the anchor people. Michelle finally had to turn off the television to escape it, so that she could get herself back together.

She wanted, so desperately, to make up for what she'd done. But she didn't even know where to start. The story was everywhere. People were condemning the American mercenaries on every news program in the world.

But Gabriel was innocent. Michelle had helped convict him in the press, without knowing who she was writing about. Now it was her turn to do her job properly, and give both sides of the story, however unpopular. She had to save him, if she could, even if he hated her forever for what she'd done.

So she went back to work. Her first act was to contact the newspaper's man in Saudi Arabia and ask him to repeat the story his informant in Anasrah had told him. Then she contacted Eb Scott and gave him the information, so that he could pass it on to his private investigator. Before she did that, she asked him to call her back on a secure line, because she knew how some of the tabloid news bureaus sometimes had less scrupulous agents digging out information.

"You're learning, Miss Godfrey," Eb said solemnly.

"Not soon enough. I know who Angel is now," she added heavily. "His sister hates me. He told her that he never wanted to see or speak to me again, either. And I deserve that. I wasn't objective, and people are paying for my error. But I have to do what I can to undo the mess I helped make. I'm sorry I didn't listen."

"Too little, and almost too late," he said brutally. "Learn from it. Sometimes the single dissenting voice is the right one."

"I won't forget," she said.

He hung up.

She tried to phone Sara back and apologize once again, to tell her she was trying to repair the damage. But Sara wouldn't accept the first phone call and after that, her number was blocked. She was heartsick. The Brandons had been so good to her. They'd made sacrifices to get her through school, through college, always been there when she needed help. And she'd repaid them like this. It wounded her as few things in life ever had.

When she tried to speak to her editor in confidence, to backtrack on the story she'd written, he laughed it off. The man was obviously guilty, he said, why make waves now? She'd made a name for herself in investigative reporting, it was all good.

She told him that Angel wasn't the sort of person to ever harm a child. Then he wanted to know how she knew that. She wouldn't reveal her source, she said, falling back on a tried and true response. But the man was innocent.

Her editor had just laughed. So she thought the guy

was innocent, what did it matter? The news was the thing that mattered, scooping all the other media and being first and best at delivering the story. She'd given the facts of the matter, that was the end of it. She should just enjoy her celebrity status while it lasted.

Michelle went back to her apartment that night saddened and weary, with a new sense of disillusionment about life and people.

The next morning, she phoned Minette Carson and asked if she had an opening for a reporter who was certain she wasn't cut out for the big dailies.

Minette was hesitant.

"Look, never mind," Michelle said gently. "I know I've made a lot of enemies in Jacobsville with the way I covered the story. It's okay. I can always teach journalism. I'll be a natural at showing students what not to do."

"We all have to start somewhere when we learn how to do a job," Minette replied. "Usually, it's a painful process. Eb Scott called and asked me, before you did the interview, if you knew who Gabriel really was. I told him no. I knew you'd have said something long before this. I should have told you."

"I should have suspected something," came the sad reply. "He was away from home for long stretches, he spoke a dozen impossible languages, he was secretive about what sort of work he did—I just wasn't paying attention."

"It amused everyone when he took you in as his ward," Minette said. "He was one of the coldest men Eb Scott ever hired—well, after Carson, who works for

Cy Parks, that is." She chuckled. "But once you came along, all of a sudden Gabriel was smiling."

"He won't be anymore," Michelle said, feeling the pain to the soles of her feet.

"Give it time," was the older woman's advice. "First, you have some work to do."

"I know. I'm going to do everything in my power to prove him innocent. Whatever it takes," Michelle added firmly.

"That's more like it. And about the job," she replied. "Once you've proven that you aren't running away from an uncomfortable assignment, we'll have a place for you here. That's a promise."

"Thanks."

"You're welcome."

Michelle convinced Eb Scott to let her talk to his detective. It worked out well, because Dane Lassiter was actually in San Antonio for a seminar that week and he agreed to meet with her in a local restaurant.

He wasn't exactly what she'd expected. He was tall, dark-haired and dark-eyed, with an easygoing manner and a wife who was thirtysomething and very attractive. She, like Michelle, was blonde.

"We always go together when he has to give seminars." Tess laughed. "At least once I've had to chase a pursuing woman out of his room." She shook her head, sighing as she met her husband's amused gaze. "Well, after all, I know he's a dish. Why shouldn't other women notice?"

Michelle laughed with them, but her heart wasn't in it. There had been a snippet of news on television the night before, showing a camp of journalists on the road that led to the Brandons' Wyoming property. They were still trying to get Sara to talk to them. But this time they were met with a steely-eyed man Michelle recognized as Wofford Patterson, who was advising them to decamp before some of Sara's friends loosed a few bears on the property in a conservation project. Patterson had become Sara's personal protector and much more, after many years of antagonism.

"I've been watching the press reports on Brandon," Dane said, having guessed the train of her thoughts. "You watch six different reports and get six different stories."

"Yes," Michelle said sadly. "Not everyone tries for accuracy. And I can include myself in that company, because I should have gone the extra mile and presented the one dissenting opinion. It was easy to capitulate, because I didn't think I had any interest in the outcome," she added miserably.

Tess's pale eyes narrowed. "Mr. Brandon was your guardian."

She nodded. He was more, but she wasn't sharing that news with a virtual stranger. "I sold him out. I didn't mean to. I had no idea Angel was Gabriel. It was hard, going against a majority opinion. Everyone said he was guilty as sin. I saw the photographs of the women and children." Her face hardened. "It was easy to believe it, after that."

"I've seen similar things," Dane said, sipping black coffee. "But I can tell you that things are rarely what they seem."

She told him about her contacts, and he took notes,

getting names and telephone numbers and putting together a list of people to interview.

He put up his pen and notebook. "This is going to be a lot of help to the men who were blamed for the tragedy," he said finally. "There's a violent element in the country in question, dedicated to rooting out any hint of foreign influence, however beneficial. But at the same time, in their ranks are a few who see a way to quick profit, a way to fund their terrorism and inflict even more horror on our overseas personnel. This group that put your friend in the middle of the controversy is made up of a few money-hungry profiteers. Our State Department has worked very hard to try to stifle them. We have several oil corporations with offices there, and a good bit of our foreign oil is shipped from that country. We depend on the goodwill of the locals to keep the oil companies' officials and workers safe. The terrorists know that, and they see a way to make a quick profit through kidnappings and other attacks. Except that instead of holding people for ransom, they threaten violence if their demands aren't met. It's almost like a protection racket..."

"That's what he meant," Michelle said suddenly.

"Excuse me?"

"Eb Scott said, 'follow the money,'" she recalled.

"Eb's sharp. Yes, that's apparently what's behind all this. The terrorist leader wanted millions in bribes to protect oil company executives in his country. The brother-in-law of the leader was selling him out to our State Department. A lot of local men work for the oil companies and don't want any part of the terrorists' plans. It's a poor country, and the oil companies provide a secure living for the village. But nobody makes waves and gets away with it. The terrorist leader retaliated, in the worst possible way, and blamed it on Angel and his men—a way of protecting his own men, whom he ordered to kill his brother-in-law to keep him from talking. It was also a way of notifying foreigners that this is how any future attempts to bypass his authority would be handled."

"I'm not telling you anything you didn't already know," she said suddenly.

"I knew it. I couldn't prove it," he added. "But you've given me contacts who can back up the protester's story. I'll have my investigators check them out and our attorneys will take depositions that will hold up in court. It will give the State Department's representatives the leverage they need to deal with the terrorists. And it will provide our news media with a week of guaranteed stories," he added coldly.

She sighed. "I think I'm in the wrong business."

"Good reporters can do a lot of good in the world," Tess interrupted. "It's just that there's more profit in digging up dirt on people."

"Amen," Dane said.

"Well, if I can help dig Gabriel out of the hole I put him into, I'll be happy," Michelle told him. "It's little enough in the way of apology."

"If you hear anything else, through your sources, you can call me anytime," he told her.

"I'll remember."

Dane went to pay the check, against Michelle's protests.

Tess smiled at her. "You really care about the mercenary, don't you?" she asked.

"More than you know," Michelle replied. "He and his sister sacrificed a lot for me. I'll never be able to pay them back. And now, this has happened…"

"At least you're trying to make up for it," she replied. "That's worth something."

"I hope it's worth enough. I'm grateful to you and your husband for meeting with me."

"It was a nice interlude between the rehashing of horrible cases." Tess laughed. "I work as a skip tracer, something Dane would never let me do before. My father planned to marry his mother, but they were killed in a wreck, so Dane became sort of responsible for me," she added surprisingly. "He wasn't very happy about it. We had a rocky road to the altar." She smiled. "But a son and a daughter later, we're very content."

"You don't look old enough to have two children." Michelle laughed. "Either of you."

"Thanks. But believe me, we are."

Dane was back, putting away his wallet. He handed Michelle a business card. "My cell's on there, as well as the office number."

"I'll cross my fingers, that our contacts can help you get Gabriel and his men off the hook," Michelle said.

His eyes narrowed. "I'm surprised that the national news media hasn't been camped on your doorstep," he remarked.

"Gabriel didn't advertise his involvement with me," she replied. "And nobody in Jacobsville, Texas, will tell them a thing, believe me."

He smiled. "I noticed the way the locals shut them out when they waltzed into town with their satellite trucks. Amazing, that the restaurants all ran out of food and the motels were all full and nobody had a single room to rent out at any price."

She smiled angelically. "I'm sure that was mostly true."

"They did try Comanche Wells, I hear," Dane added.

"Well, see, Comanche Wells doesn't have a restaurant or a motel at all."

"That explains it."

She went back to work, only to find her desk piled high with notes.

"Hey, Godfrey, can't you get your answering machine to work?" Murphy, one of the older reporters whose desk was beside hers, asked. "My old hands are too gnarled to take notes from all your darned callers."

"Sorry, Murph," she said. She was frowning when she noticed who the notes were from. "They want to send a limo for me and have me stay at the Plaza?" she exclaimed.

"What it is to be a celebrity." Murph shook his head. "Hey, there was this cool video that Brad Paisley did, about being a celebrity…!"

"I saw it. Thanks," she said, waving the notes at him. She picked up her purse and left the building, just avoiding her editor on the way out the door.

Apparently the news media had found somebody in Jacobsville who was willing to talk to them. She wondered with droll cynicism what the informant had been paid.

She discovered that if she agreed to do an exclusive interview with just one station, the others would have to leave her alone. Before she signed any papers, she spoke with an attorney and had him check out the agreement.

"It says that I agree to tell them my story," she said.

"Exactly," he replied.

She pursed her lips. "It doesn't specify which story."

"I think they'll assume it means the story they want to hear," he replied. "Although that's implied rather than stated."

"Ah."

"And I would advise caution when they ask you to name the person overseas whom your newspaper provided as a reference regarding the informer," he added. "That may be a protected source."

"I was hoping you'd notice that. It is a protected source."

He only smiled.

She sat down in front of the television cameras with a well-known, folksy interviewer who was calm, gentle and very intelligent. He didn't press her for details she couldn't give, and he understood that some sources of information that she had access to were protected.

"I understand from what you told our correspondent that you don't believe the men in question actually perpetrated the attack, which resulted in the deaths of several women and small children," he began.

"That's correct."

"Would you tell me why?"

"When I first broke the story, I went on the assumption that because the majority of the interviewees placed the blame on the American mercenaries, they must be guilty. There was, however, one conflicting opinion. A villager, whom I cannot name, said that extortion was involved and that money was demanded for the protection of foreign workers. When a relative of the extortionist threatened to go to the authorities and reveal the financial aspect, he and his family were brutally murdered as a warning. These murders were blamed on the Americans who had, in fact, been working for the government trying to uncover a nest of terrorists threatening American oil company employees there."

The interviewer was frowning. "Then the massacre was, in fact, retaliation for the villager's threat to expose the extortionist."

"That is my information, yes."

He studied a sheet of paper. "I see here that the newspaper which employs you used its own foreign sources to do interviews about this story."

"Those sources are also protected," Michelle replied. "I can't name them."

He pursed his lips and, behind his lenses, his blue eyes twinkled. "I understand. But I believe the same sources have been named, in the press, by attorneys for the men allegedly implicated by the international press for the atrocities."

She smiled. "I believe so."

"In which case," he added, "we have elicited permission to quote one of the sources. He has signed an affidavit, which is in the hands of our State Department. Please welcome Mr. David Arbuckle, who is liaison for the U.S. Department of State in Anasrah, which is at the center of this matter. Mr. Arbuckle, welcome."

"Thank you, Mr. Price," a pleasant-looking, middle-aged man replied. He was in a studio in Washington, D.C., his image provided via satellite.

"Now, from what Ms. Godfrey has told us—and we have validated her story—a terrorist cell had infiltrated the village in question and made threats against foreign nationals including ours. Is this true?"

"It is," Mr. Arbuckle said solemnly. "We're very grateful to Ms. Godfrey for bringing this matter to our attention. We were told that a group of mercenaries muscled their way into the village, demanding tribute and killed people when their demands were not met. This is a very different story than we were able to verify by speaking, under offer of protection, to other men in the same village."

He coughed, then continued, "We were able to ascertain that a terrorist cell with links to another notorious international organization was going to fund itself by extorting money from oil corporations doing business near the village. They were using the village itself for cover, posing as innocent tribesmen."

"Abominable," the host replied.

"Yes, killing innocents to prove a point is a particularly bloodthirsty manner in which to operate. The local people were terrified to say anything, after the massacre, although they felt very sad that innocent men were blamed for it. In fact, the so-called mercenaries had provided medical supplies and treatment for many children and elderly people and even helped buy food for them."

"A laudable outreach effort."

"Indeed," Mr. Arbuckle replied grimly. "Suffice it to

say that we have used our influence to make sure that the terrorists no longer have a foothold in the village, and the international community has moved people in to assure the safety of the tribesmen who provided us with this information."

"Then the American mercenaries are being cleared of any involvement with the massacre?"

"I can assure you that they have been," Mr. Arbuckle replied. "We were provided with affidavits and other documents concerning the massacre by an American private detective working in concert with the mercenaries' attorneys. They were allowed to leave the country last night and are en route to a secure location while we deal with the terrorists in question. The terrorists responsible for the massacre will be brought to trial for the murders and held accountable. And the mercenaries will return to testify against them."

"I'm sure our viewers will be happy to hear that."

"We protect our people overseas," Mr. Arbuckle replied. "All of them. And in fact, the mercenaries in question were private contractors working for the United States government, not the sort of soldiers for hire that often involve themselves in foreign conflicts."

"Another surprise," Mr. Price said with a smile.

"In this day and time, we all have to be alert about our surroundings abroad," Mr. Arbuckle said. "We take care of our own," he added with a smile.

"Thank you for your time, Mr. Arbuckle."

"Thank you for yours, Mr. Price."

Mr. Price turned back to Michelle. "It was a very brave thing you did, Ms. Godfrey, going up against the weight of the international press to defend these men. I understand that you know some of them."

"I know Eb Scott, who runs an international school of counterterrorism," Michelle corrected, unwilling to say more. "He has great integrity. I can't imagine that any agents he trained would ever go against basic humanitarianism."

"He has a good advocate here." He chuckled.

"I learned a lesson from this, as well," she replied quietly. "That you don't discount the single small voice in the wilderness when you write a story that can cost lives and reputations. It is one I hope I never have to repeat." She paused. "I'd like to thank my editor for standing by me," she added, lying because he hadn't, "and for teaching me the worth of integrity in reporting."

Mr. Price named the newspaper in San Antonio and thanked her for appearing on his program.

Back in the office, her editor, Len Worthington, was ecstatic. "That was the nicest plug we ever got from anybody! Thanks, kid!" he told her, shaking her hand.

"You're welcome. Thanks for not firing me for messing up so badly."

"Hey, what are friends for?"

He'd never know, she thought, but she only smiled. She'd seen a side of journalism that left her feeling sick. It wasn't pretty.

She didn't try to call Sara again. The poor woman probably hadn't seen the program Michelle was on. It was likely that she was avoiding any sort of press coverage of what had happened. That wasn't hard anymore, because there was a new scandal topping the news now, and all the satellite trucks had gone in search of other prey. Michelle's phone had stopped ringing. There were no more notes on her desk, no more offers of limos and five-star hotels. She didn't mind at all.

She only hoped that one day Sara and Gabriel would forgive her. She went back to work on other stories, mostly political ones, and hoped that she'd never be in a position again where she'd have to sell out her nearest and dearest for a job. Not that she ever would. Nor would she have done it, if she'd had any idea who Gabriel really was.

Michelle had thought about asking Minette for a job again. She wasn't really happy living in the city and she cringed every time someone mentioned her name in connection with the past big news story.

She still hadn't heard from Gabriel or Sara. She didn't expect to. She'd hoped that they might contact her. But that was wishful thinking.

She now owned the home where her father and, before him, her grandparents had lived in Comanche Wells. She couldn't bear to drive the Jaguar that Gabriel and Sara had given her…driving it made her too sad. So she parked it at Gabriel's house and put the key in the mail slot. One day, she assumed, he'd return and see it. She bought a cute little VW bug, with which she could commute from Jacobsville to work in San Antonio. She moved back home.

At first, people were understandably a little standoffish. She was an outsider, even though she was born in Jacobs County. Perhaps they thought she was going to go all big-city on them and start poking her nose into local politics.

When she didn't do that, the tension began to ease a little. When she went into Barbara's Café to have lunch on Saturdays, people began to nod and smile at her. When she went grocery shopping in the local supermarket, the cashier actually talked to her. When she got gas at the local station, the attendant finally stopped asking for identification when she presented her credit card. Little by little, she was becoming part of Jacobs County again.

Carlie came to visit occasionally. She was happily married, and expecting her first child. They weren't as close as they had been, but it made Michelle feel good to know that her friend was settled and secure.

She only wished that she could be, settled and secure. But as months went by with no word of or from the Brandons, she gave up all hope that she might one day be forgiven for the things she'd written.

She knew that Sara had a whole new life in Wyoming from the cashier at the grocery store who had known her. Michelle didn't blame her for not wanting to come back to Texas. After all, she'd only lived in Comanche Wells as a favor to Gabriel, so that he could be Michelle's guardian.

Guardian no more, obviously. He'd given up that before, of course, when she turned twenty-one. But sometimes Michelle wished that she still had at least a relationship with him. She mourned what could have been, before she lost her way. Gabriel had assured her that they had a future. But that was before.

She was hanging out sheets in the yard, fighting the fierce autumn breeze to keep them from blowing away, when she heard a vehicle coming down the long road. It was odd, because nobody lived out this way except Michelle. It was Saturday. The next morning, she'd planned to go to church. She'd missed it for a couple of Sundays while she worked on a hot political story.

These days, not even the Reverend Blair came visiting much. She didn't visit other people, either. Her job occupied much of her time, because a reporter was always on call. But Michelle still attended services most Sundays.

So she stared at the truck as it went past the house. Its windows were tinted, and rolled up. It was a new truck, a very fancy one. Perhaps someone had bought the old Brandon place, she concluded, and went back to hanging up clothes. It made her sad to think that Gabriel would sell the ranch. But, after all, what would he need it for? He only had a manager there to care for it, so it wasn't as if he needed to keep it. He had other things to do.

She'd heard from Minette that Gabriel was part of an international police force now, one that Eb Scott had contracted with to provide security for those Middle Eastern oilmen who had played such a part in Gabriel's close call.

She wondered if he would ever come back to Comanche Wells. But she was fairly certain he wouldn't. Too many bad memories.

Chapter 12

Michelle finished hanging up her sheets in the cool breeze and went back into the house to fix herself a sandwich.

There were rumors at work that a big story was about to break involving an oil corporation and a terrorist group in the Middle East, one that might have local ties. Michelle, now her editor's favorite reporter for having mentioned him on TV, was given the assignment. It might, he hinted, involve some overseas travel. Not to worry, the paper would gladly pay her expenses.

She wondered what sort of mess she might get herself into this time, poking her nose into things she didn't understand. Well, it was a job, and she was lucky to even have one in this horrible economy.

She finished her sandwich and drank a cup of black coffee. For some reason she thought of Gabriel, and how much he'd enjoyed her coffee. She had to stop thinking about him. She'd almost cost him his life. She'd destroyed his peace of mind and Sara's, subjected them both to cameras and reporters and harassment. It was not really a surprise that they weren't speaking to her anymore. Even if she'd gone the last mile defending them, trying to make up for her lack of foresight, it didn't erase the damage she'd already done.

She was bored to death. The house was pretty. She'd made improvements—she'd redecorated Roberta's old room and had the whole place repainted. She'd put up new curtains and bought new furniture. But the house was cold and empty.

Back when her father was alive, it still held echoes of his parents, of him. Now, it was a reminder of old tragedies, most especially her father's death and Roberta's.

She carried her coffee into the living room and looked around her. She ought to sell it and move into an apartment in San Antonio. She didn't have a pet, not even a dog or cat, and the livestock her father had owned were long gone. She had nothing to hold her here except a sad attachment to the past, to dead people.

But there was something that kept her from letting go. She knew what it was, although she didn't want to remember. It was Gabriel. He'd eaten here, slept here, comforted her here. It was warm with memories that no other dwelling place would ever hold.

She wondered if she couldn't just photograph the rooms and blow up the photos, make posters of them, and sacrifice the house.

Sure, she thought hollowly. Of course she could.

She finished her coffee and turned on the television.

Same old stories. Same programs with five minutes of commercials for every one minute of programming. She switched it off. These days she only watched DVDs or streamed movies from internet websites. She was too antsy to sit through a hundred commercials every half hour.

She wondered why people put up with it. If everyone stopped watching television, wouldn't the advertisers be forced to come up with alternatives that compromised a bit more? Sure. And cows would start flying any day.

That reminded her of the standing joke she'd had with Grier and Gabriel about cows being abducted by aliens, and it made her sad.

Outside, she heard the truck go flying past her house. It didn't even slow down. Must be somebody looking at Gabriel's house. She wondered if he'd put it on the market without bothering to put a for-sale sign out front. Why not? He had no real ties here. He'd probably moved up to Wyoming to live near Sara.

She went into the kitchen, put her coffee cup in the sink, and went back to her washing.

She wore a simple beige skirt and a short-sleeved beige sweater to church with pretty high heels and a purse to match. She left her hair long, down her back, and used only a trace of makeup on her face.

She'd had ample opportunities for romance, but all those years she'd waited for Gabriel, certain that he was going to love her one day, that she had a future with him. Now that future was gone. She knew that one day, she'd have to decide if she really wanted to be nothing more than a career woman with notoriety and money taking the place of a husband and children and a settled life.

There was nothing wrong with ambition. But the few career women she'd known seemed empty somehow, as if they presented a happy face to the world but that it was like a mask, hiding the insecurities and loneliness that accompanied a demanding lifestyle. What would it be like to grow old, with no family around you, with only friends and acquaintances and business associates to mark the holidays? Would it make up for the continuity of the next generation and the generation after that, of seeing your features reproduced down through your children and grandchildren and great-grandchildren? Would it make up for laughing little voices and busy little hands, and soft kisses on your cheek at bedtime?

That thought made her want to cry. She'd never thought too much about kids during her school days, but when Gabriel had kissed her and talked about a future, she'd dreamed of having his children. It had been a hunger unlike anything she'd ever known.

She had to stop tormenting herself. She had to come to grips with the world the way it was, not the way she wanted it to be. She was a grown woman with a promising career. She had to look ahead, not behind her.

She slid into her usual pew, listened to Reverend Blair's sermon and sang along with the choir as they repeated the chorus of a well-loved old hymn. Sometime during the offering, she was aware of a tingling sensation, as if someone were watching her. She laughed silently. Now she was getting paranoid.

As the service ended, and they finished singing the final hymn, as the benediction sounded in Reverend Blair's clear, deep voice, she continued to have the sensation that someone was watching her.

Slowly, as her pew filed out into the aisle, she glanced toward the back of the church. But there was no one there, no one looking at her. What a strange sensation.

Reverend Blair shook her hand and smiled at her. "It's nice to have you back, Miss Godfrey," he teased.

She smiled back. "Rub it in. I had a nightmare of a political story to follow. I spent so much time on it that I'm thinking I may run for public office myself. By now, I know exactly what not to do to get elected," she confided with a chuckle.

"I know what you mean. It was a good story."

"Thanks."

"See you next week."

"I hope." She crossed her fingers. He just smiled.

She walked to her car and clicked the smart key to unlock it when she felt, rather than saw, someone behind her.

She turned and her heart stopped in her chest. She looked up into liquid black eyes in a tanned, hard face that looked as if it had never known a smile.

She swallowed. She wanted to say so many things. She wanted to apologize. She wanted to cry. She wanted to throw herself into his arms and beg him to hold her, comfort her, forgive her. But she did none of those things. She just looked up at him hopelessly, with dead eyes that looked as if they had never held joy.

His square chin lifted. His eyes narrowed on her face. "You've lost weight."

She shrugged. "One of the better consequences of my profession," she said quietly. "How are you, Gabriel?"

"I've been better."

She searched his eyes. "How's Sara?"

"Getting back to normal."

She nodded. She swallowed again and dropped her eyes to his chest. It was hard to find something to say that didn't involve apologies or explanations or pleas for forgiveness.

The silence went on for so long that she could hear pieces of conversation from other churchgoers. She could hear the traffic on the highway, the sound of children playing in some yard nearby. She could hear the sound of her own heartbeat.

This was destroying her. She clicked the key fob again deliberately. "I have to go," she said softly.

"Sure."

He moved back so that she could open the door and get inside. She glanced at him with sorrow in her face, but she averted her eyes so that it didn't embarrass him. She didn't want him to feel guilty. She was the one who should feel that emotion. In the end she couldn't meet his eyes or even wave. She just started the car and drove away.

Well, at least the first meeting was over with, she told herself later. It hadn't been quite as bad as she'd expected. But it had been rough. She felt like crying, but her eyes were dry. Some pain was too deep to be eased by tears, she thought sadly.

She changed into jeans and a red T-shirt and went out on the front porch to water her flowers while a TV dinner microwaved itself to perfection in the kitchen.

Her flowers were going to be beautiful when they bloomed, she decided, smiling as they poked their little heads up through the dirt in an assortment of ceramic pots all over the wooden floor.

She had three pots of chrysanthemums and one little bonsai tree named Fred. Gabriel had given it to her when she first moved in with them, a sort of welcome present. It was a tiny fir tree with a beautiful curving trunk and feathery limbs. She babied it, bought it expensive fertilizer, read books on how to keep it healthy and worried herself to death that it might accidentally die if she forgot to water it. That hadn't happened, of course, but she loved it dearly. Of all the things Gabriel had given her, and there had been a lot, this was her favorite. She left it outside until the weather grew too cold, then she carried it inside protectively.

The Jaguar had been wonderful. But she'd still been driving it when she did the story that almost destroyed Gabriel's life and after that, she could no longer bear to sit in it. The memories had been killing her.

She missed the Jag. She missed Gabriel more. She wondered why he'd come back. Probably to sell the house, she decided, to cut his last tie with Comanche Wells. If he was working for an international concern, it wasn't likely that he'd plan to come back here. He'd see the Jag in the driveway, she thought, and understand why she'd given it back. At least, she hoped he would.

That thought, that he might leave Comanche Wells forever, was really depressing. She watered Fred, put down the can, and went back into the house. It didn't occur to her to wonder what he'd been doing at her church.

When she went into the kitchen to take her dinner out of the microwave, a dark-haired man was sitting at the table sipping coffee. There were two cups, one for him and one for her. The dinner was sitting on a plate with a napkin and silverware beside it.

He glanced up as she came into the room. "It's getting cold," he said simply.

She stood behind her chair, just staring at him, frowning.

He raised an eyebrow as he studied her shirt. "You know, most people who wore red shirts on the original *Star Trek* ended up dead."

She cocked her head. "And you came all this way to give me fashion advice?"

He managed a faint smile. "Not really." He sipped coffee. He let out a long breath. "It's been a long time, Michelle."

She nodded. Slowly, she pulled out the chair and sat down. The TV dinner had the appeal of mothballs. She pushed it aside and sipped the black coffee he'd put at her place. He still remembered how she took it, after all this time.

She ran her finger around the rim. "I learned a hard lesson," she said after a minute. "Reporting isn't just about presenting the majority point of view."

He lifted his eyes to hers. "Life teaches very hard lessons."

"Yes, it does." She drew in a breath. "I guess you're selling the house."

His eyebrows lifted. "Excuse me?"

"I saw a truck go out there yesterday. And I read that you're working with some international police force now. So since Sara's living in Wyoming, I assumed you'd probably be moving up there near her. For when you're home in the States, I mean."

"I'd considered it," he said after a minute. He sipped more coffee.

She wondered if her heart could fall any deeper into her chest. She wondered how in the world he'd gotten into the house so silently. She wondered why he was there in the first place. Was he saying goodbye?

"Did you find the keys to the Jag?" she asked.

"Yes. You didn't want to keep it?"

She swallowed hard. "Too many bad memories, of what I did to you and Sara," she confessed heavily.

He shook his head. After a minute, he stared at her bent head. "I don't think you've really looked at me once," he said finally.

She managed a tight smile. "It's very hard to do that, after all the trouble I caused you," she said. "I rehearsed it, you know. Saying I was sorry. Working up all sorts of ways to apologize. But there really isn't a good way to say it."

"People make mistakes."

"The kind I made could have buried you." She said it tautly, fighting tears. It was harder than she'd imagined. She forced down the rest of the coffee. "Look,

I've got things to do," she began, standing, averting her face so he couldn't see her eyes.

"Ma belle," he whispered, in a voice so tender that her control broke the instant she heard it. She burst into tears.

He scooped her up in his arms and kissed her so hungrily that she just went limp, arching up to him, so completely his that she wouldn't have protested anything he wanted to do to her.

"So it's like that, is it?" he whispered against her soft, trembling mouth. "Anything I want? Anything at all?"

"Anything," she wept.

"Out of guilt?" he asked, and there was an edge to his tone now.

She opened her wet eyes and looked into his. "Out of…love," she choked.

"Love."

"Go ahead. Laugh…"

He buried his face in her throat. "I thought I'd lost you for good," he breathed huskily. "Standing there at your car, looking so defeated, so depressed that you couldn't even meet my eyes. I thought, I'll have to leave, there's nothing left, nothing there except guilt and sorrow. And then I decided to have one last try, to come here and talk to you. You walked into the room and every single thing you felt was there, right there, in your eyes when you looked at me. And I knew, then, that it wasn't over at all. It was only beginning."

Her arms tightened around his neck. Her eyes were pouring with hot tears. "I loved you…so much," she choked. "Sara said you never wanted to see me again. She hated me. I knew you must hate me, too…!"

He kissed the tears away. He sat down on the sofa with Michelle in his lap and curled her into his chest. "Sara has a quick, hot temper. She loses it, and it's over. She's sorry that she was so brutal with you. She was frightened and upset and the media was hunting her. She's had other problems as well, that you don't know about. But she's ashamed that she took it all out on you, blamed you for something you didn't even do deliberately." He lifted his head and smoothed the long, damp hair away from her cheek. "She wanted to apologize, but she's too ashamed to call you."

"That's why?" she whispered. "I thought I would never see her again. Or you."

"That would never happen," he said gently. "You're part of us."

She bit her lower lip. "I sold you out…!"

"You did not. You sold out a mercenary named Angel, someone you didn't know, someone you thought had perpetrated a terrible crime against innocent women and children," he said simply. He brushed his mouth over her wet eyes. "You would never have sold me out in a million years, even if you had thought I was guilty as sin." He lifted his head and looked into her eyes. "Because you love me. You love me enough to forgive anything, even murder."

The tears poured out even hotter. She couldn't stop crying.

He wrapped her up close, turned her under him on the sofa, slid between her long legs and began to kiss her with anguished hunger. The kisses grew so long and so hard and so hot that she trembled and curled her legs around the back of his, urging him into greater intimacy, pleading with him to ease the tension that was putting her young body on the rack.

"If you don't stop crying," he threatened huskily, "this is going to end badly."

"No, it isn't. You want to," she whispered, kissing his throat.

"Yes, I do," he replied deeply. "But you're going to need a lot of time that I can't give you when I'm out of control," he murmured darkly. "You won't enjoy it."

"Are you sure?" she whispered.

He lifted his head. His eyes were hot and hungry on her body. His hands had pushed up the red shirt and the bra, and he was staring at her pert, pretty breasts with aching need. "I am absolutely sure," he managed.

"Oh."

The single word and the wide-eyed, hopeless look in her eyes broke the tension and he started laughing. "That's it? 'Oh'?"

She laughed, too. "Well, I read a lot and I watch movies, but it's not quite the same thing…"

"Exactly."

He forced himself to roll off her. "If you don't mind, could you pull all this back down?" he asked, indicating her breasts. He averted his eyes. "And I'll try deep breaths and mental imagery of snow-covered hills."

"Does it work?"

"Not really."

She pulled down her shirt and glanced at him with new knowledge of him and herself, and smiled.

"That's a smug little look," he accused.

"I like knowing I can throw you off balance," she said with a wicked grin.

"I'll enjoy letting you do it, but not until we're used to each other," he replied. He pulled her close. "The first time has to be slow and easy," he whispered, brushing his mouth over hers. "So that it doesn't hurt so much."

"If you can knock me off balance, I won't care if it hurts," she pointed out.

His black eyes twinkled. "I'll remember that."

She lay back on the sofa and looked up at him with wide, wondering eyes. "I thought it was all over," she whispered. "That I had nothing left, nothing to live for…"

"I felt the same way," he returned, solemn and quiet. "Thank God I decided to make one more attempt to get through to you."

She smiled gently. "Fate."

He smiled back. "Yes. Fate."

"Where are you going? Come back here." She pulled him back down.

He pursed his lips. "We need to discuss things vertically, not horizontally."

"I'm not going to seduce you, honest. I have something very serious I need to talk to you about."

"Okay. What?"

She pursed her own lips and her eyes twinkled. "Cow abductions."

He burst out laughing.

They were married in the Methodist church two weeks later by Reverend Blair. Michelle wore a con-

ventional white gown with lace inserts and a fingertip
veil, which Gabriel lifted to kiss her for the first time
as his wife. In the audience were more mercenaries
and ex-military and feds than anyone locally had seen
in many a year.

Eb Scott and his wife, along with Dr. Micah Steele
and Callie, and Cy Parks and Lisa, were all in the front
row with Minette Carson and her husband Hayes.
Carlie and her husband were there, too.

There was a reception in the fellowship hall and Jacobsville police chief Cash Grier kept looking around
restlessly.

"Is something going on that we should know about?"
Gabriel asked with a grin.

"Just waiting for the riot to break out."

"What riot?" Michelle asked curiously.

"You know, somebody says something, somebody
else has too much to drink and takes offense, blows
are exchanged, police are called in to break up the al-
tercation…"

"Chief Grier, just how many riots at weddings have
you seen?" she wanted to know.

"About half a dozen," he said.

"Well, I can assure you, there won't be any here,"
Michelle said. "Because there's no booze!"

Cash gaped at her. "No booze?"

"No."

"Well, damn," he said, glowering at her.

"Why do you say that?" she asked.

"How can you have altercations without booze?"
He threw up his hands. "And I had so looked forward
to a little excitement around here!"

"I could throw a punch at Hayes," Gabriel offered, grinning at the sheriff. "But then he'd have to arrest me, and Michelle would spend our honeymoon looking for bail bondsmen…"

Cash chuckled. "Just kidding. I like the occasional quiet wedding." He leaned forward. "When you're not busy, you might want to ask Blake Kemp about *his* wedding reception, though," he added gleefully. "Jacobsville will never forget that one, I swear!"

Michelle lay trembling in Gabriel's arms, hot and damp in the aftermath of something so turbulent and thrilling that she knew she could live on the memory of it for the rest of her life.

"I believe the chief wanted a little excitement?" She laughed hoarsely. "I don't think anyone could top this. Ever."

He trailed his fingers up her body, lingering tenderly on a distended nipple. He stroked it until she arched and gasped. "I don't think so, either." He bent his head and slipped his lips over the dusky peak, teasing it until it grew even harder and she shivered. He suckled it, delighting in the sounds that came out of her throat.

"You like that, do you?" he whispered. He moved over her. "How about this?"

"Oh…yes," she choked. "Yes!"

He slid a hand under her hips and lifted her into the slow penetration of his body, moving restlessly as she accepted him, arched to greet him, shivered again as she felt the slow, hungry depth of his envelopment.

"It's easier now," he whispered. "Does it hurt?"

"I haven't…noticed yet," she managed, shuddering as he moved on her.

He chuckled.

"I was afraid," she confessed in a rush of breath.

"I know."

She clung to him as the rhythm lifted her, teased her body into contortions of pure, exquisite pleasure. "I can't believe… I was afraid!"

His hips moved from side to side and she made a harsh, odd little cry that was echoed in the convulsion of her hips.

"Yes," he purred. "I can make you so hungry that you'll do anything to get me closer, can't I, *ma belle?*"

"Any…thing," she agreed.

He ground his teeth together. "It works…both ways…too," he bit off. He groaned harshly as the pleasure bit into him, arched him down into her as the rhythm grew hard and hot and deep. He felt his heartbeat in his head, slamming like a hammer as he drove into her welcoming body, faster and harder and closer until suddenly, like a storm breaking, a silver shaft of pleasure went through him like a spear, lifting him above her in an arch so brittle that he thought he might shatter into a thousand pieces.

"Like…dying," he managed as the pleasure took him.

She clung to him, too involved to even manage a reply, lifting and pleading, digging her nails into his hard back as she welcomed the hard, heavy push of his body, welcomed the deep, aching tension that grew and swelled and finally burst like rockets going off inside her.

She cried out helplessly, sobbing, as the ecstasy

washed over her like the purest form of pleasure imaginable and then, just as quickly, was gone. Gone. Gone!

They clung together, damp with sweat, sliding against each other in the aftermath, holding on to the echoes of the exquisite satisfaction that they'd shared.

"Remind me to tell you one day how rare it is for two people to find completion at the same time," he whispered, sliding his mouth over her soft, yielding body. "Usually, the woman takes a long time, and the man only finds his satisfaction when hers is over."

She lifted an eyebrow. "And you would know this, how?" she began.

He lifted his head and looked into her eyes with a rakish grin. "Oh, from the videos I watched and the books I read and the other guys I listened to..."

"Is that so?" she mused, with a suspicious look.

He kissed her accusing eyes shut. "It was long before I knew you," he whispered. "And after the first day I saw you, sitting in the road waiting for me to run over you, there was no one. Ever."

Her eyes flew open. "Wh-what?"

He brushed the hair from her cheeks. "I knew then that I would love you one day, forever," he said quietly. "So there were no other women."

Her face flushed. "Gabriel," she whispered, overcome.

He kissed her tenderly. "The waiting was terrible," he groaned. "I thought I might die of it, waiting until you grew up, until you knew something of the world and men so that I didn't rob you of that experience." He lifted his head. "Always, I worried that you might find a younger man and fall in love..."

She put her fingers over his chiseled mouth. "I loved you from the day I met you," she whispered. "When I stared at you, that day in town with my grandfather, before I was even sixteen." She touched his cheek with her fingertips. "I knew, too, that there could never be anyone else."

He nibbled her fingers. "So sweet, the encounter after all the waiting," he whispered.

"Sweeter than honey," she agreed, her eyes warm and soft on his face.

"There's just one thing," he murmured.

She raised her eyebrows.

He opened a drawer and pulled out an item that he'd placed there earlier. An item that they'd forgotten to use.

She just smiled.

After a minute, he smiled back and dropped the item right back into the drawer.

Sara was overjoyed. "I can't wait to come down there and see you both," she exclaimed. "But you've only been married six weeks," she added.

Gabriel was facing the computer with Michelle at his side, holding her around the waist, his big hands resting protectively over her slightly swollen belly as they talked on Skype with Sara in Wyoming. "We were both very sure that it was what we wanted," he said simply.

"Well, I'm delighted," Sara said. She smiled. "The only way I could be more delighted is if it was me who was pregnant. But, that will come with time," she said complacently, and smiled. "I'm only sorry I couldn't be at the wedding," she added quietly. "I was very mean to you, Michelle. I couldn't face you, afterward."

"I understood," Michelle said gently. "You're my sister. Really my sister now," she added with a delighted laugh. "We're going to get a place near yours in Wyoming so that we can be nearby when the baby comes."

"I can't wait!"

"Neither can I," Michelle said. "We'll talk to you soon."

"Very soon." Sara smiled and cut the connection.

"Have you ever told her?" Michelle asked after a minute, curling up in Gabriel's lap.

He kissed her. "We did just tell her, my love..."

"Not about the baby," she protested. "About Wolf. About who he really is."

"You mean, her gaming partner for the past few years?" He grinned. "That's a story for another day."

"If you say so."

He kissed her. "I do say so. And now, how about a nice pickle and some vanilla ice cream?"

Her eyebrows lifted. "You know, that sounds delicious!"

He bent his head and kissed the little bump below her waist. "He's going to be extraordinary," he whispered.

"Yes. Like his dad," she replied with her heart in her eyes.

And they both grinned.

* * * * *

SMOKIN' SIX-SHOOTER

B.J. Daniels

Chapter 1

"There must be some mistake." Dulcie Hughes shifted in her chair, anxious to flee the lawyer's office. "We've covered everything my parents left me in their estate."

"Not this particular part of your inheritance," he said and cleared this throat. For years Lawrence Brooks, Sr., had been her parents' attorney, but upon his death his youngest son, Herbert, had taken over his father's law practice.

Herbert was in his early thirties, only a few years older than Dulcie herself, a tall, prematurely balding man with tiny brown eyes and a nervous twitch.

Today though he seemed even more nervous than usual, which made her pay closer attention as he handed her the documents.

"What is this?" she asked, frowning. Her elderly parents had discussed all their financial arrangements with her at length for years. She'd never seen this before.

"You've been left some property in Montana."

"*Montana?*"

He tried to still his hands as he waited for her to read the documents.

"My parents never mentioned anything about having property in Montana." She read the name. "Who is Laura Beaumont?"

"You don't know?"

She shook her head. "I've never heard the name before. This is all the information you have?"

"Apparently Laura Beaumont's estate was being held for you in a trust until their deaths, taking care of the expenses. That's all I can tell you." He stood abruptly, signaling an end to their business.

Dulcie didn't move. "Are you saying this is all you *know* or this is all you're *allowed* to tell me?"

"If you want to know more, I would suggest you obtain an attorney of your own to look into the matter further," he said, tapping his fingertips on his desk as he waited impatiently for her to leave. "Or go to Montana yourself." He made the latter sound imprudent.

"Maybe I'll do that," Dulcie said, rising to her feet and tucking the papers into her shoulder bag.

"As your parents' attorney, that completes our business," Herbert said, sounding glad of it.

For the past four months, she'd been grieving the loss of her parents and not in the least interested in dealing with the financial aspects of that loss.

As the only heir of Brad and Kathy Hughes, she'd known she would be inheriting a sizable estate. Not that she needed it. Straight out of college, she and a friend had opened a boutique that had taken off.

After establishing more than a dozen such shops across the country, she and Renada had sold the businesses six months ago and made enough that she would never have to work again if she invested the money wisely, which of course she had.

She'd been trying to decide what to do next when her seventy-two-year-old father had taken ill. Her mother had never been strong, suffering from a weak heart. But to lose both of them within a few weeks had been crushing.

Now, months later, she felt even more at loose ends.

As she left the lawyer's office, her cell phone rang.

"So it's over?" asked her friend and former business partner tentatively. Renada had wanted to come along with her to see the lawyer, knowing how hard this was for her. But Dulcie had needed to do this on her own. She needed to get used to doing a lot of things on her own.

"All done," she said, patting the papers she'd stuffed into her shoulder bag.

"Up for lunch?" Renada asked.

"Absolutely. I'm starved." And she was, she realized.

It wasn't until after they'd eaten and she was feeling better for the first time in months that she told her friend about the Montana property.

"It's very odd," she said, digging out the papers the lawyer had given her. "I've been left property in Montana from someone named Laura Beaumont."

"Seriously? How much?"

"Apparently a hundred and sixty acres just outside of Whitehorse, Montana."

"Where is that?"

"I haven't a clue."

"Aren't you curious about this Laura Beaumont?"

"Yes, but it's so strange that my parents never mentioned this woman or anything about the property, even though Laura Beaumont left it to me years ago."

"Your parents never even went to Montana to see what you'd been left?"

"Apparently not. We went to Yellowstone Park one summer. Wouldn't you think they'd have mentioned the property?"

"Or taken you there. Unless it's in the middle of nowhere and they had no interest in it. You are going to check it out, aren't you?"

Dulcie knew her friend had been worried about her, urging her to come up with another business venture to help get her through her loss. "Do you want to go with me?"

Renada shook her head ruefully. "I'd love to, but I can't leave right now. I just agreed to teach some clothing design classes at the community university."

"Good for you," Dulcie said, excited for her friend. Renada had always talked about doing something like this when she had the time. Their boutiques had kept them so busy she'd never gotten the chance. Now there was nothing keeping her from it.

"It's funny," Dulcie said as they walked out of the restaurant together. "I got the feeling from the lawyer that there was something unusual about this inheritance."

"Unusual how?"

"Something he couldn't talk about. Or wouldn't."

"A *secret?*" Renada said on an excited breath. "Maybe this land is worth a small fortune. Or Lewis and Clark left their names carved in the stones on the property."

Dulcie laughed. "Don't get your hopes up. I'm sure it's just a piece of property that is so inconsequential that it skipped my parents' minds."

"A hundred and sixty acres in Montana inconsequential?" Renada scoffed. "Still, it *does* seem odd since you've never heard of this Laura Beaumont. So when are you going to Montana?"

"Right away, I guess," Dulcie said, feeling as if this was a decision that had been taken out of her hands a long time ago.

A hot, dry wind whispered in the curtains as the weather vane on the barn turned restlessly, groaning and creaking.

The air in the house was so hot it hurt to breathe. The parched land outside the old farmhouse with its ochre dried grasses seemed to ache for a drink in the undulating heat waves that moved across the prairie as far as the eye could see.

Like the land, she'd forgotten the smell of rain, the feel of it soaking into her skin. She thirsted for the sound of raindrops on the roof, the splash of mud puddles as a pickup drove past.

She lay naked on the bed in the upstairs bedroom, the hot wind moving over her lush body, leaving it glistening with perspiration. Too young and ripe to be widowed, she ached for more than a cool breeze to caress her flesh.

The noise of the whirling fan across the room covered the creak of the slow, deliberate footsteps on the stairs. While she didn't hear anyone, she must have felt a change in the air that told her she was no longer alone in the house.

"Is that you, sweetie?" she asked without expending the energy it would take to open her eyes. "I thought you'd gone down to the creek with your little friend."

No answer.

A chill skittered over her, dimpling her flawless skin. Her eyes flew open in alarm as if she heard the blade cutting through the oppressive heat.

The first stab of the knife stole her breath. She tried to sit up, but the next blow knocked her back. The attacks came more quickly now, metal to flesh to bone, burning deep as blood pooled on the clean white sheets, the blood as hot as the breathless air around her.

By the time the knife finally stilled, its wielder panting hard from the exertion in the close heat of that second-story bedroom, she lay with her head turned toward the door, eyes dull with death, the face of her killer reflected accusingly in her dark pupils.

Jolene Stevens dropped the neatly printed pages and let out the breath she'd been holding. She glanced past the glow of her desk lamp to the door of the Old Town Whitehorse one-room schoolhouse.

The door was open to let in what cool night air might be had this late spring day. Like the beginning of the story she'd just read, the heat had been intense for weeks now. There wasn't a breath of cool air and little chance of rain, according to the weatherman.

Jolene fanned herself with her grade book as she looked down at the pages again. On Friday she'd given her students an assignment to begin a short fictional story that would be told in six segments. She'd told them they didn't have to put their names on their stories, thinking this would make them less self-conscious.

Each story was typed, double-spaced, on the student's home computer so all of the stories looked the same.

While she'd instructed her students to start their stories at an exciting part and introduce an interesting character or intriguing place or event, she hadn't expected anything this disturbing.

Mentally, she envisioned each of her five students: Amy Brooks, the precocious third-grade girl; the two goof-off fifth-grade boys, Thad Brooks and Luke Raines; the sixth-grade cowgirl, Codi Fox, and the eighth-grade moody boy on the cusp of becoming a man, Mace Carpenter.

She couldn't imagine any of them writing this. Picking up the assignments, she counted. *Six?* Five students and yet she had collected *six* short-story beginnings? Was it possible one of them had turned in two stories?

For the first time since Jolene had come to Old Town Whitehorse to teach in the one-room schoolhouse, she felt uneasy. She'd been hired right out of Montana State University to fill an opening when the former teacher ran off and got married just before the school year ended, so all of this was new to her.

She rose and walked to the door to look out. Night sounds carried on the breeze. Crickets chirped in the tall dried grass of the empty lot between the school and the Whitehorse Community Center. No other sound could be heard in the hot Monday night since little remained of the town except for a few old buildings.

Her bike still leaned against the front of the school where she'd left it. Past it she could make out the playground equipment hunkered in the dark inside the old iron fence.

Beyond the playground, the arch over the cemetery on the hill seemed to catch some moonlight. She'd been warned about strange lights in the cemetery late at night. Talk was that the place was haunted.

Jolene had loved the idea, loved everything about this quaint rural community and her first teaching job. She loved the rolling prairie and even the isolation. She was shy, an avid reader, and appreciated the peace and quiet that the near-ghost town of Old Town White-horse afforded.

But the short-story beginning had left her on edge. She shivered even though the night was unbearably hot. Nothing moved in the darkness outside the schoolhouse. The only light was one of those large yard lights used on ranches, shining from down the road by the small house that came with her teaching position.

Jolene closed the door, locking it, and stood for a moment studying the tables and chairs where her students sat. Light pooled on her desk, illuminating the rest of the opening scenes waiting there for her to read.

Tomorrow her students would turn in their next segment of their short stories, the assignment to run for another five days, ending next Monday. Would there be more of this story?

Earlier she had decided to stay late and read the first of the stories here where she'd thought it might be cooler. Now, with the murder story too fresh in her mind, she changed her mind and, stepping to the desk, scooped up the assignments and shoved them into her backpack.

An owl hooted just outside the open window, making her jump. She laughed at her own foolishness. She'd been raised in the country, and having been a tomboy, nothing had scared her. So why was she letting some fictional tale scare her?

Because she couldn't believe that any of her students had written it, she thought, as she zipped her backpack shut and turned out the lamp. She moved through the dark schoolroom to the door, unlocked it and stepped out.

The heat hit her like a fist and for a moment, she had trouble catching her breath. The weather this spring was *too* much like the short story, she thought, as she climbed on her bike and rode down the hill to her small house.

Once inside, she turned on all the lights, feeling foolish. What was there to be frightened of in this nearly deserted town in the middle of nowhere? The murder in the story had just been someone's vivid imagination at work. Vivid, *gruesome* imagination at work.

She made herself a sandwich and sat down with the rest of the stories. They were all pretty much what she'd expected from each of her students and she'd easily recognized each student's work.

Just as she'd suspected—none of them had written the brutal murder story. But one of them had to have turned it in. Why?

The answer seemed obvious.

Someone wanted her to read it.

Chapter 2

Dulcie Hughes brought the rented car to a stop in front of a boarded-up old farmhouse in the middle of nowhere.

This was it? The mysterious Montana property? She couldn't help her disappointment. She hadn't known what to expect when she'd flown into Great Falls and driven across what was called the Hi-Line to White-horse.

The small Western town hadn't been much of a sur-prise, either, after driving through one small Western town after another.

She had driven under the train tracks into White-horse, telling herself she understood why her parents had never brought her here. There wasn't much to see unless you liked cowboys and pickup trucks. That seemed to be the only thing along the main street.

A few bars, churches, cafés and a couple of clothing stores later, she had to backtrack to find a real-estate office for directions to her property.

A cute blonde named April had drawn her a map and told her she couldn't miss it. Of course that wasn't true given that the land and all the old farmhouses looked alike. Fortunately she had the GPS coordinates.

The difference also was that her farmhouse had apparently been boarded up for years. Weeds had grown tall behind the barbed-wire fence. Nothing about the house looked in the least bit inviting.

"How do you feel about bats?" April had asked.

"*Bats?*"

"Whitehorse is the northernmost range for migrating little brown bats. They hibernate down in the Little Rockies and Memorial Day they show up in Whitehorse and don't leave till after Labor Day. They come for the mosquitoes. I hope someone warned you about the mosquitoes. And the wind."

"Don't worry, I won't be staying long. I've just come to see the property for myself before I put it on the market."

"So you don't think you'll be falling in love with it up here and never want to leave?" April joked.

Dulcie wondered all the way across the top of the state why anyone in their right mind lived here.

"I thought there would be mountains and pine trees," she had said to April.

"The Little Rockies are forty miles to the south. There's pine trees down there. Ponderosas. Your property isn't far from there." She'd grinned. "I guess you missed the single pine tree on the edge of town and the sign somebody put up that reads, Whitehorse County National Forest."

Funny. But stuff like that was probably all they had to do around here for fun, Dulcie had thought as she had taken the map and thanked April for her help, promising to get back to her about listing the property.

For Dulcie, who lived in Chicago, the pine trees and the mountains had been farther than she thought—about twenty miles away.

She grabbed her cell phone, unable to wait a moment longer to call Renada and give her the news. But as she flipped it open, she heard the roar of an engine and looked into her rearview mirror to find a huge farm machine of some kind barreling down on her.

Fumbling for the key in the ignition, she let out a cry and braced herself for the inevitable crash as her rental car was suddenly shrouded in a cloud of dust.

She must have closed her eyes, waiting for the impact, because when she opened them, she found a pair of very blue, very angry eyes scowling in at her.

Turning the key, she whirred down her window since the cowboy hunkered next to her rental car seemed to be mouthing something.

"Yes?" she inquired, cell phone still in hand in case she needed to call for help. "Is there a problem?"

He quirked a brow. "Other than you parked in the middle of the road just over a rise? Nope, that about covers it."

"I'm sorry. Let me pull off the road so you can get around."

"Going to take more than that to get a combine through here on this narrow stretch of road, I'm afraid."

A combine. How interesting.

"You lost?" he asked, shoving back his battered gray Stetson to glance over the top of her rental toward the farmhouse, then back to her.

He had the most direct blue-eyed stare she'd ever seen.

"No." Not that it was any of his business. "I think I've seen all I need to see here so I'll just go on up the road."

"The road dead-ends a mile in the direction you're headed," he said. "But if that's what you want to do. I'm only going another half mile. I can follow you."

Oh, wouldn't that be delightful.

"I believe in that case I'll just pull into this house and let you go by," she said and started to open her door.

"Want help with the gate?" he asked with a hint of amusement as he stepped back to let her slide from the car.

"I'm sure I can figure it out." She straightened to her full height of five nine, counting the two-inch heels of her dress boots, but he still towered over her.

Turning her back to him, she walked to the barbed-wire gate strung across the road into the house. She could feel his gaze appraising her and wished she'd worn something more appropriate.

Renada had joked that she needed to buy herself a pair of cowboy boots. She had worn designer jeans, a blouse and a pair of black dress boots with heels. As one of her heels sank into the soft dirt, she wished she'd taken Renada's advice.

The gate, she found, had an odd contraption at one

end, with a wire from the fence post that looped over the gatepost. Apparently all she had to do to open the gate was slip the wire loop off that post.

The gate, though, hadn't been opened in a while, judging from how deep the wire had sunk into the old wood. The wire dug into her fingers as she tried to slide it upward.

"You have to hug it," the cowboy said, brushing against her as he leaned over her to wrap one arm around the gatepost and the other around the fence post and squeezed. As the two posts came together, he easily slid the wire loop up and off.

"Thank you," she said as she ducked out from under his arms and stood back to watch him drag the gate out of the way. He wasn't just tall, she realized. His shoulder muscles bunched as he opened the gate, stretching the fabric of his Western shirt across his broad shoulders, and she'd gotten a good look at his backside.

The only cowboys she'd seen in Chicago were the urban types. None of them had this man's rough-and-tough appearance. Nor had their jeans fit them quite like this cowboy's did, she couldn't help noticing.

"I'd be watching out for rattlesnakes if I were you," he called after her as she turned to head for her car.

He's just trying to scare me, she told herself but made a point of walking slowly back to her rental car and hurriedly getting inside—much to his amusement.

She revved the engine and pulled into the yard of her property, glad when she would be seeing the last of him. As she did, something moved behind a missing shutter at an upstairs window.

"Just leave the gate," Dulcie said, cutting the engine

and getting out of the car. "I might as well have a look around while I'm here."

He leaned against the gatepost studying her. "Excuse me for saying so, but I don't think that's a good idea. I wasn't joking about the rattlers, especially around an old place like this. Not to mention the fact that you're trespassing and people around here don't take kindly to that. You could get yourself shot."

This last part she really doubted. "I'll take my chances."

He shrugged. "I hadn't taken you for one of them."

"I beg your pardon?"

"The morbidly curious."

Dulcie felt something in her tense. "I'm afraid I don't know what you're talking about."

"A woman was murdered in that house."

She shook her head, not trusting her voice.

"Change your mind about hanging out here?"

"No." The word came out weakly.

He tried to hide a grin. "Then I should probably warn you that if you get into trouble that cell phone you've been clutching won't be of any use. There's no coverage out here."

She lifted an eyebrow. She'd never had trouble getting coverage with her cell phone carrier. The man didn't know what he was talking about. She snapped open her phone. Damn, he was right.

When she looked up he was walking back toward his combine, shaking his head with each long stride. She could hear him muttering under his breath. "Got better things to do than stand around in this heat arguing with some fool city girl who doesn't have the sense God gave her."

"So much for Western hospitality," she muttered under her own breath, then turned toward the house and felt herself shiver despite the heat.

Jolene Stevens glanced at the clock on the school-house wall. The hot air coming through the open windows and the sound of the birds and crickets chirping in the grass had all five students looking wistfully toward the cloudless blue sky and the summerlike day outside.

"Hand in your writing assignments and you may go home a few minutes early," she said, giving up the fight to keep their attention. "Don't forget you have another part of your story to write tonight. Tomorrow we will talk about writing the middle of your story."

The air was close inside the schoolhouse, the breeze coming through the open window as hot as dragon's breath against the back of her neck.

Jolene lifted her hair as she waited for her sixth-grader, Codi Fox, to collect all the assignments. She tried not to let any of her students see how anxious she was, not that they were paying attention. As Codi put the stack of short stories on the corner of her desk, Jolene made a point of not looking at them.

Instead she watched as her students pulled on their backpacks, answered questions and wished everyone a nice evening. None of them seemed in the least bit interested in the short-story assignments they'd just turned in.

If one of the students was bringing her the extra

story, wouldn't he or she have been anxious to see Jolene's reaction? Apparently not.

After they'd all left, she straightened chairs, turned out lights, picked up around the schoolroom. The small, snub-nosed school bus came and went, taking three of her students with it. She waved to the elderly woman driver, then stood in the shade of the doorway as the parents of her last two students pulled up.

As soon as the dust settled, Jolene went back inside the classroom to her desk. Her hands were actually trembling as she picked up the short-story assignments, afraid the next installment of the murder story would be among the pile—and afraid it wouldn't.

She quickly counted the individual stories. *Six.*

With a sigh of relief and an air of apprehension, she sorted through until she found it.

It had been one those hot, dry springs when all the churchgoers in Whitehorse County were praying for rain. The small farming community depended on spring rains and when they didn't come, you could feel the anxiety growing like a low-frequency electrical pulse that raced through the county and left everyone on edge.

Everyone, that is, but her. She wasn't worried that day about the weather as she hung her wet sheets on the line behind the old farmhouse and waited—not for rain but for the sound of his truck coming up the dead-end road.

Jolene swallowed and looked up, afraid someone would come through the school's door at any minute and catch her. Reading this felt like a guilty pleasure. Gathering up her work, she stuffed everything into her backpack and biked home.

Once there, she poured herself a glass of lemonade and, unable to postpone it any longer, picked up the story again.

The sweltering heat on the wind wrapped her long skirt around her slim legs, and lifted her mane of dark hair off her damp neck as she stared past the clothesline to the dirt road, anticipating her lover's arrival.

She'd sent the little girl off to play with her new friend from across the creek. A long, lazy afternoon stretched endlessly before her and she ached at the thought, her need to be fulfilled by a man as essential as her next breath.

Over the sound of the weather vane on the barn groaning in the wind and the snap of the sheets as she secured them to the line, she finally heard a vehicle.

Her head came up and softened with relief, a clothespin between her perfect white teeth, her lightly freckled arms clutching the line as if for support as she watched him turn into the yard.

Dust roiled up into the blindingly bright day, the scorching wind lifting and carrying it across the road to the empty prairie.

She took the clothespin from her mouth, licking her lips as she secured the sheet, then leaving the rest of her wet clothes in the basket, she wiped her hands on her skirt and hurried to meet the man who would be the death of her.

* * *

Jolene took a breath and then reread the pages. She had no more clue as to who could have written this than she had the first time. Nor was she sure why the submission upset her the way it did. It was just fiction, right?

Why give it to her to read though? All she could think was that one of her student's parents always wanted to write and was looking for some encouragement.

"All my daughter talks about is the short story you're having the students write," Amy's mother had told her. "The other students and their families are talking about it as well. You've excited the whole community since I'm told the stories will eventually be bound in a booklet that will be for sale at next year's fall festival."

Was that how the author of the murder story had found out about the assignment? Which meant it could be anyone, not necessarily one of her student's parents. But one of the students had to be bringing it in to class.

Jolene got up and went to the window, hoping for a breath of fresh air. Heat rose in waves over the pale yellow wild grass that ran to the Little Rockies.

What did the writer expect her to do with this? Just read it? Critique it? Believe it?

She shuddered as she realized that from the first sentence she'd read of the story, she *had* believed it. But then that was what good fiction was all about, making the reader suspend disbelief.

Even though she knew how the story ended since the writer had begun with the murder, she had the feeling that the writer was far from finished. At least she hoped that was the case. She couldn't bear the thought that whoever was sending her this might just quit in the middle and leave her hanging.

She looked forward to seeing the next part of the story Wednesday morning and didn't want to think that she might never know who or why someone had given it to her to read. As disturbing as the story was, she felt flattered that the writer had chosen her to read it.

As she stood looking out the window, she had a thought. Had such a murder occurred in this community? The old-timers around here told stories back to the first settlers. If there *had* been a brutal murder around here, she was sure someone would be able to recall it.

Especially one involving a young widow with a daughter living in an old farmhouse one very hot, rainless spring.

Jolene glanced back up the road to the Whitehorse Community Center. Several pickups and an SUV were parked out front for the meeting of the Whitehorse Sewing Circle. If anyone knew about a murder, it would be one of those women.

Dulcie waited until the dust settled from the combine and the cowboy before she turned back to the house. Her gaze was drawn to the second-floor window again and the pale yellow curtain.

She was sure the color had faded over the years and she couldn't make out the design on the fabric from here, but something about that yellow curtain felt oddly familiar.

Careful to make sure no rattlesnakes had snuck up while she'd been waiting, she took a few tentative steps toward the house. Had she seen this house with its yellow curtains in a photograph? Surely her parents had one somewhere.

Boards had been nailed across the front door and the lower windows. There would be no getting into the house without some tools. But did she really want to go inside?

She noticed a sliver of window visible from beneath the boards and moved cautiously through the tall weeds to cup her hands and peer inside.

She blinked in surprise. The inside of the house was covered in dust, but it looked as if whoever had lived here had just walked out one day and not returned.

The furniture appeared to be right where it had been, including a book on a side table and a drinking glass, now filled with cobwebs and dust, where someone had sat and read. There were tracks where small critters had obviously made themselves at home, but other than that, the place looked as if it hadn't been disturbed in years.

Since the murder?

Dulcie felt a chill and told herself the cowboy might have just made that up to scare her, the same way he had warned her about rattlesnakes.

According to the documents, Dulcie had been left the property twenty-four years before. She would have been four.

Who left property to a four-year-old?

Laura Beaumont apparently.

Dulcie drew back, brushed dust from her sleeve

and started to turn to the rental car to leave when she heard a strange creaking groan that made her freeze.

What sent her pulse soaring was the realization that she'd heard this exact sound before. She found her feet and stepped around the side of the house to look in the direction the noise was coming from.

On top of the barn, a rusted weather vane in the shape of a horse moved in the breeze, groaning and creaking restlessly.

Dulcie stood staring at it, her eyes suddenly welling with tears. She *had* been here before. The thought filled her with a horrible sense of dread.

She wiped at the tears, convinced she was losing her mind. Why else did a pair of yellow curtains and a rusted weather vane make her feel such dread—and worse—such fear?

Chapter 3

Russell Corbett drove the combine down the road to where he'd left his four-wheeler. He hated trading the luxury of the cab of the combine with its CD player, satellite radio and air conditioner for the noisy, hot four-wheeler.

He much preferred a horse to a vehicle anyway, but he couldn't argue the convenience as he started the engine and headed back toward Trails West Ranch.

As he neared the old Beaumont place, it was impossible not to think about the woman he'd almost crashed into earlier, sitting in the middle of the road. Fool city girl, he thought, shaking his head again. Thinking about her took his mind off the heat bearing down on him.

He hadn't paid that much attention to her. Even now he couldn't recall her exact hair color. Something between russet and mahogany, but then it had been hard to tell with the sunlight firing it with gold.

Nor could he recall the length, the way she had the weight of her hair drawn up and secured in the back. He idly wondered if it would fall past her shoulders should the expensive-looking clip come loose.

He did remember her size when he'd bent over her, no more than five-six or seven without those heels, and recalled the impression he'd gotten that while her body was slim, she was rounded in all the right places. He'd sensed a strength about her, or maybe it had just been mule-headed stubbornness, that belied her stature and her obvious city-girl background.

Realizing the path his thoughts had taken, Russell shook them off like water from a wet dog. He must be suffering from heatstroke, he told himself. No woman had monopolized his thoughts this long in recent memory.

He told himself he wasn't even going to look as he passed to see if she was still parked in front of the old farmhouse. It was too hot to save her from herself, even if she had wanted his help.

But he did look and told himself it wasn't disappointment he felt at finding her gone. It was relief that she wasn't in some trouble he would have to get her out of.

He slowed the four-wheeler as he noticed the fence lying on the ground. With a curse, he stopped and got off to close it. The woman had a lot to learn about private property and leaving gates open, he thought.

Glancing at the house, he was glad to see that nothing looked any different. Not that the woman could do much damage to the place. No way could she have broken into the house—not with those manicured fingernails of hers.

He'd never paid much attention to the old Beaumont place, although he'd passed it enough times since the land just beyond it was Corbett property and seeded in dry-land wheat.

Standing next to the gate, he stared at the old house, recalling someone had told him there'd been a murder there and the house had been boarded up ever since. People liked to make houses seem much more sinister than they actually were, he thought. He was surprised he hadn't heard rumors of ghosts.

But even if nothing evil lurked in that house, it made him wonder what the woman had found so interesting about the place since, from her surprised expression, she hadn't known about the murder.

Hell, maybe she'd never seen an old farmhouse before.

As if he'd ever understood women, he thought, as he climbed back on his four-wheeler, just glad she hadn't befallen some disaster. If all she'd done was leave the gate open then he figured no harm was done. By now, she would be miles away.

Still he couldn't help but wonder what had brought her to his part of Montana in the first place. She certainly was out of her realm, he thought with a chuckle as he headed back to the ranch.

The Whitehorse Sewing Circle was an institution in the county. Jolene had noticed that when the women who spent several days a week at the center making quilts were mentioned, it was with reverence. And maybe a little fear.

Clearly these women had the power in this community. Jolene got the impression that a lot of decisions were made between stitches and a lot of information dispersed over the crisp new fabric of the quilts.

It was with apprehension that she walked over to the center and pushed open the door. She'd been inside before for several get-togethers since she'd been hired as the community's teacher. This was where all the wedding receptions, birthday and anniversary parties, festivals and funeral potlucks were held.

The wooden floors were worn from years of boots dancing across them. It was easy to imagine that hearts had been won and lost in this large open room. A lot of events in these people's lives had been marked here from births to deaths and everything in between. If only these walls could talk, Jolene thought, wondering what stories *they* would tell.

As the door opened, sunlight pouring across the floor, the women all looked in her direction. They were gathered toward the back around a small quilting frame. A baby quilt, she realized, as she let the door close behind her.

"Hello," Pearl Cavanaugh said, smiling her slightly lopsided smile. Pearl had had a stroke sometime back and was still recovering, Jolene had heard. Pearl's mother had started the Whitehorse Sewing Circle years ago, according to the locals.

"I just thought I'd stop in and see what you were making," Jolene said lamely. How was she ever going to get to her true mission in coming here?

She knew she had to be careful. For fear the story might stop, she didn't want the author of the story to find out she'd been asking around about the murder.

"Please. Join us," Pearl said.

The women looked formidable, eyes keen, but their expressions were friendly enough as she pulled up a chair at the edge of the circle and watched their weathered, arthritic hands make the tiniest, most perfect stitches she'd ever seen.

"The quilt is beautiful," she said into the silence. She could feel some of the women studying her discreetly.

"Thank you," Pearl said, clearly the spokeswoman for the group. Her husband, Titus, served as a sort of mayor for Old Town Whitehorse, preaching in the center on Sundays, making sure the cemetery was maintained and overseeing the hiring of teachers as needed.

"You have all met our new teacher, Jolene Stevens," Pearl was saying. "She comes to us straight from Montana State University."

"So this is your first teaching assignment," a small white-haired, blue-eyed woman said with a nice smile. "I'm Alice White."

"I recall your birthday party," Jolene said. "Ninety-two, I believe?"

Alice chuckled. "Everyone must think I'm going to kick the bucket sometime soon since they're determined to celebrate my birthday every year now." She winked at Jolene. "What they don't know is that I'm going to live to be a hundred."

Jolene tried to relax in the smattering of laughter that followed. "This area is so interesting. I'm really enjoying the history."

"I'm sure everyone's told you about the famous outlaws who used to hide out in this part of the state at the end of the eighteenth century," a large woman with a cherubic face said. Ella Cavanaugh, a shirttail relation to Pearl and Titus, as Jolene recalled. Everyone seemed to be related in some way or another.

"Butch Cassidy and the Sundance Kid as well as Kid Curry," added another elderly member, Mabel Brown. "This part of the state was lawless back then."

"It certainly seems peaceful enough now," Jolene commented. "But I did hear something about a murder of a young widow who had a little girl, I believe?"

She could have heard a pin drop. Several jaws definitely dropped, but quickly snapped shut again.

"Nasty business that was," Ella said and glanced at Pearl.

"When was it?" Jolene asked, sensing that Pearl was about to shut down the topic.

"Twenty-four years ago this month," Alice said, shaking her head. "It isn't something any of us likes to think about."

"Was her killer ever caught?" Jolene asked and saw the answer on their faces.

"Do you sew, Jolene?" Pearl asked. "We definitely could use some young eyes and nimble fingers."

"I'm afraid not."

"We would be happy to teach you," Pearl said. "We make quilts for every baby born around here and have for years. It's a Whitehorse tradition."

"A very nice one," Jolene agreed. She had wanted to ask more about the murder, but saw that the rest of the women were now intent on their quilting. Pearl had successfully ended the discussion. "Well, I should leave you to your work," Jolene said, rising to her feet to leave.

"Well, if you ever change your mind," Pearl said, looking up at her questioningly. No doubt she wondered where Jolene had heard about a twenty-four-year-old unsolved murder—and why she would be interested.

As Jolene left, she glanced back at the women. Only one was watching her. Pearl Cavanaugh. She looked troubled.

Dulcie drove back into town, even more curious about her inheritance. She returned to the real-estate office only to find that April was officiating a game at the old high-school gym.

The old gym was built of brick and was cavernous inside. Fortunately, the game hadn't started yet. She found April in uniform on the sidelines.

"I'm sorry to bother you again," Dulcie apologized. "Who would I talk to about the history of the property?"

April thought for a moment. "Talk to Roselee at the museum. She's old as dirt, but sharp as a tack. She's our local historian."

The small museum was on the edge of town and filled with the history of this part of Montana. Roselee turned out to be a white-haired woman of indeterminable age. She smiled as Dulcie came through the door, greeting her warmly and telling her about the museum.

"Actually, I was interested in the history of a place south of here," Dulcie said. "I heard you might be able to help me."

Roselee looked pleased. "Well, I've been around here probably the longest. My father homesteaded in Old Town Whitehorse."

Even better, Dulcie thought.

"Whose place are we talking about?"

"Laura Beaumont's."

All the friendliness left her voice. "If you're one of those reporters doing another story on the murder—"

"I'm not. But I need to know. Was it Laura Beaumont who was murdered?"

Roselee pursed her lips. "If you're not a reporter, then what is your interest in all this?"

"I inherited the property."

The woman's eyes widened. She groped for the chair behind her and sat down heavily.

Dulcie felt goose bumps ripple across her flesh at the look on the woman's face. "What is it?" she demanded, frightened by the way Roselee was staring at her—as if she'd seen a ghost.

The elderly woman shook her head and struggled to her feet. "I'm sorry. I'm not feeling well." She picked up the cane leaning against the counter and started toward the back of the museum, calling to someone named Cara.

"If I come by some other time?" Dulcie said to the woman's retreating back, but Roselee didn't respond.

What in the world, she thought, as a much younger woman hurried to the counter and asked if she could help.

"Have you ever heard of a woman named Laura Beaumont?" Dulcie asked.

Cara, who was close to Dulcie's age, shook her head. "Should I have?"

"I don't know." Dulcie felt shaken from Roselee's reaction. "Do you have a historical society?"

The young woman broke into a smile. "You just met the president, Roselee." She sobered. "Wasn't she able to help you?"

"No. Is there someone else around town I could talk to?" She dropped her voice just in case Roselee was in the back, listening. "Someone older who knows everything that goes on around here, especially Old Town Whitehorse, and doesn't mind talking about it?"

Cara's eyes shone with understanding. She, too, whispered. "There is someone down south who might be able to help you. Her name is Arlene Evans. She's… talkative."

Jolene glanced at her watch as she left the Community Center. If she hurried she could make it into Whitehorse before the newspaper office closed.

Now that she knew there had been a murder, she was anxious to go through the *Milk River Examiner* newspapers from twenty-four years ago to find out everything she could about it.

Back in the schoolhouse, she went to her desk and opened the drawer where she'd put the stories. All six were there. She had yet to read the other five, so she stuffed them all into her backpack.

Turning to leave, she was startled to find a dark shape filling the schoolhouse doorway.

"Sorry, didn't mean to startle you," Ben Carpenter said as he stepped inside. He was a big man who took up a lot of space and always made Jolene feel a little uncomfortable. She suspected it was because he seldom smiled. Ben was at the far end of his forties and the father of her moody eighth-grader, Mace.

"I was just finishing up for the day. Is there something Mace needed?" The boy resembled his father, large and beefy. Jolene had only once seen his mother, Ronda, but recalled she was tiny and reserved.

"I stopped in to see how Mace is doing," Ben said. "I ask him, but he doesn't say much. You aren't having any trouble with him, are you? If you are, you just let me know and I'll see to the boy."

Jolene didn't like the threat she heard in Ben's tone. "He's doing quite well and, no, I have no trouble at all with him."

"Good," Ben said, looking uncomfortable in the small setting. "Glad to hear it. His mother has been after me to find out."

Jolene doubted that. Ronda Carpenter seemed like a woman who asked little of her husband and got even less. "Well, you can certainly reassure her. Mace is doing fine."

Ben nodded, looking as if there was more he wanted to say, but he changed his mind as he stepped toward the door. "Okay then."

Jolene was relieved when she heard his truck pull away from the front of the school. She felt a little shaken by his visit. Ben always seemed right on the edge of losing his temper. His visit had felt contrived. Was there something else he'd come by for and changed his mind?

Was it possible he was the author of the murder

story? It didn't seem likely, but then some people wrote better than they spoke.

Locking up behind her, she biked to her little house. Then, with the installments of the murder story in her backpack, she got in her car and headed toward Whitehorse.

She took the dirt road out of town. Old Town Whitehorse had been the first settlement called Whitehorse. It had been nearer the Missouri River and the Breaks. That was back when supplies came by riverboat.

Once the railroad came through, five miles to the north, the town migrated to the tracks, taking the name Whitehorse with it.

As Jolene drove, she mentally replayed the conversation with the women of the sewing circle and was even more curious why they had been so reticent to talk about the murder.

Russell found his father waiting for him when he returned to the ranch. Grayson Corbett was a large man with graying hair and an easygoing smile as well as attitude. Grayson had raised his five sons single-handedly from the time Russell was small and had done a damned good job.

Actually there was little his father couldn't do. That's why seeing him like this was so hard on Russell.

Worry lines etched Grayson's still-handsome face and seemed to make his blue eyes even paler. Russell knew what he wanted to talk about the moment he saw his father and felt his stomach turn at the thought.

"We have to make a decision," Grayson said without preamble. "We can't put it off any longer." Clearly his father had been thinking about the problem and probably little else since they'd last talked.

"You already know how I feel," Russell said. "It's a damned-fool thing and a waste of money as far as I'm concerned. What did the other ranchers and farmers have to say at the meeting?"

"Some agree with you. But there are more who are ready to try anything if there's a chance of saving their crops."

Russell shook his head, seeing that his father had already made his decision.

"If some of these farmers and ranchers don't get some moisture and soon, they're going to lose everything," Grayson said. "I don't think we have a choice."

"So what did you tell them?"

"I told them I had to talk to my son," his father said. "This is your ranch as much as mine, more actually. You get the final word."

Russell could see that his father was worried about the others, who had the most to lose. "What choice do we have?"

If he and his father didn't go along with the rest, he doubted the fifteen thousand dollars needed to hire the rainmaker could be raised. "I'll go along with whatever decision you make."

Grayson looked relieved, not that the worry lines softened. They were throwing good money away, Russell believed. But if the ranchers and farmers wanted to believe some man could make rain, then he wasn't going to try to stop them.

"Thank you," Grayson said as he laid a heavy hand

on his son's shoulders. "At least by hiring a rainmaker, they feel they're doing something to avert disaster."

The *Milk River Examiner* was the only newspaper for miles around. It was housed in a small building along the main street facing the tracks.

Andi Blake, the paper's only reporter, a friendly, attractive woman with a southern accent, helped Jolene.

"What date are you looking for?" Andi asked.

Jolene told her it would have been this month twenty-four years ago. "I'm not sure of the exact date."

"I wasn't here then, but you're welcome to look. Everything is on microfiche. You know how to use it?"

Jolene did from her college days. She thanked Andi, then sat down in the back of the office and, as the articles from May twenty-four years ago began to come up on screen, she began to roll her way through.

She slowed at the stories about the drought conditions, the fears of the ranchers and farmers, talk of hiring a rainmaker to come to town. A few papers later, there was a small article about a rainmaker coming to town and how the ranchers were raising money to pay him to make rain.

With a shudder, Jolene thought of the murder story and her feeling that the weather conditions were too much like this year.

The headline in the very next newspaper stopped her cold.

Woman Murdered in Brutal Attack
An Old Town Whitehorse resident was found murdered in her home last evening.

Heart in her throat, Jolene read further, then back-tracked, realizing that the article didn't say who found the body.

The sheriff was asking anyone with information in connection to the murder of Laura Beaumont to come forward.

If this Laura Beaumont was the same woman that the author of the murder story was writing about, she had at least one lover.

Their DNA would have been in the house. But had law enforcement even heard of DNA testing twenty-four years ago? It wouldn't have been widely used even if they had. Certainly not in Whitehorse.

Jolene continued to read, halting on the next paragraph.

The woman was found upstairs in her bed. She had been stabbed numerous times.

Had her lover found her? Or—

Sheriff's deputies are searching for the woman's missing young daughter.

Missing?

Angel Beaumont is about four or five years old with brown hair and eyes. It is unknown what she might have been wearing at the time of her disappearance.

Jolene quickly flipped to the next weekly newspaper and scanned for an article about the murder. The girl was *still* missing a week later?

Searchers are combing the creek behind the farmhouse for the girl's body, but with no sign of the daughter. If anyone knows of the child's whereabouts or has information about the killing, they are to contact the sheriff's department at once. All calls will be confidential.

A few issues later, Jolene found the news article about the daughter.

Dulcie grabbed something to eat at a small café downtown and debated if she should call this Arlene Evans woman or drive out to her place. She opted to drive out unannounced and talk to her face-to-face.

As she was leaving the café, her mind on what she would say once she reached the Evans place, Dulcie bumped into a young woman coming out of one of the local businesses.

"Pardon me," Dulcie said as the woman, slim, dark-haired and pretty, dropped the folder she'd been carrying. Papers fluttered across the sidewalk. "I'm so sorry."

Dulcie hurried to help her pick up the scattered sheets, noticing that they were copies of newspaper articles. One headline caught her eye. *Investigation Continues in Murder Case.*

"Thank you," the young woman said, clearly upset as she hurriedly stuffed the copies back into the folder and rushed to her compact car parked at the curb.

Murder? Dulcie wondered how many murders they had in a town like this and what were the chances the article could have been about Laura Beaumont. She told herself that when she had more time and information, she'd come back and have a look at some old newspaper stories.

As she climbed into her rental car, she put the incident out of her mind and drove south to the Evans place outside of Old Town Whitehorse.

Like everything else in this part of Montana, the houses were few and far between, with a lot of prairie and gullies and sagebrush to fill the spaces.

It was late and Dulcie wasn't sure what approach to use when she knocked on the farmhouse door.

"Arlene Evans?" she asked the tall, rawboned ranch-woman who answered the door. Her hair was short in a becoming style that made her appear younger than Dulcie had expected.

"Yes?"

"I'm looking for some information and I was hoping you could help me."

"I'll certainly try. Why don't you step in out of the heat? I just made some lemonade. Would you like a glass?"

Dulcie blinked in surprise at how easy it had been to get inside this woman's home. Had this been Chicago and a stranger knocking on Dulcie's door...well, she wouldn't have opened it, let alone invited her inside for lemonade.

Dulcie noticed photographs on the wall of what appeared to be Arlene's grown children. The oldest looked to be in her thirties and rather frumpy. A woman in her early twenties was posing with a baby in her arms and a young man, presumably her husband, standing next to her. They looked as if they were crazy about each other. The third photo was of a handsome young man, but there was something sneaky in his gaze.

"Is this about my rural online dating service?" Arlene asked from the kitchen. "Have a seat," she said, motioning to the adjacent living room as she came in, and handed Dulcie a tall glass of lemonade.

It looked so good she took a sip before she sat down in the immaculate house. "This is wonderful," she said, licking her lips.

Arlene Evans smiled as she sat down across from her. The house was surprisingly cool, considering how hot it was outside.

"An online rural dating service? That does sound interesting, but I'm here about something else," Dulcie said. "Let me be candid with you. I am up here looking at a piece of property." It was the truth. Just not as much truth as she'd told Roselee at the museum. She didn't want another reaction like that one.

"Property?" Arlene repeated.

"I'm trying to find out the history of the place. I understand you've lived here all your life and might be able to help me."

"Well, like I said, I'll certainly try."

Dulcie noticed the ring on Arlene's finger as she put down her lemonade glass on one of the coasters on the coffee table. "That's a beautiful ring."

"Thank you. I'm getting married in a few months. A Christmas wedding."

"Congratulations." The diamond was extraordinary, and Dulcie wondered if Arlene was marrying some rich rancher from around here.

"So where is this property?"

"It's outside Old Town Whitehorse. I believe the last occupant of the place was named Laura Beaumont?"

"Oh, my gosh." Arlene's expression told her that she'd hit paydirt.

"Did you know Laura?"

"Not personally. I knew she was widowed. She wasn't from around here and wasn't here all that long. I heard the land belonged to her husband's family and was all that she had, so she had no choice but to live here after her husband died. She leased all of the farmland. Clearly she had no interest in farming or living in the country."

Arlene seemed to catch herself. "I shouldn't be saying anything because I didn't know her. You know how rumors get started."

Apparently Arlene was trying to live down her reputation as a gossip. "Do you know where Laura moved from?" asked Dulcie.

"California. That was another reason it was odd. Californians move to Montana all the time, just not this part of Montana, if you know what I mean."

She did. California though? Not the Chicago area. So how was it that her parents knew this woman?

"Can you tell me what happened to her?"

"You don't *know?*"

Dulcie wanted to hear it from Arlene. "Please, I really need you to be honest with me. I heard she might have been murdered?"

"Well, it's not like I'm carrying tales. Everyone knows. She was murdered in one of the upstairs bedrooms twenty…oh, my gosh, twenty-four years ago this month!"

Did that explain why Roselee at the museum had gotten so upset? "Murder must be rare in this part of the country," she said, thinking of the woman she'd run into earlier with the copies of the newspaper clippings about a murder.

"It *is* rare, but this murder..." Arlene shook her head. "It was quite vicious. She was stabbed to death over a dozen times and the killer was never caught."

Dulcie was trying to take this all in when Arlene said, "What made it all the more horrific was her daughter."

"Her *daughter?*"

"She was just a little thing, four or five, as I recall. They discovered her bloody footprints in the bedroom where she'd come in. She must have seen her mother lying there and ran."

Chapter 4

Kate Corbett saw at once that her oldest stepson wasn't himself at supper. The quietest of the five brothers, Russell also was the most grounded. He was the one who'd gone into ranching with his father right out of college. Grayson couldn't manage without Russell working the ranches with him so Kate was thankful for that.

When Grayson had sold out his holdings in Texas and moved to Montana, his sons had been shocked and blamed Kate, she knew.

Later when Grayson had asked them all to come to Montana for a family meeting, the other four had come, but not happily.

Fortunately that had changed, she thought, as she glanced around the supper table at the large family she'd married into. It had grown since they'd all been in Montana.

The second oldest, Lantry Corbett, was a divorce lawyer of all things. And while he was still in Montana on the ranch, Kate didn't expect him to stay.

Shane Corbett, the next oldest, had been on medical leave from the Texas Rangers. Kate knew that if he hadn't fallen in love with a local girl, he would have returned to Texas.

Instead, he'd hired on with the Whitehorse sheriff's department as a deputy. He and Maddie Cavanaugh had recently married in a triple wedding with his twin brothers, Jud and Dalton.

Kate certainly hadn't seen that coming, but she couldn't have been happier to see the daughter she'd never known so happy. She and Maddie had some things to work out still, but they had time, Kate told herself.

Jud was the youngest, but only by a few minutes of his fraternal twin, Dalton. Jud had been working as a stuntman in Hollywood but had fallen in love with Faith Bailey while shooting a film in Montana. The two had started a stunt-riding school on her family ranch not far from Trails West Ranch.

Dalton had fallen for the owner of the local knit shop, Georgia Michaels. That one Kate *had* seen coming and she and Grayson couldn't be more pleased.

Even though the three sons had married, they and their wives were living on the ranch until their houses could be completed. It was wonderful having such a full table and Juanita, the cook Grayson had talked into making the move to Montana, loved it. She'd outdone herself each meal, wanting to make the new brides feel at home here.

Marriage, surprisingly, was what had brought Grayson's sons to Montana. For years after his wife, Rebecca, had died, leaving him with five young sons to raise, Grayson hadn't been able to go through Rebecca's things. Nor did anyone expect him to remarry.

Kate and Rebecca had been best friends, growing up together on the Trails West Ranch in Montana until Kate's father grew ill and died, the ranch lost.

Kate also lost track of her friend who'd married Grayson Corbett and moved to Texas. It wasn't until Kate found some old photographs of Rebecca that she decided to pay Grayson a visit.

There had been a spark between them from the moment they'd met. In a whirlwind romance, they'd married and Grayson had surprised her by buying Trails West Ranch for her and moving lock, stock and barrel to Montana as a wedding present.

That was when Grayson finally went through Rebecca's things and found some old letters she had written before she died.

In a letter to Grayson, Rebecca had explained that she'd written five letters, one for each son, to be read on his wedding day. Her dying wish was that her sons would marry before thirty-five—and that the bride be a Montana cowgirl.

While Kate had heard that the brothers drew straws to see who would fulfill their mother's wishes first, she'd known the brothers well enough to know they would try to get out of the pact. But amazingly, she'd seen Rebecca's wishes coming true with all but two of her sons.

Although Lantry had no intention of ever marrying, he hadn't left the ranch. What had made them stay, Kate felt, was family.

As for Russell, well, she believed he'd never met a woman who interested him enough to pursue her.

Kate and Grayson had had a few rough spots since their marriage, but everything had finally settled down.

That's why seeing this change in Russell intrigued her.

"How was your day?" she asked Russell now, curious.

He'd been smiling to himself all through the meal. Normally he ate quickly and went back to work, excusing himself by saying he had too much to do to just sit around.

Tonight, though, he seemed lost in thought, unusually distracted, especially since his father and the rest of the ranchers and farmers were worried sick about the lack of moisture this spring.

"Fine." He looked bashful suddenly. Like his father and brothers he was a very good-looking man, with Grayson's dark hair and his mother's intense blue eyes.

"Nothing *unusual* happened?" Kate probed.

Russell realized that everyone was staring at him, waiting.

"Nothing *happened*. I just almost killed some city girl today."

"What?" Kate exclaimed.

"Don't worry, she was unscathed." At everyone's urging, he told them about coming over a rise in the combine, not expecting anyone to be on the road since no one had lived in the old Beaumont place for years and the road dead-ended a mile up.

"She was sitting in her fancy rental car, right in the

middle of the road on her *cell phone,*" he said, getting the appropriate chuckles and head shakes. Kate could tell he was embarrassed, not used to being the center of attention in this family.

"Where was she from?" Grayson asked.

"Midwest, from her accent, but definitely big city. You should have seen the shoes she was wearing." Russell shook his head. "And when she tried to open the gate..."

"Open the gate to where?" Shane wanted to know.

"The old Beaumont place, isn't that what it's called?"

"Why would she go in there?" his father wanted to know.

"Beats me. It's what she wanted so I opened the gate for her. I warned her it was private property. She didn't seem to care. I think she thought I was joking when I told her about the rattlesnakes."

"Oh, I hope she was all right," Kate said, worried. "You just left her there?"

Russell laughed, seeming to relax, maybe even enjoy himself. "She wasn't like a stray dog I was going to bring home."

"Still, if she was that inept, she could get herself into trouble."

Russell nodded. "I'm sure she will, but believe me, she didn't want my help—or my advice."

No, Kate thought, she was sure the woman hadn't, but city girl or not, she'd certainly made an impression on Russell—something not easy to do.

Dulcie shuddered. Laura Beaumont's young daughter had found her body? That poor child. That poor, poor child.

The horrible dread Dulcie had felt earlier at the farmhouse swept over again.

I wasn't that little girl.

Where had that come from? Of course she wasn't Laura Beaumont's daughter. Why had she even thought such a thing?

Just because of her earlier reaction to yellow curtains and the groaning weather vane? Just because she couldn't shake the sense of dread and fear?

Or because of the obvious? She'd *inherited* the property from a woman she'd never heard of and a woman her parents had never mentioned to her.

Dulcie recalled Renada's reaction when she'd told her. She cleared her throat. "How old did you say this child was?"

"Four or five, I think. I'm not sure anyone knew for sure."

Four or five would make the child about twenty-eight or twenty-nine now. Dulcie had just turned twenty-eight.

"What was the daughter's name?"

"Angel."

Angel. Dulcie felt a surge of relief that lasted only an instant. Of course the girl's name would have been changed if she was adopted.

Dulcie couldn't believe what she was thinking, but the kids at school and even their parents used to ask her if she was adopted because her parents were so much older than the other parents.

But if she'd been adopted, her parents would have told her. They wouldn't have kept something like that from her.

Like the way they kept the property in Montana from her?

Her heart began to pound as she thought of her elderly parents, her mother's years of trying to conceive without any luck, her mother finally getting Dulcie so late in life. Miracle? Or lie?

Everything could be a lie, including her real name.

"What happened to the daughter?" Dulcie had to ask.

Arlene sighed. "She was found drowned a couple weeks after her mother's murder."

The shock reverberated through her.

"They found her under some brush in the creek. She's buried at the cemetery at Old Town Whitehorse next to her mother."

Dulcie was so stunned it took her a moment to speak. "She's *dead*?" She couldn't be Angel Beaumont. She thought of the little girl and felt horrible for the moment of relief she'd experienced.

Arlene nodded solemnly. "It was a horrible tragedy, both mother and daughter."

"Do they think the killer—"

"No," Arlene said quickly. "The sheriff said she had fallen and hit her head and drowned. The creek wasn't very deep that spring. It had been very hot and dry."

Dulcie felt shaken. The mother murdered, the daughter killed in a freak accident. It still didn't explain how Dulcie had inherited the property. Or why she'd reacted the way she had when she'd seen the yellow curtains in that second-floor window and heard the tortured sound of the weather vane.

She downed the cold drink in her hand, suddenly

exhausted. "Thank you for the lemonade. It was delicious."

"So will you buy the property?" Arlene asked as Dulcie rose to leave.

She could see that the woman was curious about Dulcie's real reason for asking about Laura Beaumont and her daughter. Maybe even more curious why she'd want the property.

"I hope I haven't dissuaded you."

"Not at all," Dulcie said. "I'm going to sleep on it. I couldn't make any kind of a decision as tired as I am."

She left Arlene and drove back to Whitehorse. It had gotten dark, the sky deepening from dove gray to an inky black devoid of moon or stars, as if the heat had melted them. She tried not to think as she let the car's air-conditioning blow on her, but her mind raced anyway.

She *wasn't* Angel Beaumont. But it gave her no peace. Laura murdered, her daughter, Angel, drowned in the creek, the property left to Dulcie—a little girl herself at the time. Something was wrong with all this, she could feel it.

As she passed through town, the temperature sign on the bank read eighty-four degrees. It was going to be another miserably hot night.

She chose the first motel she came to on the edge of town. Once inside her room, she showered, turned up the air conditioner and lay down on the bed.

She thought about calling Renada, but didn't feel up to it even though there was a message from her friend. Tomorrow, when she didn't feel so exhausted, so depressed. If she called her now, Renada would hear

how discouraged she was and insist on coming out to
Montana. Anyway, it was too late to call with the time
difference between here and Chicago.

Dulcie expected to fall into a deep sleep almost instantly, as tired as she was. But when she closed her
eyes, she saw the yellow curtains move in the upstairs
bedroom and heard the groan of the weather vane on
the barn in the hot, dry wind.

All she could think about was that little girl. That
poor little girl.

Jolene woke to darkness and sat up, startled, to find
she'd fallen asleep in her living-room chair.

The pages from the short stories fluttered to the
floor at her feet as she reached for the lamp next to her
chair and checked the time.

Well after midnight. She must have been more tired
than she'd thought. She blamed the relentless heat,
which had zapped her energy and left her feeling like
a wrung-out dishrag.

Even this late, the air in the small house was hot
and close. She felt clammy and yearned for a breath
of cool air as she turned up the fan in the window. All
it did was blow in warm air, but even warm air was
better than nothing.

As she leaned down to retrieve the stories, she
caught sight of the murder story.

Her fingers slowed as she reached for it, remembering with a start what she'd learned at the newspaper.
Widow Laura Beaumont had been murdered twenty-
four years ago and she, like the woman in the supposedly fictional murder story, had a young daughter.

A daughter who'd been found drowned in the creek.

The short story had to be about the same woman and her child, didn't it?

She put the critiqued story installments into her backpack, although she wouldn't be returning them until the entire story had been finished, turned in and graded.

She didn't want to stifle their creativity with her comments on the earlier assignments, although her comments were very complimentary of their endeavors. The idea was to encourage her students to write freely. She understood the fear some people had about putting words to paper.

As she zipped up the backpack, she looked down at the murder story on the table where she'd left it. She would hide it in the house for now. She didn't want to take the chance that someone would find it in the schoolhouse and read it.

The story was becoming more and more like *her* dark secret and that should have made her even more uneasy than it did, she thought.

As she headed to bed, Jolene realized that the author of the murder story had gotten to her. Not only couldn't she wait for the next part, but she now felt personally involved in solving the mystery.

Reading Monday's and Tuesday's assignments in order, she had looked for some clue as to the writer. Was the writer just someone with an active imagination? Or a local gossip who thought she knew what had happened that summer, if indeed the story was about Laura Beaumont and her daughter, Angel?

There was nothing in the story that would make

Jolene believe it had been written by the killer, she assured herself.

So why did the details in the story make her so nervous? Because if she was right, the author had known this woman. Had watched the murdered woman closely. Just as the writer might be watching right now to see Jolene's reaction, she realized with a chill as she snapped off the light.

Dulcie woke Wednesday morning after sleeping later than she had in years. It surprised her given how much trouble she'd had getting to sleep last night.

She'd told Arlene Evans the truth. She'd had to sleep on it before making a decision as to what to do about the property.

Common sense told her to just list the property with the Realtor she'd met and return to Chicago and start seriously looking for her next business venture.

But even as she thought it, Dulcie knew she couldn't leave without going into that house. She had to know if she'd been there before.

She groaned at the thought. She would need to buy appropriate clothing for exploring, along with gloves, a flashlight and tools to get into the house. She sat down and made a list before heading to the local clothing and hardware stores.

"You say you'll be removing boards?" Kayla at the hardware store inquired. "You'll want a hammer and pry bar for sure, but possibly a crowbar or even a battery-operated screwdriver. Are these large boards, nailed or screwed?"

By the time Dulcie left the hardware store, she felt

equipped for an exploration to Antarctica. Kayla had suggested canvas pants and a jacket as well as work boots, and Dulcie thanked her for all her help.

Back at the motel, she changed and, putting all her equipment in the trunk, drove south. The moment the farmhouse came into view, she felt that now-familiar sense of dread and fear wash over her.

She almost changed her mind and turned around. She was even more persuaded against staying when she saw that someone had closed the damned gate.

Jolene watched as Thad Brooks, one of her fifth-grade boys, collected the writing assignments. She'd felt antsy all morning, waiting for the next installment of the murder story, afraid this would be the day that the story stopped as mysteriously as it had begun.

She could hear the dried grasses outside the open window rustling in the hot, dry wind and fanned herself as the student placed the stack of papers on the edge of her desk.

"How are you all doing on your stories?" she asked and listened to a variety of complaints from being stuck to being bored.

"At this point in your stories, I want you to sit down and write down ten things that could happen next," she told the class. "When you get stuck and can't think of anything else to write about your character, it helps if you do what is called brainstorming. Let your imagination run as you write down as many things as you can think of that could happen."

"What if you can't think of anything?" whined Luke Raines, her other fifth-grader.

"Then you have to think harder. Concentrate. Think about your characters. Think about the weather. Think about where you are in the story. The middle parts are the hardest because you have to keep the story going. It helps if something exciting happens that changes the direction of your story. What is the worse thing that could happen to your characters? What is your hero or heroine most afraid of? For instance, what if there was a huge storm? What if your character was caught in it? What if someone new came to town? What if some old enemy came to town? What if your character found out a secret?"

Jolene saw Mace Carpenter writing like crazy. Amy Brooks was also writing. Thad and Luke were mugging faces at each other. Codi Fox was staring at the ceiling, but Jolene could see her mind working.

"I need the next segment of your stories tomorrow, so keep up the momentum."

"Do we really have to write something every night this week?" Thad asked.

"Yes—and this weekend you will write the ending, to be turned in on Monday for a total of six parts of the story."

Thad and Luke groaned.

"That's why you have to brainstorm more ideas," Jolene said. "Open your mind to new possibilities. What kind of trouble can your character get into? Today is only Thursday. You have another night. Now make a list. I want at least ten things that could happen before you leave today."

She waited until each student had at least ten things written down before she dismissed the students for recess. She hadn't planned to read any of the stories until later at home. But she had to see if the murder story was in the stack.

Hurriedly she thumbed through them, trying to keep an eye on the door just in case one of the parents should stop by. Ben Carpenter's visit yesterday had spooked her. That and realizing that the author of the story was probably *now* keeping an eye on her just as he had Laura Beaumont, twenty-four years ago.

She was trying to imagine Ben authoring the story when, with a start, she realized the murder-story installment wasn't in the stack.

Frantically, she leafed through the stack again, this time more slowly. With relief she found it sandwiched between sixth-grader Codi Fox's and eighth-grader Mace Carpenter's.

Her heart sped up again. Had Mace turned this in with his? Then she remembered that Luke Raines had been gathering the assignments and putting some on the top of the stack and others on the bottom.

She thought about picking up the assignments herself tomorrow, but that might alert whichever student was bringing the extra copy. No, she didn't want to call attention by changing things. The chosen student enjoyed being the one who got to collect the papers each day. Tomorrow though, she would pay more attention when the student was collecting the stories.

She pulled out the murder story, glancing toward the door before she read the installment quickly, guiltily.

Dusk had settled over the land, but the heat was relentless as her lover sneaked away from the old farmhouse, believing she loved him and only him.

She stood at the window and watched him go, but he hadn't gone far down the road before a restlessness overtook her again.

She pulled the lightweight yellow robe around her. Her favorite color, yellow. She liked it because she said it made her feel good.

Colors altered her moods, she said. Green calmed her. Blue made her nostalgic. Red, well, red made her amorous. As if she needed any encouragement.

He hadn't been gone long, the air stifling, heat radiating up from the baked, dry earth, before she poured herself a bath.

She slipped down into the big claw-footed tub full of cool water and closed her eyes. Her fingers teased the water around her body as she daydreamed of another life far away from this dusty, hot farmhouse.

In the next room, her daughter played quietly, ignoring the sound of the vehicle that pulled into the yard, the heavy footfalls on the stairs, the creak of the bathroom door as it opened and closed.

As voices rose from an argument behind the bathroom door, the little girl covered her ears and sang a song her mommy had taught her until she heard the bathroom door slam open and the angry footfalls on the stairs again, and finally the sound of her mother crying softly across the hall.

Russell Corbett couldn't believe his eyes. The city girl's rental car was parked in front of the old Beaumont place again.

But that wasn't what had him throwing on the brakes and skidding to a dust-boiling stop.

The woman had a crowbar in her gloved hands and appeared to be trying to remove the boards barring the front door.

"What the hell do you think you're doing?" he demanded as he strode past the gate lying oddly in the dead grass. "Tell me you didn't cut the barbed wire on that gate to get in here."

She turned slowly to give him a droll look. "Okay."

He snatched his gray Stetson from his head and smacked it against his jean-clad thigh in irritation. "You can't go around cutting people's gates and vandalizing their property, even if it is abandoned."

She cocked her head as if seeing him for the first time. He was starting to lose his temper when she said calmly, "This *is* my property."

"What?" He thought he had to have heard her wrong.

Smiling, she nodded, seeming to enjoy his surprise and loss of words.

"You *bought* this place?" he asked, his tone making it clear nothing could make him believe she wanted to live here.

Her hands went to her hips, the crowbar hooked between the fingers of her right hand. "I'm sorry, I missed the part where it was your business."

The woman had some mouth on her, he thought, his gaze going to her bow-shaped, full pink lips. His own lips twitched in response to the mad detour his mind took as it tried to imagine what it would be like to kiss that mouth of hers.

He held up his hands in surrender. "Don't let me keep you then." He started to turn away, planning to stalk back to his four-wheeler, cursing all the way under his breath.

"Wait. I'm sorry. I'm just hot and frustrated." She sighed. "I can't seem to get this last board to come loose. Since you're here, would you mind?"

He pulled up short, her soft, seductive tone like a lasso dragging him back. He told himself to keep walking. If he turned around he'd regret it. This woman was trouble in a pair of dirt-smudged canvas pants.

Turning slowly, he eyed her from under the brim of his hat the way he would eye a rattler about to strike. He didn't trust this change of tune on her part. She couldn't get the last board so now she was going to turn on the feminine charms, thinking they would work on him?

"I wouldn't want to make it my *business*."

She transformed that magnificent mouth of hers into a lazy grin. One hand was on her shapely hips now, the other beckoning him with the crowbar. "I *said* I was sorry."

He felt himself weaken in spite of every instinct to keep his distance from this one. But he'd been born and raised in Texas, where a man came to the aid of a lady. Although it was debatable this woman was a lady.

"I really would appreciate it," she said in that same come-hither tone. "This last board just won't budge."

Russell let out a deep sigh, mentally kicking himself in the behind, as he stepped to her, took the crowbar from her without a word and pried off the board, the nails screeching as they gave way.

He tossed the board to the side where she'd thrown the others and handed her back the crowbar. The plan was to tip his hat like the gentleman he was and get the hell out of there without looking back.

"Dulcie Hughes," she said, tugging off her glove and holding out one perfectly manicured hand.

He slowly wiped his hand on his jeans and extended it grudgingly, telling himself he wasn't going to let her rope him into anything else. For all he knew the woman could be lying about owning this place and he'd just helped her commit a crime.

Her hand was cool and smooth as porcelain as it disappeared into his larger, calloused one. "Russell Corbett," he said, his voice sounding as rough as his hand.

Her molasses-brown-eyed gaze met his. Humor seemed to jitterbug in all that warm brown. "Thank you, Russell Corbett. I do apologize for earlier. I hate it when I can't handle something myself. It makes me testy."

He nodded, familiar with that feeling.

"So what is a Southern boy like yourself doing out here in Montana?" she said, smiling.

He told himself he had work to do and no time for standing around in this heat chitchatting, but he'd pay hell before being rude to a woman.

"I came up from Texas to work the Trails West Ranch." He made a motion with his head to the west, wondering why he hadn't told her he was co-owner of the family ranch. Because it was none of her *business*.

"I take it the ranch is down the road apiece?" she asked with a grin. "Everything up here seems to be down the road apiece."

He couldn't tell if she was having fun at his expense or not. Whatever she was doing, she seemed to be enjoying herself and he kind of liked her when she wasn't on her high horse.

She wiped a hand across her forehead, skin glistening in the heat, and left a smudge of dirt just above one finely sculpted eyebrow. It made her look a little less in control, something he thought probably rare.

"Mind if I ask what you're planning to do here?" He gestured toward the house.

"Just going to take a look around, then put the place up for sale. I inherited it sight unseen and was just curious."

"Inherited it, huh. Is your family from around here?"

"No. Would you be interested in buying the property?"

He noticed the way she had quickly changed the subject. "Might be interested. So you aren't related to the Beaumonts?"

"Did you know the woman who lived here? The one who was murdered?"

"Before my time." Russell was getting tired of her not answering his questions, but then again, who was he to ask? He started to leave, but couldn't help himself. "If you're determined to go in there, you should know the floors might be rotted through, rattlers probably have nested inside, not to mention bats and mice and every other rodent known to man."

She cocked her head at him. "You like scaring me, don't you?"

"Just trying to give you some friendly advice, which is clear you aren't going to heed." He took a step back, telling himself that no matter what she said or did, he was out of there. She wasn't his responsibility.

* * *

"Thanks for the advice," Dulcie said to his retreating backside. Not a bad backside. For the first time, she understood the expression "cowboy swagger."

The man *was* blessed. Not only did he have the looks, he came fully equipped with broad, strong shoulders, slim hips and long legs. And damn but didn't he look good in his Western attire.

She couldn't help grinning as she watched him kick a small stone with the toe of his boot, sending it flying into the sizzling heat. Her grin broadened as she listened to him mutter under his breath just as he had last time.

"Stop by anytime," she called after him and smiled as she watched him swing a leg over his four-wheeler, crank up the engine and take off without a backward glance, the tires throwing gravel.

An errant thought idled past. She hoped she got to see Russell Corbett on a horse before she left town. The man was classic cowboy. What the devil was he doing on a four-wheeler? She shook her head, disappointed to have her illusions about the West and real cowboys crushed.

This time tomorrow she would be flying back to Chicago. Russell Corbett would be just a memory, the only pleasant one she feared she would take from Montana.

With growing dread, Dulcie turned back toward the house and the job ahead of her. Russell Corbett was wrong. It wasn't morbid curiosity that drove her. She just hoped he was wrong as well about the rotten floorboards and the critters nesting inside.

Among the documents her parents' lawyer had given her she'd found a key. She'd assumed it was for the front door. Taking it from the pocket of her new canvas pants, she tried it in the lock. The key turned as if the lock had been opened only yesterday—not over twenty-four years ago.

A still, breathless silence had settled in along with the heat. Dulcie listened for a moment to the steady, quickened beat of her heart, then grasping the knob, she slowly turned it and felt the door begin to swing in.

Chapter 5

"What do you know about the old Beaumont place?" Russell asked his father when Grayson met up with him later.

Grayson seemed distracted for a moment as he pulled his gaze away from the cloudless sky. "Not much. Why do you ask?"

"I just met the owner. At least she claims she's the owner. She says she might be putting the place up for sale."

Grayson studied his son. "*She?* This isn't the city girl you were telling us about at supper, is it?"

"One and the same." He shook his head. "She's over there now exploring that old house."

Grayson looked worried. "By herself? Son, do you think that's wise?"

Russell snorted. "I think it's crazier than hell. But the woman doesn't take advice well."

His father laughed. "What woman does? Maybe it's

the way you gave it though. If she's serious about selling that property, I definitely think we should make an offer. That land connects up with ours and has laid fallow all these years. I think we could get a pretty good wheat crop out of it, not to mention the property's got water on it. Why don't you see what she wants for the place," Grayson said, rubbing his jaw.

Russell studied his father for a moment in the dim light of the barn. "You talk to the other ranchers and farmers?"

Grayson nodded. "We all kept telling ourselves that we're bound to get some moisture, but every day it seems to be hotter and drier. If we don't get some rain soon..."

Hiring a rainmaker was a desperate measure and they both knew it. Russell remembered so-called rainmakers being run out of town in Texas after they failed to make it rain and talk had turned violent.

"They've suggested a rainmaker who's been here before," Grayson said, reaching into his pocket to pull out a slip of paper. "I got his name and number."

"I'll make the call," Russell said and saw his father's relief as he handed over the information.

One inch of rain was worth a million dollars in this part of the country. Fifteen thousand to make it rain was cheap. If this Finnegan Amherst could make it rain, then he would be worth every penny.

"And go check on that woman," Grayson said as he started to leave. "Make her an offer she can't refuse," he added with a wink.

Dulcie pushed the door of the old house all the way open and was hit with a blast of stale, putrid air. She recoiled, questioning her sanity. Did she really have to go into this house? What more could she hope to learn about the former owner and her daughter in a house that had been empty for the past twenty-four years?

She didn't know, but she had to find out what the connection was between her and Laura Beaumont. If it was in this house, then she had to look. This was *her* house now, she reminded herself.

Screwing up her courage, she took a tentative step inside. Instantly she was as fascinated as she'd been when she'd looked in the window the day before. The house seemed to have been frozen in time. Nothing out of place. Obviously forensics hadn't torn the house apart like they would have nowadays at a crime scene.

She tried the floorboards, testing them with her weight as she recalled what Russell Corbett had said and mugged a face at the thought. The man was infuriating, but he had gotten her into the house, and for that she would forgive him his oh-so-male arrogance.

The dusty, worn wooden floor creaked and groaned a little, but seemed solid enough as Dulcie entered the room. She left the front door open for the air. Even hot air from outside was better than nothing. It also let in light so she could see better. Both good reasons, although the truth was she wanted the door wide open in case she needed to make a run for it.

The living room was just as it had appeared through the window. She moved slowly through the room, trying to imagine the woman who'd lived here sitting in that chair with the glass and book next to it on the table.

How was it possible that she had been left this property and knew nothing about Laura Beaumont or her daughter? Her parents must have befriended the woman, helped her out maybe through some organization.

As kind and generous as her parents had been, Dulcie was convinced that had to be it. At some point, her parents must have come up here after the murder and brought four-year-old Dulcie with them. That would explain these odd almost-memories she kept feeling.

Laura, wanting to repay the Hugheses, had in turn left all she had in the world to them. It was a great scenario except for one thing. Laura Beaumont hadn't left her worldly possessions to Dulcie's parents. She'd left this house and land to Dulcie.

That, she reminded herself, was what worried her. No one left property to a four-year-old unless it was their own child.

At the kitchen door, she stopped, shocked by what she saw. Dishes still on the table. A bowl and a spoon in front of one chair, an overturned cereal box and what appeared to be signs of those critters Russell had told her about.

In front of the other chair was a small plate with a knife next to it and a coffee cup. Dulcie could imagine two shadowy figures sitting there, the daughter having cereal, the mother having toast and coffee. Neither having a clue how horribly this day would end.

She blinked and drew back, knowing she was putting off going upstairs. She'd been afraid that the house would feel familiar, that she would remember being inside here.

But as she stood there, she realized she felt nothing. She hadn't been *inside* this house. At least she couldn't recall this part of the house.

Retracing her footsteps, she moved to the bottom of the stairs and looked up. With the shutters closed up there, it was much darker at the top of the stairs.

Dulcie hesitated. She'd been called bold and daring because of her business ventures. But when it came to this sort of thing, she was far from fearless. She had a yellow streak a mile wide.

Unfortunately, she also possessed a stubborn streak that, while it had seen her through some tough times, right now it meant she wasn't leaving here until she went upstairs. So she might as well get it over with.

She clutched the banister, then quickly let go, grimacing as she brushed the cobwebs from her hand onto her canvas pants. Testing each stair with a tentative step, she climbed upward into the dim darkness.

A few of the locals had stopped by right after Jolene was hired to finish out the school term for the teacher who'd run off and gotten married. The locals had brought homemade bread, cinnamon rolls and homemade canned goods from their root cellars.

She'd felt welcomed by their visits and their gifts.

But now as she saw Midge Atkinson drive up in front of her house, Jolene wanted to hide and pretend she wasn't home.

Unfortunately, she feared Midge had seen her pedal down the road from the school only moments before.

From the window, Jolene watched Midge climb out of her SUV and glance around as if looking for a charging dog. Or looking to see if anyone was watching her. She carried a wicker basket to Jolene's front door and knocked.

Making sure that the murder story was carefully hidden in a bottom drawer and the house was neat enough for visitors, Jolene answered the door.

"Hello," she greeted her guest warmly. She'd been warned about Midge Atkinson.

Midge's husband, John, owned half the businesses in town and Midge spent the money from them, was the way Jolene had heard it. "No one crosses the Atkinsons," one woman had whispered conspiratorially to her. "Midge likes to wield her power. I don't think I have to tell you who wears the pants in that family."

As a matter of fact, Midge was wearing pants today, a pair of purple ones with a matching large, garish print blouse. "I brought you a little something," she said, slipping past Jolene and into the house without waiting to be asked.

As Jolene closed the door, she noticed Midge inspecting the place. Her visitor's gaze fell on the table where Jolene had left the students' short stories she still had to read.

"Here, let me take that," Jolene said of the basket Midge was holding. She set it down on the table and quickly put the stories into her backpack, zipping it closed. "Please sit down. What can I get you to drink?"

"I can't stay long," Midge said as she took a seat near the fan in the window. "Something cool to drink would be nice though."

"I have sun tea. Do you take sugar or lemon?"

"Lemon."

Jolene went into the small kitchen and opened the refrigerator. As she took out the tea and a lemon, she heard the chair Midge had been sitting in squeak and turned in time to see Midge slip across the room to the table.

She filled two glasses and put a slice of lemon on the side of each before she returned to the living room. Midge was sitting at the table.

"That fan is too noisy," Midge complained. "This is fine here." She took the glass of tea and Jolene joined her at the table, trying not to look again in the direction of her now-open backpack.

She had zipped it closed, hadn't she? But why would Midge open it? Only one person would know about the murder story—the author. And of course Jolene. And the student who was bringing it to her. And maybe the friend of the author.

Jolene groaned inwardly at the thought of how many people might know about the story.

"Aren't you curious about what I brought you?" Midge asked, sounding perturbed. Perturbed because Jolene hadn't thanked her yet? Or because she hadn't found what she'd been looking for in Jolene's backpack?

Pulling the basket toward her, she saw that it was filled with store-bought muffins. In this part of Montana, bringing store-bought anything was almost an insult.

"How thoughtful. Thank you."

Midge gave a slight shrug. "I hadn't welcomed you since you were hired. How are things going?"

"Fine. No problems."

Midge took a drink of her tea, winced and said, "It's bitter. I think you left it out in the sun too long.

I've had enough anyway." She shoved the nearly full glass away and rose.

Jolene got up to see her out, but Midge didn't make it to the door before she turned, hands clasped in front of her and said, "I heard you were asking questions about some unpleasant business from years back." She tsked. "You really don't want to concern yourself with that sort of thing. We like our teachers to concentrate on making a pleasant, educational environment for our students. I would suggest you restrict any research projects to the part of our history for which we have pride, such as our early homesteaders."

Jolene was so shocked she couldn't reply at first and then she had to bite her tongue to keep from telling Midge Atkinson what she thought of her suggestion.

Midge's quick smile was more a grimace as she turned abruptly toward the door. "Oh, and I would like my basket back when you've finished with the muffins."

"Of course." As the irritating woman drove away, Jolene closed the door and leaned against it, wondering who in the Whitehorse Sewing Circle had ratted her out.

Dulcie stopped at the top of the stairs and took a shallow breath. The air up here on the second floor of the farmhouse seemed even more foul and stagnant than the floor below. She looked down the hallway toward the front of the house. Four doors stood partially open.

Behind the one closest to her, she saw a broom closet with an ancient vacuum leaning against one wall and a ratty broom.

Stepping lightly, she edged toward the next door.

The room was nearly empty except for an old treadle sewing machine sitting against one wall.

Dulcie moved to the next door and peered in. The little girl's room. Someone had painted a blue-and-white ceiling resembling sky and clouds. On the walls around the bed were painted half a dozen angels, complete with wings and cherubic sweet faces. Had the mother painted these?

As Dulcie stepped into the room, she saw that the artist had signed his or her name in the bottom of one corner of the room. M. Atkinson.

The name meant nothing to her. She glanced again at the paintings. A roomful of angels for a little girl named Angel. She tried to picture the little girl who'd lived here. Tomboy or doll-playing princess?

Nothing about the room felt familiar. With a sigh of relief, Dulcie told herself she'd never seen it before. If she'd come to Whitehorse with her parents for whatever reason, then she'd stayed outside this house—outside where she could see the yellow curtains in the second-floor bedroom window and hear the weather vane on the barn.

A small, once-white dresser stood against one wall. She pulled out a drawer. Empty. She tried another. Also empty. How strange that everything else in this house seemed to be just as it had been left twenty-four years ago, except that Angel's clothes were missing. Why take a dead child's clothing?

Russell called the number his father had given him, surprised when a girl answered the phone. For a moment, he thought he'd dialed the wrong number.

"Is there a Finnegan Amherst there?"

"My grandfather. Just a moment." The phone dropped but a few moments later a raspy, deep-throated voice asked who was calling.

"Russell Corbett from the Trails West Ranch outside of Whitehorse, Montana."

He heard a soft, dry chuckle. "I wondered when you'd be calling."

"Then you must know what I'm calling about," Russell said, hoping his father and the other ranchers and farmers weren't about to throw their money down a rat hole. The rainmaker definitely *sounded* like someone's grandfather, old grandfather.

"You need a rainmaker," Finnegan Amherst said.

"We need *rain,*" Russell corrected.

Again the man chuckled.

"So are you interested?"

The rainmaker sighed. "Let me think about it. If I decide to come up, I'll be there tomorrow. Otherwise I'll call."

With a curse Russell realized that the man had hung up.

"Might as well go waste some more time," he said to himself as he headed for his pickup, sure Dulcie Hughes would drive a hard bargain for her land.

Directly across the hall from Angel Beaumont's room was the bathroom. Dulcie could make out a large old claw-footed tub against the back wall.

She moved cautiously toward the front bedroom. Through the partially open door, she could see part of the faded yellow curtains billowing in the hot air stealing in through a broken pane.

A chair was positioned by the window, a book lying on the floor, open and facedown and like everything else in the house, covered with dust.

Dulcie hesitated at the threshold to the room. She touched the door, pushing it all the way open. Nothing came scampering out, but she heard the sound of tiny feet overhead and thought of those critters Russell had warned her about.

When she stepped in, she saw the wallpaper and felt a jolt. She *knew* this pattern of old-fashioned tiny yellow flowers. It was so familiar that her knees threatened to buckle under her as she tried to fight the crush of dread mixed with terror.

She *had* been in this room. The room where Laura Beaumont was murdered. Her parents wouldn't have brought her up here. So how was it possible?

Feeling sick, she gripped the doorjamb for a moment until the light-headedness passed.

Dulcie had made a point of not focusing on the high double bed with its antique iron frame. But suddenly she couldn't stop her gaze from going to the soiled mattress. Cringing, she looked away to see a large chest of drawers against the wall.

As if sleepwalking, she crossed the room and opened the top drawer to find it filled with women's undergarments. The second drawer had more of the same. The third and fourth held shirts and blouses, jeans and slacks.

Someone had taken the child's clothes, but left the mother's?

She opened the closet. Dust-coated dresses hung limp from metal hangers. Shoes were scattered across the closet floor. A closet full of high heels and pretty dresses.

Yellow must have been her favorite color. Just as it was Dulcie's. She closed the closet door, ready to flee as she wished on a ragged breath that she'd never come here.

With a start, she caught movement on the other side of the room. A scream rose in her throat but she quickly tamped it down as she realized what she'd seen. Her own reflection in a cloudy mirror over a vanity on the opposite wall.

The top of the vanity was cluttered with a brush, a mirror, an assortment of bottles and jars, all coated with thick dust.

Dulcie suddenly needed fresh air, even brutally hot air. She started to close the closet door, bumping into the dresser. Something slithered down the wall to the floor.

She stepped back, ready to scream, but stopped when she saw what had fallen. Squatting, she gingerly picked up what appeared to be a snapshot that had fallen from behind the dresser and landed face-down on the floor.

She turned it over and stared into the face of a little girl. A face so like her own, it could have been her twin. Or Dulcie herself.

Chapter 6

From the floor below came a thunk as if something had been knocked over. Startled, Dulcie stuffed the photo in her pocket and looked around for anything she could use to defend herself.

She was thinking about critters when she tiptoed down the hallway toward the top of the stairs. She grabbed the old broom from the small closet and positioned herself on one side of the stairs, ready for anything that came racing up.

A stair creaked under the weight of a heavy boot heel. It must be a pretty large critter, she thought. Russell Corbett? Had he come back to see if she needed protecting? Or maybe to give her more advice?

As the footfalls neared, she clutched the broom in both hands, planning to use it like a bat if necessary. But even as she stepped to the top of the stairs, armed and ready, she was hoping to see Russell Corbett's handsome face looking up at her.

No such luck. This man was barrel big, his face round and beefy, his look murderous. She swallowed back the scream that rose in her throat, tightening her grip on the broom handle, ready to start swinging.

"What the hell do you think you're doing?" the man demanded, stopping halfway up the stairs. His face was enflamed with anger. "You have no business being in this house. You're trespassing and you're damned lucky I haven't called the sheriff."

"You come one step closer and I won't be responsible for what I do with this broom."

They both started at the sound of footfalls behind the man.

"Ben? What are you doing here?" Russell asked from the bottom of the stairs as he looked from the big, angry man to Dulcie and her broom.

"I was just asking this trespasser the same thing," the man said as he shot Dulcie a withering look. "I'm about to take that broom away from her."

"I'd reconsider that if I were you, since you're threatening the owner of this place and could end up in jail yourself," Russell informed him.

Dulcie loosened her grip on the broom, but didn't put it down as the man retreated back down the stairs. She followed after a moment to find both men standing in the living room, looking at her with anything but pleasure.

"He says you own the place?" demanded the man Russell had called Ben. "You have any proof of that?"

"I do."

It took a few moments before the man realized she had no intention of showing it to him.

"And you are…?" she asked.

"Ben Carpenter. I was just driving by."

Russell raised a brow. She could tell he didn't like the man.

Ben scowled at Dulcie. "You thinking of moving in here?"

The question was so ludicrous even Russell seemed to have a hard time keeping a straight face.

"I'm not sure of my plans," she said.

Ben shook his head. "Give it some thought. Your kind don't last long here."

Her *kind?*

Russell tensed, all cordiality gone. "I think you've said quite enough, Ben."

"Yeah?" He looked like he might argue, even throw a few punches, but apparently changed his mind. "I guess I'll just leave the two of you to whatever it is you're doing," he said with a nasty sneer before stomping out the door, angling toward an old pickup parked on the road.

"You just make friends wherever you go," Russell said, shoving back his hat to grin at her.

"It's a knack," she agreed. "Who *is* he?"

"One of your neighbors. He manages a ranch a few miles down the road in the other direction."

"So he wasn't just driving by."

"Nope," Russell said, rubbing his jaw thoughtfully as he looked out the door after Ben.

As he turned to her again, she said with a grin, "So he probably wasn't just driving past like *you* were."

He smiled and glanced around. "You find what you were looking for?"

"Who said I was looking for anything?"

He chuckled at that. "Have you had dinner, what they call supper up here?"

She shook her head. "The kitchen's a mess," she joked.

"I know a place that cooks up a pretty good steak in town. Unless, of course, you're one of those *vegetarians*."

"Do I look like a woman who can't handle her beef?"

"No siree, you look like a woman who can handle most anything. But what exactly *were* you planning to do with that broom?"

Jolene was surprised and delighted when Tinker Horton called to ask her out. She hadn't expected him back before the weekend.

"I know this is late notice, but I'm in town and I really was hoping you'd be up to having supper with me."

The thought brightened her day instantly. It had been a terrible day and supper out was always a treat.

"I would love to," she said with a laugh as she returned the unread short stories to her backpack again. At the rate things were going she wasn't going to get them read and graded until later tonight.

"Do you mind if we meet in town? I've done all the driving I can stand for one day. I'll make it up to you by taking you to Northern Lights."

"You're on. What time?"

They agreed on a time to meet and Jolene headed for the shower to get ready.

She'd met Thomas "Tinker" Horton her first week in Old Town Whitehorse. They'd run into each other at the Whitehorse Community Center when he'd asked her to dance. Tinker traveled from rodeo to rodeo as a bull rider. She got the feeling he didn't make much money, but that he loved the notoriety since he was famous in this part of the state.

It seemed that he made it back home to Whitehorse more often since they'd met, she thought with a smile.

Tinker was four years older, thirty-three, but he didn't act it. Nor did she see him as a potential boyfriend. They got along fine and seemed to enjoy each other's company. But when he was gone, she didn't miss him and suspected he felt the same way.

Tonight, though, she decided to wear her best dress. It was too fancy for even the Northern Lights, but she was so happy to be getting away from everything for the night, she was going all out.

The dress was the color of autumn leaves. It brought out the reddish highlights in her dark hair. She checked herself in the mirror, pleased. Nothing could ruin this night.

As Jolene went out the door, she grabbed the muffins Midge had brought her. Tinker ate anything when he was on the road. He'd appreciate the muffins and now she'd be able to take Midge's basket back to her. This was working out well.

As she walked toward her car, she noticed that there was something stuck under the windshield wiper on the driver's side.

She plucked a small folded sheet of white paper from beneath her wiper. There was just enough light from the overhead farm light to read the crudely written note.

Watch your step.

"You clean up nice," Russell said when he picked Dulcie up at her motel.

She smiled. "I could say the same of you." And just when she thought he couldn't look more handsome. He wore a pale gray Stetson, a red-checked Western shirt, jeans and boots. While he was dressed much like the first time she'd seen him, there was definitely something different about him tonight.

He looked shy and ill at ease. He didn't date much, she thought, and she found that charming. So what had made him ask *her* out, she wondered, amused.

He opened the passenger-side door of his pickup for her, so chivalrous, and went around to slide behind the wheel. She felt as if she was going to her first prom. It gave her an odd, almost old-fashioned feeling.

Country music came on the radio as he started the truck. She was disappointed when he reached over and turned it off.

Whitehorse was hopping tonight and the Northern Lights restaurant was no exception. Dulcie counted a couple dozen pickups parked along the main street. She could hear more country music coming from one of the bars down the street as she and Russell entered the busy restaurant.

It surprised her a little to realize he'd reserved a

table for them. But then Russell Corbett didn't seem
like a man who left much to chance.

"So want to tell me what this is really about?" she
asked once they were seated and the waitress had taken
their orders for two large T-bone steaks, medium rare.

"I wanted a steak?" he said.

She smiled and shook her head.

"I wanted to get to know you better?"

That made her chuckle.

"What if I told you it was a spur-of-the-moment invitation that I regretted the minute I asked?"

She laughed. "That's more like it."

He seemed to relax. "I *am* curious about you."

"How so?"

"I can't figure you out. You're obviously a city girl
and yet you've got grit. I couldn't believe it when I saw
you with that crowbar. Not many women would have
gone into that house."

"Confession? I didn't want to. I almost chickened
out."

"Then why put yourself through it? You can see by
looking at that house that it's not worth anything. Any
value is in the land."

"I wasn't *appraising* the place," she said, looking
into his warm, open, handsome face. "It's hard to explain."

He seemed to settle into his chair as if he had all
night.

There was something about him, a peacefulness, a
strength, an old-fashioned integrity and honesty that
garnered her trust.

"As I told you, I *inherited* the property. Where the

problem comes in is that my elderly parents, in the years before they both died, insisted I know everything about their estate. They had wanted to make it as painless for me as possible by gifting me as much as they could over the years."

"They sound like very loving, responsible parents."

"Exactly. So imagine my surprise when this piece of Montana property comes at me from out of left field."

"You like baseball?"

She blinked.

"The baseball analogy? I thought you might be a Cubs fan."

She had to chuckle. "I am. My father took me to many of their games." She could see by Russell's smile that he liked her a little better. Being a fellow Cubs fan was all it took?

"Sorry, I didn't mean to interrupt your story."

"That's just it. There isn't much more to tell. I inherited the property, apparently from Laura Beaumont, via my parents. I'd never heard of her. Then I find out she was murdered and that she had a *daughter*. It brought up the obvious questions. Why hadn't the daughter inherited the property unless she was deceased—or…"

"Or *you* were the daughter?"

She nodded, glad he was tracking her thoughts.

"Is that possible?" he asked.

"Apparently not, since little Angel Beaumont was found drowned in the creek after she went missing following her mother's death. So how did I inherit property at the age of four from a woman I've never heard of? And why didn't my parents ever mention it? All I can figure is that there is a connection between me and Laura Beaumont. But what is it and why would my parents keep this from me?"

He shook his head and waited as if he knew there was more.

Dulcie drew out the photograph and handed it across to him. "To make things worse, I found this in the house today. I looked just like the girl in the photo at that age."

He studied the photo, then her and handed it back. "Is it possible this girl is related to you?"

She shrugged. "I used to have an imaginary friend. I told everyone she was my little sister. I called her Angel." Dulcie looked over at him, her gaze locking with his as she felt a shudder quake through her. "Just another coincidence? Or is it possible that my whole life is a lie?"

Jolene tried to forget about the stupid note she'd found on her car. Midge had probably put it there.

Except it sounded…threatening. But would she have found it threatening if she wasn't secretly getting the murder story?

Midge had warned her not to go digging around in Laura Beaumont's murder. Why would she care unless there was something to find? And what business was it of Midge's what Jolene did?

Jolene thought back to when she'd tried to question the members of the Whitehorse Sewing Circle. She recalled the way Ella Cavanaugh had looked at Pearl, as if afraid to say something she shouldn't.

Jolene couldn't believe what she was thinking as she drove toward Whitehorse. That the whole community might be involved in keeping a secret about the murder. Did they know who killed Laura and had been protecting that person for the past twenty-four years?

That seemed even more far-fetched. Maybe it was just as Midge had said, an unpleasant part of the area's history that the community didn't want dug up. So why didn't Jolene believe that?

Like the books she loved to read, she knew a good mystery when she found one. She also understood that in any good mystery there were clues that needed to be uncovered. In this case, finding those clues meant digging into the murder even further.

Word had gotten out much too quickly in this isolated, small community that she'd been asking about the murder. Anything more she did would be known and even possibly jeopardize her job.

But as she hit the outskirts of Whitehorse, she was thinking about the next segment of the story—and planning to pick up the assignments herself on Thursday in the hope of finding out where the murder story was coming from.

What worried her most was why someone had chosen her to tell their story to—true or not. She couldn't shake off the feeling that the writer was feeding her information about the murder for a reason other than a critique of the writing.

But why not give the information to the sheriff if the author knew something? Unless the story was actually a confession...

Another thought struck her. What if the author was tired of being part of the conspiracy and had decided to tell an outsider the truth, that outsider being some-one safe and trustworthy like, say, the schoolteacher?

Jolene desperately wanted to talk to someone about the murder story and bounce her theories off them. But the moment she saw Tinker's face, she knew she wasn't going to mention it to him.

"Hi, beautiful," he said, brushing her cheek with a kiss. "You look good enough to eat."

She smiled. "I take it the rodeos went well?" He was always in a good mood when he won the bigger purses.

"Well enough to buy you the best meal this side of Miles City."

"You're on, big spender," she said as she took his arm and let him lead her toward the restaurant.

It startled Dulcie when Russell reached across the table and covered her hand.

"I can see this has you upset," he said. "But aren't you jumping to conclusions without any real basis? A lot of kids resemble each other and aren't related."

"Women have a God-given right to jump to conclu-sions without any basis. Comes with the genes," she joked, hiding how serious this was for her.

He shook his head. "Not you."

"And you base that on...?"

"Being around you a total of five minutes."

She smiled. "Normally, you would be right. But in this case given these feelings I keep having—" She had to swallow the lump in her throat. It was one thing to let her mind run off in this direction, it was another to voice her suspicions.

"What feelings?" he asked as if seeing how upset this had her.

"When I first saw the house, actually when I saw the yellow curtains in the upstairs window, I had this sense of having been there before. In some other areas of the house, I got a horrible feeling of dread, followed almost at once by an irrational fear."

He was studying her openly.

"I heard that Laura Beaumont's daughter might have found her body," Dulcie said, needing desperately to voice her worse fears. "What if she saw the killer?"

She had to take a sip of her wine to steady herself. She hadn't even told Renada, her best friend, and here she was baring her soul to this cowboy she'd just met.

"That's a lot of what ifs," Russell said.

"There must have been evidence taken from the murder scene," she said after a moment. "If there is any DNA to test…"

"You're that afraid that you're Angel Beaumont?"

"It's the only thing that makes any sense. You understand now why I have to find out the truth one way or the other?"

He squeezed her hand. "I do. But if you're right, then I'm sure your parents had a good reason for not telling you about this, and that it was done out of love."

Tears burned her eyes at his kindness and she had to look away not to cry. A young couple had just come in the door. The cowboy was good-looking in a cocky, got-it-all-going-on kind of way. But it was the woman who caught Dulcie's eye. She was tall and pretty with a mane of chestnut hair. There was something familiar about her…

"There has to be a simple explanation that will clear this whole thing up."

"Thank you," Dulcie said to Russell as she turned back to him and pulled herself together. "I just needed to say all of that out loud. I feel better."

He grinned at her. "I'm glad I could help."

Their salads arrived just then and they lost themselves in the food and talking about other things. She asked about Texas and Whitehorse. He asked about Chicago and the Cubs games.

The evening passed in a pleasant blur of good food and equally good conversation. There was a lot more to Russell Corbett than met the eye—and in his case, that was saying a lot.

As they were leaving, she again noticed the young woman whom she'd seen with the cocky cowboy. As Dulcie passed their table on the way out of the restaurant, the woman looked up, a smile coming automatically to her lips, then a look of recognition and surprise.

That's when it came to Dulcie why the woman had looked so familiar. She was the one Dulcie had run into coming out of the newspaper office—the one who'd dropped the copy of the article about the murder investigation.

What surprised Dulcie was the tear in the young woman's face at seeing her again.

Chapter 7

Russell noticed the change in Dulcie as they were leaving the restaurant. "Anything wrong?"

"That young couple we passed as we were leaving, do you know them?"

He'd seen Dulcie hesitate at that last table. "That's Tinker. You probably don't follow rodeo. Thomas 'Tinker' Horton's a pretty famous bull rider in these parts."

"I was more interested in the woman with him," Dulcie said, surprising him. Most women would have been more interested in Tinker.

"That's the new schoolteacher in Old Town Whitehorse, Jolene Stevens."

"Not that tiny school I saw next to the community center?"

He grinned at her obvious surprise as he opened his truck door for her. "It's your old-fashioned one-room schoolhouse. I think I heard she has five students this year, grades three through eight."

"I had no idea," Dulcie said as he slid behind the wheel. "I thought one-room schools were a thing of the past. So she drives to and from Whitehorse every day?"

"The community provides her with a house in Old Town. It's that cute little white one past the center and down the hill a ways. Why all the questions about the schoolteacher?"

Dulcie shrugged. "I ran into her the other day in Whitehorse. I was just curious who she was."

He cut his eyes to her, knowing there was more to it.

She gave him an innocent look. "What else could it be?"

His question exactly. Dulcie looked out the side window as they drove to the motel, clearly not going to tell him what her real interest was in Jolene Stevens.

"You never told me what you do," he said as he pulled up in front of her motel room.

"Do?"

"For work. You do work, don't you?"

"Why? You think I have so much money I don't have to work?"

"I've heard tell of such a thing." He hadn't had to work for financial reasons his entire life, thanks to the Corbett wealth, but he thought everyone needed a job, a goal, something to do.

"I owned a business with a friend. We just sold it. I'm looking around for something else to keep me out of trouble."

"No small order that," he said as he got out to open her door. "I enjoyed dinner, especially watching you eat that steak. You are a woman after my own heart," he said as she stepped out into the starlight.

"Oh?" She cocked her head, grinning at him.

"You aren't flirting with me, are you?"

Her soft laugh was all music. "Would that be so bad?"

No, he thought, unless he was foolish enough to lose his heart to this city girl. But there was no chance of that. Especially if he didn't make the mistake of kissing her under the starlight.

Damn, but she *was* asking for it though.

Tinker grew quiet as he walked Jolene to her car. She hadn't been able to get a word in edgewise all during dinner. Tinker did love to talk about himself.

But with the night winding down, she thought this might be the perfect time to ask if he remembered the murder. "So you've lived here in Whitehorse your whole life."

"I don't like to think about it," Tinker joked as he leaned against her car and grinned at her. "I just come home now to see you."

"You don't have family here?" she asked, surprised.

"My mom," he said. "She remarried when I was little. My stepfather and I don't get along. But she loves the bastard so…" He straightened, clearly not wanting to talk about it.

"Do you remember a murder twenty-four years ago outside of Old Town Whitehorse?" she blurted out.

Tinker looked surprised, then annoyed. "Why ask me?"

She wished she hadn't. For some reason the question had ruined Tinker's good mood. "It's nothing. Just something I was curious about."

He was shaking his head, clearly angry. "That's a damned odd thing to be curious about."

"It's just that I thought you might have known the daughter, Angel Beaumont. She would have been younger than you…"

"Did someone tell you I knew her?" he demanded.

"No, I just—"

"Just heard that my stepfather was the ranch manager on the Atkinson place across the creek," he said angrily. "Well, he got fired because of Laura Beaumont, okay? We had to move to a run-down old place and my mother…" He shook his head, clearly agitated now. "I don't know what some busybodies have been telling you—"

"No one's been telling me anything."

He glared at her. "Why are you digging up this old crap after all this time?"

She shook her head, at a loss since she couldn't tell him about the murder story, especially now. "I'm sorry. I—"

"Oh, that's right, you've got Mace in your class."

Mace Carpenter? Now she really was confused. "Wait a minute, Ben Carpenter is your stepfather?"

"As if you didn't know that."

"I didn't. I swear." Ronda Carpenter was Tinker's mother?

He looked away and when his gaze returned to her, there was a coldness to it. "I knew Angel, okay? I felt sorry for her. Her mother was a tramp who didn't pay any attention to her. I'd already lived through my mother's divorce and her remarrying Ben. I could relate so I tried to watch out for the kid."

She didn't know what to say. Tinker was the friend from the murder story?

"Angel was a sweet little girl. She didn't stand a chance though. I wasn't surprised when her mother got herself murdered and Angel..." He shook his head again. "I don't like talking about any of this."

"I'm sorry. I really had no idea." She should have, though, given how small the community was.

He glanced at his watch. "I've got to go."

"Thanks for supper."

"Sure." He started to step away, but turned back. "I wouldn't go talking to anyone else about this if I were you. People around here don't like you digging up bad memories." He left her standing beside her car, feeling awful for spoiling their evening out.

But at least now she knew. Tinker had to be the friend in the murder story. He would have been nine, Angel four or five. Why else would he have been so upset?

Still she couldn't help but feel strange about him telling her not to talk to anyone else about it.

First the Whitehorse Sewing Circle, then Midge, now Tinker. Her conspiracy theory raised its ugly head again. Who were they all trying to protect?

Russell walked Dulcie to her motel-room door under a canopy of starlight and just a sliver of a moon. There was no one around, the hot night breathlessly silent.

She made the mistake of looking over at him, their gazes locking. "Thank you, Russell, for—"

He reached for her, bunching a handful of her wild mane at her nape in his fist as he pulled her to him.

Her brown eyes fired with a heat he hadn't seen for a long time—even longer, felt.

Her lips parted. He dropped his mouth over hers, felt the soft remnants of a smile disappear as he kissed her—and she kissed him back.

He encircled her with his arms, holding her as the kiss ended. Slowly, he drew back to look into her eyes. Her gaze was as dark as the night. It stirred a fire in him, sparking a yearning that had lain dormant far too long.

If only it had been with some other woman…*any* other woman.

He let go of her and started to open his mouth to speak.

"If you say you're sorry for kissing me so help me I'll slug you," Dulcie said, narrowing her eyes at him.

He laughed because that's exactly what he'd been about to do. He brushed a lock of her hair back from her cheek with his thumb. "What will you do now?"

"Go to bed."

"No, I mean—"

"I know what you mean." She looked up toward the heavens. "I never make decisions at night, especially after a big steak and—" she lowered her gaze to him "—an amazing kiss. Can't trust your judgment at times like that."

He smiled. "You're a smart woman."

"Aren't I, though? Good night, Russ. Sweet dreams." She turned and went inside.

He stood smiling after her, then walked to his truck. It wasn't until he was almost to the ranch that he realized he hadn't made an offer on her land. He hadn't even broached the subject.

But then it wasn't good to make a decision after a big steak and an amazing kiss, now, was it?

When Jolene started toward school the next morning, she noticed a pickup parked out front and feared there was a problem with one of her students.

The schoolhouse door was propped open. As she approached it, she wondered who in the community had a key besides her.

Titus Cavanaugh was sitting behind her desk, leaning back, eyes closed. For a moment she thought he was asleep.

Titus, a large, white-haired man with a powerful voice and a strong handshake, was pretty much in charge of everything in Old Town Whitehorse.

He opened his eyes as she approached and she saw that he hadn't been sleeping. "Hello." He smiled broadly. "I just came by before class to see how you were doing."

"Fine, I think," she said, sliding into one of her students' chairs.

"Good." He crossed his arms and leaned over her desk to look at her. "No trouble with that Carpenter boy?"

She shook her head. "Should I be having trouble with him?"

Titus laughed. "The last teacher found him…temperamental."

Jolene debated how much to say. "I did wonder if he might not have some issues at home."

"Indeed," Titus said with a nod of his head. "How about his father? The last teacher also had trouble with him."

"Ben stopped by yesterday to ask how his son was doing in school. I told him Mace was doing fine."

"Good." Titus rose to his feet. "I just wanted to make sure you weren't having any problems. Ben can be kind of a bully. If you have any trouble with him, you let me know." His blue eyes glinted as he smiled. "It sounds as if you're doing a fine job. Oh, by the way, the door was open when I arrived."

"I locked it last night. At least I would have sworn I did." Jolene worried that she'd been distracted and might *not* have locked it.

"I suppose there could be some keys floating around from former teachers," he said. "Don't worry about it. No harm done. It's not like there is much to steal."

She walked Titus out. Back at her desk, she noticed that one of the drawers was partially open. Had she left it like that?

Opening the drawer, she glanced at the short stories she'd already read and graded. Someone had gone through the stack.

When Dulcie opened the door to her motel room the next morning, she found Russell Corbett leaning against his pickup, waiting for her. She was instantly reminded of their kiss and felt a pleasurable warmth flow through her bloodstream.

"How do you feel about breakfast?"

She smiled, surprised how glad she was to see him. Last night, she hadn't told him why she was asking questions about the schoolteacher because she'd seen how scared the teacher had been at seeing her again.

Whatever it was about, she felt she needed to keep the teacher's secret.

Nor was she going to talk about her problems. She only had a few more days here and she wanted them to be pleasant. Russell Corbett made them pleasant.

"I'm *for* breakfast."

"Good, because I worked up an appetite standing around out here," he said, opening her door.

"You could have just knocked on my door," she said as she slipped into the passenger seat.

"And disturb your sleep? I couldn't chance that you're one of those people who's crabby if she doesn't get enough sleep," he said, starting the engine.

She smiled to herself as she studied him, his big hands on the wheel, and with that almost arrogant confidence about him that drew her in spite of herself.

"Okay," she said later, after she'd put away a large slice of ham, two eggs, hash browns and toast. "Let's hear it."

"Hear what?"

"Two meals, compliments and all this chivalry? What's this about?"

"I don't know what you mean."

"Sure you do. This is not how you spend your mornings *or* your evenings." She reached for his hand, turning it over to expose the thick callouses. "This time of the morning you'd be working if it wasn't for me. So why aren't you? I saw the look on your face. You were upset to see the way I was dressed this morning. If this is about keeping me away from that house—"

"Now that you mention it," he said, frowning as he

pulled his hand back. "I don't like the idea of you going back there by yourself."

"That's sweet, but what does your boss say about you missing work to babysit me?"

He hesitated just a little too long.

"What?"

"I wasn't completely honest with you about my job. Trails West Ranch is a family-owned operation."

"And you're one of the family." She couldn't be angry with him, given that she hadn't originally been completely honest about the businesses she'd started with Renada.

"We're interested in buying your property if you decide to sell it."

"So that's it." What had she thought? That he might be interested in *her?*

"Not entirely," he said, but she was already on her feet.

"You're more than welcome to make an offer when I sell the land. I'll let you know. Thanks for breakfast. No, please, stay and enjoy your coffee. I'd prefer to walk."

"Dulcie—"

The door slammed behind her. "Handled that well," she muttered under her breath, angry with herself for making it so obvious how much that had hurt.

Jolene collected the short-story assignments herself, counting them as she went. She hadn't gotten much sleep last night. Her thoughts kept circling around her conspiracy theory about Laura Beaumont's murder.

Nor did it help to find Titus waiting for her this

morning after someone had been in the schoolhouse and gone through the drawer with the stories in it.

When Jolene had gotten back to Old Town Whitehorse last night, she'd been spooked remembering the note she'd found earlier that night on her windshield. She'd gone through her small house, checking all the windows and doors to make sure they were locked and the closets were free of any intruders.

It had felt silly and yet she couldn't shake the feeling that all this was about more than some aspiring author using her for a free critique of his or her work.

This morning she'd finally admitted her worse fear—that Laura Beaumont's killer had resurfaced, if he'd ever left to begin with, and now he was writing his story just for her.

Suddenly she stopped in the middle of her classroom and counted the short-story assignments she'd collected. There were only *five.*

She counted them again. Just as she'd feared, the murder story wasn't among them.

"Don't you want that one?" asked her third-grader, Amy Brooks.

Jolene turned and looked at the girl. Amy was pointing at the corner of a table in the back of the classroom where stapled-together papers were lying on it, facedown.

"Does anyone know who left this here?" she asked her class, glancing at each of the five. Blank faces stared back at her. "Has it been here every time you collected the stories?" she asked her students.

Amy nodded. "Isn't it from your other student?"

"My *other* student?" Jolene repeated.

"Don't you have one who can't come to class and sends things in?" she asked. "You know, like an on-line student?"

"A ghost student," her fifth-grader brother, Thad, said with a laugh.

"Yeah, *ooooooo*," Luke chimed in. "Ghosts."

"All right, that's enough. It's Thursday so that means we have one more day of writing the middle of the story and then you will have the weekend to complete the end."

There was a groan from the two fifth-graders.

"You're about to wind up your story. What else do you need to tell your reader before the ending? That's what you should think about when you write tonight."

She picked up the pages from the small desk at the back and turned them over. More of the murder story. She felt her pulse quicken with both relief—and dread. Monday it would end.

But how?

The searing wind was a demon moving over the lifeless land. With no sign of rain in the forecast, the tension had grown until it was like a wire strung too tightly. Everyone waited, knowing it was just a matter of time before something snapped.

Among the farmers and ranchers there was a grow-ing sense of panic. The men talked among themselves in quiet desperation. The women tried to keep the chil-dren from irritating their fathers.

A silent fear had settled in. If it didn't rain soon, there would be no crops, no money. They had been

*through hard times before, but this time might be the
final straw that broke the camel's back.*

*While she fanned herself and watched the road or
slogged through chores that couldn't be put off, the
rest of the community hung on each blistering breath
and prayed and cursed and worried.*

*Not that she was immune to the growing strain in
the country and people around her. She was part of
it, this pressure that pushed some to the edge, for she
had grown bored and restless. Her lover had to sense
it and feel another kind of quiet desperation.*

*The hottest day that spring, she lifted her head as
if sniffing the air. An old pickup clattered up the road,
the metal pipes he carried in the back humming like
a siren call. Did he glimpse her standing at her bedroom window, lifting her long, richly burnished hair
from her slim neck?*

*Or did he first see her on her porch scantily dressed
one night as she searched for a cool breeze?*

*In the days that followed when he tried to work his
magic in the pasture near her farmhouse, he watched
both the sky and the woman.*

*How different things might have been if the rain-
maker had resisted her. Or if the rain hadn't come
too late.*

*How lucky though that the little girl had a friend she
met at the creek. He was older, one of those lost souls
who had seen too much in his young life and expected
to see much worse before it was over.*

*He liked the girl, felt protective of her. He watched
the farmhouse and he knew what went on there. That's
why on that horribly hot day he lured the little girl*

away from the house. Not to help the killer, but to save his friend.

If only he could have kept her from going back to the house, from finding her mother like that, from seeing the killer—and the killer seeing her.

"I take it you didn't have any better luck this morning than you did last night?" Grayson Corbett asked as Russell stalked into the main house, scowling.

"That woman is impossible," he muttered as he poured himself a cup of coffee from the carafe behind the bar.

Kate was smiling at him. "How was supper at Northern Lights?"

"Fine." He didn't want to talk about his date. "She's going back over to the house today. If she doesn't break her fool neck, maybe I'll go over and try to talk some sense into her."

"You might just want to keep it strictly business," Grayson suggested.

"Or you might want to ask her out again," Kate said.

Russell shook his head. "I doubt either will do me any good. Maybe I should just leave it to you," he said to his father. "You might have better luck with her."

Grayson shook his head. "Kate's probably right. A woman likes to be courted—even in business."

"Flowers are always a nice gesture," Kate suggested.

Russell scoffed inwardly at that. He'd already done too much courtin' of Dulcie Hughes when he'd kissed her last night in front of her motel room.

No wonder she'd gotten angry this morning at breakfast. She thought that kiss was about getting her land when her property had been the last thing on his mind.

"I've got work to do," Russell said. "I'll go over later and see what I can do to rectify things."

"It's no big deal if we don't get the property," Grayson said. "I understand if you want to forget it."

What he wanted to forget was Dulcie Hughes.

"Any word from that rainmaker?" his father asked.

"No. He said he'd come on up here or he'd call. He hasn't called. I'll get back to him."

Russell tried the rainmaker and got his voice mail. He left a message. As he was driving past the Atkinson place, he swung in. John Atkinson owned that property behind Laura Beaumont's place at the time of the murder. If Russell could find out something for Dulcie, he might be able to help her solve this mystery so she could get back to Chicago and he could get back to work and get her off his mind.

It had nothing to do with getting back into her good graces. She'd just think it was about buying her land and get mad again anyhow.

Dulcie ducked into the newspaper office since she was walking past it anyway. It didn't take long to find out what year Jolene Stevens had been looking at and deduce which murder the schoolteacher had made copies of. Why would a schoolteacher be interested in Laura Beaumont's murder?

As Dulcie went through the same stories Jolene had, she noticed something odd. There was no mention of Laura Beaumont's past. No mention of Angel's father. No obit with Laura's maiden name or any background.

Leaving the newspaper, she drove out of town more convinced than before that something was very odd about all of this. Leaves scuttled across the dusty street, propelled by the blistering, dried-out wind. It was early in the morning and yet the temperature was already in the seventies.

She had stopped for gas at Packys on the way out of town, all unpleasant thoughts of Russell Corbett disappearing as she felt the tension growing in the community. It was as if a spark could set off the locals, just as it could ignite the tinder-dry grasses outside.

The talk everywhere was of the need for rain.

Dulcie found herself caught up in it, anxious and nervous and expectant. She watched the sky for any sign of relief and silently prayed for the heavens to open up and douse them all in reviving moisture that would save not only the crops, but also the peace.

The feeling that she was perched on a powder keg about to blow grew stronger as she pulled past her cut barbed-wire gate lying in the dry grass and parked in front of the old farmhouse.

This empathy she felt for the ranch and farm people surprised her. Growing up in Chicago, she couldn't have been farther from the land and her food source. Here though, she felt as if she were a part of it. Or possibly had been.

You aren't Angel Beaumont.

Wasn't she? she thought as she looked up at the second-floor window and saw the yellow curtains. What felt like a memory nudged her, but refused to come into focus. She was a part of something here and damned if she wasn't going to find out what.

Opening the car door, she stepped out and moved through the tall weeds toward the house—ever vigilant of rattlesnakes.

Hurriedly she climbed the steps, glad to be where she could see what might be next to her. When she reached the front door, though, she paused.

Yesterday she'd locked the front door as they'd left. She remembered testing it, standing on the porch with Russell. It *had* been locked.

But now as she reached for her key, she saw that the door was slightly ajar. Goose bumps spread over her flesh even in the breathless heat. Her blood pounded in her ears and yet past it she could hear the annoying weather vane moving restlessly in the searing wind.

A new sound set her teeth on edge. The rhythmic clinking of metal on metal coming from behind the house.

Dulcie stepped to the edge of the porch and looked toward the creek and the property beyond her own. Through the branches of the cottonwoods, she could see a man with a sledgehammer, pounding what looked like pipe into the ground on the other side of the creek.

He stopped as if sensing her watching him and looked in her direction. She couldn't see his face under the dark hat he wore, but she could feel his hard, staring eyes on her, his gaze hotter than the spring day.

She stepped back quickly, feeling strangely violated. How was it possible she could feel both hatred and lust, fear and shock and pain in a look?

She knew what Renada would say. This place was making her imagination run wild. Dulcie shook her head at her own foolishness but was thankful when the man resumed his banging.

Just the thought of Renada made her too aware that she hadn't called her friend. Nor had she answered the messages Renada had left. She promised herself she would call her tonight, if only to let her know she was all right.

She knew why she hadn't called and told her about what had been going on. Renada would be on the next plane out and Dulcie would have loved nothing better. But it would mean taking Renada away from her design classes and something she'd wanted for far too long.

Walking to the front of the house again, Dulcie took a breath and, holding it, flung open the door. It was impossible to tell if there were any new tracks in the dust.

She stepped in, leaving the door open, and moved cautiously toward the kitchen in the back. She hadn't taken two steps when the front door slammed with a loud bang.

She jumped, heart leaping to her throat. Something stirred the air around her. Wind like a blast furnace. Moving toward the source, she found the back door wide open. Hadn't it been boarded up like the front door? She'd never checked.

Dulcie closed and locked it, using the dead bolt. Then she stood, listening. No sound came from upstairs. But she couldn't convince herself that she wasn't alone in the house until she went upstairs and checked.

She listened again, thankful when she heard the man she'd seen driving pile still working. When she listened really hard, she could hear the creak and groan of the weather vane, but no sound coming from inside the house.

What was she doing here? What more did she hope

to find? She wished she knew as she cautiously climbed the stairs, drawn to the front bedroom.

At the doorway, she watched the wind breathing the yellow curtains in and out. She caught a scent on the air, faint but so seductive, it drew her into the room. Yesterday, she'd seen the assortment of bottles thick with dust atop of the vanity.

Now she saw that someone had moved them, leaving tracks in the dust. Avoiding looking in the cloudy mirror, she spotted a perfume bottle, the dust smudged.

Carefully she picked it up, that faint scent she'd caught earlier tempting her. Opening the bottle, she took a whiff. Her throat closed, eyes brimming with tears as she dropped the perfume onto the vanity and stumbled back, her hand clamped over her mouth to keep from crying out.

In the mirror, she saw herself again, saw her terror, and fled the room to stand in the hallway. While the yellow curtains and the sound of the weather vane in the wind had jarred some memory, the scent of Laura Beaumont's perfume had struck a chord so deep in her that it felt as if the very foundation she stood on was crumbling beneath her.

Dulcie slid down the wall to the dusty floor and dropped her face into her hands as her heart thudded wildly and she tried to catch her breath. The scent of Laura Beaumont's perfume was inextricably linked in her mind with that of a crying, terrified little girl—and blood, lots and lots of blood.

Chapter 8

Arctic cold air-conditioning blasted Russell as John Atkinson opened the door of the ranch house.

"Russell?" John said, seeming surprised to see him. John Atkinson was a contemporary of Russell's father, a large man in his early sixties with a thick head of salt-and-pepper hair and a weathered face.

"Sorry to drop in without calling, John."

"No, come in. Midge just made a fresh pot." This was rural Montana where a pot of coffee was always on and drop-in visitors were always welcome.

The house had recently been remodeled with all new furnishings that Russell suspected had to do more with Midge's tastes than John's, including the hand-painted flowery borders in every room.

Russell led him into the large ranch kitchen and offered him a chair at the table. While John filled two mugs with coffee, Russell glanced out the window at the view of the Larb Hills etched against the skyline.

John and Midge still had several ranches to the south, but had moved closer to town in the past couple of years. Unlike other ranchers who turned the place over to their grown sons or daughters and son-in-laws, John and Midge had never had children, so his ranches were leased.

"I heard you called in a rainmaker," John said, handing Russell one of the mugs filled with coffee before joining him at the table.

"Finnegan Amherst."

John's head came up with a jerk. He let out a curse, something unusual for John.

"He's the same one that was used some twenty years before. He did make rain the last time, didn't he?"

John waved a hand through the air. "I'm just surprised he's still alive."

An odd thing to say, given that the rainmaker was supposedly younger than John himself.

"Was he in ill health?" Russell had to ask when John didn't say more.

"No, no, I just thought someone would have shot him by now. Or strung him up."

Russell was confused and said as much.

John took a sip of his coffee as if he'd said too much already. "It's his way with women, other men's women."

"Finnegan is a lady's man?" Russell said with a laugh, remembering the man's deep, raspy voice. "I doubt he is anymore. He sounded on the phone as if he was ninety."

"Really? He's closer to fifty now, I'd say. Making rain must have aged the man."

John's sarcasm and obvious dislike of the rainmaker confused Russell. Was it possible Finnegan Amherst had gone after Midge?

The idea made him scoff. Midge Atkinson wasn't the type of woman that attracted men. There was something too brittle about her. Ah, hell, the woman was a bitch, plain and simple.

"So when is he coming?" John asked.

"Good question. I'm waiting to hear from him." Russell glanced at his watch and remembered why he'd stopped by.

"I don't know if you've heard, but the owner of the old Beaumont place is in town. She's interested in finding out more about the murder."

All the blood drained from John's face. His coffee mug clattered to the table, coffee spilling everywhere.

John shoved back his chair and hurried into the kitchen to grab some paper towels.

Russell righted the coffee mug. "I take it you remember the murder. I guessed you would, since you had the ranch behind the place," he said as John sopped up the coffee. "You knew Laura Beaumont then?"

Russell hadn't heard Midge Atkinson enter the kitchen until he heard her sharp, low cry behind him. He turned to see her ashen face and the way she looked at her husband.

"I spilt a little coffee. No big deal," John said as she rushed over to snatch the sodden paper towels from him, clearly furious. But was it over spilled coffee or what she'd heard when she'd entered the room?

"I was just asking about Laura Beaumont," Russell said.

"I heard," Midge snapped. "Don't you men have some work to do?"

Russell finished his coffee quickly as she reached for his mug. Taking it from him, she returned to the kitchen and turned on the water in the sink.

He glanced over at John, who shook his head as if to say, "Let it go." As she started to wash out the mugs, he saw her grip the edge of the sink as if hanging on for dear life.

"I've got some things to pick up in town," John called to his wife and motioned for Russell to follow him outside.

"She doesn't like talking about Laura's death," John said once they were out by their trucks. "So I'd really appreciate it if you didn't mention it again."

"Sure," Russell said, wondering if that was all there was to it. But before he could ask why, John ended the conversation by heading to his pickup.

Dulcie slowly became aware of her surroundings. As she lifted her head from her hands, her whole body tensed. Listening, she heard…nothing. The banging on the other side of the creek had stopped. Had the wind died down as well? She couldn't hear the weather vane.

Her gaze shot down the hall toward the window and the slack, unmoving yellow curtains. No wind. No sound. It was as if she'd suddenly gone deaf.

Get out of the house! Now!

Irrational panic filled her. She shot to her feet, teetering for a moment at the top of the stairs as she looked down into the dim darkness below her. Her feet faltered, but only for a moment as she rushed down the steps.

She only had two steps to go. She'd already taken them in her mind, had already seen herself grasp the doorknob, turn it and fling the door wide, bolting out into the heat and sunlight.

The man appeared at the bottom of the stairs as if materializing out of nothing.

Her scream was bloodcurdling as she grabbed for the stair railing in an attempt to keep from crashing into him. Her fingers slipped on the dusty rail, and finding no purchase, she fell the last two steps, slamming into him.

He looked so fragile, she'd thought the two of them would fall to the floor. Tall and thin, dressed all in black, including his felt hat, it surprised her at how solid he felt, how strong.

His fingers bit into her shoulders as he grabbed her. She fought to free herself and heard him swear as he righted her, holding her away from him, staring into her face.

Dulcie stared back, flinching at what she saw under the soft brim of his beat-up hat—a gaunt face stretched over hard angles and startling dark eyes that shone with something so black it was like falling into a bottomless pit.

She jerked back, repelled by the man, and found her voice. "What are you doing in my house?"

"*Your* house?" The sound of him surprised her as much as the sight of him. A rasp of a voice, well-deep and just as cold.

"*My* house," she repeated, screwing up her courage. "You're trespassing and you know what they do to trespassers up here."

His laugh was hollow, the shine in his eyes hypnotic.

"Get out!" she ordered, her voice spiraling with her fear. "Get out or I'm going to call the police."

His smile showed shockingly uniform white teeth and for a moment she glimpsed what he must have looked like when he was younger.

Her breath caught. As she staggered backward, she threw her hand up as if to ward him off. His hand shot out, brushed her sleeve. Her scream was a shrill cry of raw terror.

"Dulcie? Dulcie!" Russell burst through the front door, stopping short as she shoved past a tall, thin man dressed all in black and ran into his arms.

Russell held her to him and demanded of the man, "Who the hell are you?"

"I'm afraid I frightened her," the man said in a raspy, deep voice that Russell recognized at once. The man turned to face him, giving a slight courtly bow without removing his hat. "Finnegan Amherst, at your service. And you are…?"

"Russell Corbett."

"Ah, the rancher who called requesting my talents. I have already begun my work."

So he *had* shown up. "I hope you aren't planning to make rain inside this ranch house," Russell snapped.

The rainmaker chuckled, a sound like dead, rustling leaves.

He could still feel Dulcie trembling and knew how

much it took to scare this woman. What had this man done to her?

"Again, I am sorry if I frightened you, miss." He tipped his hat to Dulcie. "I've set up across the creek. The same place I did last time with much success." His gaze raked over Dulcie, making her shiver again before he left them, closing the door behind him.

"Are you all right?" Russell asked, looking into Dulcie's brown eyes. His fingers brushed back her hair.

She nodded, her eyes locking with his as she held tight to him. Her eyes filled, her full lower lip trembling.

"You're all right," he whispered as he traced a thumb over her lower lip. Her lips parted, the tip of her tongue brushing his rough skin.

Dulcie heard his groan and pressed her body to his. His arm dragged her to him. His mouth came down hard on hers. She gasped as she felt the tip of his tongue tease the inside of her lower lip.

Her breasts, crushed against his hard chest, ached and as her arms encircled his neck, she felt him lift her from the floor.

She hung on, his mouth never leaving hers, as he backed her up against the wall at the bottom of the stairs, holding her there with his body as his fingers opened her shirt, slipping inside to cup her full, round breast in his warm palm.

She cried out softly, her head lolling back as his thumb found the hardened tip of her nipple. Her arms slipped from around his neck to grasp the front of his Western shirt and pull, the snaps coming undone to reveal his smooth, tanned flesh and the dark trail of fine hair that disappeared in a *V* into the waist of his jeans.

"Dulcie," he said on a ragged breath.

She closed her eyes as she felt him bare her breasts to his mouth, to his hands, and squirmed against him, wanting him like she'd never wanted any other man.

She opened her eyes and reached for his belt. His mouth came down on hers again as he lifted her higher and worked her canvas pants down. She felt the heat and hardness of him and nothing on earth could have kept her from fulfilling this desire burning in her as he pulled back to look into her eyes.

She reached for him, rocking against his hips, as he took her to the edge of climax and then even higher before quenching her aching need.

Russell held her against the wall and tried to catch his breath. They were both covered in sweat, their bodies glistening. He slowly lowered her feet to the floor.

"I'm sorry. That wasn't the way I…" His voice trailed off as he realized what he'd been about to say. *That wasn't the way I envisioned making love to you.*

She laughed softly. "Oh. And what *had* you planned?"

He couldn't help but smile. "A bed?"

She shook her head as she slowly began to button her blouse, her brown-eyed gaze locked on his. "I wouldn't have had our first time be any other way. I wanted you as much as you wanted me."

"I doubt that." Their *first* time? He told himself there wouldn't be a second. He could see that she wasn't taking this as seriously as he was. Hell, the woman wasn't taking any of this as seriously as he thought she should. Just being in this house was dangerous. Investigating an unsolved murder could be deadly.

"I know you drove out here to scold me," she said as she dressed.

He couldn't help himself. He leaned toward her and gently kissed her. "I want you to be safe."

"I know." She cupped his face in her hands and, smiling, brushed a kiss over his lips before letting go.

He stepped back, determined that if they ever made love again, it wouldn't be in this old house against a wall and it would be for the right reasons. It wouldn't be lust or fear.

He could hear the rainmaker driving his metal pipes into the ground again. He could see that Dulcie was listening as well. "What did that man want with you?"

"Nothing," she said as she hugged herself, rubbing her arms with her hands even though they were both perspiring in the heat of the closed-up house. "Nothing."

"He had to have wanted *something*. I saw the look on your face. Dulcie—"

"I'm fine. I'm sorry I scared you."

"Scared *me?* It's you I'm concerned about. That man is going to be working just across the creek from you. If he touched you or threatened you—"

"I told you, he didn't *do* anything. He just…startled me, that's all, and I overreacted."

She was lying and for the life of him he couldn't imagine why. What would have happened if he hadn't come along when he did? Yesterday it had been Ben Carpenter. Today that damned rainmaker.

Worse, Russell had made love with her and complicated things even more. He wanted to cross the creek and pummel the truth out of that old man, but he had a feeling he'd get the same answer from him.

"That man," she asked. "What kind of work is he doing across the creek?"

"He's a rainmaker."

"You hired him to make *rain?*"

Russell wasn't in the mood to debate this and said as much. He had enough doubts of his own.

She must have seen that he was angry with her as he shoved back his hat and prepared to leave, because she didn't argue the issue. "He said he was here before."

He studied her for a long moment. "Twenty-four years ago." He saw her expression and felt the import of his words on her.

The last time the rainmaker had been here would have been that hot, deadly dry spring when Laura Beaumont was murdered.

The school day seemed to drag. During recess, Jolene sat in the shade and read the short stories, but her mind wandered.

When the time came to dismiss the students, she was relieved. Monday the school term would end. Since she'd been hired for the coming year as well, she would be allowed to live in the small house down the road for the summer.

She'd been looking forward to the time to read and explore the area. But the heat this spring had curbed her enthusiasm. That and the murder story.

No wonder she felt restless. Tomorrow was Friday.

There was only one more segment of the short story. Then the ending on Monday. Would Friday's be waiting for her on the corner of that used desk in the morning when she opened the classroom?

Or would the killer?

She shivered at the thought.

"See you all in the morning. Don't forget," she said as she watched her students noisily preparing to leave. "Keep working on your stories."

She watched from the window as they loaded onto the bus or climbed into waiting pickups and SUVS, then began to gather her belongings, anxious to get home.

At the sound of footfalls, she looked up to find a woman standing in the doorway, looking around as if she'd never seen a one-room schoolhouse before.

"Can I help you?" The woman was studying the birthday wall, where everyone had posted their upcoming birthdays, hers included, complete with photographs.

As the woman turned, Jolene recognized her. It was the woman she'd bumped into on the street that day outside the newspaper office. The same woman she'd seen at dinner last night at Northern Lights.

"Jolene Stevens?" the woman asked. "I'm Dulcie Hughes. Do you have a minute?"

The teacher's hand was ice-cold as Dulcie shook it. "What is this about?"

"Laura Beaumont's murder." Dulcie saw the young woman's surprise. "Don't bother to tell me you don't know who I'm talking about. I saw the copy of the newspaper article you dropped on the street that day. I checked at the newspaper office and found out which stories you copied."

"I don't understand why—"

"I recently inherited Laura Beaumont's house. Is there somewhere we could talk about this privately?"

Jolene Stevens seemed to hesitate, but only for a moment. "Let's go to my place." She pointed down the dirt street to a cute little cottage. "Just let me lock up the school."

Dulcie waited in the car with the air-conditioning running. She had tried to pull herself together after Russell had left her at the farmhouse. He'd been angry and she couldn't blame him. They'd shared an intimacy that a man like him didn't take lightly. Nor did she, even though she'd let him believe she had.

Even now she couldn't regret what happened, but she also couldn't let it happen again. She'd gotten too close to Russell Corbett.

He'd realized that as well and that was one reason he was so upset with her. He knew she was keeping things from him. But explaining what had happened between her and the rainmaker before Russell had burst in was impossible.

She still didn't understand it herself.

After he'd left, she'd thought about going upstairs to do more digging. She'd already found one photograph. There had to be more since nothing seemed to have been taken but the child's clothing. Wasn't it possible there were old letters? Something that could provide the answers she so desperately needed, especially now?

She had started back up the stairs, her legs still

weak, her heart still racing from their lovemaking, but the sound of the rainmaker's hammer clanging against the pipes reverberated inside her skull and sent her rushing from the house. That and the memory of the rainmaker's face.

Dulcie brushed the thought away as she waited for the schoolteacher. Jolene had been investigating Laura Beaumont's murder and apparently didn't want anyone to know. Dulcie couldn't wait to ask the schoolteacher why.

Jolene came out of the school and double-checked the door to make sure it was locked. Dulcie thought of how she'd done the same thing at the farmhouse. Was Jolene worried that someone had been getting in—just as Dulcie was? What else did they have in common? she wondered, as she followed the teacher to her house.

"I have some iced tea," Jolene said as she parked her bike against the side of the house and opened the front door.

"I'd love some."

Fans whirred in the windows, circulating the hot air. "Sorry, I don't have air-conditioning. Just have a seat anywhere," Jolene called from the kitchen.

Dulcie remained standing until Jolene returned. She took the tall, sweating glass offered her and sipped the tea. "This is wonderful. Thank you."

Jolene nodded, looking nervous. "I really don't know anything—"

"Let's sit down," Dulcie said, taking a seat across from her. "Why are you researching Laura Beaumont's death?"

"I was just curious."

"Why would you be interested in her murder? I know you aren't from around here. All I can assume is that you learned something about her death that made you curious."

"If you inherited the house then you know more about—"

"I never heard of Laura Beaumont until after my parents died and I was told I'd inherited property in Montana," Dulcie said. "I didn't even know there was a house on the land, let alone that the woman who'd left it to me had been murdered—or that she'd had a little girl."

Jolene took a sip of her tea.

Dulcie saw that her hands were trembling. "Jolene, some very strange things have been happening from the first time I laid eyes on that house. If you know something, please, help me."

"What kind of strange things?"

Dulcie sat back, holding the glass in both hands as if she could soak up the cold. She started at the beginning, telling about her elderly parents, her mother's trouble conceiving, the complete shock of the Montana property, her fear that she was Angel Beaumont.

"When I saw those yellow curtains…" She shook her head. "I know it sounds crazy, but I knew I'd seen them before. That wasn't all. There's a sound out there on the place…" Her voice broke.

"You felt you'd been there before?"

"I *know* I have. How else can I explain these feelings of déjà vu? I need to find the connection. Why leave this property to *me?*"

Jolene put down her glass. "You can't be Angel

Beaumont. They found her drowned in the creek. She's buried up on the hill. I had planned to go up there—"

"What if she didn't drown in the creek? Come on, have you seen how shallow the creek is right now and this spring is just like that one. There wasn't enough water in the creek for her to drown."

Dulcie sighed. "I guess I want to believe she is alive because it would explain why I inherited the property."

"But that would mean…"

She nodded. "That I'm Angel Beaumont. My parents had to have had a reason for keeping the Montana property a secret. I feel as if it was something they couldn't bring themselves to talk about. Something they had to let me discover on my own. I know that sounds strange."

"Not really."

"It's like they were…ashamed to talk about it. See? Crazy."

"Maybe not so crazy."

Dulcie studied the young woman over the rim of her glass. Jolene knew more than she was saying. If there was one thing Dulcie had learned in business, it was to be patient. Let the other person fill the silence.

"You're going to think *I'm* crazy now," Jolene said finally and gave a nervous laugh.

"Try me," Dulcie said.

"I get the feeling that the community knows something about the murder but they've made a secret pact not to tell."

"A conspiracy?" That didn't sound crazy to Dulcie at all.

Jolene nodded. "What if the little girl discovered

her mother's body and she saw the killer? Since the killer was never caught and for all we know he still lives here, what if the community is protecting him?"

"Or protecting Angel Beaumont," Dulcie said. "Isn't it possible the community faked her death so the killer wouldn't find out she was alive?"

Jolene shivered and put down her glass. "The killer could be a woman."

Dulcie stared at her. "Why would you say that?"

"It's a possibility, isn't it?" Jolene picked up her tea again, avoiding Dulcie's gaze.

She'd been right. Jolene knew something. That's why she'd researched the murder at the newspaper office.

"You never told me what got you interested in this murder case," Dulcie said.

Jolene slowly raised her gaze to meet hers. "How do I know I can trust you?"

"Because I can tell you're terrified for some reason," Dulcie said. "So am I."

Jolene studied her openly for a moment, then rose and went to the drawer in a cabinet. She took out some papers and, holding them against her chest, returned to her chair and sat down.

"I gave my students a short-story assignment. The story is to continue for six days with a small part turned in each day until the story ends on the last day."

She glanced down at the papers she held tightly against her chest. "The first day I got an extra story. Someone had left it on an empty desk in the school-house. The story is about the murder of a widow who had a young daughter."

Dulcie wasn't sure what she'd expected but definitely not this. "Laura Beaumont?"

"That would be my guess."

"Who is leaving you the story?"

"I have no idea. Apparently, some of the residents have keys to the school, so it could be anyone."

"This story, do you have reason to believe it's not fictional?"

"It takes place during a hot spring just like this one. It reads as if it was written by someone who knew the murder victim, someone who watched her and her daughter."

Dulcie felt her heart begin to race faster. "Someone who might know who killed her?"

"Possibly."

Her gaze went to the pages Jolene held. She was trying to be patient. "Why would this person give it to you, do you think?"

"At first I thought they just wanted me to read their story and critique it."

"And now?"

"Now I'm afraid it might be a confession."

Dulcie sat forward. "May I read it?"

Jolene seemed to hesitate for a second before she handed it over. "It's only the first four days' worth. There are still two more segments. One tomorrow, with the ending on Monday. At least I hope there is an ending."

"We already know how it ends," Dulcie said absently, her attention on the papers in her hands.

"Do we?" Jolene said. "I'm not so sure about that."

Chapter 9

Russell spent the remainder of the afternoon making sure Finnegan Amherst didn't return to Dulcie's farmhouse.

Watching the rainmaker work only convinced him that he and the other ranchers and farmers had just thrown away fifteen thousand dollars.

"So where did you learn this?" he'd asked Finnegan.

"I met an old Indian who could make rain. He taught me everything he knew."

Finnegan had driven a series of steel pipes into the ground near the water along the creek. Occasionally he would stop, listen for a long while, then uproot a pipe and sink it elsewhere.

"And the purpose of the steel pipes?"

"They act as an antenna to redirect the energy flow." He must have heard the skepticism in Russell's voice.

"I don't *make* rain, Mr. Corbett. Only God makes it rain. I *influence* the weather. The earth is your mother." He lifted his arms and raised his face toward the heavens. "I reach out to her to redirect the jet stream." As he dropped his hands, he added, "Prayer is good, too."

"Have you ever *not* made it rain?" Russell had to ask.

The rainmaker smiled his twisted smile, the dark eyes shining. "Ranchers have been known to string up men who don't make it rain. I'm still alive, aren't I?"

When Finnegan finally quit for the day to return to his tent at Trafton Park in Whitehorse, Russell had gone by the farmhouse to check on Dulcie.

Seeing that she'd gone left him torn between disappointment and worry. What would she do next? Maybe she'd given up on this quest to find out more about Laura Beaumont and had returned to Chicago. Without saying goodbye?

That thought filled him with a sense of loss for a woman he'd known less than forty-eight hours. But then again, a woman like Dulcie Hughes got under a man's skin immediately.

He told himself she wouldn't leave without telling him goodbye, but he wasn't completely sure about that. He was, however, sure she wasn't the kind to give up easily and he doubted she'd solved the mystery this afternoon in that old house.

As he drove toward the ranch, he thought he must have conjured her from his imagination because a car like Dulcie's rental was headed down the road toward him right now, coming from the wrong direction.

Why would she be coming from Old Town White-horse?

He slowed the pickup, pulling to the side to let her pass.

She slowed and then seemed to reluctantly pull to a stop next to his pickup. He waited as she whirred down her window and smiled but not before he'd seen the exhaustion in her face.

"You look tired," he said.

She didn't deny it, confirming that she was dead on her feet. The strain of her quest, no doubt.

"Have you had anything to eat?"

"Breakfast," she said with the quirk of her mouth. "It gave me indigestion."

"I don't think it was the food. Park your rig in that turnoff behind you and come with me. No arguments for once in your life."

She smiled at that and surprisingly didn't put up a fight, instead backing her car into the turnoff to a pasture. He pulled up, reached over to open the passenger's-side door and she climbed in. As he drove toward the ranch, she leaned back in the seat and closed her eyes.

"Where are you taking me?" she asked, sounding as if it really didn't make any difference.

"You'll see. How was your day?"

"Fine." She opened her eyes and looked over at him. "I don't want to talk about it, okay?"

He glanced at her, saw her expression and said, "Okay."

She closed her eyes again and they drove in a companionable silence until he slowed for the turnoff to the ranch.

She sat up. "Trails West Ranch?" Glancing over at him, she asked, "Are you sure this is a good idea?"

It was a terrible idea for a lot of reasons, he thought. "I thought you'd like to meet my family."

"If this is about buying my property—"

"This is about getting you a good meal," he said. "Nothing more."

She cut her eyes to him as he parked in front of the main house.

"I hope you like margaritas," he said as he got out and led her toward the front door.

Dulcie stepped into the cool, inviting ranch house and was drawn to the voices and muffled laughter. She breathed in the smell of tantalizing Mexican food cooking somewhere close by and could almost taste the sharp, tangy salt on the rim of a margarita as Russell took her arm and called out, "I brought a friend for supper."

The night passed in a pleasant blur of good food, drink and company. The Corbetts were a handsome and charming bunch and she liked their stepmother, Kate, a lot. She complimented Juanita on her amazing culinary masterpieces and thanked Kate and Grayson for allowing her to join them.

"You should have warned me," Dulcie said on the way back to her car after the evening was over.

"Would you have gone with me if I had warned you about my family?"

"You know I didn't mean your family," she said, humor in her voice. "You're one of those wealthy ranchers I've heard about."

"I work."

"I know you do," she said, taking his right hand from the wheel and running her fingertips along the callouses. "That's one of the things I like about you."

"*One* of the things?"

"You? Fishing for compliments?" she said, shoving his hand away with a laugh. "I wasn't exactly honest with you either about my work." She told him about Renada and the boutique they started that grew into a wildly successful enterprise.

"What will you do now?" he asked.

"I don't know. Not sit idle, that's not me. But truthfully, I'm out of ideas at the moment. This thing with the property and that house…"

"I visited this morning with someone who used to own the property behind yours by the creek."

"Where your rainmaker is working."

His rainmaker. He grimaced inwardly. "John and Midge Atkinson. They moved into town after the murder, I think. I was hoping to get some answers for you, but…"

"But people don't want to talk about it, do they?"

"No."

"Doesn't that tell you something?" she asked, glancing over at him, her face intent in the glow of the dashboard lights.

"What it tells me is that people don't like talking about the brutal murder of a young woman who lived near them, someone they knew. I get the impression that Midge Atkinson was a friend of hers."

Dulcie started. "Midge Atkinson? No wonder the name sounded familiar. An M. Atkinson painted angels on the wall in Angel Beaumont's bedroom upstairs. Do you know if Midge paints?"

"Could be. All the borders were painted at her house. But if she was a friend, then that could explain why some people don't want to talk about the murder."

"Maybe they don't want to talk because the killer was never caught…and he's someone in this community and they're all covering for him."

Russell shot her a look. "Is that what you think?"

"I'm not the only one who thinks that." Dulcie regretted the words instantly.

"Someone told you *that?*" He slowed as her car came into view.

"I'm sorry I said it."

"But not because it wasn't true." He stopped the pickup and looked over at her. "Dulcie, you're scaring me. If you know something, you have to go to the sheriff. Or talk to my brother Shane. You met him tonight. He's a deputy sheriff. He'll help you." Shane had left just before them for his late shift.

"I don't know *anything,* that's the problem. It's all speculation."

He studied her openly in the dashboard light. "You aren't going to let this go, are you? Then let me help you. I don't want you to have to do this alone."

"Thank you. For the offer. For supper. For including me in your family tonight."

"I'm serious about helping you," he said.

It was tempting to accept his help. But what could he do? The locals weren't apt to talk to him any more than they were to her. Russell hadn't been here long enough that he knew the community's secrets. Maybe you had to go back five generations for that.

"I know you are serious about helping me and I appreciate that. I just don't know how you can help me right now."

"You're going back to the house tomorrow."

She nodded. It was all she had.

"Then let me come with you. I'll scare away the snakes and do whatever you need."

"And make sure your rainmaker doesn't come back?"

"That, too."

She shook her head. Tomorrow she planned to cross the creek and talk to the rainmaker. After reading the murder story Jolene had given her, Dulcie had some leverage to use with him. The only way she might get the rainmaker to talk to her, though, was if Russell Corbett was nowhere around.

"If I need you, I'll let you know." She opened the passenger's-side door. "I liked your family."

"Well, that was only because they were on their best behavior tonight."

"Oh?" She hadn't meant to sound so suspicious.

"My father and I are the only ones who discussed purchasing your land—if and when you put it up for sale."

"So why were they on their best behavior?" she asked.

"It's embarrassing."

"They thought I was your girlfriend?" She laughed. "They must be horrified. You and a fool city girl? I heard what you muttered under your breath the first day we met."

He leaned back, smiling over at her. "Now I *am* embarrassed."

"No, you're not. Anyway, it's true. I *am* a fool city girl out here and gone in the wilds of Montana." She glanced away for a moment. "I don't even know what I'm doing here."

"Looking for answers."

"That's what I keep telling myself. But I'm not sure I want to hear the answers."

"Then why keep looking? You can walk away right now."

She laughed at how outrageous that was.

"I'm serious."

"I know you are, but nothing could get me to quit at this point. I have the feeling that the reason my parents didn't tell me about this property was because this was something I had to do myself and they knew it."

He shook his head. "This is no way to find it out about a murdered woman and her dead child." He sounded angry.

"You didn't know my parents."

"Did *you?*" he shot back.

She started to step out of the pickup.

"I'm sorry, you're right, I didn't know your parents. I should keep my opinions to myself."

She couldn't be angry with him. Russell had been there for her when she'd needed him and she hadn't forgotten when they'd made love in the house.

But he couldn't solve this for her—as much as he wanted to. "Thank you again for this evening. I can't tell you how much I needed it but then I think you knew that, didn't you?"

"You give me too much credit."

"No, I don't." She thought about leaning back into

the pickup's cab and kissing him. But she knew how dangerous that would be. The two of them being intimate again wasn't a good idea.

Instead, she smiled, stepped out of the truck and closed the door.

He waited, just as she'd known he would, for her to start her car and drive down the road before he turned around and headed back to the ranch.

She didn't let herself think about the copy of the murder story Jolene Stevens had given her until his pickup's taillights disappeared from her rearview mirror. Shuddering, she glanced over at the story stuffed in her shoulder bag.

Was it just fiction? Or was Jolene Stevens right? Could it be a confession? But why write it for the teacher of the one-room schoolhouse?

And where, if anywhere, did that leave Dulcie?

The headlights came out of nowhere. One minute there was no one behind her. The next a pickup was tailgating her, its bright lights blinding.

Dulcie slowed a little, pulling to the side to let the impatient driver pass.

The pickup started past her, then swerved into her rental. The loud crunch of metal filled the car as she was thrown against the door. Her car veered to the right. She fought to keep it on the road as it swerved wildly.

At first she thought the truck had hit her accidentally until the driver swerved into her again, jarring her vehicle in a roar of engine and screaming metal.

Ahead the road narrowed, dropping off steeply on both sides. The truck swerved away from her after the impact, but she could see it heading for her again.

She sped up, knowing her only chance was to outrun the driver.

The pickup fell in behind her, the lights filling the cab as it stayed with her. The road dipped and rose. The car caught air over a rise and came down hard.

Behind her, the truck came off the top of the rise airborne. It was going so fast that for a breathtaking instant, she thought it would land on her.

The pickup came down in a cloud of dust directly behind her. She felt it slam into the back of her car, shooting her forward before the truck started to fishtail in some loose gravel on the edge of the recently graded road.

In her side mirror she saw the truck leave the road, barreling down into the barrow pit and back up the other side. It hurtled through a barbed-wire fence before coming to rest in a mushroom cloud of dust in the middle of a wheat field.

Dulcie sped up, racing toward town. In her rearview mirror she saw the truck's headlights sweep around as the driver headed back toward the road.

Fear had her gripping the wheel and continuing to glance at the rearview mirror. She was driving as fast as she could without going off the road herself, afraid any moment the pickup's headlights would appear again over a rise.

But a few turns in the road, she looked back and saw nothing but darkness behind her. Either the pickup hadn't been able to get out of the wheat field. Or whoever had tried to run her off the road had given up, having successfully sent their message.

She didn't slow until she reached the outskirts of

town. Her heart was still pounding as she drove down the main drag looking for the sheriff's department.

The office was in a small, brick building. She was glad to see Shane Corbett as she rushed in.

"What's wrong?" he asked as he saw her face.

"Someone just tried to run me off the road." She motioned toward her rental car parked outside.

"Let me have a look. Stay here." And he was gone. A few minutes later he returned. "Come into the office and I'll take your report."

By then she wasn't shaking anymore and was able to tell him what she could about the truck. "Dark colored." She saw by his expression that the description wasn't going to help. "There are a lot of dark-colored trucks around here, aren't there?"

He nodded. "But the driver left some paint on your rental car. The pickup was brown and I would imagine you left some bright red paint on his pickup. We'll look for it and have the body shop watch for it."

She doubted the truck would be turning up. The driver would be a fool not to park it in his barn and leave it there.

"Any reason someone would want to run you off the road?"

"No." Even as she said it, she wondered if she was wrong.

"Did the driver appear to be drunk?"

"Not really."

"I guess what I'm asking is if you were going too slow and taking up the road?" he said, looking embarrassed.

"You mean being a city girl?" She sighed. "No, I

was going normal speed and I even pulled over to let him go around and he wouldn't."

Shane nodded. "Didn't mean to insult you. Just trying to figure out why anyone would want to run you off the road."

"I haven't been here long enough to make enemies, but I have been looking into Laura Beaumont's murder."

He nodded slowly. "Russell mentioned that. You know—"

"You aren't going to tell me that I might be putting myself in danger by doing that, are you?"

Shane smiled. Those Corbett men really were good-looking. "I might have thought about warning you that sometimes locals don't take kindly to a newcomer butting into their business."

"That's what I thought. But isn't it more likely that, since the murder was never solved, I'm making someone nervous?"

"A twenty-four-year-old murder? The killer's gone free all this time? Seems kind of stupid for him to try to run you off the road and give himself away when you don't have any evidence against him, right?"

He did have a point.

"Not yet," she admitted.

"Yeah, that's the part that makes me nervous," he said. "What exactly are you thinking of doing to find this evidence?"

"Just doing a little more digging."

He raised an eyebrow. "You think that's a good idea?"

"Someone is trying to scare me off. That means there is something to find and I don't scare off easily."

"I'm beginning to see why my brother is so taken with you—and why he's equally as worried."

"He's *taken* with me?" she asked with a grin.

"You tell him I said that and I'll deny it. Seriously, we're a small sheriff's department. There's no way we can protect you."

"But you could *help* me," Dulcie said. "You could let me see the file on Laura Beaumont's murder."

She ran blind from her mother's bedroom, leaving bloody footprints. The killer raced after her, calling her name, as she ran down the stairs and burst out the front door.

She could hear the killer behind her as they both disappeared into the darkness. It wasn't until she reached the road that she realized she'd run the wrong way.

Had she run toward the creek, she could have hidden in the trees. Or called her friend for help. He would've saved her.

But instead she'd run to the road.

She looked back, hearing the killer coming behind her, knowing now that she didn't stand a chance of getting away. The killer was almost to the open gate. On the road the killer would have no trouble catching her.

Lights came over the small hill, blinding her. She closed her eyes at the screech of brakes and thrown gravel as the vehicle skidded to a stop. She was caught in the headlights like a deer about to be slaughtered.

The door opened. "Angel? My God, Angel, is that blood on you? Where's your mama? Tell me where your mama is, girl. Stop your crying and pulling away, I'm not hurting you. Tell me what's happened. Stop it and tell me what your mama has done now."

It rained the day of Angel Beaumont's funeral. She was buried on the hill overlooking Old Town White-horse. The whole county turned out, huddled under a sea of black umbrellas, as Titus Cavanaugh read from the Bible and prayed over the poor helpless child.

During the funeral the rainmaker drove by in his beat-up truck, his magical pipes singing against each other. The mourners dispersed soon after. A few days later, the community had joined again at the cemetery to lay to rest the mother now beside the child, just as they had lain to rest the truth.

Jolene looked up at her Friday class, heart pounding. All but one head was bent over the math assignment she'd handed out. Her unruly fifth-grader, Thad Brooks, was chewing on the end of his pencil and staring out the window, daydreaming.

She cleared her throat, catching his attention. He ducked his head and went back to work. She read the pages again.

Last night she'd tossed and turned for hours, afraid she'd made a mistake by giving Dulcie copies of the murder story. She'd been anxious this morning to get the next assignment, equally afraid the author would find out what she'd done and quit sending it.

Now she'd been given another piece of the puzzle and she couldn't wait to see what Dulcie thought about it.

When her students had finished their math assignment and turned it in, Jolene said, "Monday is the last day of your writing project, which means you have to wind up your story. Today we're going to talk about endings. Can someone tell me what we need to do to make a satisfying ending?"

"What if we can't end it?" Mace Carpenter asked. "Cuz it has no ending?"

"For this assignment, you need to end it," she said. "The ending of your story must satisfy all the questions the person reading your story might have. For instance, the reader will want to know what happened to your character. Why it happened. And feel satisfied that the character will be all right in the future."

"That's called a happy ending," Codi spoke up. "Which means your character can't die, isn't that right, Miss Stevens?"

"For this assignment I think it best if your characters continue living, yes." She wasn't sure why she'd just told them that the stories had to have a happy ending. They didn't. Maybe because she hoped there would be a happy ending to the mystery in the murder story.

At recess, Jolene made a decision. She called the cell phone number Dulcie had given her, planning to leave a message. She was surprised when Dulcie answered and said as much.

"I'm in town. I had to wait until my new rental car was delivered. It's a long story. Did you get another part of the murder story?" she asked excitedly.

"Yes." She glanced around to make sure no one was nearby listening and then read the story.

"The girl is alive," Dulcie cried.

"Not necessarily. The person who found her certainly wasn't very compassionate."

"What are you saying? That you think the person in the vehicle killed her? That the killer had an accomplice?"

"Maybe. I don't know. I guess it depends on who found her that night and why that person wasn't very kind to her, if you believe the author of the story."

Dulcie was quiet for a moment. "I still think she's alive, but you're right. It doesn't mention what happens to the killer. I wonder what the author of the story is trying to tell us?"

Tell *us?* Jolene shuddered. The author was trying to tell *her* something, but Jolene wasn't sure what exactly.

"If Angel lived, then that would explain why no one wants to talk about what happened to the girl. She saw the killer. She could identify him."

"So why didn't she identify him?" Jolene asked in a whisper.

This time Dulcie was silent for much longer. "I hadn't thought of that. She was old enough to identify the killer. Unless she didn't recognize him. Still, she could have described him. Unless she was too traumatized to do so."

Jolene knew where Dulcie was headed with this. "So you think the community secreted her away so the killer couldn't find her."

"Or so she *couldn't* identify the killer."

Jolene shuddered at the thought.

"They found someone to adopt her. Apparently Laura didn't have any family. It makes sense. Especially if I'm Angel Beaumont."

It *did* make sense, Jolene thought. And that's what was scaring her.

* * *

The moment Russell saw his brother drive up, he knew something had happened and he feared it had to do with Dulcie Hughes.

"I'll be back in a minute," he told the ranch hands he'd been working with on the new section of fence and hurried toward the patrol car as Shane got out.

Russell had been out since sunup, hoping to work off some of his frustration. He would have liked to forget all about Dulcie Hughes, but there didn't seem much chance of that. Now, he was convinced he'd had every right to be worried.

"What's she done now?" he asked before his brother had a chance to open his mouth.

"She got into a little fender bender on the way home last night," Shane said, knowing at once who he was referring to. He quickly added, "She wasn't hurt."

"A fender bender?"

"A pickup tried to run her off the road."

Russell swore as his mind raced to make sense of it. "Why would someone…" His voice trailed off as he realized his brother hadn't driven all this way out here to tell him that.

"We found a pickup that matches the description she gave us. It has some of her fancy rental-car paint on the side of it," Shane said.

"*Who?* Did you arrest the son-of-a-bitch?"

Shane held up a hand. "It's a little more complicated than that. The pickup is a beater John Atkinson keeps down in his barn on his old ranch."

"Let me guess, he told you he keeps the key in the ignition?" Russell demanded sarcastically.

"On the floorboard. He swears he hasn't used the truck in months and didn't know it was missing until this morning when he happened down that way and found it in the ditch with a flat tire."

"And you believe him?"

"I do. The pickup reeked of alcohol. If John had tried to run someone off the road in it, seems kind of dumb of him to just leave it in a ditch right beside the road since it didn't take five minutes to trace the truck back to him."

Russell swore. "You're telling me you think some drunk kids borrowed the truck for a joy ride?"

"Looks that way."

"Bet Dulcie didn't see it that way," Russell said, narrowing his eyes at his brother.

Shane sighed. "Nope. She thinks someone is trying to scare her off this investigation she's doing of Laura Beaumont's murder. She even asked to see the file."

"Did you let her?"

"You know better than that on an unsolved case." He shook his head. "I did go dig the file out of cold-case storage. Brutal murder. The woman was stabbed thirteen times."

"A crime of passion?"

"She did have some men friends, apparently."

"John Atkinson?" Russell saw that his brother wanted to deny it, but couldn't.

"He *was* questioned. He had an alibi for the time of the murder. He was with his wife."

"Midge." Russell thought about his visit to the Atkinsons. Now their reactions made a hell of a lot more sense. "Did you ever think that Dulcie might

know what she's talking about? That the killer is still around?"

"I'm not arguing that. I just don't believe that's what was going on last night, given the evidence."

Russell wanted to argue further, but he could see it would be a waste of breath. That and the fact that Shane Corbett was a damned good law-enforcement officer who'd been a Texas Ranger and was now a local deputy with a hell of a lot of experience.

Not that even the best weren't taken in on occasion by a clever criminal. But this criminal didn't sound clever. Laura's killer sounded like someone who'd lost control. Or maybe never had much control.

"Just tell me this," he said to his brother. "Was Ben Carpenter one of the other men who were questioned during the murder investigation?"

Shane seemed surprised. "No, should he have been?"

"Maybe." Russell saw that his brother was chewing on his cheek and realized there was more, something Shane was debating whether or not to tell him.

"What else did you find in the file? I know there's more."

Shane looked away for a moment. "The file had been sealed by a local judge."

"Sealed?" Russell asked in surprise. "In an unsolved murder case? I thought they only did that when a juvenile was involved?"

"I guess they did it because of the little girl."

"Angel Beaumont. But she's dead."

Shane said nothing.

"She is dead, right?"

"Her death certificate was signed by the same judge." Russell swore.

"Now don't go jumping to conclusions," Shane warned. "The judge was probably acting as coroner back then."

"Don't give me that. You think something is wrong with this case or you wouldn't have just told me about this."

Shane cocked his head at him. "How involved are you with this woman?" He swore as he caught Russell's expression. "Hell, Russell."

"It isn't like I'm falling for her." Russell couldn't regret making love with Dulcie, no matter how big a fool move it had been. "She'll be gone back to Chicago soon."

Shane was shaking his head and frowning. "Look," he said. "I found something in the file. I'm sure Dulcie is going to find out about it sooner or later. Maybe sooner and from someone who cares about her would be better."

Russell held his breath.

"Laura Beaumont's maiden name was Hughes. She was the daughter of Brad and Kathy Hughes of Chicago—and the mother of *two* daughters. Angel was the *oldest*."

Chapter 10

After making plans to meet Jolene later, Dulcie called Renada. She felt terrible for not doing it sooner.

"Honey, you sound awful. Put the property up for sale and get out of there," Renada said.

"It's not that simple." She had skipped telling her friend about Laura's murder or about Angel Beaumont. "I still don't know why it was left to me and until I do, I can't leave."

"How did I know you were going to say that? Have you at least met a handsome cowboy?"

"Actually…"

Renada laughed. "I can't wait to hear all about it. You're sure you don't need me to come out there?"

"Positive. How is the design class going?"

"Wonderful! I am having so much fun. I'll tell you all about it when you get back. Back soon, okay?"

"Okay." Dulcie hung up and felt like crying. She missed her friend, but she knew it was more than that. She was scared. She'd been scared ever since she'd heard she'd inherited the property in Montana.

And it had only gotten worse once she'd arrived here and found out what had happened to Laura Beaumont and her daughter.

She was convinced she was Angel Beaumont. It was the only thing that made any sense, she told herself, as she drove to the farmhouse. And if there was one person who might tell her the truth it was the rainmaker.

She'd seen his shocked expression yesterday on the stairs. For a moment she would swear he'd thought she was Laura Beaumont. Was it possible she resembled the woman?

According to the short story, the rainmaker had known Laura intimately. He would have seen the little girl.

Dulcie followed the banging of his hammer, heard it slow as she approached, and then cease. The rainmaker raised his head as if he'd sensed her more than had seen her coming.

With one filthy hand, he pushed back his hat and leveled those malevolent dark eyes at her.

"What do you want?" he asked, his sandpaper voice grating

"You knew Laura Beaumont."

His expression didn't change.

"I know you were her lover."

One eyebrow lifted, but he still said nothing.

"I need to know about her and her daughter."

He chuckled at that, a dry, rusty sound. "You need to mind your own business."

"It *is* my business. If you know who killed her—"

"If I knew, he'd be dead." The words snapped like a whip.

Dulcie swallowed, not doubting for an instant that he meant it. "I saw your expression yesterday when you glanced up as I came down the stairs. Do I look like Laura?"

"I have work to do." He reached for his sledgehammer.

She grabbed his arm. It was hard and strong as the steel he pounded. "Please, I have to know why you thought I was Laura Beaumont."

"You're not." He jerked his arm free.

"I could be her daughter, Angel."

The dark eyes narrowed. "You're not."

"How do you know that?"

A thin, cold smile curled his lips. "I'm sure. Go home before you get hurt."

"Are you threatening me?" Her voice betrayed her and broke, making him smile as he picked up the sledgehammer.

"Leave me alone." He turned his back on her. As he swung the hammer, she had to jump back. He brought the sledge down hard on the top of the steel pipe. The deafening sound rang in her ears long after she left.

Russell had ridden out this morning to help with the fence. Now he realized that he could get to the old Beaumont place faster by horseback than returning to the ranch for his pickup.

He needed the fresh air anyway. The news his brother had given him only made him more afraid for Dulcie.

That Dulcie had been right about a possible cover-up

only made him more anxious. Now there definitely seemed to be a question as to whether or not Angel Beaumont was really dead. If Angel had seen the killer, that would explain why her mother's murder file had been sealed. Someone had wanted the townspeople to believe that Angel was dead.

But was she?

It was all speculation with few facts and he knew better than to jump to too many conclusions at this point.

Or had sealing the file been about protecting the second daughter so she didn't end up like Angel?

As he rode past part of the Atkinson place, he saw John standing out by his barn and on impulse rode over. John shielded his eyes and, seeing him, let out a curse.

"Let's see this old truck my brother told me about," Russell said as he dismounted.

"What are you doing, getting involved in this?" John demanded. "It doesn't have anything to do with you."

"Seems to have something to do with Dulcie Hughes, though, doesn't it?"

John shook his head irritably. "I told your brother—"

"I know what you told my brother and I know what you told me yesterday. How about telling me the truth?"

"Damn it, I didn't have anything to do with that woman being run off the road last night."

"But you did have something to do with Laura Beaumont."

"I suppose your brother the deputy already told you I had an affair with Laura."

"Actually, I figured that out on my own."

"Midge knows all about it."

"Is that why she gave you an alibi the day of the murder?"

John looked angry again. "I didn't kill Laura. I loved her. I was planning to leave Midge for her if—"

"If what?"

"If she hadn't dumped me for someone else, all right?"

"Who?"

John looked away, his jaw set, and for a moment Russell thought he wouldn't answer. "Ben Carpenter. At least that's who I saw going into her house right after I left."

"You must have been angry enough to kill her."

John swore and started to walk away, but turned back. "I *loved* her. I wouldn't have hurt her for..." He wagged his head, looking miserable. "I would have done *anything* for her."

"What about Midge?"

"What about her?"

"If she found out about you and Laura, maybe—"

"She'd known for months. She was the one who told me there were other men. I didn't believe her until I saw it for myself."

"And you did *nothing?*"

John let out a humorless laugh. "Wrong. I did something. I crawled back to my wife and begged her forgiveness."

"Is that when you moved to the other ranch?"

John nodded, looking shamefaced. "And before you bother to ask, I was cleaning out one of the bedrooms to move our stuff in when I heard about Laura. It damn near killed me. I've never gotten over Laura. I never will."

"So tell me what you know about Laura and her two daughters."

* * *

Dulcie had searched the house for hours. She had just stepped out for a breath of fresh air when she saw the lone rider coming over the hill across the road.

She'd wondered if Russell's brother would tell him about the pickup that had tried to run her off the road. It had surprised her she hadn't heard from Russ. She'd expected him to come tearing up, angry and scared and dispensing more good advice.

One look at the expression on his handsome face now, though, and she knew he must have only just heard about last night.

She leaned against the side of the house in the shade and watched as he rode the large buckskin horse into her yard. He swung off the horse like a man as at home in a saddle as on a four-wheeler or driving a combine.

She hadn't been able to help the small thrill she had felt seeing him astride the horse. Riding to her rescue, she thought with a grin.

"Something amusing?" he asked as he walked to the bottom of the porch steps.

"Just admiring you in the saddle."

He climbed the steps in long strides that brought him right to her. She could tell by the look on his face that he wasn't here to make love to her again.

"My brother tell you that he found the pickup that ran you off the road?" he asked. "He thinks some kids took it from an old barn, picked up some booze and went for a joy ride."

Her brown eyes narrowed. "What do *you* think?"

"I think anyone who knows John knows about that pickup. They probably saw your car parked where we left it yesterday evening and just waited at a distance for you to return."

"So you think it was a warning, too?"

He shook his head. "A warning would have been a note tacked on your door."

She thought about the note Jolene told her had been tucked under her windshield wiper. *Watch your step.*

She nodded, her gaze locked with his.

He dragged his away. "You look good."

"I'll just bet after being in that house all day, digging into every dirty corner I could find."

"I take it you didn't find anything?"

She shook her head.

Russell glanced toward the house behind her. "You searched the whole place?"

She nodded.

"Then maybe it's time for you to go back to Chicago."

That took her by surprise. "Just when we're having so much fun?" she said, trying to make light of it.

"I stopped having fun when someone tried to hurt you," he said quietly, his incredible blue eyes locking with hers.

Dulcie swallowed the lump in her throat as she saw that he was no longer teasing. He was dead serious and she felt the intensity of his gaze all the way down to her toes.

"There is something I need to tell you," he said and she felt her heart drop. "You've been trying to find out about Laura Beaumont's past…"

She saw it in his face. He was about to deliver some devastating news.

"Laura's maiden name was Hughes. She was the

daughter of Brad and Kathy Hughes of Chicago. She had two daughters."

Dulcie grabbed the porch railing as the world tilted crazily and suddenly she could no longer get enough oxygen into her lungs.

Russell stepped up behind her and wrapped his arms around her. He could feel her shock, her pain, her disbelief in the rigid muscles of her body.

He'd feared what this would do to her, finding out that the murdered woman who'd lived in this house had been her mother and that the little girl who had died was her sister.

Dulcie was strong, stronger than any woman he'd ever met, but was she strong enough to get past this?

Her words came out a whisper. "The oldest daughter? What was her name?"

"Angel Lee."

"And the youngest?"

He swallowed. "Dulcie Ann."

"I don't understand."

"John Atkinson told me that Laura had gotten in a lot of trouble when she was young. She'd run away and married Darrell Beaumont against your grandparents' wishes. They disowned her."

He felt Dulcie stiffen, waited a moment, and continued. "Laura had two children right away, one right after the other. When Darrell was killed in a motorcycle accident, Laura contacted your parents for help. She was living here in the old Beaumont place, Darrell's family was helping out, but Laura was lonely and lost. Are you sure you want to hear this?"

She nodded, but didn't turn around.

"Your grandparents came to Whitehorse. Laura apparently thought they'd come to take her back to Chicago but when she realized it would be on their terms, she turned them down. They saw the way she was living here and insisted on taking you back with them since you were the youngest, only three at the time. They apparently raised you as their own."

Dulcie shook her head and stepped out of his arms to go to the end of the porch. "I can't believe they would do that."

"This is only Laura's side of the story through someone else. Angel refused to go with them. She said she had to stay and take care of her mother." He knew she deserved to be angry, but said, "I'm sure your grandparents didn't know how to tell you after everything that happened."

She turned. Her face was still pale, but her eyes were fired with heat. "Yes, how could they explain what they'd done? Taking me, leaving behind my sister to…" She waved an arm through the air. "And then not telling me all those years, letting me walk into this minefield?"

"Parents make mistakes."

"Don't even try to defend them."

He stood listening to the pounding of his heart and realized he could no longer hear Finnegan Amherst sinking the metal pipes. Glancing at the sky, he saw nothing but blue sky. Not a cloud in sight. "Dulcie—"

"It makes sense now, doesn't it," she said with a bitter laugh. "Me inheriting the property. I knew there had to be a connection, but I never dreamed…"

"I'm sorry you had to find out this way. John told me that Laura wore a locket around her neck with your picture in it. She would never take it off. He said losing you broke her heart."

Dulcie's eyes welled with tears. She quickly turned away.

He started to go to her, but stopped himself, giving her the space he knew she needed. "John said Laura feared they would come back for Angel as well. He thinks it was the reason she wanted to remarry, but only someone she could love as much as your father. I'm so sorry you had to find out this way."

"So they left Angel and then Laura was murdered and Angel…" She turned around. "What happened to Angel?"

"She died, Dulcie. You were the child everyone was trying to protect."

Dulcie shook her head. "That can't be right." She glanced at her watch. "I have to go."

"*Go?* Dulcie—"

"I'll be all right." She stepped to him to lay her palm against his cheek. "Thank you for telling me. I know how hard it was for you. I knew it was going to be something like this. I thought I must be Angel…" She shook her head and turned to go down the porch steps as if she had somewhere she had to get in a hurry.

Russell wanted to call her back, afraid for her.

She stopped at her car, looked back at him and smiled. "I want to ride a horse before I leave Montana. Promise?"

He nodded as she ducked into her car and stood watching her go, telling himself she needed time alone to digest all of this.

But as he watched her drive off, he knew that nothing would stop her from looking for the killer now.

Dulcie told herself that nothing had changed. She was still the same person she'd believed herself to be all these years. But she was lying—just as everyone had lied to her.

She didn't know who she was, wasn't sure she could get past this. Her entire life had been built on the facade of a solid foundation that had now crumbled to dust and she felt herself sinking into the mire of lies.

Her mind whirled as she drove. A mother and father she'd never known. Her parents...*grand*parents, the two people she trusted the most. She could see their faces, the worry in them from the time she could remember. So much older than all her classmates' parents.

"Why didn't you tell me the truth?" she cried, slamming her fist against the steering wheel. "Because you were cowards? Because..." The answer came to her as if plucked out of the blue sky overhead.

"Because you didn't want to tell me about my mother." She said the words on a ragged breath, her voice breaking as she thought of the murder story and the way Laura Beaumont had been portrayed. An alley cat in heat. A mother who ignored her little girl.

But why hadn't her grandparents taken both girls? Why had they left Angel?

As she hit the brakes to make the curve in the road, Dulcie realized she was driving too fast. The car fishtailed wildly, the back tires sliding off into the shallow barrow pit. The sound of the dirt and gravel scraping across the underbelly of the rental car drowned out everything except the erratic pounding of her pulse. She was going to wreck another rental car. As if that was her biggest concern.

She got the car under control and slowed, her hands trembling on the wheel, her whole body shaking. The tears finally came in a rush, a wall of water that forced her to pull over and stop. She leaned on the steering wheel and cried for the mother and father and sister she'd never known, for the two people who had raised her, for herself.

When the sobs finally ceased, she wiped her eyes and pulled herself together. She might not know who she was—but she knew what she had to do. She straightened up and got the car going again, telling herself she'd always been strong. Now more than ever she needed that strength for what was coming.

She felt a small shiver of fear prickle her skin as she saw the Old Town Whitehorse cemetery ahead.

After school, Jolene waited until everyone was gone before she walked up to the cemetery on the hill to meet Dulcie. The afternoon sun hung low in the sky after another torturous day of heat.

She stopped to catch her breath and pick some of the wildflowers that grew at the edge of the road. As she took her small bouquet and passed under the wrought-iron arch that read Whitehorse Cemetery to climb the hill, each breath burned her lungs.

The quiet up there was eerie. A stray gust of breeze stirred a bouquet of plastic flowers on a nearby grave. The air that brushed her face was hot as a fevered touch. She drew back instinctively and stood for a moment, trying to catch her breath.

She had to stop letting her imagination run away with her. There were no ghosts in this graveyard. The stories of the lights were nothing more than rural legends.

But the fear she felt was real as she saw Dulcie's rental car parked at the back of the cemetery. Was she waiting in her car? Or had she already found Angel Beaumont's grave?

Jolene wished she hadn't agreed to meet here. Normally she found cemeteries interesting. She liked the headstones, the history, the feeling of peace.

But today she felt jumpy.

Dulcie looked up as she approached. Something in her face made Jolene's heart lodge in her throat. Dulcie had discovered something. What?

All her fears came in a rush, filling her with terror. Perspiration beaded on her upper lip. She wiped at it and forced herself to walk over to where Dulcie waited.

She sucked in an arid breath, tears suddenly burning her eyes as Dulcie stepped to her.

"Why are you looking at me like that?" Jolene demanded, her voice a hoarse whisper. "What's happened?"

Dulcie shook her head and Jolene saw her hurriedly brush at her own tears. "I need to ask you something. How did you get the teaching position here?"

Suddenly she felt dizzy, a little confused. She shook her head as if to clear it. "Someone called down to the university looking for a teacher. Why?"

"You didn't apply for it before that?"

"No, I—"

"Are you adopted?"

Jolene took a step back, her heart a thunder in her chest. "Tell me what's going on."

"You *were* adopted?"

"My mother was a teenager. She couldn't keep me." The words tumbled out. "Why are you asking me this?"

"Because I've been trying to understand why someone is sending you the murder story," Dulcie said.

"I know it doesn't make any sense."

"It didn't—until I realized that the person writing it has just been waiting for me to inherit Laura Beaumont's property and return to Montana and find Angel Beaumont."

Jolene stared at her, eyes widening. "*You're* Angel Beaumont?"

"No," Dulcie said, shaking her head as she reached to take Jolene's hand. "*You* are."

The words barely registered as Dulcie led her to the tiny headstone next to Laura Beaumont's. An angel had been carved into the granite with the child's name cut in the wings: Angel Beaumont

But it was the smaller letters carved in the bottom that squeezed Jolene's heart like a fist: June 5, 1980–May 11, 1985.

June 5, 1980. Jolene's birthday.

Chapter 11

Jolene felt numb. This was so surreal. She shook her head. "No, you're wrong." She felt faint, the heat so intense, she thought she might have to sit down.

Dulcie pulled her over into the shade of a large tree. "I'm sorry you had to learn it this way. I'm sorry we both did. But Laura Beaumont had *two* daughters," she said, taking both her hands in hers. "Do you hear me? *Two* daughters. Dulcie Ann born in 1981 and Angel Lee born in 1980. We're *sisters*."

Jolene stared at the stranger standing in front of her. She heard the words but they didn't register. She and Dulcie were sisters? "That's not possible."

"I know this is hard to believe. I'm having the same trouble, but it's true." Dulcie went on to talk about a locket and grandparents and secrets. Jolene listened but felt no connection to the people Dulcie was telling her about.

"Jolene, you *are* Angel," Dulcie said when she'd finished.

She was Angel Beaumont? The daughter of Laura Beaumont? The little girl who'd witnessed her mother's murder? The little girl someone had saved?

She shook her head and pulled her hands free. "There's been a mistake."

Dulcie studied her for a moment. "There's one way to prove it. We can have Russell's brother at the sheriff's department run DNA tests. Then will you believe me?"

The sooner they cleared this up the better, Jolene thought, just wanting to leave the cemetery and go home. Since she was a little girl she'd always lost herself in books and that was what she wanted to do right now—curl up with a book, forget about all of this.

"Don't you see, this is why you're getting the murder story," Dulcie said. "Someone knows who you really are."

Jolene felt herself surface as if she'd been swimming up from the bottom of a deep, dark pool. "The killer's wrong." She felt her first pulse of panic. "If the killer thinks I'm Angel…"

Dulcie's expression softened. "Don't worry. I won't let anything happen to you." She smiled. "I always wanted a sister. I used to have an imaginary friend, at least that's what my parents told me it was. Her name was Angel. Don't you see? I remembered you."

Jolene brushed at the sudden tears that flooded her eyes. "It isn't that I don't believe you…"

"It's okay," Dulcie said, putting an arm around her for a moment. "Are you going to be all right?"

Jolene nodded, although she wasn't sure of that at

all. "If what you're saying is true, why can't I remember? Why was none of this familiar like it was for you?"

"I suppose you repressed it because you couldn't handle what you saw. You were so young." Tears filled Dulcie's eyes again. "I'm so sorry."

Was that what she'd done? Buried the memory? "You think that's why I came back here? Why I took this job?"

"Maybe."

She studied Dulcie. *Her sister?* "What if the killer got me back here?"

"Let's not jump to conclusions."

"Jump to conclusions?" Jolene cried. "One minute you're telling me you're Angel. The next you're telling me I am." She shook her head and stepped back. Her life had always been dull. Older parents. No siblings. Her only friends on the isolated farm where she lived were the animals and the characters in the stacks of books she read. Was it any surprise she wanted to believe this was fiction?

"It's going to be all right," Dulcie said, trying to comfort her.

But Jolene knew better.

Dulcie wasn't sure how she'd expected Jolene to react to the news. She'd hoped she would be as happy as she was about having a sister. She'd handled it poorly. But she'd suspected the truth the moment she'd heard Laura had two daughters.

The gravestone with Jolene's birth date on it only proved it. Angel Beaumont was alive, back in Whitehorse and someone was sending her the murder story.

That's why Dulcie had to find the killer fast.

Back at Jolene's tiny house, she watched her sister in the kitchen pouring them each a glass of tea. She understood why Jolene didn't want to believe this.

Still, she seemed too calm and Dulcie worried that Jolene didn't understand how much danger she was in. Or didn't want to face it, the same way she didn't want to believe she was Angel.

They'd said little after they'd left the cemetery and driven into town to the sheriff's office. Shane had taken DNA from each of them and promised to put a rush on the results, then they'd come back to Jolene's house.

Dulcie knew that Jolene had to have buried the memories of her first five years here in Whitehorse along with the murder of their mother. "Maybe you should talk to someone. A health care professional who's dealt with this sort of thing before."

"A psychiatrist?" Jolene shook her head. "Let's just wait for the DNA test results, okay? Because you're wrong."

Unfortunately, the results might not come soon enough, Dulcie thought. Who else knew Angel Beaumont was alive? Deputy Sheriff Shane Corbett, Russell Corbett, the person who'd saved Angel that night on the road, whoever had faked Angel's death, whoever had whisked her away to be adopted illegally to hide her from the killer, and the killer?

A lot of people knew Angel Beaumont was alive. But how many knew Jolene Stevens was Angel?

"You can't stay here," Dulcie said. "It's too dangerous." She couldn't bear the thought of finding a sister she never knew she had only to lose her.

Jolene handed her a glass of tea and plopped down

on the couch in front of the fan. The hot air lifted the russet hair that had escaped her ponytail. Dulcie saw with clarity that her older sister's hair was a shade darker than her own.

"I *have* to stay here. If I leave, the killer won't give me the ending of the story."

"You already *know* the ending," Dulcie cried.

"No, I don't. There is so much I don't know. If I'm who you say I am, then I don't know why our mother was killed. I don't know who saved me. I don't know who it is I have to fear."

Dulcie couldn't believe this. "You think the killer is going to confess all to you?"

"I do. Why else give me the other parts of the story? He—or she—wants me to *understand.*"

Dulcie was shaking her head. "It's too dangerous. The killer can't let you live once you know, don't you see that?"

"I've made up my mind. The killer won't act until he's finished the story. He wouldn't kill me before then."

"There is just one flaw in your logic. What if the killer isn't writing the story?"

"He is. No one else knows what happened that day but the killer."

And Jolene, Dulcie thought with a shudder. But she could see her sister wasn't going to change her mind. At least Jolene wasn't completely denying that she was Angel and she seemed to have pulled herself together. "I swear you're as stubborn as—"

"You?"

She stared at Jolene for a moment then began to

laugh. "We *are* sisters. You'll see. That's why you can't expect me to sit back and wait all weekend."

"I didn't expect you would, knowing you just the short time I have."

"We have to find the killer before you get the last of the murder story," Dulcie said, with renewed determination. She pulled a pad and pen from her purse and began making a list of what they did know.

"Midge Atkinson befriended Laura, then her husband had an affair with Laura. Both definitely suspects. Midge should also know who the friend was who Angel played with at the creek. Also there is the rainmaker and a man named Ben Carpenter who knew Laura." She looked up. Jolene had an odd expression on her face. "Is something wrong?"

"No."

"It's not much, but at least it's a place to start, right?"

"I still think the answer is in the murder story."

"We've both read it a dozen times—"

"I'm going to read it again. There has to be something in it that points to the killer."

Dulcie studied her sister. "If you're that sure the person writing the story is the killer, then maybe we should turn the story over to the sheriff."

Jolene was shaking her head. "The story isn't over. The killer will finish it if we just wait."

But finish it how?

"Monday I'll get the end of the story. In the meantime…" Jolene glanced toward the table. "I need to return that basket to Midge Atkinson. Maybe we could do it tomorrow? I'm really tired today and I want to reread the murder story. I'll be fine here alone. I need to be alone, okay?"

Dulcie knew she had little choice. Jolene was determined that the killer wanted her to read the ending and that she would be safe until then.

She just hoped Jolene was right and they had until Monday morning to find the killer.

"I need your help."

Russell couldn't believe his ears. He'd spent an afternoon in hell, worrying about Dulcie. Just the sound of her voice on the phone made his heart lift like helium.

"You know you have my help. What can I do? Did I mention I'm glad you called?"

He heard her chuckle on the other end of the line. "Meet me in town at my motel?"

"I'll see you in fifteen minutes, ten if you need me there sooner."

She laughed. "Fifteen will be fine."

Russell wavered between being relieved that she'd finally asked for his help—and worried, since he knew what it would take for her to ask.

This was about Laura Beaumont's killer, he was sure of that. The killer had stayed hidden for twenty-four years. Did Dulcie really think she could flush him out?

Of course she did. And she would, if humanly possible, and no matter the consequence. That, he knew, was what terrified him. He couldn't bear the thought of losing her.

That thought made him laugh. He would lose her to Chicago even if he could keep her from getting herself killed here in Whitehorse. It was just a matter of time until Dulcie left. She was a city girl, after all. He could already feel the hole she would leave in his life.

It was crazy how she'd gotten under his skin. All these years, he'd barely dated. He met women, but none of them could hold his interest. Then again, none of them had been Dulcie Hughes.

What if the killer *was* still around? And worse, what if he'd had help concealing his crime? Maybe not help from the entire community as Dulcie suspected, but from someone close to him. Someone as determined as the killer to keep the secret.

As he pulled up in front of the motel fifteen minutes later, Dulcie came out and slid into the passenger side of his truck. "Thanks for coming."

His heart did a little Texas two-step at just the sight of her. "How are you?"

"Fine." The lie seemed to freeze on her lips. "There's something I need to tell you. Angel Beaumont isn't dead."

He listened in shock as she told him about Jolene Stevens and handed him what she said was a copy of a short story the teacher believed the killer had been writing for her.

"You need to take this to my brother at the sheriff's department," he said when he finished reading it.

"No. And neither can you. I promised Jolene. Shane knows about Angel. He's getting DNA tests run for us."

"Do you realize how dangerous this is, not just for you, but for your sister?" He saw her expression and quickly backed off. "All right. But you need help."

She smiled. "That's why I called you. I know you

haven't been here long, but you know more people than I do. I have to find the killer before Monday morning. Will you help me?"

He'd move heaven and earth for this woman if possible. "Do you have something in mind?"

"We need to know who was in Laura Beaumont's life."

He noticed that she hadn't said "her mother's life." "Okay."

"The problem is no one will talk to me about it."

He wasn't sure anyone would talk to him either, but he couldn't let her down. He started the pickup and headed toward downtown Whitehorse.

Jolene sat down with the murder story, but she couldn't concentrate and finally put it away and walked to the window to stare out at the landscape. The late afternoon sun hung at the edge of the horizon, gilding the dry grasses with its golden light.

The rolling prairie, with the Little Rockies dark and constant against the horizon, had brought her a sense of peace. How was that possible, given the horror of what she must have seen when she'd lived here?

And why hadn't she started remembering? Was the truth buried so deep that even coming back here hadn't triggered it?

She shook her head, reminding herself that she didn't believe she was Angel Beaumont. Or did she?

Dulcie believed it and so did the killer, apparently. But why the story? Was he afraid she would remember someday and, upon hearing about the writing assignment, had decided to tell her his side of the story?

Was it possible that for twenty-four years the members of this community had lived with a murderer in their midst? Had they protected the killer the same way they'd protected her years ago? Who, she wondered, had saved her that day? Not just saved her, but found a couple willing to adopt her—illegally.

Her parents had explained to her that they couldn't adopt through normal channels because of their advanced ages.

Like Dulcie's parents, Jolene's were also gone. She'd lost her father first four years ago, then her mother passed away while she was still in college. There would be no answers coming from them.

Someone in this community knew though and as her gaze took in the vehicles parked outside the community center, Jolene told herself that this time someone in the Whitehorse Sewing Circle was going to tell her.

When Russell arrived in town, he'd made the acquaintance of Bridger and Laci Duvall. The two owned the Northern Lights restaurant and had recently had a baby boy.

Laci had been born and raised here so it was her Russell hoped to talk to when he pulled up in front of the restaurant.

He knew one of the Duvalls would be there cooking something for the supper crowd that evening and lucked out when he found Laci sliding a batch of her flourless chocolate cake into the oven.

"Russell," she said, giving him a kiss on the cheek. "I see you survived the wedding."

"Barely," he admitted. Three of his brothers had

recently wed in a triple ceremony that wouldn't soon be forgotten in Whitehorse. Laci and her husband had catered it.

"Only two Corbett bachelors left," she said with an exaggerated sigh.

"Don't start," he warned playfully, then introduced her to Dulcie and told her what they needed.

"I know how people here are about their secrets, especially in Old Town Whitehorse." Laci thought for a moment then smiled broadly. "I know just the person. Her name is Nina Mae Cross and you can find her at the rest home. I should warn you. She's a little irascible."

Jolene pushed open the door to the Whitehorse Community Center and stepped inside. It felt cooler in here in the large, dim, shadowy room. At the back, all of the quilters turned to see who had come in—just as they had last time.

Only this time, no one looked pleased to see her.

She walked to the back where they were gathered over the same small quilt they'd been working on the other day. She hadn't paid much attention then, but she did remember the small squares of bright colors. Today the women seemed to be embroidering tiny flowers along the edge of the baby quilt.

"Did you change your mind about learning to quilt?" Pearl Cavanaugh asked, looking hopeful.

"No," Jolene said. "I changed my mind about letting you get away without telling me about Laura Beaumont. I want to know what really happened to her daughter."

The room was instantly, deathly quiet.

Pearl put down her needle and thread. There was a trembling in her hands as she reached for her cane. "I don't believe you've ever seen our kitchen," she said, pushing herself up.

Jolene stepped back to let her lead the way and followed, afraid at how unsteady Pearl seemed on her feet.

They passed through a doorway. "Close the door behind you," Pearl said over her shoulder.

Jolene did as she was told, noticing that the other women were staring after them, but none had moved.

Suddenly Pearl turned to face her and Jolene saw that she was furious.

"What has possessed you to come in here and demand—"

"I have *every* right if I'm Angel Beaumont."

The rest of Pearl's words died on her lips.

"I am, aren't I?" The words came out a whisper.

Pearl leaned into her cane, swaying slightly. She took a step toward one of the chairs next to a small table and dropped into it.

As Jolene stared at the woman, she thought of the baby quilt the women were making—and the tiny embroidered flowers along the edge and had to sit down in one of the chairs herself.

"I have a quilt like that one out there you're making," she said, her voice breaking. The Whitehorse Sewing Circle had made her a quilt when she was a baby? Or when she'd been secreted away and adopted by parents in Seattle?

"You didn't know when I got the teaching job that I was Angel?"

Pearl shook her head. "The name was Thompson."

Why hadn't Jolene thought of it? Her adopted father had died when she was six. Her mother, Marie Thompson, had remarried and changed her name. Larry Stevens had adopted her.

Pearl met her gaze and Jolene saw the compassion in those pale blue eyes. She felt tears burn her own eyes.

"You can't stay here. It isn't safe."

"It never was safe, since I believe my mother's killer is the one who got me back here." She brushed away her tears, angry that so many people had lied to her. She didn't need a DNA test. She'd seen the truth in Pearl's face. "Have you been protecting my mother's killer?"

"Of course not," Pearl snapped.

Jolene got to her feet. "You must have had your suspicions twenty-four years ago about who murdered her. Or maybe I told you."

"You weren't…talking. You didn't talk for months afterward. I don't know who was responsible and I'm certainly not going to speculate."

"But you do know who found me that night on the road."

Pearl's gaze widened. "You remember being found on the road. If you're starting to remember—"

"Just tell me who found me."

Nina Mae Cross was a tiny gray-haired woman with twinkling blue eyes and dimples. Russell had been warned that Nina Mae was tough as nails and quite outspoken.

But he hadn't been ready for this little waif of a woman. "Nina Mae Cross?"

"Who wants to know?" the wiry little woman asked, one hand on her hip as she stood in the middle of her room.

"My name's Russell Corbett."

"Never heard of you." She started to turn away.

"But you have heard of Laura Beaumont."

She stopped and turned back toward him, eyes narrowing. "Everyone's heard of that one," she said.

"Mind if we sit down? This is my friend Dulcie Hughes."

"Never heard of her either," Nina Mae said but waved them into the two available chairs. She lowered herself to the edge of the bed and looked from one to the other with an intent gaze. "Friends, huh?" She chuckled.

"Can you tell us about Laura Beaumont?" Dulcie asked.

"What's to tell? She's dead."

"We're trying to find out who killed her," Russell said. "You have any ideas?"

"Lots of ideas. Could have been a jealous wife. Could have been a jealous lover."

"Like John Atkinson?" Dulcie asked, lowering her voice.

Nina Mae smiled sagely. "So you already know about John. He'll be doing whatever Midge says till his dying day." She shook her head as if she couldn't imagine anything worse.

"What about Ben Carpenter, John's ranch manager? Was he one of the men?"

"John thought so. He fired Ben, sent him packing. Couldn't have been a worse time with Ronda pregnant and then when she lost the baby…" Nina Mae wagged her head sympathetically. "Ben had wanted that baby so bad. It changed him for the worse, Ronda losing that baby. Ronda had her son from her first marriage, Tinker, but Ben and the boy never got along."

"I heard Laura's little girl played with a friend at the creek. Was it Tinker?" Dulcie asked, her heart in her throat.

Nina Mae nodded.

Tinker, the friend. The boy who'd tried to protect her. And the cowboy Dulcie had seen her with at the restaurant. Did he know Jolene was Angel? Is that why he'd asked her out?

"Tinker took that little girl's death hard. Before that he'd been such a good boy, but after, he was in trouble all the time. Before that, he idolized Ben. After…" She shook her head. "There was a time I thought the two of them would kill each other."

Tinker and his stepfather? "That must have been hard on Tinker's mother, Ronda," Dulcie said.

"Ronda loved Ben and stuck by him although I wouldn't have," Nina Mae said.

"We've heard that Laura might have fallen in love and was breaking it off with the others," Dulcie said.

Nina Mae's sharp eyes shone. "Funny you should say that. I heard talk that it was John, but I always figured it had to be Ben. Then again it was that hot, dry spring so that rainmaker…"

"That's quite enough," snapped an elderly woman from the doorway.

Dulcie turned at the shuffling sound to see a handsome woman leaning on her cane and understood at once why her voice had sounded odd. She'd had a stroke at some point. One side of her face hung lower than the other.

"You've said quite enough, dear," the woman said to Nina Mae more kindly. "Perhaps you'd like to go down to the nurses' station for some juice."

"Juice?" Nina Mae bristled. "I'd rather have a beer." But she rose and left anyway.

"She won't remember what she was going for by the time she reaches the nurses' station. I'm Pearl Cavanaugh." She said it as if the name should mean something to them.

Clearly someone at the nursing home had alerted Pearl about Nina Mae's company. She must have raced right in to make sure Nina Mae didn't spill the beans.

"You're one of those Corbett men," Pearl said, nodding to herself. "I heard you were all handsome, but clearly that was an understatement. What are you doing bothering Nina Mae? Didn't anyone tell you she has Alzheimer's? You can't believe anything she says."

"Can't we?" Dulcie asked, wondering how long Pearl had stood outside the room listening.

Pearl turned to scrutinize her. "You must be the woman who bought the old Beaumont place."

Dulcie had heard about Pearl and Titus Cavanaugh from Jolene. They were like royalty in Old Town Whitehorse, running everything from the school to the Whitehorse Sewing Circle. If anyone knew the truth about Laura Beaumont's murder, it was this woman.

"Actually, I *inherited* the Beaumont place." Dulcie couldn't miss the surprise in the woman's eyes and then the realization of who she was. "I'm Dulcie Hughes, but then I suspect you know that and a whole lot more."

Chapter 12

Midge Atkinson opened the door and looked surprised to see that Jolene wasn't alone.

"I brought your wicker basket back," Jolene said when Midge made no move to invite her and Dulcie inside. "I brought a friend, too."

"I see that." Midge was a large-framed, thick woman, shapeless in a purple sweatsuit, her face set in a permanent scowl. "Well, come in then." She reached for the basket, stepping back with obvious irritation.

Dulcie and Jolene followed her into the kitchen. After her run-in with Pearl Cavanaugh the day before, Dulcie didn't expect Midge Atkinson to be any more forthcoming that Pearl had been.

"I like your borders," Dulcie said. "Did you paint them?"

"Yes," Midge said as she put the wicker basket on

the top shelf and turned toward them. "But you aren't here to return my basket or compliment my artwork. What do you want?"

Clearly word had spread about the Beaumont girls. "We're here to ask you about Laura Beaumont," Dulcie said.

Midge swung her gaze to Jolene. "I warned you about digging into things that don't concern you. If you care about your teaching job—"

"Actually, it does concern us and I think you know it," Dulcie cut in. "We know you painted Angel Beaumont's room and that you were friends with Laura Beaumont."

"I want you both to leave. *Now.*" Midge started to take a step toward the phone as if to call for help, when Jolene finally spoke.

"You were the one who saved Angel that night."

All the air seemed to be sucked from the room. Midge swung around, almost lost her balance and had to grab the countertop to keep from falling.

Dulcie also turned in shock to look at Jolene. Why hadn't Jolene told her this?

Midge looked as if she might have a heart attack right in front of their eyes. She stumbled to the table and sat down heavily in one of the chairs. "Who told you that I—"

"It doesn't matter," Jolene said, sounding calm as she took a seat and Dulcie did the same.

Midge was staring at Jolene. So Midge really hadn't suspected that Jolene was Angel?

"Were you also responsible for me coming back here?" Jolene asked.

"A committee of parents were involved in the hiring," Midge said. "I don't know who suggested you. I didn't know…"

"Why were you on that road that night?" Dulcie asked.

"I went there looking for John," Midge said in a tiny voice. "His pickup wasn't there."

"You must have seen the killer."

Midge shook her head. "All I saw was Angel. I started to go toward the house, but I couldn't leave the girl. I could see that something horrible had happened. She had blood all over her." Her voice broke. "I got out of there. I took the girl and went home. John was there. He'd been there the whole time cleaning so we could move into the house."

"He hadn't just gotten back from Laura's?" Dulcie asked.

"He hadn't been near Laura's. I checked his truck. The engine was ice-cold. He told me she'd broken it off with him, said she'd fallen in love."

"With Ben Carpenter?" Dulcie asked.

Midge pursed her lips. "That's what I heard."

"You were the one who put the note on my car, weren't you?" Jolene said.

Midge looked embarrassed. "I was trying to protect you."

"Or protect yourself?" Dulcie said.

Jolene rose to leave. "Thank you," she said to Midge and started toward the door.

"That's it?" Dulcie said when she caught up to her sister outside Midge's house.

"I'm sorry I didn't tell you what I'd discovered," Jolene said. "Midge found me. She got Angel…me to some people who located a couple interested in adopting me illegally. It's still a shock and it's going to take me a while to…"

"It's okay," Dulcie said, understanding. They were strangers. Sisters, but strangers. In time maybe…

They turned as Midge came out of the house. "You want to know who killed Laura?" She sounded angry. "Ask Ronda Carpenter. But don't let that timid act of hers fool you. That woman is capable of murder. She and Laura were the best of friends until she lost her baby." Midge seemed glad to finally unburden herself of this news. "I heard Ronda and Ben fighting that night. Could hear them clear up at the house from that old trailer they lived in on our property. Who knows if Ben pushed her or she fell like she swore later, but she lost her baby and Laura Beaumont was dead by that evening. So you tell me who killed Laura."

With that Midge went back into the house and slammed the door.

"Are you all right?" Dulcie asked.

"Please stop asking me that," Jolene said as Dulcie drove them away from the Atkinson Ranch. "I know I'm Angel Beaumont, but still, it's as if everyone is talking about someone else."

"I only asked because it's hard for me to hear these things about our mother," Dulcie said, her eyes on the road. "I thought it might be for you, too."

Jolene stared out the window. "I want to go by her house."

Dulcie shot her a look. "I don't think that's a good idea."

"I have to see it. You said yourself that we need to

find the killer. If I saw him that day, going to the house might make me remember."

"You don't know what kind of reaction you might have."

"If you don't take me, then I'll go alone."

They drove in silence to the old farmhouse. As Dulcie pulled up in front, she let out a curse. "I locked that door," she said, cutting the engine. "Someone keeps leaving it open. Don't you dare say ghosts."

Jolene wasn't about to say it but if there were ghosts, then they would most assuredly be in this house, she told herself as she got out.

The house loomed in front of her. She stood, waiting to feel something, some sense of having been here before, to hit her like a brick, to make her remember.

She could feel Dulcie watching her expectantly as she walked toward the house. At the front door, she hesitated, some of her courage deserting her.

"You don't have to do this," Dulcie said at her side.

Jolene stepped in and grimaced at the smell, but was determined not to let Dulcie see how truly afraid she was.

As she walked through the living room toward the back of the house, she expected any moment to see something that would send her into some kind of shock.

She found the kitchen at the back. On the table were a bowl and spoon, a small plate and butter knife. Her last meal with her mother?

She tried to imagine herself sitting there. Tried to imagine the woman sitting across from her. Her mother.

"Jolene?" Dulcie asked behind her.

She shook her head as she moved away from the

table and headed for the stairs. Might as well get it over with.

"Honey, I'm not sure—"

Jolene didn't wait to hear what Dulcie had to say. She'd come this far. She had to go upstairs. Part of her prayed that she would remember. She wanted these people to mean something to her. Laura Beaumont. Angel Beaumont. Dulcie, the sister she never knew she had.

As she hurried up the stairs, her heart a-thunder in her chest, she heard Dulcie at her heels.

At the top of the stairs, Jolene slowed. All her senses were on alert as she turned. One room caught her eye. A child's room. Angels painted on the walls. They were as striking as Dulcie had said they were.

She moved toward the room like a sleepwalker. Angel Beaumont's room. *Her* room. At the door she stopped and was surprised when she burst into tears. She felt Dulcie's hand on her shoulder.

"Jolene? Do you *remember?*"

She shook her head. "I just suddenly felt so sorry for this little girl," she said, wiping her tears. "There is so much sadness in this room. Loneliness. Can't you feel it?"

Dulcie nodded.

"Where is her room?" She couldn't bring herself to call Laura her mother. And yet calling her Laura felt wrong, too.

"Down there."

Jolene walked toward the open door to the room at the front of the house. She could see part of a faded yellow curtain billowing in and out on the hot wind.

Jolene had to force herself, one foot in front of the

other, to enter the room. The vanity against the wall, the dresser... She froze as she saw the stained bed. The murder story leaped into her mind and she could see the woman lying on the bed, the killer standing over her, the glint of the knife's blade in the light.

After a moment she let the breath out she'd been holding. She could feel Dulcie's gaze on her, a look of fear and wonder in her eyes—and hope.

She felt nothing. Even when she told herself that her mother had died here. She couldn't remember that mother, couldn't remember this life at all. Thank God.

"Sorry," she said to Dulcie as she turned and left the room.

"Nothing at all?" Dulcie asked as they descended the stairs.

"Nothing." Jolene was surprised how relieved she felt. She'd been terrified of what she might remember and how she would react. Now she just felt empty as she and Dulcie left the house.

At the car, Jolene heard a sound that made her turn and look back. The weather vane on the barn groaned in the wind. Just like the one her adoptive father used to have on his barn—before he had it taken down.

"I think we'd better go see Ronda Carpenter."

"Son?"

Dragged from his thoughts, Russell turned to find his father standing at the edge of his cabin porch. He'd been mentally kicking himself and hadn't heard him approach.

After seeing Nina Mae yesterday, Dulcie had been

upset. He'd tried his damnedest to get her to come stay out at the ranch, but she'd refused.

"I need to be alone for a while," she'd said. "Truthfully, I have trouble thinking when you're around." She'd smiled that incredible smile that made his knees weak and kissed him before shoving him out the door.

He'd known it was the best thing she could have done. If he'd stayed there in the motel room with her...

"I was hoping we could talk before supper," Grayson said, taking one of the porch chairs beside him.

Russell saw the lines of worry etched in his father's face and felt a stab of guilt. Of course his father was worried. He'd gone along with the other ranchers and farmers in hiring the rainmaker. And now...

"I'm sorry, I said I'd talk to the rainmaker..." Russell swore. He'd been so involved with Dulcie that he hadn't given the rainmaker or rain a thought.

"The ranchers and farmers are losing their patience," Grayson said. "If this rainmaker doesn't have some results soon I'm afraid what some of the hotheads of the bunch might do, true enough. But that isn't what I wanted to speak to you about."

Russell hadn't been on the ranch much either the past few days. "Is something going on I should know about?"

"That would be my question," Grayson said.

"I'm sorry. I've been involved in... Dulcie, the woman I brought to dinner, she found out that she's one of Laura Beaumont's daughters. Now she's more determined than ever to find the person who killed her mother."

"She's a lovely, intelligent, determined woman. I

can understand why you're concerned about her. Surely your brother is looking into this."

"Shane's doing his best since the sheriff is out of town, but the trail is twenty-four years old and the community isn't talking."

His father raised a brow. "You think the community is protecting the killer?"

"Maybe. Someone tried to run Dulcie off the road. Shane says he doesn't think it's connected."

"But you do."

Russell nodded. "I've tried to reason with her."

His father chuckled, then turned serious. "You care a lot about this woman."

Russell realized now what was bothering his father. "I would never leave the ranch."

Grayson smiled ruefully. "Love makes a man do things he swears he never would."

"Can you imagine me in Chicago?" He shook his head. "No matter how I feel about her, nothing will get me away from Trails West Ranch." Even as he said the words, Russell realized that Dulcie had *already* gotten him away from the ranch. All his thoughts for days had been about her and only her.

At the rural mailbox with the word *Carpenter* crudely printed on the side of the rusted metal, Dulcie turned off the dirt road and into the yard of the run-down farmhouse.

Two mongrel dogs came charging out, barking. As she cut the engine, she looked over at Jolene, who also was debating whether to get out with both large dogs barking wildly just outside the car.

The front door of the house swung open. Ronda Carpenter called off the dogs, frowning, as Jolene got out of the car. Her frown deepened when she saw Dulcie.

Ronda was one of those tiny women, small-boned, late forties and beat-down looking. Jolene had seen her only once before. At her interview for the teaching job. Ronda had been on the parent committee that recommended hiring her.

"If this is about Mace he isn't here," Ronda called. "He and his father went to Havre. Is he in trouble?"

"No," Jolene said. "Mace's fine."

Ronda looked relieved but not much. "If you're here about money for the school or something…"

"I'm not. Could we step in out of the heat for a few moments?"

Ronda looked worried as Jolene and Dulcie followed her up the steps and into her kitchen. "I need to get supper made. Ben and Mace will be back soon. I hope this won't take long."

Jolene stood for a moment watching the woman's trembling hands as she put some water on to boil, took out a large bag of elbow macaroni, a can of cream of mushroom soup and two cans of tuna. Dulcie was glancing around the old farmhouse, seeing, Jolene was sure, the tattered furnishings.

"I need to ask you about Laura Beaumont," Jolene said.

Ronda froze. Slowly she put down the can opener she'd been using on the tuna-fish cans.

"I heard she was a friend of yours," Jolene said. "I was hoping you could tell me a little about her."

Ronda didn't turn around. "That was so long ago. Why would you care about—"

"It's important or we wouldn't come here and ask you questions that might upset you," Jolene said. "We need to know what Ben's relationship was with Laura."

"What?" Ronda clutched the edge of the counter.

"What she's asking is, if Ben was having an affair with Laura," Dulcie said and shrugged when Jolene shot her a warning look.

"No. Ben? No." Ronda turned around. She looked sick. "Who are you?"

"I'm sorry," Jolene said. "This is Dulcie Hughes. She owns the old Beaumont place."

Ronda's gaze swung to Dulcie, her eyes widening.

"I'm sorry, but we have to ask you these questions," Jolene said. "Midge Atkinson told us that her husband fired Ben because he was having an affair with Laura."

"John was *wrong*. He was the one—" Ronda clutched the apron material tied at her waist in both fists. "Ben was never with Laura. She was *my* friend. You have it all wrong."

"Then help us," Jolene said.

She was shaking her head, her eyes dull with pain. "Please, you both need to leave now."

"I know Tinker tried to protect Angel Beaumont the day her mother died," Jolene said.

"Tinker?" Ronda's gaze cleared. Anger shone in her eyes. "You leave my Tinker alone, you hear me?" She picked up the can opener from the counter and advanced on them as if she meant to strike them. "Get out and don't you come back. If Ben catches you here…"

Jolene took a step back and Dulcie was already

headed for the door when they heard a vehicle coming up the road.

"Go," Ronda cried. "If Ben finds you here, he'll think it's about Mace. He doesn't want Mace turning out like his stepbrother."

Dulcie opened the door and they both stepped out on the porch as a truck drove past but didn't stop.

Ronda stood in the doorway, hanging on to the knob as if her relief had turned her knees to water. Just before she slammed the door, Jolene saw the hateful look she shot the two of them.

As the sound of the door slamming died off, Jolene thought she heard someone sobbing on the other side. Huge racking sobs that tore at Jolene's heart. How many lives had Laura Beaumont destroyed before losing her own?

"What do you make of that?" Dulcie asked, once they were in the car and far enough away there was no chance of running into Ben Carpenter.

"I think Ronda is afraid of her husband," Jolene said.

"Then why is she still with him after everything he's done to her? I told you what Nina Mae Cross said about the fight Ronda and Ben had and Ronda losing the baby after a fall. You know the bastard pushed her, just as you know he was having an affair with Laura."

"Maybe there's more to the story." Jolene hoped so. "We'll know in the morning," she said with a sigh.

Dulcie glanced over at her. "You can't still expect the end of the murder story? Jolene, if the killer is writing it, then he knows what we've been up to. You don't still think he—"

"The killer will finish because he wants me to know why he killed Laura," Jolene said.

Dulcie was shaking her head. "Why is he going to confess? We are no closer to finding out who killed Laura than when we both arrived in town. The killer has no reason to give himself—or herself—up. Not after twenty-four years. There isn't going to be any more short story. You have to face the fact that we may never know the truth."

Russell looked up as Dulcie made her way to his table at Northern Lights restaurant. When he'd called earlier to see if she would have dinner with him, she'd sounded discouraged. Now as she walked toward the table, he could see it in her face.

"Bad day?" he asked as he rose to help her with her chair.

There were dark circles under her eyes and she looked as if she carried the weight of the world on her shoulders.

"I feel as if I'm beating my head against a wall." She filled him in on the talk with Midge Atkinson and Ronda Horton Carpenter as well as what Jolene had found out.

"I think Ronda Carpenter is in major denial but after meeting her husband, Ben, I can't imagine how my mother could have been in love with him."

"Nina Mae said he changed after the loss of his baby," Russell reminded her. "If he and your mother were truly in love, her death must have changed him as well."

"Of course there is always the chance that Midge is lying, and John was the man my mother was in love with and Ben was the man who got dumped."

"I see why you feel like you're beating your head against a wall," Russell said.

"That's just it. We have no idea who is lying and who is telling the truth. On top of that, Ben's son, Mace, is one of Jolene's students and Jolene has been going out with Ben's stepson, Tinker. What a tangled mess."

"Small-town Montana," Russell said.

"Do you think Tinker knows who Jolene really is?"

Russell shrugged. "I wouldn't worry about it, though. Didn't he try to protect her when they were kids?"

"Yes." She rubbed her temples. "Give me some good news. What did you find out about my mother's locket?"

Russell wished he had good news. "The locket wasn't on the body, according to the coroner's report."

"Are you telling me the killer took it?"

"Or it was misplaced during the investigation. I'm sorry. Shane got the DNA reports back." Russell nodded. "You and Jolene are sisters."

"Does Jolene—"

"She knows. Shane just let me know. He said she took the news fine. Sounds as if she's accepting that part of it at least."

Dulcie shook her head. "I don't like Jolene out there alone. I wanted to stay with her. I even offered to put her up at the same motel where I'm staying. I'm worried about her."

"I'm worried about *you*." He met her gaze. All he wanted was to take her in his arms and comfort her. They hadn't made love since that one and only time at the old farmhouse and that hadn't been his idea of making love.

He wanted to get this woman in a proper bed and

make love to her the way she deserved. He leaned toward her and said as much.

She gave him a broad smile, light shining in her dark eyes, along with a challenge. "So what's stopping you?"

"I want your undivided attention." He wanted more than that, but he was smart enough not to voice it. He got the impression she wanted this to be casual. He didn't do casual.

She sobered and looked toward the bank of dark windows. "I can't give you what you want right now."

"I know," he said. "So what now?"

"We wait and see if the killer finishes the murder story," Dulcie said. "Or did you mean with me and you?"

After Dulcie left Russell in the parking lot by the restaurant with little more than a brief kiss, she felt restless. She'd hoped he would change his mind and come back with her to the motel.

But she understood how he felt. He was the kind of man who fell hard when he fell for a woman. He was afraid of falling for her and with good reason.

She knew she wasn't going to be able to sleep. Just as she knew that she'd purposely let herself be distracted with Laura Beaumont's murder. She didn't want to think about what her grandparents had done.

Nor did she want to examine too closely how she felt about Russell Corbett.

Back at her motel, she thought about the farmhouse because it was easier than thinking about the rest of it right now. The house hadn't been broken into, which meant someone had a key.

Laura Beaumont had given someone a key to her

place? The man she'd fallen in love with, Dulcie thought with a start.

It made perfect sense if what the writer of the murder story and Midge had told them was true. Laura had fallen in love. She'd broken it off with the other men, which explained that scene in the murder story where one of the men was arguing with Laura in the bathroom. John Atkinson? Ben Carpenter? The rainmaker? Or had there been others that even the storyteller hadn't known about?

Excited that she might have stumbled onto something, Dulcie changed her clothes, dressed for a long night of it, and equipped with water, a flashlight and pepper spray, drove toward the farmhouse. Tonight she would find out who Laura had given a key to. Find out who the man was that Laura had fallen in love with.

Dulcie was putting her money on Ben Carpenter. That was the reason she'd brought the pepper spray. The man scared her.

On the drive to the farmhouse, she debated calling Russell until it was too late. No cell service.

She parked up the road and walked, telling herself that all the rattlesnakes had gone back under their rocks for the night. At the house, she found a spot where she could hide to wait and settled in.

An hour later she was wondering if her theory was as ridiculous as her hiding out here when she heard a sound coming from off in the darkness. The swishing sound became recognizable. Someone was moving through the tall, dry grass toward her.

Chapter 13

A black shape emerged from out of the darkness. Dulcie couldn't see a face, just a large, man-size form as he passed within feet of her. She pressed herself against the wall and didn't dare breathe until he turned the corner of the house.

She heard the clomp of his boots on the steps and across the porch, then using his key, the man entered the house.

Just as she'd thought. He *had* a key.

But who had it been? She crept around the corner of the house. He'd left the door wide open. She could hear him climbing the stairs, his footfalls labored.

She waited until she heard nothing then she edged to the porch steps and glanced inside. Pitch darkness and putrid air filled the house.

Was she really going inside?

A light flashed on in the upstairs front bedroom, making her jump. The man was in Laura Beaumont's bedroom. The faint glow shone through the yellow curtain.

What was he doing in Laura's room? Just touching her things, remembering? Or was he searching for something? Evidence that she'd overlooked?

She debated what to do, knowing what Russell would say about her impetuous behavior. Taking the bull by the horns, so to speak, she crept up onto the porch and entered the house. She didn't dare use her flashlight. But she checked to make sure it and the pepper spray were still in her vest pockets. They were.

The blackness inside the house was complete. It made her feel dizzy, screwed up her equilibrium. She closed her eyes, envisioning where everything was as she inched to the bottom of the stairs, her hands out like a sleepwalker.

She tried not to think about what she would do if she touched flesh and blood. Listening, hearing nothing, she started up the stairs.

Five steps, stop and listen, another five. At the top, she stumbled and froze, afraid her clumsiness might have been heard.

A strange sound was coming from the front bedroom. A high keening sound like that of a wounded animal. Her blood turned to ice.

Was it the man? Who else? No one but he had gone into the house and she didn't believe in ghosts, did she?

Dulcie found the wall in the dark and worked her way carefully along it. The keening had changed to something almost more frightening, a horrible choking sound.

She moved toward the dim light and the sound, determined to get a look at the man and then run like hell.

As she reached the doorway she saw the man on his knees beside the bed. His flashlight lay on the bed, the shaft of light splashed across the room.

He was hunched over, holding something in his right hand, his body convulsing with what she realized were sobs.

The sight gripped her. She watched him, his hands balling into fists, his body quivering, choking out sobs as if bringing them up from some deep, dark well inside him.

The muscles of his right hand flexed, the fingers opening. In the light from his flashlight lying on the bed, she saw what he held. A gold locket on a chain.

Her heart stopped. All breath rushed out of her. Time seemed to freeze as her muscles turned to mush.

The man spun around so fast she didn't see the blow coming, couldn't have moved even if she had. His fist caught her on the side of the head, knocking her back into the wall. She smacked her head and felt the light sparkle as she slid down the wall and hit the floor, the lights going out completely.

Russell jerked up out of a bad dream, confused for a moment where he was. It took a few seconds to realize what had awakened him. The phone.

He grabbed it up. "Hello?"

"It's Shane. I didn't want to wake Dad, but I thought you should know. I just arrested Finnegan Amherst."

The rainmaker? Russell sat up and tried to clear away the cobwebs of the dream, the remnants of sleep. He'd been dreaming about Dulcie. She'd been in trouble. He shook it off. "Why would you arrest—"

"I think you might want to come down here. I had

the other deputy on duty take Dulcie Hughes to the hospital for—"

"What?" Russell was on his feet now, fear sending his heart into overdrive.

"Just for observation. I wanted Doc to look her over to make sure she didn't have a concussion."

"What the hell?" Russell swore as he snapped on a light and looked around for some clothes.

"She's all right, okay? She had a run-in with Finnegan Amherst."

"I'll kill that bastard."

"Settle down. He's behind bars and that's where he's going to stay. We picked him up as he was leaving town."

Leaving town? "That son-of-a-bitch."

"I knew you'd want to know about Dulcie. Russell? It looks as if she might have found Laura Beaumont's killer."

"The rainmaker? After I check on Dulcie, I want to see him."

"Not happening," his brother said.

"Where's the sheriff? I'll ask him."

"The sheriff's out of town. But he wouldn't let you see Finnegan Amherst either."

"I'm not going to kill him. I just want to talk to him."

"If you're thinking of beating a confession out of him, forget it. Anyway, he swears he didn't kill Laura."

"He swore he could make it rain, too."

Dulcie looked up to see Russell coming through the door of her hospital room and felt her heart do a little jitterbug. Just the sight of him made her eyes fill with tears. She quickly brushed them away.

"Are you all right?" He looked both scared and re-lieved and angry. She didn't have to guess why.

"I'm fine. It's only a slight concussion." She smiled even though it hurt her jaw to do so.

Russell swore as he stepped to her, gently turning her head with his fingers to look at the dark bruise that ran from her cheekbone to her chin.

"It looks worse than it is," she said and saw him clamp down on his teeth, the muscles in his jaws bunching with fury.

"How in the hell…" His words ran out.

"It's a funny story," she said, making his eyes nar-row. "I couldn't sleep so I decided to stake out the house. I knew someone was coming in at night and I had this idea that since whoever it was had a key, Laura must have given it to him. Which meant he had to be the man she'd fallen in love with and why she'd broken it off with the others."

"Get on to the part that's funny," he snapped.

"The rainmaker *was* the man. He used his key to get into the house. I followed him upstairs. I found him kneeling beside her bed…" She felt odd telling this part. "He was crying and I saw that he had something clutched in his hand. It was her locket."

Russell flinched. "Your mother's missing locket with the photo inside?"

"When he realized I was behind him, he spun around and…"

"He hit you."

"I blacked out for a few minutes. When I woke I heard his pickup leaving. I drove down to Arlene Ev-ans's and got her to call the sheriff's office. Then Arlene drove me in to see Shane and he insisted I come over here. End of story."

Russell glared down at her. "You went out to that house in the middle of the night, by yourself, looking for a killer."

"Actually, I was looking for her lover—not the killer."

"How could you do something so rash? So irrational? So damned dangerous and stupid?"

She bristled. "Reckless yes, dangerous as it turned out, but not irrational or stupid. I took pepper spray and I knew what I was doing."

"Did you?" His gaze went to her bruised face and she watched as his expression softened. "Damn it, Dulcie." He stepped to her and pulled her into his arms.

She leaned her uninjured cheek against the warm, soft fabric of his shirt and breathed in his scent. She *had* been rash and reckless and a little crazed. Kind of like her feelings for this man.

"You're coming home with me until you have to leave for Chicago," he said.

"The killer is behind bars."

Russell pulled back to look into her eyes. "Exactly, and I have your undivided attention for a few days before you have to leave, right?"

She grinned even though it hurt her jaw. "You *did* promise me a horseback ride and I could use a few days of R & R." She touched his cheek. "Are you sure about this, Russ?"

He nodded and leaned down to kiss her softly on her lips. As he drew back, his gaze locked with hers and she realized just how risky this was. For the first time in her life, she felt as if she was in over her head.

* * *

Jolene had awakened late Sunday after a sleepless night. She'd stumbled into the bathroom to shower and stood for a long time studying her face in the mirror.

She was Angel Beaumont. She'd waited for the name to trigger a memory. Nothing. Just like her visit to the house. And to the jail, after Dulcie's call.

She'd looked at the rainmaker, seen nothing but a man who'd aged badly over the past twenty-four years, and felt not even the slightest stirring of recall.

"Give it time," Dulcie had said when she and Russell stopped by.

Word had traveled through the county about the arrest. Jolene had wanted to feel something. Relief. Anger. Anything. But instead, she'd felt only a little sad. With the rainmaker in jail she would never get the end of the story.

She didn't mention this to Dulcie, knowing how foolish her sister would find it. Dulcie was convinced Jolene knew the ending, knew it probably better than anyone.

Deputy Sheriff Shane Corbett had called with the DNA results. Jolene had been expecting the outcome. She and Dulcie were sisters. DNA from the murder scene proved they were the daughters of Laura Beaumont.

By then, all things that Jolene had known. Still, she'd thought that when she got the DNA results she would feel that bond with Dulcie that sisters were supposed to feel. She'd hoped she would. She hadn't.

Maybe it was as simple as the fact that she didn't want to be Angel, didn't want to remember those first five years of her life or her mother's murder or what she must have seen.

She sighed now, wishing she could quit thinking about it. She'd read most of the cruelly hot afternoon, but even a good book couldn't distract her from her thoughts.

Putting down her book, she walked to the window, surprised it was getting dark. She felt restless, thought about going into town, but didn't have the energy or any reason. It was still unbearably hot, but now the breeze coming in the open window felt muggy.

She dreaded tomorrow. There would be no ending to the murder story. She would grade her students' assignments, then hand them all back, keeping copies for the promised anthology. School would let out early for the year. It would be over.

And yet it wouldn't be over for her until she remembered.

She couldn't bear to think about spending a long, hot summer here now. But where would she go? Dulcie had talked about her coming back to Chicago with her. Jolene wasn't ready for that.

She turned away from the window. The house felt unbearably hot. Maybe she'd take a cool shower. She wandered into the bathroom and stripped down. As she stepped under the icy spray, she thought of Tinker and felt her stomach turn. He'd been the boy she'd played with at the creek, the friend who, according to the author of the murder story, tried to save her the night her mother was murdered.

As she shampooed her hair, she wondered if Tinker knew who she was, had known since the first time he'd asked her out at a Whitehorse Community Center dance.

The thought sent a chill through her. She turned up the hot water and stood under it for a few seconds.

Had Tinker known his father sneaked over to see Laura? He was nine, plenty old enough to know what was going on. Or had Ronda been telling the truth and Ben had never been Laura's lover?

Turning off the shower, Jolene rubbed her temples, feeling a headache coming on, if she kept this up. But she had to know who'd been writing the murder story.

As she pulled on a tank top, shorts and sandals, she padded back into her living room and glanced at the computer sitting on the desk in the corner.

She hadn't even turned it on since the one at the school was newer and had Internet service. But hadn't Titus Cavanaugh mentioned that the two computers were networked together?

Moving to the desk, she stood for a moment, staring down at it, thinking of the murder story and what had bothered her about it. *Let me be wrong.* Slowly, she touched the on button. It took a moment for the computer to boot up.

Jolene jerked back as the murder story came up on the screen.

Do you remember yet?

Remember the crushing heat that night, wading in the warm creek water, the feel of the grass on your bare feet? Remember sitting on the bank whispering a secret in the dark?

You have a secret, don't you? That's why you don't want to remember that night and the sound of the weather vane groaning in the wind.

You know who killed your mother. You've always known. But you don't want to remember the blade of the knife, dripping bright red with your mother's blood, or the hand holding it.

Jolene covered her mouth as tears flooded her eyes. She shot out of the computer chair, stumbling back, almost falling. As if she could run away from the words on the screen.

Through the open window, she could smell rain in the air and feel the cool blowing in. She snatched up the phone and dialed Dulcie's number. There'd been enough secrets. Enough lies. She could no longer live with hers.

The call went straight to voice mail. The trees just outside the window whipped back in the wind, the branches scraping the side of the house like fingers across a blackboard. Dark shadows flickering shapelessly against the coming night.

"If you would like to leave a message…"

"Dulcie, I know. I know what happened that night. I—" The words caught in her throat as she saw something through the thrashing branches.

There was a light on in the schoolhouse.

After their horseback ride, Dulcie soaked in the hot tub, hoping to relieve some of her aches and pains and then showered. "Riding a horse isn't as romantic as it looks," she called from the bathroom. "Thank you for taking me, though. I loved seeing the country. It is so beautiful down in the Missouri Breaks. I see why you love it here."

When she didn't get an answer, she pulled on her clothes and, finding the bedroom empty, discovered Russell sitting in the living area reading something.

As she moved closer she was startled to see that he was reading the copy of the murder story that Jolene had given her.

The worry in his gaze as he looked up at her scared her.

"Why are you reading that?"

He set the copies aside and sighed. "What if Jolene receives the ending tomorrow at school?"

"That's not possible. The rainmaker is in jail."

"What if he isn't the one writing it?"

Hadn't she thought there might be someone else, an accomplice to the murderer who had helped him or her stay free the past twenty-four years?

But she'd discarded the theory when Finnegan Amherst had been arrested for the murder. The rainmaker was a loner, an outsider. No one in this town would have helped him.

"You're scaring me."

"I'm sorry. It's just that after reading this again…" He met her gaze. "The writer is too intimate with what happened."

"Of course he is. The killer's the only one who knows the whole story."

"Except for Angel."

Dulcie felt her breath rush from her lungs. "You think she's writing it. That's she's always been the author."

"I think it's possible. Maybe more than possible. She repressed the past and yet she took this teaching job.

What if her writing the murder story is Angel's way of dealing with her past?"

She bit her lip to hold back the tears. "What happens if she writes an ending to the murder story and it's on that empty desk in the morning where she found the others?"

"She'll know the truth," he said flatly.

Dulcie felt ice slide up her spine. "Russ, no. You can't think… She was only *five*. She couldn't—"

"I don't want to believe it either, Dulcie. But—"

"No. It was the rainmaker. He had the locket—" She felt the tears on her cheeks. Not her sister.

Her fury at her grandparents gripped her heart like a fist. How could they have left Angel behind, left her in such an awful situation? It didn't matter if Laura refused to give up Angel. They should have taken her anyway. They should never have separated her from her older sister.

"I'm going to call her," Dulcie said.

"Be careful what you say," Russell said behind her. "I'm afraid of what she might do when she remembers."

Dulcie didn't hear him as she listened to her sister's message.

Jolene stared at the light through the trees. She felt the faint push of memory. The feel of the warm creek water on her bare feet. The night pitch-black. The scorching wind carrying the scent of dust and dry grass and the smell of desperation.

Crying on the bank of the creek, rubbing her eyes with her fists, her hands as dirty as her clothing. Her stomach aching because she hadn't eaten since breakfast. A bowl of cereal.

She'd gone home for lunch, but her mother had been napping and the refrigerator was empty. Was that when she'd first gotten really scared? She'd kept telling herself that her mommy would get better.

Jolene had a flash of memory: her mother sitting across from her, talking too fast, scary happy, eyes too bright just as she'd seen her before, too many times.

"Everything is going to be all right now, sweetie. Fin is going to take us far away from here. Don't cry. He'll be your new daddy. He'll buy you things. He'll take care of us. He isn't like the others."

The memory fell over her, the weight of it stealing her breath, the pain of it making her want to curl up in a ball on the floor.

"Stop it! *Stop it!*" She couldn't think about this now. She had to get up to the schoolhouse. Stepping into the kitchen, she opened the top drawer. The butcher knife was long, the handle warm in her hand. As the blade caught the light, she flinched as if she could feel the blade cutting through flesh.

She started to put it back, repulsed, her stomach revolting as she remembered the smell of blood. Blood pooling on the once-white sheets, her mother's vacant eyes. She stumbled back from the open drawer, afraid she might black out, the knife gripped in her hand.

Fighting back the darkness that threatened to pull her under, she stepped out the back door and, keeping the knife hidden behind her, started up the hill. She could see the light burning in the schoolhouse, knew who was waiting up there for her.

Do you remember yet?
You know who killed her. You've always known.

"Jolene?" Dulcie glanced over at Russell next to her standing on the steps of the small house and knocked again on Jolene's door. The lights were on inside the house and both her car and her bike were out front.

When she didn't get an answer, Dulcie tried the door and found it unlocked. Her heart in her throat, she opened the door. *"Jolene?"*

The house looked empty. She stood rooted to the floor and Russell hurried past her to search for her sister.

Dulcie felt numb, too afraid almost to breathe, let alone help him search.

"She's not here," he said when he returned.

The house had felt empty, empty as she felt inside. She glanced at the computer sitting on a desk under the window in the corner.

"I'm going to go look for her," Russell said, heading for the door.

"Wait. I don't want you going alone. I want to check something." If Jolene had been writing the murder story, wouldn't it be on her computer?

She stepped to the desk, pulled up the chair and with trembling fingers touched the mouse. The screen lit up, the words leaping out at her.

You know who killed her. You've always known. But you don't want to remember the blade of the knife, dripping bright red with your mother's blood, or the hand holding it.

"Oh, God, Russell. It's here on the computer. At least

part of it," Dulcie cried. "It looks as if she is in the middle of writing it—"

More words began to appear on the screen. "She's typing it right now from another computer. The schoolhouse. The computers must be connected."

"There's a light on at the school," he said, opening the front door. "I'm going up there. Stay here."

Before she could stop him, he was gone, the door closing behind him. She looked down at the computer screen.

It's hard to admit, isn't it? This secret you've been keeping all these years. You wanted her dead. You wished it that night on the creek. Loving her was so hard. Sometimes you hated her.

You wanted to be with your sister, with your grandparents in their nice house your mother told you about.

Dulcie had to stop reading to rub her eyes to clear them of tears.

You wanted to be the chosen one who got to leave your mother and didn't have to listen to her crying at night and laughing with men and that horrible squeak of the bed springs when she told you to go play at the creek.

She's dead because you

Dulcie stared at the screen. Why had she stopped typing? Russell couldn't have reached the school yet.

The night was black. Earlier the wind had been hot and stinging. Now as Russell walked up the road, he sensed something had changed.

He looked to the west, past what was left of Old Town Whitehorse, and thought he saw something glitter behind the Little Rockies. Lightning? A low, distant rumble followed.

The air around him suddenly felt cooler, the wind in his face smelling of rain. He couldn't believe it. Rain? Finally this horrible hot, dry weather would end.

As he neared the schoolhouse, he told himself a lot of things would end tonight. The thought scared him. Dulcie and her sister had been through so much. They were strong, but were they strong enough to face this?

He glanced back, wishing now he hadn't left Dulcie alone in the house. But bringing her with him was out of the question. He had no idea what he would find at the schoolhouse.

Was there any doubt now that Jolene was the author of the murder story? Was she even aware of it? He could see that, like tonight, she might have gotten up in the middle of the night to write it and then taken the story to the schoolhouse to leave it for her conscious self to find.

How disturbed was Jolene? They'd all thought that her being unable to remember was because she'd seen her mother's murderer. But what if they'd been wrong? What if she'd killed her mother? That could explain why she'd buried the memory so deep that it could only surface as if someone else was telling the story—and why the town had banned together to protect her.

At the schoolhouse, he stopped to listen. A bolt of lightning splintered the sky; this time the answering boom of thunder followed close behind. The wind kicked up, moaning along the eaves. Closer, the limbs of the old cottonwood scraped against the side of the building, making his skin crawl.

He reached for the doorknob and realized it was sticky and wet with... The door swung open. He stared down at his hand in the dim light. Blood.

His gaze shot up at a sound. Jolene stood just inside the door. Her face was distorted in fear, her mouth open. She was saying something but the wind was stealing her words before they reached him. Or maybe he didn't hear what she was saying because he was too busy staring at the butcher knife clutched in her hands, the blood dripping from the tip onto the hardwood floor at the feet.

Her mouth opened but he never heard her yell.

The blow came out of the darkness. Something hard and cold struck his temple. He reached, his fingers brushing fabric as he fell, a familiar face peering down just before the darkness closed in around him.

Dulcie waited anxiously for something more to appear on the screen. She could hear the howl of wind and looked up to see tree branches whipping in the gale outside. Shadows flickered wildly. She could barely make out the dim light at the schoolhouse.

Russell must have reached the schoolhouse. That's why Jolene had quit typing the story. She glanced out the window toward the faint light glowing through the blackness.

She started to push away from the computer when words began to appear again.

You killed your own mother.

And now you have to kill yourself the same way you killed her. It's the only way your story will end.

Dulcie stared at the screen in horror. Jolene wasn't the one writing this. She shot up out of the chair and ran to the door, praying she wasn't too late.

Chapter 14

"Russell! Russell!" The wind tore away her words and lashed her hair around her face as Dulcie ran up the road toward the schoolhouse. Lightning flickered on the horizon. A soft boom sounded like gunfire in the distance.

Up the road she could see the dim light in the building. A shadow moved in front of it, making her catch her breath. Jolene? Or Russell?

The first cold drops of rain splattered on the dusty ground, pelting her as they began to fall harder. The rain mixed with her tears of fear as she topped the hill and, turning into the school yard, came up short.

The door into the schoolhouse stood wide open.

"Russell?" She mounted the steps cautiously. "Russell?" No answer and yet she'd just seen someone inside when she was coming up the hill.

She stepped through the small cloakroom with its hooks and shelves for coats and boots. As she rounded the corner, she saw her sister.

Jolene stood at the front of the classroom, her back to the wall. A large, bloody knife on the floor at her feet. Her sister didn't seem to hear her come in.

Oh, God, where was Russell? "Jolene?" Dulcie said cautiously.

"Run!" Jolene yelled. "Run, she has a—"

Gun. Dulcie saw the gun before Jolene got the word out.

Ronda Carpenter stepped out from behind the door to the supply room, holding a semiautomatic in both hands, the barrel pointed at Dulcie's chest. Her face was twisted into a nasty sneer and the left side of her blouse was soaked with what looked like blood.

A trail of blood drops led from Ronda to the computer on the side of the classroom. Next to the chair was a small pool of blood where Ronda had apparently been sitting. Sitting typing the murder story, Dulcie realized.

"Close the door and lock it," Ronda ordered.

"Where's Russell?" Dulcie asked, her voice cracking as she closed the door and pretended to lock it. She was soaked to the skin and shivering, terrified for the man.

"Now go over and stand by your sister," Ronda ordered.

Dulcie met Jolene's terrified gaze and read more than fear in it. "Where is Russell?" she asked, this time of Jolene.

Jolene looked as if she were in shock. "I'm starting to remember," she whispered. "It's my fault. I wished our mother dead. I—"

"That's right," Ronda said. "You killed her."

"No, I loved her. I didn't want her killed."

"You told my son you wanted her dead!" Ronda cried. "You told my son. My beautiful boy."

Jolene was crying now. "I didn't mean it. I was angry at her for making me go with the rainmaker to live somewhere else. I knew things wouldn't be better there. I knew."

Dulcie thought she understood now. Nine-year-old Tinker Horton wanting to help his little friend, wanting to protect his pregnant mother because he thought his stepfather was having an affair with Laura. Wanting to spare Angel from trying to take care of a self-absorbed mother.

"Ben *was* having an affair with Laura," Dulcie said. "Was he going to leave you, and Tinker thought he could keep Ben from going and you from being hurt by killing Laura?"

Ronda laughed. "Ben hated Laura because she was encouraging me to leave him. I was the one leaving Ben—until he found out I was pregnant. He didn't give a damn about me, but he wanted his kid." Bitterness rimmed her voice. "Tinker thought Ben threw me down the stairs to get rid of the baby because he wanted to be with Laura. He'd seen Ben coming from Laura's house. He didn't know that Ben had gone over there to threaten Laura to stay away from me and quit putting fool ideas into my head."

"How could you stay with a man who threw you down a flight of stairs?" Dulcie asked.

Ronda shook her head, anger and bitterness burning in her eyes. "I threw *myself* down the stairs. I knew if I had that baby, I'd never be free of Ben. Laura was my best friend. She promised to help me leave him."

Dulcie felt her blood turn to ice. This woman was crazy. Or maybe worse, completely sane and evil. "But you *stayed* with him."

"He was blackmailing me! He knew Tinker killed Laura. He was going to the sheriff unless I stayed with him. He said I owed him a baby."

Mace. Mace had been the baby she owed Ben? "Why would you make a bargain like that?" Dulcie demanded, horrified. "You had to know that one day it would come out. That Jolene would remember..." The rest of her words died away as she realized that Ronda was the one who'd gotten Jolene back to Whitehorse.

Russell came to in the dark to the sound of driving rain. At first he thought he must be dreaming, it had been so long since he'd heard rain like that.

His head ached and he felt confused. He touched his temple and came away with blood on his fingers. It took a moment for him to remember what had happened.

He sat up with a start, his head swimming. Dulcie! He'd left her at Jolene's house but, knowing her, she wouldn't have stayed there long. She would have come looking for him. She would have—

He shoved away the thought as he remembered Jolene standing in the schoolhouse, a bloody knife in her hand.

Rain pounded the tin roof overhead. He realized that he must be in the garden shed next to the schoolhouse because he'd seen the lawnmower and some garden tools in the flash of lightning.

Staggering to his feet, he tried the door, not surprised to find it locked from the outside. He felt around in the dark shed until he found a hoe and using it as a lever was able to force it between the shed door and the wall.

The cheap latch on the shed door gave with a snap. Still holding the hoe, Russell listened but could hear nothing except the storm. He'd been so wrong about who killed Laura Beaumont, he thought, as he shoved open the shed door and looked out into the rain.

He moved quickly, the hoe in both hands like a bat in case he ran into the person who'd hit him. But there was no one outside the shed nor along the side of the schoolhouse. He reached the front, saw that the door stood open, just as before.

Only this time, he was ready in case Tinker Horton was lying in wait for him.

"Why did I stay with Ben? Tinker was my baby," Ronda said, choking on tears. "I would do anything to protect Tinker—"

They all froze at the sound of a key in the school house lock. Dulcie realized that whoever was coming in didn't realize that she hadn't locked the door.

Ronda smiled as Tinker came in, soaked from the rain. He didn't bother to close the door, seeming in a hurry. "I took care of it for you, Mama," he said, then saw his mother's bloody blouse and staggered back. "Oh, no. What happened?"

"It's okay, baby. It's just a flesh wound," Ronda

said. "I'm fine. *We're* fine. But there are a couple more things you're going to have to take care of for me, sweetheart."

Tinker seemed to see Dulcie and Jolene then. His eyes widened and he began to shake his head as he saw the bloody knife on the floor.

"Now don't get queasy on me, Tinker. Once we clean this up, it will be over," Ronda said soothingly. "No one will ever know what you did."

"Tinker didn't kill Laura," Jolene said.

Ronda's gaze narrowed. "Ben saw him with the knife. He had blood all over him. He was crying. He—"

"I startled the killer," Jolene said, her eyes glazed, her voice sounding strange, as if she were back there in that room that night. "The killer dropped the knife. Tinker had followed me to the house. I saw him as I ran out. He must have picked up the knife." Her gaze seemed to clear. "Tinker didn't kill Laura." She looked at the rodeo cowboy. "You didn't kill her."

"Now don't you go trying to confuse my boy," Ronda said. "He knows what he did and he—"

Dulcie saw Jolene swing her gaze to Ronda. "*You* killed her, Ronda. I *saw* you. I heard what you were saying. You'd found out she was running off with the rainmaker. She'd lied about helping you when you left Ben. In fact, she's the one who told Ben you were pregnant, wasn't she?"

"You let your son believe all these years that he—"

"Shut up!" Ronda snapped, cutting Dulcie off. "Don't listen to her, Tinker. She's the one who told you she wanted her mother dead, remember? She's the one who's to blame for this."

Dulcie caught movement out of the corner of her eye. Russell had entered the schoolhouse and was sneaking along the cloakroom wall behind Tinker and his mother. Dulcie's heart soared, then came crashing down. Ronda had a gun. She had to warn him. Or at least distract Ronda.

"Once we take care of things," Ronda was saying, "I can leave Ben for good, just like you've always wanted me to do, Tinker."

"You didn't stay with Ben because of Tinker," Dulcie said. "Ben must know the truth. That's why you stayed with him. He *was* blackmailing you, but not about Tinker."

Tinker suddenly went pale. "No, tell me that isn't why you had me..." His voice broke and Dulcie felt as if she might be sick.

"Ben was a bastard," Ronda said to her son. "You did the world a favor." She glanced down at her bleeding side. "Look what your precious Angel did to me. She tried to kill me because of you."

"She's lying, Tinker," Jolene said, sounding more calm than Dulcie right now. "Your mother took the knife from me and stabbed herself in the side."

"That's a lie," Ronda snapped then laughed. "Why would I stab myself?"

"She has a gun," Jolene said. "Would I stab a woman holding a gun? She is going to blame all of this on you, Tinker. She's going to let you take the fall for all of it."

Tinker looked to his mother. Like Dulcie, he must have seen Ronda's hand holding the gun waver as she considered turning it on her son.

Russell had moved closer, his eyes on Dulcie. She

knew it was now or never. She looked down at the knife on the floor, then up at Russell. He nodded.

Things got crazy after that. Dulcie shoved her sister and kicked out at the knife. She heard it clatter across the old wooden floor toward Russell as she threw her sister and herself behind Jolene's large desk.

The gunshot boomed in the small school. Behind Dulcie, the blackboard shattered, raining down onto the floor beside them. A second shot followed and a third on its heels.

Dulcie was on her feet, terrified what she would see when she rose from the floor.

Over the sound of pounding rain, she saw Russell standing over the bodies of Tinker Horton and his mother. Tinker still had the gun that he'd taken from his mother in his hand. Ronda lay on the floor next to the computer, the words she'd typed still visible across the room.

She was holding her chest where her son had shot her before taking his own life. Her eyes were wide with surprise, even in death. Just as Laura Beaumont's had been.

Epilogue

Dulcie didn't hear Kate Corbett approach. It wasn't until she sat down next to her in the large Trails West Ranch living room that she stirred from her thoughts.

"Beautiful view, isn't it?" Kate said. "I never tire of sitting here. But it must be very different from Chicago and what you're used to."

Dulcie knew Kate hadn't joined her to talk about the view. "I was just thinking about Russell."

"I know," Kate said. "He's in love with you. But your life is in Chicago, isn't it?"

"It used to be," Dulcie said.

"He'll go back with you, if it's what you want," Kate said. "I know Russell. He'd do anything for you."

Dulcie knew he would. She'd fought him when he'd tried to protect her, believing she had to hang on to her independence. But something had changed since the night at the schoolhouse. It gave her nightmares to think how Tinker could have just as easily wrenched the gun from his mother's hand and turned it on Russell instead of his mother and himself.

A brush with death changed people. It had changed her. Just as this man and this land had changed her.

"I wouldn't ask Russell to go back to Chicago with me," she said. "I know how much he loves ranching with his father. It isn't just the ranch. His family is here."

Kate rose to her feet. "There are worse things than him leaving his family and the ranch. I couldn't bear to see his heart broken. I know Russell. He doesn't love easily. There won't ever be anyone else but you. Let him go with you. If you love him."

Left alone with only the view of the Montana prairie and the Little Rockies in the distance, Dulcie thought about Russell, her feelings for him and what was waiting for her back in Chicago. Then seeing the time, she hurried to her car.

On the drive into town, she found herself reliving the night at the schoolhouse. In a flash of lightning, she'd seen Russell rush to her, drag her into his arms and lead her and Jolene outside. Life and death. Only a flash of lightning between them.

Russell had kept saying her name, over and over, as he held her. Water ran from the brim of his hat and the soft, dark strands of hair at the nape of his neck. He blinked back the rain, his blue eyes alight with the storm and her.

"I love you!" he'd yelled over the pounding rain. "I love you, Dulcie Hughes!"

He'd held her tight, rain and the tears running down her face in the darkness. She had turned her face up to the rain, letting her tears finally come. Around her lightning flashed, thunder boomed and she'd cried for the mother she never knew and for her sister, the blessing, she'd almost lost.

Laura Beaumont had lost herself here. Her youngest daughter had found herself, Dulcie thought. And found a sister she'd never known she had.

Would she ever be able to forgive her grandparents? In time. She told herself that they had known she would find Jolene. And save her? Or was that just her way of dealing with it, believing there'd been a plan bigger than herself?

She knew they had blamed themselves until their dying days for leaving Angel. For leaving Laura.

But Angel had survived it. She smiled at the thought of her sister, Jolene. A strong woman like herself. Jolene would be fine. In time.

Speaking of Jolene, Dulcie thought. Her sister would be waiting for her at Northern Lights.

Jolene looked up as her sister came into the restaurant. Her sister. She'd always wanted siblings. She smiled and rose to give her a hug. They held each other for a long moment.

"I hope you're hungry," Jolene said. "Laci insisted on cooking us something special for lunch."

Dulcie laughed. "I'm starved, but then I always am."

Jolene studied her. "How are you?"

"Better. How about you?"

Jolene nodded. "I feel lighter." She laughed. "I took

your advice. I'm seeing a psychologist. Talking about it helps."

She understood why she'd hidden her truth for so long and so deep. She'd believed she'd caused her mother's death because of one weak moment on the creek that night when she'd wished her mother gone.

"I just feel bad about Tinker. Maybe if I had remembered sooner…"

"Don't do that to yourself," Dulcie said. "Ben knew the kind of woman he was living with. How is Mace, though?"

"The Whitehorse Sewing Circle is finding him a home," Jolene said. "Pearl assured me that they would find him a good one and make sure he was all right."

"Here, I want you to have this." Dulcie pulled some papers from her shoulder bag and slid them across the table.

"Dulcie—"

"It's the money from the property and half of the estate our grandparents left us."

"Dulcie, no. They left that to you."

Her sister shook her head, smiling. "No, you see that's the thing I figured out. Why they didn't tell me about you, about the Montana property, about our mother. I think they felt their hands were tied, but they knew me. They knew I wouldn't give up until I got to the bottom of it. Until I found my sister and made things right."

Jolene looked down at the check, then back up at her sister. "It's so much."

"Enough so that you never have to work again."

Jolene shook her head. "I love teaching. I didn't get

into it for the money, that's for sure," she added with a smile.

Dulcie reached across the table and took her hand. "I'd hoped you'd say that. You're a great teacher."

Laci appeared then with a huge tray. "I made you samplers of all my favorites."

They dug in, complimenting each dish and thanking Laci for her thoughtfulness.

After she was gone, Jolene asked her sister, "What about you? What will you do now?"

Dulcie shook her head, a faraway look in her eyes. "Russell has invited me to stay out at the ranch for a while."

"How are things with the two of you?"

"I've never met anyone like him."

"I'm sure he's never met anyone like you," Jolene said with a laugh. "I'm glad you're staying for a while. We have a lot of catching up to do."

Dulcie's gaze locked with hers. "You were always in my heart and no matter what the future holds I'm never going to be more than a phone call away."

It had clouded up again by the time Dulcie drove back toward the ranch. As she passed the Whitehorse Cemetery, she slowed when she saw the rainmaker's truck parked beside the road.

She could make out his dark silhouette standing on the hill by Laura Beaumont's grave. She saw him put the small bouquet of flowers by the headstone and turn to leave. Stopping the car, she rolled down her window as she waited for him.

Finnegan Amherst saw her but there was no longer

any malice in his expression, just grief. "Maybe now she can rest in peace. Maybe we all can."

"I'm sorry I misjudged you," she said as he started past her car.

He stopped and looked back at her. "You *do* look like your mother. She was a beautiful woman. But she wasn't strong. Not like you. She would have been proud of you and your sister…and sorry." He nodded, tears shining in his dark eyes.

With a tip of his floppy black hat, he walked to his pickup and climbed in as large drops of rain began to fall.

Dulcie sat, thinking about her mother. Had the rain-maker been the love of her life? Or had it been Dulcie's and Angel's father? Or would Laura Beaumont have spent her life looking for that one man who would love her the way she so desperately needed to be loved?

The way Russell loved her, Dulcie thought.

The rainmaker's pickup engine started, rumbling roughly, and he drove away, the metal pipes in the back of his truck clinking softly to the sound of the rain.

Russell saw Dulcie drive up and went out on the porch. She'd been quiet all morning and when he saw her face he knew she'd made a decision.

She stepped out of the car and stood, her face turned up to the rain. He'd never seen a more beautiful woman, never loved her more than he did at that moment. He had to let her go. He'd known that from the start. Just as he knew he would go with her—if she let him.

She must have sensed him standing there because she looked in his direction, a big smile spreading across her face. "I love you!" she called through the pouring rain. "I love you, Russell Corbett."

He realized it was the first time she'd said it. He felt his heart take off at a gallop. "I love you, Dulcie," he called back.

"Marry me and build me a house over there on that hillside."

He met her gaze and was off that porch in a heartbeat, lifting her off her feet to whirl her around as the rain fell, beading in her lashes and running down her face. And they were laughing and he was telling her how much he loved her and then his mouth was on hers and slowly he was lowering her to the ground.

As he pulled back, both of them soaked to the skin, he had to ask, "Are you sure, Dulcie? This is no Chicago."

She laughed. "No, Russ, it's not. But this is where our children will grow up and, if we're lucky, our grandchildren. This is where my heart is."

* * * * *

We hope you enjoyed reading

Texas Born

by *New York Times* bestselling author

DIANA PALMER

and

Smokin' Six-Shooter

by *New York Times* bestselling author

B.J. DANIELS.

Both were originally Harlequin® series stories!

From passionate, suspenseful and dramatic
love stories to inspirational or historical,
Harlequin offers different lines to
satisfy every romance reader.

New books in each line are available every month.

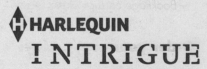

**SEEK THRILLS. SOLVE CRIMES.
JUSTICE SERVED.**

Harlequin.com

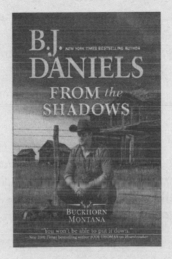

SPECIAL EXCERPT FROM

HQN

*Everyone says the hotel Casey Crenshaw inherited is
haunted. She wants to sell it as quickly as possible, but
Finn Faraday is throwing a wrench into her plans. He's
determined to figure out what happened at the hotel
years ago, but Finn and Casey will soon discover that
digging into the past can be dangerous...*

Read on for a sneak preview of From the Shadows,
the second book in the Buckhorn, Montana *series
by* New York Times *bestselling author B.J. Daniels.*

Chapter One

Finn lay on the dusty floor of the massive, old and allegedly
haunted Crenshaw Hotel and extended his arm as far as it
would go into the dark cubbyhole he'd discovered under the
back stairs. A spider web latched on to his hand, startling
him. He chuckled at how jumpy he was today as he shook
the clinging strands from his fingers. He had more to worry
about than a few cobwebs. Shifting to reach deeper, his
fingers brushed over what appeared to be a notebook stuck
in the very back.

Megan Broadhurst's missing diary? Had he finally gotten
lucky?

The air from the cubbyhole reeked of age and dust and
added to the rancid smell of his own sweat. He should have
been used to all of it by now. He'd spent the past few months
searching this monstrous old relic by day. At night, he'd lain
awake listening to its moans and groans, creaks and clanks, as

if the place were mocking him. *What are you really looking for? Justice? Or absolution?*

What he hadn't expected, though, was becoming invested in the history of the place and the people who'd owned it, especially the new owner—who would be arriving any day now to see the hotel demolished. Casey Crenshaw had inherited the place after her grandmother's recent death. Word was that she'd immediately put it up for sale to a buyer who planned to raze it.

Finn had been looking for a place to disappear when he'd heard about the hotel, which had been boarded up and empty for the past two years. He'd known it would be his last chance before the hotel was destroyed. It had felt like fate as he'd gotten off the bus in Buckhorn and pried his way into the Crenshaw. He'd been in awe of the hotel, which had once been popular with presidents, the rich and famous, and even royalty, the moment he stepped inside.

He'd only become more fascinated when he'd stumbled across Anna Crenshaw's journals. That was why he felt as if he already knew her granddaughter, Casey. He was looking forward to finally meeting her.

His fingers brushed over the notebook pages. He feared he would only push it farther back into the dark space or worse, that its pages would tear before he could get good purchase. Carefully he eased the notebook out.

This was the first thing he'd found that had been so well hidden. He hoped that meant it was the diary that not even the county marshal and all his deputies had been able to find.

Don't miss
From the Shadows *by B.J. Daniels,*
available March 2021 wherever HQN books
and ebooks are sold.

HQNBooks.com

H HARLEQUIN

INTRIGUE

SEEK THRILLS. SOLVE CRIMES.
JUSTICE SERVED.

Save $1.00

on the purchase of

ANY Harlequin Intrigue book.

Available wherever books are sold,
including most bookstores, supermarkets,
drugstores and discount stores.

Save $1.00

on the purchase of ANY Harlequin Intrigue book.

Coupon valid until May 31, 2021.
Redeemable at participating outlets in the U.S. and Canada only.
Not redeemable at Barnes & Noble stores. Limit one coupon per customer.

52617049

5 65373 00076 2 (8100)0 12496

BACCOUP9964!